I0527011

A River Divides

BOOK TWO
BEYOND THE WOOD SERIES

A River Divides

BOOK TWO
BEYOND THE WOOD SERIES

MICHAEL J. ROUECHE

Vesta House Publishing

Copyright

A River Divides

ISBN-10: 0983756767
ISBN-13: 978-0-9837567-6-7
LCCN: 2013942644

Vesta House Publishing
1893 Mapleview Dr., Ste. B
Bountiful, UT, 84010
www.vestahousepublishing.com

One luminary clock against the sky
Proclaimed the time was neither wrong nor right.
I have been one acquainted with the night.

Acquainted with the Night
Robert Lee Frost

Chapter 1

February 1864, Just Outside Staunton, Virginia

She felt free to breathe—at last, and she did, heavily, with a deep rising and falling of her chest and a slight inadvertent sigh at the end of each exhalation. She was conscious for the first time of the sweat on her back as she leaned heavily against the icy-cold front door. Her body shook gently, and she used the door to steady herself. She was an extraordinarily lovely woman, but her momentarily starkly pale skin—almost a death-like mask—emphasized a healing cut across her cheek.

It was cold . . . bitterly cold. For a number weeks, it had been warm, but the respite was over, and temperatures had fallen. But she didn't feel the cold. She was aware only of her wet back and her growing relief as she watched him mount his horse and ride from the house.

She wondered briefly how he'd heard of the trouble and confessed to herself that she'd never been more frightened than at his call. His visit had seemed interminable. She reviewed the interview, finding she hadn't given too much away. Or had she? Her relief dissolved as she began to think again through the details of their conversation—what she'd said, and how he'd responded. What did those responses mean? What did he know? What did he suspect? Did he believe her? Just a few weeks ago, she wouldn't have worried. She would have been sure he'd accepted every offered word and nuance, but now . . . .

He'd arrived an hour earlier, unannounced. Her elderly slave, John, had opened the door to him and formally announced him to Betsy Henderson, widow of Captain Thaddeus Henderson of Stonewall Jackson's 5th Virginia. Mrs. Henderson, who wore her blond hair pulled back in a bun, rose and approached her visitor as the sheriff entered the library. Indirect winter sunlight augmented by gas-light blaze illuminated the room. Mrs. Henderson smiled broadly at the sheriff, her green eyes sparkling. She offered her hand, and said, "Sheriff, an unexpected pleasure. Won't you come over here and sit . . . sit here in this chair . . . near the fire? You look as if you perish of cold."

The stocky, older man approached Mrs. Henderson, taking her hand gently and respectfully with his ungloved right hand, while his left held his worn slouch hat and glove at his side. She was elegant in her red wool and silk jacket that flared at her slender waist to cover the top of her matching skirt. Her delicate lace collar and cuffs spoke of wealth and refinement. He was balding and his long graying hair was pushed backward, reaching nearly to his collar. He smiled generously, exhibiting heavily stained teeth. His big, beefy hand was cold as it touched the widow's, and she inadvertently winced at the sensation. This man had years ago been sheriff and recently reassumed the office as younger men— more energetic men—were gone to war.

"My dear, Mrs. Henderson," he began with ingratiating courtesy. "I've received the most distressing news imaginable and come to offer my assistance."

She was assured by his tone. He wasn't here to trouble her, and she determined to keep the discussion focused as narrowly as she could. As they sat down, she tried to distract him. "Sheriff, you've come on business, but won't you join me . . . for a cup of coffee?"

"Coffee? Haven't had that in a year. Real coffee?"

She smiled. "Yes, I can still offer you coffee . . . at least for now." She was comforted. He suspected nothing, still considered her superior and was in awe just being with her. "John, bring coffee for the sheriff . . . for us."

The slave, lingering near the door, nodded affirmatively and stepped out. The widow watched him, then turned to the sheriff.

He was smiling at her. "I'm sorry . . . so sorry to intrude. Hope it's not . . . in the end a bother."

"Sheriff, surely it won't be. You're welcome. Although I know of nothing requiring your concern."

"I hope it's so." He lowered his eyes, placing his hat carefully on the floor beside his chair. "I couldn't ignore the rumors anymore . . . not without visiting you. They seemed unlikely, and if I may be intimate, they troubled me. I don't . . . couldn't believe them, but circumstances bear them out. Hopefully we'll quickly agree they're merely stories from someone's fertile imagination . . . or deranging fever."

Betsy turned to better face the sheriff in apparent excitement. "Sheriff, this sounds more interesting than anything in my life. I can't imagine what would be so intriguing—so troubling—to bring you here in such frosty weather."

The sheriff sniffled, shivered and cleared his throat, finally beginning to warm after his cold ride from Staunton. He smiled again, shifted in his chair toward her, positioning one arm comfortably on the armrest nearest Betsy.

He spoke so softly Betsy could scarcely hear him and watched his mouth and listened intently.

"Well, I heard . . ."

Betsy interrupted. "Why don't we wait for the coffee? You must still be frozen. The weather's taken quite a turn."

"Yes."

The visitor was visibly uncomfortable with social chatter, and she imagined he would have been more at ease discussing his business. But she wanted him off balance, muddled, unable to ask probing questions or examine answers too closely.

"What do you hear of the war?" she asked abruptly.

"Only what I read in the paper."

"Sheriff, I'm disappointed. I thought you would have official reports . . . or, at least, gossip."

He offered, "I have heard there's not much food in the valley, and someone told me they're going to devalue the currency soon."

"Devalue the currency! It has so little value now, how can they devalue it further? But never mind, I've given up buying anything. Most of what we get now we trade for—a little grain for something we need. But we're running out of grain. We're running out of everything." Betsy lightened her tone and shook her head, "Now listen to me. I've taken our conversation in the wrong direction. Maybe I should stop deferring your business. It's just so nice to see a friendly face." John was entering the room with a tray of coffee and teacakes, and she smiled and said, "Ah, rescued." She looked warmly at John, and he responded with an affectionate nod.

The guest noticed the warmth Betsy showed her slave. Betsy poured out the coffee, passed a cup to the sheriff and offered him a teacake. He took a sip of the coffee, inadvertently sighed, thanked her, laid the coffee cup on a nearby table and took a sweet—immediately putting it entirely into his mouth with visible pleasure.

"And your business, Sheriff," Betsy prompted as soon as his mouth was full.

"Ah, my business," he said, picking up his cup, swallowing the cake and licking his lips to clear the crumbs. He enjoyed the process and waited until he had fully tasted the crumb's slight flavor before continuing. "I understand Mr. Walthrope—the fellow that supervised your factory—I understand he's gone . . . disappeared."

"Yes, he has," she responded, feigning disinterest.

"It's not just he's disappeared, is it?" His voice was suddenly louder, more direct. "I understand, if I may be straightforward, he may have been the killer . . . may have murdered your foreman. We never did find his killer."

"Yes, I know." Her throat tightened as she perceived a competent mind behind the sheriff's facade. "I've followed news of your investigation closely . . . in the newspaper."

"Mrs. Henderson, I know this is terrible for you, but I must ask some questions . . . and questions are such indelicate things, especially in the presence or even worse . . . when asked of a lady. I do apologize, but . . . I've heard this Walthrope bothered you. That's why I've come. I want to know everything, so nothing else happens . . . to you."

"Nothing's happened to me . . ."

He cut her short. "I don't mean to be disagreeable or rude, but that cut . . . the cut on your face suggests otherwise. I'm embarrassed to even mention it."

Her hand rose reflexively and touched the right side of her face—the fresh scar—before she realized what she'd

done. Feelings overwhelmed her. She remembered the day
. . . the anger, the shame. She thought of Walthrope and hated
him. He'd almost been her husband, but he was a murderer.
She'd only been saved from the indignity of marrying him by
a woman who had hinted at the worst. She didn't know who
the disreputable woman was or where she'd gone, but she'd
saved Betsy.

Walthrope had been charming, wedging his way into her
life, bit by bit, and all—as it became too apparent—for
her wealth and position. There had been clues, tiny suggestions, but she paid no heed and denied what he truly was,
because she wanted comfort and love. He offered both, she'd
thought, and she'd been so alone.

The sheriff watched her complexion go from shades of
red anger to a ghost-like hue of horror, and thought, "Then
it's true." But he said nothing. He'd wait. She'd tell him all.
Maybe not everything today, but slice by slice, she'd give
him details till she'd given him the entire apple.

When she realized he waited for her to say something,
she steeled her emotions. "Yes, you're right. I do believe he
killed the foreman."

"You believe this because?"

She looked at him, keenly aware of his dignity. The gentle voice and crude exterior hid a shrewd, tenacious mind. A
slight fear nipped her. She would tell him about Walthrope.
That would divert him from her true secret, which she could
not reveal. "Sheriff, I was foolish."

"Foolish?"

She recounted how she'd discovered Walthrope had
killed the foreman, a Mr. Stokes. Walthrope and Stokes
had used her woolen factory to smuggle and hoard supplies,
speculating—all without her knowing. But the conspirators

had a falling out, and Walthrope had killed Stokes. Betsy had been furious, embarrassed, humiliated, when she found out about the smuggling and murder. She wanted to show Walthrope he hadn't fooled her, and she'd confronted him. The encounter had gone horribly wrong, with her mother and friends put in harm's way, and her own face left with the hideous cut. She'd vanquished Walthrope by telling him she'd called for the sheriff, that he was on his way. Walthrope only left because he thought all was lost—that he was in danger.

She wished she had told the sheriff, but once Walthrope ran, she didn't think it would make a difference . . . and she was humiliated. They'd never catch him.

The sheriff heard her confession, feeling she'd told the truth. It squared with her behavior, her healing wound—which to him didn't look hideous—and everything he'd heard. He looked at her compassionately and said, "I'm sorry to dredge this up. I do wish you'd sent for me. I could have stopped him, but I understand your feelings . . . your actions. I'd like to think I'd have done . . . or rather that my wife would have had the courage to do as you did. And I regret his harming you."

Betsy looked sad, almost tearful, "I do, too. But it could have been much worse, and for that I'm grateful."

They sat quietly for a moment, looking at each other until the sheriff smiled kindly and said, "Another matter, Mrs. Henderson."

She tensed and paled again. He saw it. What did it mean? She was hiding something. She may have told the truth about Walthrope, but she hadn't told him everything. Could he stumble onto her secret?

"Yes," she said, uncomfortable with the pause in the conversation following such a crucial comment.

"Surely you've noticed soldiers . . . civilians around, begging food."

She smiled warmly, relaxed, letting her chest and head slump slightly forward. "Yes, we have them here at all hours. It was just soldiers, but now, it's everyone. It's impossible not to feel for them. We give what we can. I fear we'll all be in that condition soon . . . the way things crumble."

He hadn't hit on exactly what she hid, but he didn't worry. He had time. Even if it didn't come out today. The thought of coming again—eating her cakes, drinking her coffee, hearing her voice—delighted him. But he feared for the lady. Was someone else, now that Walthrope was gone, threatening her? He revolted at the idea as he found Mrs. Henderson warm and kind and appealing. He smiled, remembering her last comments. "I'm sure you're generous with everyone." He paused. "My concern, Mrs. Henderson—if I may be a bit too direct once more—is your safety. You're not in town. I worry some who pass might not be satisfied . . . want more than offered."

"That hasn't happened," she quickly responded. "The possibility never occurred to me. Do you think . . . we're at risk?" She tried to look frightened.

"No . . . perhaps not." He hesitated, smiled at her clearly feigned, fearful expression. He looked down at the empty tray in front of them and wished there were more teacakes, as he'd finished them all. "Because of what happened to you, I urge vigilance. I've heard of one soldier who took advantage of someone's hospitality . . . even refused to leave." There, he saw it again. She paled. Her body stiffened. "But it probably won't happen here. You've your servants . . . and family, I believe?"

"Yes, I still have some servants. I've got my mother with me, and I think that would be enough." She smiled as she thought of her mother confronting an intruder. "I did have the new foreman from the factory—a former officer—living here. But he's in town now. His fiancée lives here till their marriage in March."

"Yes, I know of him. Lieutenant . . . ?"

"Moore. Caleb Moore."

"Yes. Caleb Moore."

"Do you think we should have him move back? Maybe it would be better . . . safer to have him here."

"Perhaps. I do worry about soldiers . . ."

"Surely, they wouldn't do . . ."

"I wish you were in no danger . . . but let me be frank. I heard one was bothering you." He'd never heard it.

She stuttered as her face flushed. "Not . . . not out here. We haven't . . . had that. No one is bothering me."

He pressed his advantage. "Sometimes, they don't admit they're deserters."

Her breaths involuntarily shortened to shallow, continuous panting. She was close to panic. Did he know about Hank? How could he? No one would tell. Perhaps others had seen something. She looked at the sheriff carefully, trying to peer into his soul. What did he know? What was he doing? As she watched him, she began to regain her control. He knew nothing. He was just reporting rumors. He was here to protect her. He was kind. You could see that in his gentle brown eyes and feel it in the humble way he'd taken her hand. She would say nothing more.

He was uncharacteristically uncomfortable with her anxiety and tried to ease it by saying, "Just be vigilant."

She wasn't listening. Her mind had again panicked. She imagined Hank had never escaped Staunton, that this fat sheriff—not really so benevolent—had captured him and forced him to tell all. Was the sheriff here to entrap her?

She responded coldly, superficially, "Thank you."

Chapter 2

Weeks Earlier, Near Staunton, Virginia

The man moved quickly toward the woods. His stomach cramped and ached, and it was growing dark and cold. So many emotions and thoughts attacked simultaneously, stupefying his mind, leaving his legs moving of their own accord toward his destination.

It was time to leave. That was clear. He could stick around, create problems for some—he'd like that, and desire welled up at the thought—but it was too risky. He walked with trembling strides. If only he could strike down just one of them. But he couldn't, not now. He'd had his chance and failed. Maybe later. Definitely later! He'd hunt them down, one by one, destroy them . . . slowly, painfully.

The more he thought about it, the more his legs trembled, and the angrier he became. He abruptly screamed in rage, his voice rebounding through the bare trees before dissipating into far reaches of the forest. He stopped and listened. Had anyone heard him? He gritted his teeth. If someone had, he knew what he'd do. Maybe rendering a violent blow would help him cope. Perhaps then his fury would abate, and he'd be able to think clearly. But no one came, and his wrath-filled body stumbled forward, driven by increasing choler.

Finally at his destination, his mind came back to the task at hand. He tried to steady his still-wobbling knees before crouching. "I need you to hold me up," he thought. He kept his cramped stomach straight, and with his right hand brushed back decaying leaves, matted and damp beneath a small bush. He felt what he sought, pulling it from concealment. He no longer had a gun or knife—he'd lost them in his struggles, so he sought his last and most powerful weapon—the money he'd gathered while in Staunton. With the uncovered shovel in hand, he rose quickly and walked, still shaking, several paces from the bush.

He stopped, stared at the ground and began dragging the shovel across the earth, pulling back leaves, revealing in the diminishing light recently disturbed ground. He thought of the new French novel he'd started to read at Betsy's insistence and chuckled at the irony. He owed Betsy credit for this simple plan, he thought angrily. He never finished the book, but read far enough to steal the idea. Yes, Betsy and that thief Valjean, they'd given him his final weapon. He dug briskly, proud of this precaution, else all would have been lost.

He quickly scraped the metal of a box, then slowed his effort till he'd uncovered its top. He knelt down, unthinkingly, in the moist leaves and swore as the wet penetrated his pants. He cursed himself. The stains and dirt would show after the pants had dried. Only later would he cuss the chill of the now-icy-wet knees. On feeling the moisture, he instinctively rose—even though it was too late—to a crouch. His stomach cramped again from the effort, and he damned the petty Union private for the gut punch and spasms.

He carefully dug around the box, loosening and pulling it out, resting it on the ground. He'd buried it earlier, returning whenever he had money to add. He opened it and touched the coins. This money was all he had in the world, but it would be enough, ample seed money for a rich harvest of revenge.

Later the same evening, a dark-haired young lady, Emily Graham, sat at a writing table, drafting a note to an acquaintance, recounting a most disparaging and delightful rumor about Richmond society. She wore a high, jewel-neck mauve dress. White lace trimmed the collar. Her bodice was fitted with decorative buttons and bishop-style sleeves—tight at shoulder and wrist, ballooning loosely at the elbow. She was unwillingly interrupted when a slave entered the room to announce a visitor.

Emily responded abruptly, "I told you I wasn't to be disturbed. I'm not home." She put down her pen and turned her head to look at the servant. "Stupid girl."

The slave, with dark skin and eyes, was thin, small and mousy. She stood with her head bowed, accepting the scolding silently. She was in a simple, worn blue dress with loose sleeves ending at the wrists in tight, ragged-from-use cuffs. Afraid to say anything, she waited for instructions, further scolding or a sharp blow from her mistress.

Mrs. Graham had forgotten the slave, thinking instead of the possibilities of a surprise visit. She was curious. "What visitor? Didn't you get a name . . . a card?"

"Yes, Ma'am. Got his name."

"What is it?"

"Lucius Walthrope. He give me his card."

The mistress's brown eyes narrowed and an unconscious grimace crossed her face. What did he want? He was her cousin's love, and she wanted nothing to do with either of them. "I won't see him," she declared flatly and looked down to continue writing her note. "If you'd followed my instructions . . . Tell him I'm not at home."

"Yes, Ma'am. He says yuh'd say that. Says he got news yuh'd like . . . wants to tell it hisself."

Her mistress kept her head lowered as if to write, but she was busy weighing the latest revelation. He wouldn't have come unless he had something appealing to her refined senses. She would see him. "Show him in," she commanded, raising her head just long enough to eye the slave coldly. "Give me that carte de visite."

"Yes, Ma'am."

As soon as the slave left the room, Emily positioned herself before a chair that stood in front of a high, arched, heavily draped window. She glanced briefly at the picture on the carte de visite and smoothed the folds of her skirt. When the slave and Mr. Walthrope didn't enter the room immediately, she sat, leaned slightly forward and studied the card. Emotions—strong and exciting—enlivened her.

Emily gave the slave girl a disgusted look when she finally led her guest into the room, but disgust melted to surprise when she saw Walthrope. He wore no overcoat or jacket. His shirt and pants were wrinkled and soiled, especially the wet and dirt-browned knees. His cheeks were bright red from the cold. He shivered. His filthy hands made it clear something extraordinary had happened. She was glad she'd seen him.

She'd planned to greet him warily, but seeing his condition, she rushed forward, unconsciously grasping his soiled hands, exclaiming, "What's happened, my dear Lucius? Your face . . . your hands—they're ice." She rubbed his hands gently in hers.

The man, even with his cold-red complexion, was handsome. He was tall, blond with light blue eyes. He wore a full beard, and she thought he looked exactly as he had the last time she'd seen him, but for the red of his cheeks.

He stared for several seconds into her eyes before responding. "Ah, Emily, my dear, it is so good . . . a gracious gift to be in your presence. I was beyond hope moments ago, afraid you'd turn me away. I thank the gods for this salvation."

"Not see you?" She smiled sheepishly, then added, "It's as it should be. Friend saving a needy friend."

"You're a blessing," he said in an earnest tone, towering over her as she continued massaging his hands.

"A blessing? Yes, of course." She looked at him warmly and said without irony, "What have I saved you from?"

"From freezing to death, and . . . the clutches of your cousin and her evil, wily Yankee spy."

"Yankee spy?" she queried skeptically.

Walthrope anticipating her surprise, quickly responded, "I knew you too were taken in by their treachery. You'd never tolerate such traitorous thoughts and acts."

"Of course, I would never betray the Confederacy, not for her . . . not for anyone." Guilt burned in Emily. She was again maligning her innocent cousin Betsy. She loved her, but Betsy knew the truth about Emily's husband, a cowardly soldier. Betsy had gone north to help Emily retrieve him from a Confederate hospital. But in time, Emily couldn't bear Betsy knowing of his cowardice.

In Emily's eyes, Betsy was the epitome of their sex, a perfect Confederate lady, and because of Emily's embarrassment, she felt lessened in Betsy's presence. When Emily brought her recuperating husband home, it seemed easier to let distance grow between her and Betsy, and it had. But she couldn't conceive of Betsy with a Yankee spy.

As hard as it had been for Emily to accept, Betsy had once loved a Yankee soldier, a boy she'd known before the war. Perhaps that was the Yankee Walthrope accused of spying. But none of that mattered because Emily had long known Betsy and Walthrope would marry. It was obvious to her. They were both beautiful, faithful to the Rebellion, so capable of goodness.

She smiled. This was nothing more than a green-eyed pout. Perhaps he'd discovered Betsy once loved this boy and petty jealousy had enraged him. A lovers' tiff, a misunderstanding. Emily would help them sort it out. "Lucius, you know it's not true! Remember how much you love Betsy . . . how much she loves you." Her voice was soothing, condescending.

He hadn't expected her reaction. Because of her estrangement from Betsy, he'd expected her to anger quickly and offer him help. He was briefly confused about how to control the conversation. Should he play it as a jealous madness or stay the course, claiming traitors among them? He blurted out sullenly, "She's a traitress, with a Yankee soldier . . . a private, not even an officer."

"You don't believe that," she responded patiently.

"Dear Emily, I saw the proof with my own eyes. He attacked me, because I stood loyal to the Revolution."

"Attacked you?" She looked at him suspiciously.

"With a knife. I fought him, but had to flee. He tried to kill me because I am . . . faithful. Look at my sleeve! The proof! Look at the blood!" He pointed to blood stains.

"Are you hurt badly?" Her tone changed to motherly concern. "Let's bandage that arm."

"Don't worry about that. I stopped the bleeding . . . bandaged it best I could. I was nearly killed by some crazy Confederate widow and her Yankee lover."

"Don't say such things! I can't believe it."

"You would if you'd been there." He looked frightened. "She invited me to her library. We were having a wonderful time, then she said she had a special friend she wanted me to meet. She walked to the door, opened it. There he was— the Devil incarnate. Before I could do anything, he rushed me, slashing wildly with a knife. He nicked me a couple of times—that's the blood. But I fled . . . without jacket, coat . . . horse. I was lost, with no idea what to do, who to confide in, who to turn to in my need . . . in the country's moment of danger. Then, in my madness . . . my desperation, I thought of you—my savior. She . . . you are a lady, I thought, a friend . . . patriot and true. I knew you'd help a man persecuted merely for loving our country. I knew you were a faithful Rebel, a trusted friend."

"This happened?" she asked, but then answered shaking her head. "No . . . no . . . it can't be. I'm beginning to think you play an April Fools' joke in January." She let go of his hands, which she'd held tightly throughout the conversation, and considered the situation aloud. "I half expect Betsy to come through the door. I half hope . . . no, I completely hope this is some ruse cooked up to bring us together . . . family. What a blessing it would be." She stopped, looked at him sternly. "What you say cannot be. It is . . . too terrible to even consider. Betsy . . . traitress, willing dupe of a Yankee . . . not even an officer."

He looked hard again into her eyes and said sadly, "Have you known me to lie . . . to do anything dishonest . . .

to deceive? Think . . . remember all I've done for you . . . for Betsy. How could you imagine deceit in me . . . as I'm standing here in my own blood. I swear it by that blood which I shed today for our country that Betsy Henderson is a traitress. On my own blood!" He raised his stained sleeve.

She was devastated. There was the proof. His oath, his blood. Never did she suspect it was Betsy's blood, that he'd run when discovered false, that he'd attacked and been bested by the Yankee private.

"What can I do?" she said despairingly in rhetorical surrender.

"Help me!"

She looked puzzled. "Why do you need help?"

"I'm frightened of the Yankee spy. He attacked me once, and promises to do it again . . . if he finds me. He threatened to kill me. Hide me, Emily!"

"I most certainly will not," she said indignantly.

"Emily, you've always been kind to me . . . and I to you. Help me escape our enemy!"

Emily looked at his sleeve and the blood stains. Where was the cut? How could he have been cut without visible holes in his clothes? Why didn't he go to the sheriff? Something didn't make sense.

"Emily, won't you help a neighbor beset upon?"

His comment angered her. "You think me a child. I know who my neighbor is, and I'm not sure you're one. You didn't get stabbed by a Yankee. You probably got cut shaving. Out with it! What do you need? You're inconveniencing me, Mr. Walthrope. You're becoming—I hate to admit—a bore. There, I've said it. You've become a bore."

He was tired of being found out, but he could see she wouldn't probe. She wanted him gone, and he was going to get clean, dry clothes. "Loan me a jacket . . . a coat. I'm going to freeze if I don't get clothes."

"Why come to me for clothes? I'm no shopkeeper."

"Could I buy some of your husband's clothes? I'll pay handsomely. You once said he was about my size."

"Why not just go to town and buy your own clothes? My husband's fond of his."

"Because, Emily . . . my dear, faithful Emily, I need them now . . . and I'm afraid he'll find me. We have been such wonderful friends, even as Betsy's proven false to us both. Remember our friendship. Such kindness would cap it . . . even as it ebbs because of your unending love for an unworthy woman."

She looked at him with relief. "It will end, then? You won't bother me again?"

He nodded.

She needed only give him clothes, and she'd be rid of him. Emily beckoned her slave and gave specific instructions on which trousers, shirt, coat, gloves and jacket to bring.

Once her slave, Ruth, left the room, Emily became agitated. She wanted to send Walthrope to the back porch to wait, as if he were a beggar, but knew she couldn't muster the courage. She certainly wouldn't invite him to sit. He was filthy, and she now felt her furniture would be morally soiled if he were to sit on it. She stepped from him and pointed him closer to the room's fireplace. "Warm yourself." She glanced dartingly in disgust at the dirt transferred from his hands to hers.

He smiled as she distanced herself. He disdained the insipid, self-absorbed, superficial woman. He moved slowly to face the fire, holding his hands downward towards the flame.

Coming here had been perfect. She'd never again be of use to him, but he could get clothes and slip into the dark. He closed his eyes and enjoyed the warmth on his face, hands, chest and legs.

Chapter 3

February 1864, Staunton, Virginia

The sheriff couldn't dismiss from his mind even the smallest detail of his visit with Betsy—her sudden paleness; her kindness; her gentility; her lovely features; her delicate, clean, white hands; the still-red scar; the flavor of the coffee. The memory of the coffee lingered agreeably. Unsettling thoughts of Mrs. Henderson worked on him day and night, keeping him awake as he lay in bed coveting the sound sleep of his wife.

There was something missing in his picture of the widow. Something was wrong with the portrait she so carefully had created, and when something felt wrong, the sheriff's mind relentlessly revisited the memory, searching for some minute detail he'd failed to notice or understand. The elegant Mrs. Henderson had seemed disturbed, and he wasn't yet sure why.

He smiled in the dark as he wondered if there was something unseemly at work in him, something confusing his well-developed ability to find answers in the smallest gesture or misspoken word. He was attracted to her. He acknowledged it for the first time. Before the confession, he would unhesitatingly have rejected the possibility as an absurdity, rivaling the folly of the war around him. After all, he smiled again, he was old enough to be her father—grandfather! And he was very attached to his wife.

But there was something about this woman, so strikingly attractive in looks and pleasant in manner, that when he had interviewed her he was young again. The sensation arose anew whenever he thought of her. He was relieved he could now acknowledge this affection—to himself only, of course. Perhaps now he'd be able to join his wife in slumber. But the emotion didn't make him sleepy, and he scrunched his face as he tried to gain the upper hand in his internal conversation.

At some point during the night, he recognized his problem. When he thought of her, his mental discipline evaporated and his mind flitted from pleasurable image to pleasurable impulse. He pictured her thick, blond hair—he'd once allowed himself to imagine touching it. He could hear her warm voice. He envisioned her green eyes—he could look at such emeralds all day. To have them stare back would be pure joy. He remembered her kindness, especially the teacakes, and savored the memory of being with her. At his weakest, he imagined she was his, but sudden stern remorse punished him.

His moral will eventually regained the upper hand, and his mind landed firmly on his official responsibility. He needed to protect her. Yes, that was it. He would bend this improper attraction till it aligned with duty. His motives were beyond reproach. They were nothing more than the praiseworthy fondness he'd feel for a daughter, for any virtuous young women. So to protect her . . . his daughter, he had to know more. His wife shifted in her sleep. The next day his inquiries began in earnest.

His investigation commenced with Caleb Moore. Moore saw war's beginning as a cadet at the valley's Virginia Military Institute, but he had been bred in slave-rich Tidewater. As a lieutenant, Moore had lost a leg at Gettysburg. Mrs. Henderson, who met him before the war, rescued him from a makeshift Confederate hospital where doctors had lost hope for him. Moore had become her confidant, and she'd asked him to manage her substantial estate.

While her interest in her two grain mills, woolen factory and farm had waned much earlier, it evaporated entirely after Walthrope's attack. For her and without murmur, Moore had taken on her estate when Walthrope, who previously managed much of it, had been unmasked. The soldier's relationship with Betsy was now clear to everyone as the-ever-loyal saved to the savior.

The sheriff reviewed these facts methodically as he approached the woolen factory. He'd never met Moore and was curious about him, slightly jealous of his proximity to the widow, but appreciative of a man true to Betsy.

He stopped outside the factory, drew a deep breath, turned the knob, and pushed the door. But his entrance was blocked by a tall, lean man wearing a worn slouch hat and hair covering the top of his ears. He was dressed in a dark business suit and leaned lightly on a crutch. They were both startled, and the sheriff stepped back as the man, nearly losing his balance, bent forward.

The sheriff, first to recover from the awkwardness, spoke. "Do excuse me, sir. I didn't expect anyone to be right there . . . right behind the door."

The dark-haired man took in the sheriff, noting his short stature, his pudgy, undistinguished face and the long hair flowing from underneath his hat. Resting on his crutch, the man responded, smiling warmly, "If you'd arrived a minute earlier or later, you would have found the way clear." He extended his hand to the sheriff and said, "I presume I've the pleasure of meeting our sheriff."

"You do. And you are the courageous Lieutenant Moore?" he asked, shaking Caleb's open hand vigorously.

Caleb ignored the compliment. "Come in." Doubt crossed his face, and he added, "You are here to see me?"

"Yes. Were you expecting me?"

"Well, come in then. We can visit in the office. And yes, I was expecting you. I'd heard you were concerned for Mrs. Henderson . . . and from your reputation, I thought you'd persist."

The sheriff wondered why Mrs. Henderson would have warned Moore. Was she frightened of an investigation? Frightened of someone who might hear about the investigation? Frightened of Moore? Frightened by some indiscretion?

His questions abandoned him as he watched Caleb's gait. The former soldier hardly used the crutch and barely limped. The sheriff, so enthralled by what he was witnessing, didn't notice the nerve-rattling factory noise and commotion. When they arrived at the office, Caleb stepped aside, removed his hat and motioned with the sweep of his hand for the sheriff to enter first. The sheriff obliged, and Caleb followed. "Won't you be seated?" he said congenially but loudly to be heard above the factory din.

The sheriff sat quickly, waiting for Caleb to close the door—which barely cut the noise in the office—and move gingerly to a desk chair. The former soldier lowered himself with a sigh. As he passed, the sheriff surreptitiously stole a glance at Caleb's legs. He couldn't tell them apart, but for the faint limp.

Caleb saw him, ignored the look and said loudly, "There. The racket still grates, but it's quieter than with the door open. How can I help your investigation?"

The sheriff smiled, "Lieutenant, I need not tell you the purpose for my call."

Caleb chuckled. "No need for formalities, then. What do you specifically want to know of Walthrope?"

"You get around well," the sheriff said.

Caleb paused, struggling briefly to understand the sheriff's intent. "You mean . . . without a leg?"

"Exactly. I expected a man hobbling on two crutches, maybe a peg leg. Instead, I find you walking as if nothing much had happened, on a leg that looks . . . a lot like the other. I'm not sure which is real." The sheriff smiled, revealing his upper row of yellowing teeth.

"But much has happened," Caleb responded gloomily, "and I get around only because of Mr. Hanger's limb."

"I imagine it's convenient to be here where Mr. Hanger makes them."

"Yes, I suppose, but I'd rather forgo it altogether. I find the loss of my leg disadvantageous . . . and painful, even where the leg is gone. No one warned me about that." There was bitterness in his tone, yet his expression betrayed a slight smile.

The sheriff grimaced. "I've overstepped propriety. Forgive me." He watched for Caleb's response.

"Yes, you have, but everyone does. My leg . . . or rather, Hanger's limb gets all the attention. They stare when they realize what it is. I understand, and for the most part, I'm delighted to tout it. Embarrassed as I am to admit it, I'm glad Mr. Hanger was the first to lose his leg in the war. It gave him a motive to invent it. Now, he can make them for the rest of us." He looked carefully at the sheriff, then added, "I haven't worn the leg long, so I'm not totally comfortable, still a little unsure. You have to learn a new way of moving, thinking, leaning, resting. So I keep the crutch nearby . . . for now. And no matter how impressive it seems, it's not as comfortable as my leg was."

Without further comment, Caleb rose and walked around the desk till he was beside the sheriff. He leaned against the desk, pulling up his pant leg to reveal wood barrel staves joined, carved and finished into the appearance of a leg. He explained to the sheriff that the artificial leg was hollow, making it lighter and compensating for heavy metal hinges at knee and ankle.

The sheriff was intrigued. "Your life is different than it would have been."

Caleb wasn't sure whether the sheriff had asked him a question or was making a comment. "My life is different, as is everyone's."

"Yes, but . . . but you've made a great sacrifice, and you'll be asked about that leg for the rest of your life."

"Probably," he said, pulling his pant leg down over the limb and retreating to his own side of the desk.

"It's not quite the same thing, but I'm always being asked about my name. 'Is that your real name?'"

"I wondered about that. Sheriff Sheriff," Caleb repeated to hear how it sounded. "An unlikely coincidence."

"If my mother had known I would end up a sheriff, she might have married a Smith."

Caleb smiled, "Are you running for reelection?"

"No. I didn't run last time. I came back for a few months to fill in because I was needed. Started just a little while after the foreman was killed. Now more men are available . . . interested. I'll leave it to younger men . . . more energetic men—men like you—and I'll retire again."

"Not men like me. My hands are full."

"Yes. Managing the Henderson estate . . . by yourself—that's a heavy burden. But it must have benefits . . . in wages . . . if nothing else."

"I'm pleased to do it."

"Why?"

"Why? Why am I pleased to do it?"

"Exactly."

"I . . . I . . . What else could I do to help in the war?"

"You're in the home guard. You're helping the war there. So tell me, why do you really do it?"

Caleb's face grew darker, his eyes narrowed, his lips compressed. "You think I have a hidden motive?"

"Just trying to understand how you benefit from your relationship with Mrs. Henderson."

Caleb, irritated, stared as if to penetrate the sheriff's mind. "Are you accusing me of something? If you are, I believe I'd be obligated to challenge you, sir."

"No. No, of course not. No need for that. I didn't mean anything by it, but I do think Mrs. Henderson is in difficulties. There may be people waiting to take advantage—as Walthrope did—of her good will . . . her generosity."

"I'm not Walthrope and don't appreciate the comparison." He meant to stop there, but vexed by the sheriff's accusatory questions, he pushed on. "She saved my life. She's family . . . closer than my family. I'm making sure she's well. If you were to arrest me, question me, hang me, you would find no other motive."

"Well," the sheriff smiled pleasantly, "That's not even a possibility. Arrest you? Nonsense, even in jest. No, you're doing great service. No doubt of that. And you're doing well for yourself." The sheriff hesitated before continuing. "You probably make a good wage . . . have the means to make more."

"What does that mean?" Caleb said, openly angry.

"I've upset you. How clumsy I am. I didn't mean to do that or—oh, I abhor the thought—to fault you . . . of anything. I've let my tongue get out of my mouth till I've tripped on it. I'm embarrassed. No, your loyalty to Mrs. Henderson is renowned . . . beyond reproach."

Caleb didn't respond for a long time, and the sheriff sat quietly, waiting. "Sheriff, how do you know when they're calling you by your last name, rather than your office?"

"It's confusing, making me especially grateful mother gave me a different first name." Both men laughed.

After a brief silence, Caleb spoke with resignation, "Sheriff, I don't take advantage of her. I saw Walthrope attack her . . . and I could do nothing. In my unfit-for-battle condition, I can stay . . . protect her now. I'm not trying to . . ."

The sheriff cut him short, "Do you suspect anyone is?"

Caleb thought. "No, I don't see anyone . . . besides Walthrope. Why these questions? You must suspect something." He bit his lip, then continued, "Otherwise, you wouldn't put me through this inquisition."

"Inquisition? I hope I haven't made you feel . . . I apologize. I've clearly gone too far. Now you understand why they won't run me for reelection. I just don't think clearly, not anymore . . . and I'm getting grumpy. I'm ashamed, having provoked such a man as yourself . . . a hero." He paused. "I don't know of anyone trying to harm her." The sheriff leaned toward the desk, lowering his voice till it was barely audible over the cacophonous machinery, "But I do worry—like you—and want to make sure she's not harmed." He sat back, raised his voice and added, "Anything else you can tell me?"

Caleb shifted slightly in his chair, and the sheriff noted it. "No, nothing more."

"Do you have an idea where Walthrope might have gone? Or what his real name is? I assume not Walthrope."

Caleb laughed. "Sheriff, I don't know where he went. I was one of the people he tried to kill. He hates me, and that's fine because . . . I hate him. A strong word, I know, but if you list people who would like to harm him . . . kill him, include me first."

"Is there someone else who would know where he went?" Caleb's last comment unexpectedly struck the sheriff, and he added, "He did get away? No, don't answer that."

Caleb thought for a moment, looking carefully at the sheriff. Did he suspect they'd killed Walthrope? He shrugged. "There is another person, Emily Graham. I never met her. She's Mrs. Henderson's husband's cousin." He smiled. "Got that? Mrs. Henderson lived with her a while, and I've heard Mrs. Graham liked Walthrope . . . very much. She and Mrs. Henderson had a falling out, so maybe she kept in touch with Walthrope."

"Falling out? About what?"

"Don't know. Mrs. Henderson never said exactly, but I heard her once say Emily was embarrassed about something. So Emily cut her."

"When?"

"Before she brought me to Staunton. They—Mrs. Graham and Mrs. Henderson—went to Winchester to bring back Mr.

Graham. He'd been injured at Gettysburg. That's when Mrs. Henderson rescued me. I don't remember much of that time, and I don't have any memory of the Grahams. I'd lost my leg. I was feverish. It wasn't healing. They'd given up on me, so they let Mrs. Henderson take me. Odd they'd do that. There was a lot of confusion then. Probably thought she'd save them a burial . . . one less body." He chuckled. "But she kept me alive. I don't know how that works, but her strength kept me going. At least that's what Mrs. Henderson's mother told me." He paused, his gaze drifting downward. "I wouldn't have lived without Bet . . . Mrs. Henderson."

Sheriff looked sympathetically at the man. Undeniable sincerity permeated the soldier's voice and manner. This wasn't the man perturbing Mrs. Henderson. But Caleb wasn't telling him everything. Both he and Mrs. Henderson were holding something back. But what was it, and why wouldn't they share it?

Chapter 4

February 1864, Eastern Kentucky

The man walked unseeing—his feet bare—through the woods. It was light, but late afternoon winter light—low and cool, coming from just above the horizon. His britches were worn at the knees, leg bottoms frayed and tattered. He walked slowly, aimlessly, holding close a blanket that covered his hole-pocked shirt. His broad feet, toughened by weeks of walking, still ached from the cold. He looked old and worn, like his britches. But there was a dignity in him. He walked with his back straight, singing quietly, repeating tune and words that spoke of a promised land. Once in a while, a tear slid down his cheek from his reddened, watery eyes. At every tear, a quick movement of the blanket dried his high, dark cheekbone before it could drip into a long, unkempt beard.

He carried a powerful frame, but his legs seemed heavy, barely able to step forward. At one point, he stopped and gazed toward his black feet. He groaned deeply and cried, "Why, Lord, why?" Suddenly, he jerked his head upward and tears—that he no longer stanched—streamed freely into the beard. "How long, Lord?" he yelled in despair. "How long?" His cry echoed indistinctly in the trees.

He lowered his head and renewed his slow, stumbling march, dabbing again at his cheeks. He came to a clearing in the woods, stopped, moved his head to gaze from one side of the meadow to the other, then feebly stepped into the clearing. Halfway across, he stopped at a tree stump and stared blankly at it. His head began an assenting nod, and he carefully twisted and lowered his frame till his back rested against the stump. He pulled the blanket more tightly to him, tucking his feet under it.

He was sleepy but forced his mind to consider the dried grass of the field, the distant trees. He looked up for one last glimpse of the sun through the winter-bared trees. He began to rock, again singing quietly of the promised land. He sang and sang and sang, softer, softer, softer, till his head fell gently forward jerking his body to the ground.

The boy had followed him a long while, listening to his woeful song, curious about who he was and why he walked through the woods. Strangers were in the woods and on the roads nearly every day now, and he carefully avoided them. He wasn't even supposed to be near the forest. If his mother knew. He winced imagining the punishment. These were perilous times and dangerous men were about. But this man was different. He seemed so sad. The boy was sure the stranger's sorrow was the heaviest burden he'd ever seen, and he'd seen men heft heavy logs and boulders.

"You see, Mama," he imagined himself explaining, "I had to see what was wrong." He had witnessed the man enter the clearing, sit by the stump and sway till he fell. The boy expected him to struggle to his feet. When he didn't, he—Adam—ran swiftly along the tree line, disappearing into the woods, breathing heavily as he ran.

The woman scrambled after Adam as quickly as she could, furious he'd again done exactly what she'd forbidden. She understood he was too energetic to be kept at home, that he wandered no matter how she disciplined him or how great the trouble in the area. The boy was small for his nine years, unnaturally innocent, and her fear for his life and freedom tortured her days and nights.

He had far outpaced her, and with no hope of catching him, she slowed. In spite of the dangers, raids and war around them, Adam had never seen a corpse outside a box, so she accepted his curiosity, and she hadn't discouraged him from returning for the body. But she had no intention of doing anything with the corpse—she and the boy couldn't carry a man's body. She was just letting Adam learn and wearing him out so she could have a few moments of peace.

The boy was out of sight, but she knew he could navigate the woods and fields. She followed in the direction he'd disappeared. She was a healthy woman, able to walk for hours without tiring, but she didn't want to walk. She wanted to be at home, preparing supper. Approaching the field Adam had described, she could barely see him waiting. He didn't hurry her, but she could tell he was troubled by what he saw.

She approached the body carefully and was surprised to see a black man. She looked at him, curled on his side, legs together, one arm slightly behind him, the other slack in front, resting on the frozen earth. She stepped between the body and the boy, looking at her child.

He asked, "He . . . he . . . he's dead, isn't he?"

"Yes, he is."

"I . . . I . . . I've never seen a . . . um . . . ah . . . dddead body before."

"Yes, you have, just not where it died." She reached down, put her arm on his small back, blocking his view.

"I . . . I liked him, Mama. He was mmmy . . . friend."

"Hush now. You don't know him. Friend? Ridiculous."

"I know," he responded dejectedly. He thoughtfully added, "BBBut I liked him."

She didn't look at the body again, but gently turned her son's shoulders homeward. "Time we go. I've work to do, and so do you. I'm glad you brought me. It was good to care," she said as she lightly pushed the boy.

He looked up at her with dark eyes. "Aren't we go . . . go . . . going to bring him?"

"How? You know we can't. He's too heavy."

"We ccc . . . ," his head jerked forward, "can't leave him."

She could feel him resist her physical guidance. She'd have to be careful now, or she'd not get him home tonight. "We'll get help. Tomorrow. We can get him then."

She knew the argument hadn't worked when he pulled free from her grip and ran toward the body. She'd lost the battle. He was strong-willed. Once he fastened something in his mind, he couldn't be turned. She sighed as she watched him lean over the body to examine it. She loved her son and moved closer to him. "He's too heavy."

His eyes pled hopefully. "I could get a . . . um . . . sho . . . sho . . . vel . . . a shovel. I'll dig a hole, bury him in the hole."

She gazed at his caramel complexion with patience. "We shouldn't be out here." She resigned herself to using fear. "Do you want to be kidnapped? Do you know what they'll do to you . . . a little black boy?"

His expression didn't change. "They won't ccc . . .catch me, Ma. They won't be able to. I can run fa . . . fa . . . fast."

"Oh, you can run fast, but they'll have horses, dogs. They'll catch you . . . and beat you. Then they'll take you down to Harris' and auction you off, sell you to some master down in Alabama . . . and you'll break your mama's heart."

"I . . . I . . . I'll tell them I'm . . . I'm not a . . . a slave."

"Oh," she laughed in a sort of snort. "They won't listen. They'll say, 'Maybe you is, maybe you isn't a slave, but we caught ya now. We'll be selling ya at Harris'.' Then you'll be a slave for sure. And they'll do just that. They'll sell you right down there at Harris', and you'll have to go work all your life for some mean ogre down south in the cotton fields, and he'll beat you. And you'll deserve it, too. Oh, yes you will. Adam, you were freed soon after you were born, and you don't know what it's like to be a slave."

She wanted to stop, but wanted to go home more, so she persisted. "When they've sold you, you're not going to want to do what your master commands. You won't like him one bit. You'll look for little ways to do what he forbids. You'll look for secret ways to punish him. Once in a while you'll get caught. Maybe you'll steal something—and you know that's not right—or you'll talk about freedom to other slaves. And the overseer—he's a bad man who hates slaves—he'll tie you to a tree and whip you till your back bleeds and swells up. Maybe he'll pour salty water on your back. You'll put on your shirt, and it will hurt. It will stick to your back till it won't ever come off. Yes, you'll just moan the whole day and night. That's what's going to happen when you get caught."

"MMMa, you're just making that up. No one's going to kidnap me. YYY . . . You said slavery was over. You're just trying to sssc . . . care me. Besides, the judge would speak for me. They'd listen to the jjjudge."

She couldn't help but smile at him, grateful he was so protected. Odd that his stuttering had softened the world to him. He believed people mistreated him only because he stuttered, never suspecting it was his ancestry. She couldn't keep up the fear-mongering. "Adam, I do hope the judge would take care of you."

"I'll bu . . . bu . . . bury him!"

"Do you know how hard it is to dig a hole deep enough for a body? You can't bury it right under the ground, or the rain will wash away the dirt and animals will dig it up. You've got to bury it deep, and this Kentucky clay is almost harder than rock, especially when it's so dry . . . so frozen."

"How de . . . de . . . deep?"

"Big enough to stand in it without seeing over the top . . . maybe deeper."

"Th . . . Th . . . That's deep!"

"Yes. Too much work for you. Let's go home before it's dark. Come."

"I cccan do it, Ma."

"Not today, you can't!"

"Bu . . . Bu . . .But," his head jerked forward again, "I can start today, finish tttomorrow."

"Do you know how hard it will be to move the body? When a man's dead, he's extra heavy. All the food he's ever eaten . . . all that weight comes back on him!"

"I can just pppush him into the h . . . h . . . hole."

"Try pushing him," she said, reaching down to show the boy how useless it was. She shoved, and as expected the limp body resisted. But a slight shock passed through her. The body was warm, too warm for a dead man in the cold.

Chapter 5

February 1864, Eastern Kentucky

It was dark as Adam led the men to the field. The boy would scamper ahead, then come back, then scurry ahead again. Lanterns in hand, the judge and two slaves followed him, making their way slowly, carefully to the opening. They'd brought a wagon and hidden it near the road. A slave had been left behind to protect it should it be discovered. He was frightened of slave patrollers and had suggested the wagon would be safe left alone. But the judge insisted he guard it.

It was dangerous for all of them, and only the judge's long and deep attachment to Adam's mother had brought them on such an errand. Eastern Kentucky was a difficult place in 1864. It was a legally loyal slave state, but only some citizens shared the Union allegiance.

Because it remained in the Union, Kentucky was untouched by the Emancipation Proclamation. But slaves were restless, often escaping to nearby free states or attempting—to the consternation of owners—to enlist in the Northern Army. Enlistment bought freedom, so slave patrols, tasked with preventing wandering slaves, worked vigilantly to stop them from escaping to the army.

The judge, in his late twenties, tall, slender, studious-looking, owned a number of slaves and kept most by paying them low wages. He assured them, unlike many neighbors, that he'd keep families together. A few slaves, nonetheless, anxious for freedom, had run to the army. He quickly learned he couldn't even visit former slaves once they were in military hands. The auburn-hair judge had insisted in those cases, with spotty success, that he be compensated by the government.

One escaped slave found army life another form of servitude with a less-personal and personable master. He yearned for the greater freedom he'd enjoyed with the judge and wrote his former master begging for a restoration to his family. The judge had approached the army, hoping to help the young slave, but it was for naught as he was quickly, adamantly denied contact with the lad.

The judge wrote the slave explaining he could do nothing. He reminded the new soldier that he had a new master and should conduct himself with courage, obedience and dignity. Perhaps, he wrote, when the war was over, he could enjoy the freedom that had enticed him to enlist. Shortly after sending the letter, the judge took government compensation and forgot about the slave.

The night was moonless, and the men anticipated alert slave patrols. Never far from their minds was the added possibility they might run into Confederate or Union raiding parties. Before they set out, the judge had given each slave a pass, and each man had nervously, carefully secured it in his clothes—fear of patrollers and raiders dwelt deep in slaves and freedmen.

As the rescue party came to the fallen man, patrollers rode near the hidden wagon. Isaiah, the slave left to guard it, could feel the nervousness of the harnessed horses and worked hard to keep them calm and quiet, patting and petting them, whispering pleadingly in their ears.

The concussion of hoofs on the ground increased, and he could soon hear pattyrollers laughing. They slowed their horses as they neared. They no longer laughed, but rode silently, listening. Isaiah prayed they would keep moving, not stop, not hear the horses. He would have run, but he told himself he was loyal to his master, obliged to protect the wagon. Closer to the truth, he feared his master's wrath should he or the wagon be gone when needed.

The patrollers were laughing again. Isaiah could hear one brag about catching a slave the night before. The slave had been trying to enlist, but when they finished with him and delivered him to his appreciative owner, the slave couldn't crawl. Expletives, curses, approvals greeted the story, along with verbal hopes the current night would yet yield another wayward slave.

The pattyrollers stopped, listened again . . . just feet from Isaiah and the horses. Isaiah, sure they would find him, panted in short, shallow breaths as sweat beaded on his face. He wanted to run, but he knew running offered no real promise. They'd catch him, and if they didn't find him quickly, slave catchers would come with dogs. He felt faint. His head was light. He leaned against one of the horses to stay upright.

Isaiah had been whipped many times and no longer thought himself brave. He didn't want to be whipped, especially by these men who had no interest in seeing he could work again. He'd once been proud, resisting the will of his masters as much as he could, anytime he could, any way he could. He'd stolen from them, because they stole everything from him. He'd refused to work, because they'd not given him adequate clothing. He'd run away because they'd sold his children to passing slave traders. But his masters had beaten resistance and rebellion from him. Whipping after whipping. Scar after scar. Isolation. Tied in the scorching sun for days. They'd worn him down. He was, in his own mind, a broken man.

He didn't care now what he had to do as long as it didn't end in a whipping. He cursed the judge under his breath for leaving him to guard the wagon. Any other slave would have been a better choice. They weren't stronger—no one was stronger—but they were braver. He still slumped against the horse.

The patrollers were so close he imagined he could hear their breathing. He closed his eyes and pleaded silently with Jesus to deliver him. He stopped the prayer unfinished to again curse his master. Oh, the agony. He prayed, reminding the Lord they both knew what it was like to be beaten and whipped. Protect me, Jesus, from these bullwhip-carrying Pharisees—these crackers—whose whips shatter the frozen, dry night air. He knew the day of Jubilee was coming. It had to. Lord Jesus, keep me from whipping till that day.

His prayers were answered. One of the pattyrollers, trying to better his compatriots, said he had a good story—the humbling of a slave. "It was a woman we found. She don't have no pass, and we done catched her and . . ." The story trailed off as the patrollers, again jovial, moved away.

Isaiah collapsed onto the ground. He thought about his wife and wondered if the story the man was telling was true. His wife was gone, sold by her master as his financial circumstances had deteriorated. The judge, while sympathetic, was unable to buy her. Isaiah didn't know where she was. His heart pounded, sweat saturated his shirt, and he allowed his breathing free rein.

He again cursed the judge for leaving him behind. He thought the judge an honest master, but he wasn't sure he was wise . . . or smart. He prayed again to Jesus for the Jubilee.

Adam led the judge to the man. Laying his lantern on the ground, the judge and a slave moved close to the prostrate man. The slave without command raised his own lantern while the judge crouched, feeling the man's forehead.

"What's your name, and what are you doing here?" the judge asked. He beckoned the slave who carried a litter.

Adam, at the judge's side when he stood up, stammered, "Is he ssstill alllive?"

"He's alive." The judge said, not looking at the boy.

The two slaves laid a blanket they'd brought on top of the stretcher and positioned it next to the unconscious body. They struggled to move the man to the litter, lifting, pushing, shoving, eventually rolling him onto it and wrapping the blanket around him.

The judge turned, bent over Adam and said sternly, "Don't run ahead. Stay with us, or your mother will punish you. We can't lose you now . . . and don't make noise. Do as I tell you, boy, so . . . ." He didn't finish the statement. Instead, he stood up and peered at Adam. He added, hoping to entice the boy to good behavior, "I want you to stay by the litter. Make sure he's comfortable. Can you do that?"

A wide smile broke across Adam's face, "I c . . . c . . . can," he said with his mouth opening awkwardly and his head jerking slightly forward, then back.

The judge said softly to the stretcher-bearing slaves, "Go ahead. Careful."

The patrollers returned. Isaiah didn't know why, but as his broad-shouldered, tall frame lay on the ground, exhausted by their last visit, he heard them. Silent prayers began anew. He could hear what they were saying.

"The path be here . . . along here somewheres."

His fellow pattyroller responded gruffly, "Well, you'd better find it, or we'll know it was a yarn."

"It be here. We'll find . . ."

"What's that?" whispered the second patroller—the patrol captain.

"What?"

The captain spurred his horse in Isaiah's direction. "In the trees."

"I see it!" Someone added.

Isaiah, instantly alert, leaped to his feet, shielded from view by the horses.

"A wagon."

"Why be it here?"

The captain moved his horse to the wagon. "Light the torch! Mischief's afoot," he cried.

The patrollers crowded the wagon's side as one lit a torch. It cast a faint, warm yellow light on the wagon and horses and ghostly shadows into the dark.

"Don't see no one."

"A man don't leave his wagon and horses in the middle of the night, not without some plan. Mischief's afoot. Give me that torch, Abner. Look around."

"Massa."

Slightly startled, the pattyrollers looked down on a well-groomed black man of broad nose, full lips, tight-cropped hair and high forehead.

"Where'd you come from, you . . . ?"

"Left wid the wagon, Massa."

"Ain't yours!" Another patroller called out, laughing.

"No, Massa. Ain't none of mine. Belongs to the judge."

"Judge?"

"Yes, Massa, the judge."

"Why you here? Show us your pass, you . . . ."

When he finished the abuse, Isaiah answered "Yes, Massa. Here it be, Massa. I gots a pass, Massa." Isaiah showed humility, but no fear. He handed his pass to the horseman, ignoring the two patrollers who had dismounted and now stood behind him. One was cracking a whip.

The captain held the pass in torchlight to read it. "This don't look like a real pass." The pass touched the torch's blaze, and the patroller turned the paper so the flame rose along the note, then tossed it to the ground. "Don't believe you got a pass, you . . . ."

Isaiah didn't argue or respond, but his body stiffened, ready for an assault. He could run—but they'd catch and beat him mercilessly. He could resist and fight, but they'd pummel him more viciously, especially for any good punches he might throw. He could submit passively, and they'd still thrash him. The only difference in outcome would be the extent of his bodily injury. Anger like the pent up pressure of a volcano exploded.

He heard a crack close behind him and spun just as a second whip lashed at him, catching his chest, tearing his overcoat. He was momentarily grateful for winter, and leaned away from the blow, while with a sudden arm thrust, he grabbed the whip's receding tail and pulled vigorously. A man fell at his feet, and he spun around just as another man dived at him, attempting to grab him. He cat-like stepped aside, and the man fell hard on the ground, grunting. Another whip lashed his arm, and without thinking, he sent the handle of the whip he held in the direction of the lash, catching it and wrapping itself like a snake around the first whip. Then he felt a blow, hard against the back of his head, and still holding the whip, stumbled forward toward the ground. Dazed, he let go of the whip and reached out to break his fall.

"What ruction!" commented a quiet voice.

The torch, resting on the ground, was raised toward the voice, illuminating the judge as he calmly surveyed the combatants.

"Jud . . . Judge," the captain sputtered. Looking suddenly sheepish, he added, "Glad you're here."

"Looks as though I've come just in time." He added in his mind for personal amusement, "to save you."

"This slave . . . no pass," stuttered the captain.

The judge looked at Isaiah sternly. "What'd you do with that pass? Can't you even take care of a pass? You . . . ."

Isaiah listened to the judge's vile insults, staring humbly toward the ground. "No, Massa. Must'a lost it."

"We'll beat him for you, Judge," a pattyroller offered.

"No, that pleasure will be mine." The judge then said patronizingly to Isaiah, "Let this be a lesson, you . . . ."

"Yes, Massa," Isaiah said, his head still downcast.

"Now, gentlemen," he said turning to the patrollers. "Thank you for your vigilance. I hope you would have been lenient with him—he's got work to do. I'm so glad you came when you did." Conversationally he added, "Now that you're here, would you help get this man in the wagon. He collapsed, and we've come to take him home, but please be gentle. He's hurt badly . . . and worth a lot—don't want to lose him. Please, lift him gently into the wagon."

Without saying anything, the patrollers gathered around the stretcher laid on the ground.

"Judge, why can't your slaves do this? Didn't realize you had so many with you," the captain queried.

"Not gentle enough, not these . . . . They'd injure the man. Takes a white man for careful endeavors."

The slaves moved from the body and watched, quietly giddy, as the patrollers lifted the man into the wagon.

When the body lay motionless in the wagon, the judge smiled warmly. "Thank you for that . . . for your diligence. I release you to proceed with your patrol."

As the patrollers silently mounted their horses, the judge said, "Oh, you've forgotten your whips. Here. Here they are." He moved to where the whips curled on the ground and handed them to the captain. "Thank you again," he said warmly. "Goodnight."

The patrollers rode off dispirited, humiliated. The judge knew he played a dangerous game, that their emotions would later coalesce into anger—anger especially dangerous for his slaves—but he felt mischievous, and he couldn't constrain himself.

Isaiah, his head throbbing from the earlier blow, climbed into the box to drive as Adam and the other slaves clambered carefully into the back of the wagon. The judge watched the patrollers ride from sight, then climbed up with Isaiah and said offhandedly, "There now, Isaiah, I told you nothing would happen while we were gone."

Isaiah didn't respond, and the judge, not expecting an answer, laughed softly, then began whistling happily.

Chapter 6

February 1864, Richmond, Virginia

The uniformed man shifted the second letter nervously hand to hand, feigning to read it again. He was thinking, not ready to speak. He glanced at the calling card on his desk, the visitor's name—Oskar Dante—written elegantly at its center. He thought it odd the stranger had inadvertently given him a carte de visite with its image of the man before him in a flamboyant Confederate uniform, then quickly snatched it, apologizing for the mistake. It was meant, he had explained, for an evening social call.

The soldier sized up his visitor. He was blond, lean but strong, with a full beard and bothersome light blue eyes that stared and pierced. Dante was well dressed . . . too well dressed for the captain's taste. His right arm rested in a sling. Did he like this man? Not at all. His impression was aversion, disgust. He was too smooth, too aristocratic, not trustworthy. But trust might not be needed. Dante might be useful, so the soldier restrained his revulsion.

He glanced at Dante's staring eyes, then dropped his head quickly. When the soldier finished considering options, he spoke. "Notable letters . . recommendations—a general . . . a governor."

Dante blustered, but quickly softened his tone. "Yes, they are. I hope they convey the respect they hold for me . . . my talents, loyalty."

"Yes, your loyalty," the interviewer said dismissively. "I have just one question. Why do this? With your battle record, you could land notable appointments anywhere in the government . . . perhaps more in the public eye."

"Yes, surely. But I'm not interested in that. I am, if nothing else, selfless. I need no stage nor clamoring crowd. Give me the quiet salon."

Selfless? The question ran slowly through the captain's mind, tickling even its hardened corners. The Confederate restrained the impulse to smile.

Dante continued, "I don't want prominence . . . nor fame. Simply to serve our grand Revolution. My grandfather fought the first—the English tyranny. I'll be true to his legacy and repel these foreigners, throw off this Northern tyranny. Is that wrong? I hope we haven't debased ourselves such that we do all now merely for fame."

No prominence? No fame? Selfless? The officer thought it unlikely. He would have wagered his family's dwindling wealth to bet that Dante lived for fame, fortune and money. His dissembling talk of humility was meaningful, but the captain couldn't quite understand why.

"To be honest, I've seen battle enough for any man," Dante continued. "The war's hard fought in the west—as it is here. I've been intimately involved in much of it out there, and would that I could fight to see independence assured. But an arm like this . . . useless . . . at jeopardy of losing it outright any day." His words ended abruptly as he nodded to his slinged right arm. "Useless to the army. If you lose a leg, they can strap you on a horse. Lose an arm, it's harder." He looked again at the sling, then at the officer. "I want to do what I can do, because I can no longer do what I would."

"I see."

"But that's not all," Dante pressed passionately.

The officer expected more exquisite fabrications.

"To be frank, I miss society. This is a way . . . to be part of the Revolution and enjoy the company of Richmond . . . ladies." He winked at the officer.

The officer was embarrassed to see the wink. It made him feel a guilty conspirator against Richmond's female gentry. He looked down, one eyebrow twitching nervously. Dante made him feel sordid, but the captain thought he'd finally heard a remnant of truth. "You think you can do in Richmond what the governor claims of you in Atlanta?"

"Claims? I don't have to prove what I've done, sir. Not to you . . . not to anyone." Dante pounded the desk methodically for emphasis, discomforting the officer.

Dante was visibly agitated, and the officer regretted the word "claims." He'd used it to jab his guest, but when he saw his visitor's rage, he was frightened the man might challenge him . . . or leap across the desk to beat him.

Oskar Dante continued, each word enunciated perfectly, elongated for emphasis. "I can do what I did in Atlanta . . . and more. There are more traitors here, so close to the North. Be assured, I will unmask . . . ." He paused, not finishing the thought, looked at the floor and added in a subdued tone, "If you'll let me." He quickly raised his piercing eyes to peer at the officer and spoke still softer, "I'm anxious to get to work. The government needs my service to end this wretched invasion. We must unmask Northern sympathizers who pass information through the lines."

The captain was irritated. "Save your lectures," he said gruffly. He immediately regretted his words, again fearing a formal challenge. The officer had once seen a duel. It had left him with a recurring dream in which he died of a pistol wound in a hastily arranged affair of honor. He unconsciously slid back in his chair.

Dante's face flushed, but he said nothing.

The officer continued in a more cordial tone. "I'll consider it. We . . . we have spies here in Richmond, of course."

"Yes," Dante responded condescendingly, "but none to provide information on the highest society . . . not as I can." His voice rose in volume and confidence. "Information . . . names. Whatever I discover is yours. Feathers in your cap—yours alone. I'm not interested in recognition for my great contributions. I assure you I want no fame—you'd never have to reveal who told you."

"You'd want something."

"Nothing. I do this for our nation . . . and for the society of the ladies, as I've confessed." He smiled at the captain. "Of course, I must have resources to look the part. I lost everything when the barbarians overran my New Orleans plantation. I must have money. That's part of the scheme, don't you see?" Dante noticed the officer's face sour, and quickly added, "I ask a lot, but when I bring you what no one else can . . . Don't get me wrong. I want to live well, and that's part of my reason . . . why I'm willing to sacrifice like this. And that's exactly why it will work so well . . . for us both. You need information to win this war. I, who have served the country so well in Atlanta, then in the field . . . now crippled," he peeked at his sling, "I just want a few creature comforts. We're not naive . . . you and I. Prudent men. We know the world. We get what we want." Dante stopped briefly to watch how his words affected the man and continued when he saw the officer no longer resisted. "Agreed, then?"

"You promise a lot."

"I proved myself in Atlanta. I gave them vital information."

"I'll consider it." He rose.

"We can't agree now?" Dante said in unveiled surprise.

"What you're asking will take time . . . arrangements."

"But I don't want to . . ."

"I'm sure you'd like me to decide now, but I can't."

Dante glared at the officer, but said only, "Thank you. I think you'll find my offer a blessing to our nation."

"I'll contact you. Adieu." The officer nodded at his now unwelcome guest, sat down, opened a drawer and slid Dante's two letters of recommendation into it. He drew out different papers and, without acknowledging Dante further, began reading.

Dante smiled, stood and said, "Thank you for seeing me. We'll accomplish much together."

The officer without looking up, waved his left hand.

As Dante moved toward the door, the officer called out forcefully, "Close the door."

Dante stepped through the door, closing it softly. He hurried out of the Mechanics Institute Building, passing its double doors into the sunny, cold winter morning.

Created to encourage technology and education, the building had narrowed its focus to destructive weapons technology and an education for war. From the use of its big hall by the secessionist convention to its division into the bureaucratic beehives of the Confederate War, Navy and Patent departments, the building had been reborn, and Dante smirked thinking of it.

But he really didn't care, his thoughts shifting quickly to his next appointment. He pulled a watch from his vest with his left hand to check the hour. He had enough time to walk the few blocks to his next appointment.

Dante was pleased. He'd get what he wanted from this Confederate cringing tiger. The captain—timid, frightened, bureaucratic—just needed to flex scrawny muscles to show he had them, but Dante had seen how weak they were. He reveled in conquest.

He moved along Franklin Street, from the Capitol to the corner of 8th. There he stopped, seemingly confused. He looked in every direction, then turned south, ambling aimlessly for a half block before he stopped again, furtively glancing around. With no one in sight, he quickly and effortlessly removed his sling, letting his right hand drop easily to his side. It moved in natural rhythm as he made his way rapidly toward a warehouse on Canal Street.

A man, also appearing to be in his late twenties, stood outside a warehouse watching Dante as he approached. He was shorter than Dante and wore a bowler, with a scarf tied high around his neck which disappeared into his knee-length overcoat. A red beard without mustache covered his chin and jawline. His nose was red from the cold, but he smiled warmly as Dante approached. "I'm so pleased to see you, dear old friend."

"Matthew, thank you for meeting me."

"Why wouldn't I?" jovially asked the red-haired man.

"You know what happened? You heard, I'm sure."

"I did. Unfortunate."

"I almost had it all." Dante laughed. "I was . . ."

"You killed a man."

"Had to. He would have revealed me."

Matthew laughed deeply, and in a mischievous voice said, "In his death, he did reveal you."

Dante was uneasy. This was not the topic he'd expected. "What do you mean?"

Matthew grinned, putting his hand on the taller man's shoulder. "I just note his death defeated your best plans. Unfortunate."

Dante was expressionless. "It was unfortunate."

"Yes, for the victim." Matthew laughed again.

Dante blinked nervously.

"Come, let's walk," suggested Dante's acquaintance.

"I'm cold. Let's go to your office."

"Yes, we could . . . No, let's walk. We'll walk down toward the iron works. It's a pleasant stroll on such a sunny day. You can tell me all that's happened and about this business scheme of yours. I just hope it doesn't include another widow. The last one didn't work out." Matthew chuckled happily again.

Dante peered nervously at Matthew. Something was different. In spite of the smiles, Matthew radiated hostility. Yes, he'd failed to marry Mrs. Henderson and get control of her wealth. He'd settled for less than he hoped, but he got a small fortune—stuffed in that box in the woods. Why should any of it matter to Matthew? He looked at Matthew's laughing eyes and pleasant smile. "Matthew, what is it? Don't speak riddles. Acknowledge the corn. We've known each other too long for this."

Matthew laughingly asked, "Lucius, do you really believe it's been that long?"

Dante, not dressed nearly as warmly as Matthew, suggested again going inside.

"No," Matthew said flatly, ignoring Dante's discomfort.

Dante shivered as he realized Matthew didn't want to be seen with him.

"Why did you do it?"

"What?"

"Kill the man."

Dante sighed. "How do you know about that?"

"I heard he died. You told me his name last time we met. Stokes wasn't it? When I heard he was killed, I knew. But you haven't told me why. Something happened, and before we do business . . . again, tell me what it was."

Dante looked toward Tredegar Iron Works, where much of the artillery and iron for the Southern war effort was manufactured. He thought the murder behind him, and now to have Matthew, of all people, bring it up.

He'd killed Stokes because Stokes had failed. He'd been responsible for part of Dante's last scheme—defrauding Betsy Henderson by using her woolen factory, which Stokes oversaw, to smuggle and hoard valuable commodities. Stokes was to make the factory appear ever busy weaving cloth for butternut uniforms. But he failed, and their unwitting patron became suspicious. Stokes tried to deflect blame for Betsy's doubt onto Dante, and his accusation had provoked Dante to explosive violence. Dante responded, "Why care about Stokes?"

Matthew halted, turned, squared his shoulders and looked into Dante's blue eyes. A brief stern look melted to a friendly smile. "Oh, Lucius. I didn't know this Stokes fellow and don't care what happened to him. I've grown quite used to death." His smile faded as he spoke, but his eyes still danced merrily. "What I don't under . . . what I need to

understand is why you killed him. Until I do, there won't be
. . . an opportunity to work together, regardless of how marvelous your scheme."

"Humph." Dante groaned in resignation. He thought
briefly and spoke carefully. "He died, because he was destroying my effort to overcome Betsy."

"Destroying?"

"He didn't keep Betsy's factory looking busy."

"Incredulous! I don't believe it. You'll have to tell me
more if you want my help."

"That was it."

"Lucius. You're wanted for murder in Staunton."

"That's hundreds of miles . . ."

"Hundreds of miles! Maybe a hundred, and that's nothing. Everyone's moving around the state right now. I have to
force myself to believe it's you . . . here. A sane man would
be somewhere in Georgia or New York or . . . Europe. You
can't hope to live here . . . not safely . . . not in Richmond . . .
not in Virginia . . . maybe not in the Confederacy. Someone,
somewhere will remember you from Staunton or Wilmington
. . . or some other town. So you need to tell me exactly why it
happened, and your plan had better be rewarding . . . to
make it worth my friendship to help you."

"Friendship!" Dante said with disgust.

"If, then . . . dear friend, there is no friendship, you'd
better explain it especially well."

"I lost my temper. Is that what you want me to say?"
Dante spat out with rising anger in his voice.

Matthew's smile broadened. "That wasn't so bad was it?
The truth. I suspect it's new to you." He laughed from his
belly.

Dante's anger dwindled to nervous laughter.

"Doesn't it feel better to share the truth with a friend?"

"I do feel better."

"I knew you would. Even when you thought I wasn't your friend, I was looking after you."

Dante feigned a smile.

"Stopping like this . . . I feel the cold. Let's keep walking." Matthew began strolling leisurely again.

"Now, can I tell you what I've got in mind?"

"Of course," Matthew said haltingly. "But before you delve into details, explain why you struck an innocent woman . . . one you were stealing from . . . one you had planned to marry . . . further fleece? Seems to me, she should have slapped you." He laughed again. "You did deserve at least that."

Dante's anger flashed again. He wanted to hit Matthew. Matthew could feel it, and he smiled to himself. Too many people were passing them, Lucius wouldn't dare strike. One of the comforts of this mid-winter stroll, he thought. This is why he no longer wanted to work with Lucius. His anger. It got Walthrope in trouble. And the new, more intense anger that brought murder in Staunton and Betsy Henderson's assault portended worse.

Matthew feared Walthrope's anger was becoming uncontrollable. He would have walked away from him without looking back, if he dared. But Lucius knew too much about him to be dismissed. He had to manage the man carefully. He spoke calmly, kindly again. "Lucius, I must understand. Did you have to hit her?"

Through gritted teeth, he growled, "I had to teach her!"

"Teach her! Did the student . . . did the honorable Mrs. Henderson learn the lesson? What was the lesson? Don't get involved with thieves!" Matthew laughed loud enough that a boy passing by turned to look. "It's just so comical, ludicrous burlesque. You teaching our widow."

"That's not the teaching I'm talking about." Dante wanted to grab Matthew and throw him to the ground.

"Don't cohort with smugglers? Was that the lesson? Or don't be tempted by the Devil and loneliness to fall in love with murderers?" Matthew was pushing hard.

"That's enough. I don't want to hurt you."

"Nor do I want to be hurt," Matthew said jovially.

"Do you want to do business? If so, let's get on with it. I don't know what you're about, but I won't put up with it."

"You won't?" Matthew responded harshly, "I suggest you get and keep control of yourself. I'm not a lackey you can bully, threaten . . . or attack."

"What do you want?" Dante asked despondently.

"Ah, good, friends again." Matthew spoke in a happy pitch that grated on Dante. "A simple question. Why strike that poor, beautiful woman?"

Dante said sadly, "I hated her."

"I thought you loved her?"

He said earnestly, "I may have loved her. I think about her . . . wish it had been different. If nothing else, it would have been easier."

Matthew chuckled.

"I wished, just then . . ."

"When?"

"When she told me she knew I'd killed Stokes. I'd been so close to holding her . . ."

"And her money."

Dante ignored his comment. "I was so close, but it melted . . . collapsed."

"Can I assume then you would have done more if you could? A slap across the face seems so controlled . . . so little for what she'd done to you."

Dante considered the question, remembering his rage. He'd wanted to kill Betsy, her mother, Betsy's plain friend and that hobbled soldier. He'd been so close to having her and her money. She did deserve more. When he got his hands on her again, he'd . . . . He broke off the thought. For now, he'd be satisfied with the back-hand, diamond-ring-enhanced slap that bloodied her face.

Matthew saw Dante's body tighten, his hands flex as if squeezing something. He shuddered at his friend's increasing darkness and fear warned him away, but he was trapped.

"She did deserve more," Dante answered. "A simple slap . . . nothing for what she'd done. But fortune smiled on me." He proudly pulled off his glove and raised the ring for Matthew to see. "She was bleeding when I left. That is my solace."

"But surely you left with money. Money's solace."

"Yes, I'd banked, as it were, money."

"If it makes you prouder," Matthew said reassuringly, "she was left with a scar across that beautiful face. That's what I've heard. I haven't seen it, mind you." He laughed. "You left a great impression on her."

"A scar?" Dante chuckled.

"Makes you feel better, then . . . the scar."

"It must make her think of me every time she looks in a glass. She'll remember me." He paused. "Things worked out better than I thought."

"To be remembered by a past love is consolation, isn't it? But then, Lucius, I imagine to be remembered fondly is better." Matthew snickered.

"To be remembered is enough." Dante said coldly. "And her lover . . ."

"Lover?"

"I told you about him. A Union soldier. Met him on my way out of her house. I beat him. Perhaps he's scarred, too. I left him writhing on the ground. I should have killed him." His eyes glowed with anger.

"What an interesting end to your story, although . . . it really isn't over. I wonder what will yet happen."

"Why's that important?"

"Not important. Just interesting."

"Don't call me Lucius."

"What shall I call you?

"I'm Oskar Dante."

"How poetic. Now, what's your scheme?"

The two men slipped into comfortable conspiratorial tones as they continued their stroll.

Chapter 7

February 1864, Staunton, Virginia

Robert Sheriff awaited his third interview filled with increasing ardor for Mrs. Henderson. He still claimed it was fatherly concern, but when he examined his motives closely, he became uneasy. He was waiting to meet Betsy's cousin Emily Graham. Her falling out with Betsy was well known, although no one would say what caused it.

The sheriff had given his card to the small, nervous servant woman, and she'd disappeared toward the back of the house to present it to her mistress. He looked around the hall admiringly, noting its elegance, attention to detail, fashionable decor. His heart was light. He felt a ripple of excitement at meeting such a lady, but the feeling immediately embarrassed him. Had he descended so low as to get excited each time he met a young woman?

The question discouraged him, and his previous excitement gave way to anxiety. It was good he'd be doing this job only a few more months. He tried to corral his thoughts. He was here to get information, a formal inquiry. He couldn't allow feelings or fashion to distract from truth. Then thoughts of Mrs. Henderson crept in. He reassured himself yet again that it could only be fatherly feelings. He was right in wanting to protect her—that was part of his occupation and . . .

"Sir, de mistress will see yuh. Please folla me."

The shrill-voiced slave interrupted his thoughts, and he found he was gazing blankly up the wide staircase, lost in analysis and self-justification. He smiled to himself and without responding followed the slave.

"Sheriff, it's an honor to have you here in our home. A wonderful surprise, and at such an hour! We don't have callers so early in the morning . . . not usually."

The sheriff didn't have time to notice the room because Emily greeted him as soon as he'd crossed the threshold. He noted her elegant green cashmere morning dress, but smiled nervously as she was clearly reprimanding him for such an early, unannounced social call. She was expecting an apology, but he wouldn't give it. "Mrs. Graham, I'm here on official business."

She smiled, "Ah, that would explain the time . . . and the manners." But she quickly changed her expression to a frown, and exclaimed, "Official business. That sounds serious. Nothing sad, I hope. I particularly don't like to be sad. Is your business sad, Sheriff?"

"I'm here on inquiry."

"Inquiry? About what?"

"May we sit down?"

"If you must." She motioned to a chair in front of a tall window and, with a sweep of her hoop-skirt, moved to a similar chair nearby. "Oh, heavens, the surprise of an official visit has caused me to forget my manners. Sheriff, may I offer you something to eat or drink?"

"Coffee?" the sheriff suggested hopefully, leaning forward to place his hat in front of him on the floor.

"I'm sorry. We don't have coffee. You know the domestic economies," she paused briefly, "required to support the nation. Perhaps tea?"

"Thank you, but no. I want to know about a friend."

"Yours or mine?" Emily smiled faintly. "I want to help you . . . if I can. I'm mindful of duty."

"Very well." The sheriff was beginning to feel the rift parting Emily and Betsy was Lilliputian compared to the chasm between their characters.

"What acquaintance?" Emily betrayed a slight nervousness in the question.

Sheriff hesitated answering, hoping to add to her anxiety. Did her nervousness reveal something? He smiled, feigned coughing, cleared his throat. Emily's eyes darted from object to object in the light-filled room, avoiding the sheriff's gaze. He cleared his throat again.

Emily shifted in her chair. Eventually, Emily's eyes rested on the sheriff. "Your inquiry." she stated firmly.

"My inquiry," the sheriff repeated slowly, letting the words linger.

Finally fully composed, Emily waited patiently. She looked carefully at the sheriff for the first time. "What a queer man," she verbalized in her mind. His silly, long hair emphasized his baldness. She glanced at his worn hat on the floor, his dirty shoes, his unfashionable dress. She didn't like him and was offended to have him in her house . . . on her furniture . . . his hat soiling her floor.

"Mrs. Graham, can you tell me about your cousin?"

"My cousin? Whi . . ."

"Mrs. Henderson."

"Ah, Sheriff, she's no cousin, not by blood . . . not in any way now. She did marry my dear cousin, Thaddeus." She smiled knowingly, trying to cover her guilt at speaking ill of a woman she was desperately jealous of. "Only a cousin by marriage. Now he's gone. Is she still my cousin? No, I don't believe so. She's no relation of mine. She's from up north . . . Winchester. Farther north, and she'd be foreign, but then there was always something foreign about her."

The sheriff smiled congenially. "Yes, I knew she was a cousin by marriage."

Her eyes dimmed. "Thaddeus died at Manassas."

"I knew he died, but not where. Sorry to speak of it."

"Oh, it's fine. A long while ago. But he was a wonderful soldier . . . and man—my cousin. My husband, you must know, was severely . . . heroically injured at Gettysburg. It happens to so many . . . among the most valiant Virginians. No shirkers . . . my husband and cousin. We just have to live with it, don't we? The will of God. I doubt Mrs. Henderson— it's a pity she still carries the name—will ever accept the will of the Almighty. Sheriff, whatever Mrs. Henderson's done, I've nothing to do with it."

The sheriff had expected negative comments about Mrs. Henderson, knowing the two women were estranged, but he was surprised at Emily's harsh tone. "I'm sorry. I didn't know your husband passed."

"Where did you hear that? From that woman? She lies even about that!" She laughed sarcastically, hating herself again for her own untruth.

The sheriff paused before responding. "No," he drew out the word. "Actually, I just thought you said it. I thought you said they were both courageous."

"They were . . . when they fought in the war. Luckily, God smiled on our family—understandably so—bringing my husband home to me. I thought it clear, Sheriff. I was refer- ring to their courage when they fought in the war." She sounded annoyed. "My husband did not die. He was only injured, as I said. But I must remind you again I've nothing to do with that woman and what she's done. It is so hard to bear . . . that she carries a name she's not worthy of. Scandalous. My cousin's death ended all connection between us, regardless of what you heard."

"Ah, no connection."

"No, none whatsoever."

"Odd, I thought she helped you retrieve your husband . . . after hers was killed. Was it Gettysburg? Where do these rumors come from?"

"Well . . . yes, she did. I wasn't thinking of that."

"What were you thinking of?"

She hesitated. "A general statement. I wasn't thinking about anything. Do you have other questions?"

"You just want me to know you're not close to Mrs. Henderson, so you said you had no relationship with her after Captain Henderson's heroic death."

"Precisely so, Sheriff. I see we understand each other, in spite of your station. I'm pleased. We . . . that woman and I do not speak. Unfortunate, but it has to be. She caused it. Nothing I could do."

"Why not on speaking terms?"

"Countless reasons, Sheriff," she said, exasperated at his probing and her own willingness to disavow Betsy so easily. "Is this really so important? There are times, honestly, I regret we're not close. But it can't be."

"You'd like to be close to her, but you can't be?"

"No, not under the circumstances. It's impossible. Unfortunate, but impossible."

"Impossible?"

"Yes, impossible. She's always judging my husband."

"Your husband? She judges your heroic husband?"

"Yes, there you have it. My husband made mistakes . . . minor errors—what man doesn't? Thoughtful mistakes—the kind great men make." She paused. "He didn't think it right to invade the North, so he stayed behind when the army went to Sharpsburg. But he went to Gettysburg, so you can see it was his conscience . . . not cowardice."

"Invading the North—I remember it was long argued. But how is Mrs. Henderson involved?"

"She found out. She was always prying, questioning me about him. But," her face evidenced a slight sneer, "from that instant . . . the moment she knew, she was always there. She never said anything, but she was always judging . . . condemning a hero of the nation."

She looked at the floor and the sheriff's hat. Her jaw was tight, her eyes narrow, her heart breaking. "Yes, all right, I admit, there were a few indiscretions, but nothing, Sheriff . . . nothing to mention. But there she was, always thinking about them. I could hear her . . . always judging him. She couldn't look at him . . . at me, without thinking of it. She seems saint-ly . . . on the surface. There you have it. She judges harshly . . . not correctly . . . not as a Christian. She judges and con-demns. I think she takes joy in damning him. Yes, you heard me. She damns him to hell."

"That isn't Christian. It must be hard to have her judge you . . . your husband like that. I wouldn't have expected it, after having met her. She seems . . ."

Her voice rose. "Of course you wouldn't expect it. She's . . . she puts on that front . . . that . . . that goodness."

"A facade of goodness?"

"Yes, exactly. A facade—that's the word. I'm pleased you saw through it. Not many do. I'm glad we—the two of us— can share our concerns . . . suspicions openly. She always says and does exactly the right thing. Never the wrong word. But I know she looks at me . . . at good Mr. Graham . . . and is ever thinking of what he did . . . condemning us." She rocked backward and forward.

"May I ask what else he did?" He regretted the question instantly. He'd lose ground with it. He could see the offense and hurt in her eyes.

"He did nothing! I told you of his act of conscience. That wasn't wrong! He was wounded in battle. Doesn't that tell you it was lies . . . the rumors . . . the gossip. Just lies. He's a proud, courageous . . . Virginian and soldier. Why should she judge him a coward? It disgusts me."

Her feelings of guilt and love for Betsy were slipping into dislike. She was finally feeling free of obligation to her cousin's wife. To talk so openly, to relinquish control, to let resentment flow out, it was invigorating. "How dare she?" The hint of a sneer was there again. "And what she was doing. There's no innocence in her."

"What was she doing?" He felt pity for the woman, but pressed forward in spite of the pathos. He was here to find out who threatened Mrs. Henderson, and that was a greater purpose than easing this woman's fragile mind and overwrought feelings. "Can you confirm it for me?"

Emily's anger simmered. What had Betsy done? She remembered, and before she could stop herself—with fury in her eyes—said, "You know of her treason, then. Is that why you've come? Her lover! The Yankee!"

She saw the sheriff's surprise and her anger collapsed of its own weight, leaving her grimacing in horror. What had she done? Betsy would never betray the cause of liberty. It was Emily's own doing, her jealousy's progeny. She resented

Betsy for knowing of her husband's cowardice. She resented Betsy's perfection. Betsy had always been so kind to her. Yes, Betsy loved a Yankee. She'd known him before the war. She openly admitted that to Emily, and Emily had sworn to never reveal it.

Stunned at what she'd divulged to this paunchy, unkempt sheriff, she didn't know how to extricate herself. She felt beyond redemption. The sheriff hadn't known about the Yankee. He'd come on a different errand, and she'd denounced Betsy's innocent love.

Shock registered on her face as she remembered her clandestine visit from Lucius Walthrope. He'd seen the soldier at Betsy's. Was it possible then that she was a traitress? Had the soldier convinced Betsy to reveal Confederate secrets? She must have betrayed us! Else why would the sheriff ask such questions? Betsy . . . a traitress! She'd betrayed Emily, her husband and Virginia.

She was calming down and sneered. She was again free to hate Betsy, and she did. How could perfect Betsy betray everything for a squalid Yankee . . . a private? She deserved Emily's contempt. Emily had been right to uncover it to this sheriff. Her expression changed to a smug smile.

The sheriff watched in wonder as Emily's face migrated through its series of expressions and emotions.

"There," she finally said, "I can't be expected to keep her secrets . . . not when they harm our country."

"No . . . no, you can't," the sheriff said hesitantly. "And you mustn't." His voice firmed. "Your duty is to tell me everything. The soldier . . ."

"Then you already know about her lover . . . that foul Yankee. I told her to forget him. He visited her, didn't he? I'd heard that, but didn't want to believe it. I always believe the best about people, Sheriff. As a Christian, I must. You understand. I know you do. But now . . . Has she told him war secrets? I hope you caught them. Are they in prison? Will they be executed? Don't wait long, Sheriff! They may escape. Traitors have their friends." She paused, looked at the ceiling, then added with determination, "Traitors must be dealt with firmly, quickly."

She was so agitated the sheriff could hear her panting. He was confused. Too many possibilities had accumulated to follow up on. He wanted to be meticulous. Unmasking a traitress. That hadn't been his intention. He began tentatively, "Mrs. Graham . . . may I ask you how you know a Union soldier visited Mrs. Henderson . . . enlisted her to spy?"

Smiling, Emily replied, "A friend of mine visited. The Yankee attacked this dear friend. That woman had invited my friend to her house, but she had her Yankee lover hiding and commanded him to strike . . . to kill my faithful friend. I saw the blood on his shirt."

"May I ask the name of this friend?"

"He's a patriot. Done great things for the Confederacy."

"His name?"

"Mr. Walthrope. The honorable Mr. Lucius Walthrope." She looked satisfied.

He was now irritated by Emily's waffling and twisting facial expressions. This last claim was too much. He poked at her. "Mrs. Graham, Lucius Walthrope is a murderer."

"Murderer? Sheriff! Incorrigible, he is that." She laughed softly as she thought of him. "But murder? Is that what Betsy said? I imagine she would . . . to protect her treason," she said spitefully.

"She did tell me that."

"Well, Sheriff, you can't just accept what people tell you . . . especially those who hide secrets. Protecting her lover . . . probably a whole web of spies. I've heard of such things in Richmond, but I never thought . . . not here in Staunton. I'm glad you discovered it, Sheriff. I assure you I had nothing to do with it. She did live with me while my husband was away . . . in the army. I pitied her after her husband died. She was so weak. She needed me. But I knew nothing of her spying. Now . . . I find I knew nothing about her."

The sheriff was sure she was mad, vacillating as she did on everything, but he said nothing.

"Sheriff, she's accusing wonderful Lucius of murder . . . when he would hurt no one. He's gentle . . . kind. A faithful Rebel. He was in love with Betsy, and they'd have married, but for that Yankee spy. Who did she claim Lucius killed?"

"The factory foreman—Mr. Stokes."

Emily gasped, leaned back, horror in her eyes.

"It was Mr. Walthrope who was not who he seemed. He used the factory to hoard and smuggle supplies to both sides. For some reason, he killed Stokes."

Mrs. Graham sported an expression of timidity, and the sheriff marveled at her inability to hide thought or feeling.

He explained further, "Mrs. Henderson learned about the murder from a woman—a stranger—and confronted Walthrope. He tried to kill her in front of three witnesses. He definitely killed Stokes, and he'd willingly kill others."

Emily was horrified. She remembered again his visit, the blood on his shirt. She'd helped him escape. She was not going to tell the sheriff of the escape.

The sheriff was still talking, "I knew you and Mrs. Henderson didn't speak, but I had hoped for your help."

"My help? How can I help?" she asked fearfully. "I had no idea of who this Walthrope was. I knew him only as Betsy's friend. She spoke so highly of him. But Sheriff, maybe he attacked her . . . because she'd betrayed us."

The sheriff had wearied of the woman. "Walthrope. Do you know where he is?"

Emily stared blankly at the sheriff. "I'm sorry, I don't." She was speaking mechanically. "I haven't seen him since I returned with my husband."

"Are you sure? Think about it. Didn't you say . . ."

"Sheriff, I am sure. I haven't seen him since returning from Winchester. There's nothing more. Please, leave. I'm tired. It's early. You really should have come later."

"Yes, but now I need to know more about the Yankee . . . and Mrs. Henderson. I think you'll want to tell me. Your loyalty . . . patriotism—yours . . . your husband's. He paused, dropped his eyes to his hat and lowered his voice. "It might look like you were helping them." He raised his eyes suddenly to stare accusingly at her.

Panic spread over her face so quickly the sheriff almost laughed. "Sheriff, we are patriots. I had nothing to do with this treachery. Nothing. It was her!"

"Was it?" he said disdainfully. "She did live with you. How did she spy from your home without you knowing?"

Emily was concluding that Betsy had brought this on herself. She was foolish to love a Yankee. Emily had to choose between the Confederacy and Betsy.

Emily told the sheriff that Betsy had known Hank Gragg in the lower Shenandoah Valley before the war. They hoped to marry, but some row had separated them. He joined the Union Army—although she didn't understand how a Virginian could ever do that. She supposed he was born with a treacherous heart.

Evil fate brought Betsy and Hank back together. He'd been with Betsy's husband when he died. She now suspected Hank killed him. The cursed Yank claimed he'd promised to deliver Thaddeus' last letter to Betsy, but he didn't know he was taking a letter to his former lover. Based on what Walthrope had told her, the Yankee had finally succeeded.

The details swirled in the sheriff's mind. "And you last saw Mr. Walthrope?"

"A few weeks ago."

"I thought you didn't see him after Winchester."

Horror swelled on her face. "Sheriff, you obviously didn't understand."

"No, I didn't." The sheriff stopped, and turned in his chair to look out the window. When he was sure his long silence had discomforted her, he turned back and asked softly, "When you say they were spies . . . how can you be sure?"

"Isn't it obvious?"

"Obvious?"

"Yes," she snorted. "Why would he come so far to meet Betsy? They probably exchanged secrets for a long time, but he wanted more . . . wanted to hear the traitorous news directly from Betsy's deceitful mouth. Maybe . . ." She interrupted herself to think. "Maybe . . . Sheriff—it's becoming clear—he came because she beckoned him with Southern secrets. Why else would he be allowed to come? The Yanks depended on her." She looked earnestly at the sheriff. "You must stop them, before the information gets to Lincoln."

"So important it would get to Lincoln?"

"I'm sure of it. You must stop them."

"But the boy didn't know who Betsy was when he promised your cousin that he would deliver the letter."

Her eyes were briefly blank, then alive again, darting around the room. "Oh, my! Everything was a lie! They spied from the beginning. She married Thaddeus to spy for the North . . . with the Gragg boy."

"How would she know her husband would be killed? How would she know Virginia would secede? Why would she marry someone she didn't love . . . to spy in a war she didn't know was coming?"

Emily cried out. "Oh, Sheriff, spare me! She didn't ever love Thaddeus! It's too painful. Thaddeus was so beautiful . . . so wonderful. And she never loved him. She's horrible . . . evil. Tell me no more, Sheriff. My gentle nature cannot tolerate such . . . such betrayal. Oh, please stop. It's too much for me." She whined, "She didn't even love him!"

"That's not what I meant," the sheriff said calmly, but she didn't hear him.

"She married him after the war began," she said flatly. Her back arched, and she added passionately, "She's a traitress to the cause. I'm glad I broke off relations. I must have known . . . felt it. My cousin died at the hands of that Yankee . . . spittle." She choked on her last words.

The sheriff had lost her. She was clearly so sapless and frightened that she was losing her sanity. But he couldn't restrain himself from adding, "Why not come forward earlier? Why didn't you tell me or the provost marshal?"

"Isn't that obvious?"

"No."

"I was deceived by that . . . that fancy woman!" she shrieked.

The outburst embarrassed them both. The sheriff responded quickly, thanking her for her patriotism. He picked up his hat and without escort made his way to the front hall and out to the street.

Emily remained seated. She looked for a long time across the room, then said to no one in particular with a warm smile, "Yes, I am a Patriot."

Chapter 8

March 1864,
Near the Rappahannock River, Virginia

Oskar Dante had not weathered the weeks well.

His friend Matthew had agreed to help him in his smuggling scheme if Dante secured his planned informal relationship with the government. But Dante's expectations were dashed when the bureaucratic officer declined his offer. Dante suspected it was because he had asked for money to set himself up.

The officer had offered to pay him "appropriately" if he brought important news, and Dante had already taken him worthwhile information. A lady—Elizabeth Van Lew—was passing secrets to the North, and Dante shared his discovery with the captain, expecting excessive financial reward and the respect he merited from the ill-informed, gray-clad, small-minded Rebel.

The officer listened politely, distantly at first, but when he heard the name Van Lew, his expression changed. He stared at Dante for an uncomfortably long time. Dante squirmed till the officer began laughing. Dante smiled nervously in response.

"Is that the best intelligence you have?" the man had asked. Dante's smile faded, and the officer's mocking laugh stopped abruptly. "Mr. Dante, your Miss Van Lew is a lady of prominence and wealth. She does talk too much about the government and surely sympathizes with the Union. But we watch her, and if she passes information to the North, we'll know. But a lady like that . . . would not betray us."

When the captain realized Dante was glaring angrily, his expression and voice softened. "Honestly, she's harmless . . . a spinster, Mr. Dante." But the officer couldn't contain his contempt, and a smile curled the corners of his mouth. He looked at Dante's enraged eyes, and the hint of a smile became a mocking laugh again. "Thank you. This is true treasure. You must keep up your inquiries. I see now your exceptional abilities. I'm only sorry we didn't make our affairs formal."

The officer's gaze drifted to the ceiling as if something interesting were happening in its corner. He regarded it for a long time, then spoke, "We'll need no more information from you." His eyes dropped to Dante's face. "We'll be too busy following up on Miss Van Lew." He laughed. "Don't bother me again."

The officer never said goodbye.

Humiliation always took Dante back to his earliest memory. He no longer saw it through his own eyes, but as if he'd watched it from above.

He was young—he guessed four or five. He saw a big room—a saloon—full of adults. His mother had sent him to bring his father home. From outside the room, he peeked timidly into the bar, frightened, fearing his father, fearing the loud adults, fearing his mother's wrath if he didn't bring his father home.

His father was there, across the broad floor. Drunk as usual, he was boisterously telling with huge graceful gestures a story from his endless repertoire of tales. To Dante, his father was the center of everyone's attention.

His father didn't see him peek in, or see him as he crept along the front wall, then the side wall, or as he slipped among the people standing at the bar. In mid-sentence and in keeping with the flow of his story, the man looked down. There he was, young Dante, standing by his— as Dante remembered them—enormous black boots, silently awaiting discovery.

"What're you doing, boy?" his father roared, before he raised a dried-mud-covered boot and pushed it into Dante's little stomach. The man laughed and said, "Gentlemen, an imbecile! Just like the wench!"

"Ma wants you home," the boy whispered, faithful to his mother's charge.

"What is it boy! Did you speak?" his father bellowed.

Dante repeated more loudly, "Ma wants you home."

"Ma wants you home," his father reprised mockingly. "His ma wants me home." He tightened his jaw and in his deep voice growled menacingly, "You tell that trollop to come get me herself . . . if she dares."

The child Dante, frightened, ashamed of himself and oddly proud of his father's power, felt all eyes on him. In his young mind, they were angry and hostile eyes—directed at him, a stupid boy. They shared his father's loathing for him. Dante loathed himself. Why couldn't he be like his pa? Why did his pa hate him? Why did he have to beat his mother and him?

He backed slowly from his father, frightened at what might happen if he turned his back on the man-sized viper. The saloon was silent. He bumped into someone who gently *lifted him and set him down closer to the door. He backed farther till he hit his head on a table edge. When he heard responding laughter, he turned and ran out the door. The laughter faded only when he was far from the saloon.*

Humiliation, from that moment, possessed and ruled Dante, and he could only hide its pain by layering it with a smooth coating of revenge and anger, an anger that years later drove him to beat his father senseless, almost to death. He never knew if his father recovered for he never saw him or any other family member again. Remembering the scene, the adult Dante wanted to cry for the frightened child, but he quickly smothered the emotion with ire directed toward the rejecting captain and, for the first time, at the Confederacy.

He futilely tried to remember the boy's name, but he'd buried it so deeply, he couldn't even remember it. He'd become Lucius, and his surname had shifted as circumstances required. He liked the name Lucius, and only recently abandoned it to become Oskar Dante—the same man, but with a strong new name.

The memories and thoughts of his name were interrupted by a quiet, nervous voice nearby in the dark, saying, "Have we been forgotten?"

Another voice whispered, "It's your first time. You get used to these waits . . . delays. Never goes as planned. One time it's a cavalry patrol, the next unexpected boats passing. Always something. Just slows everything down. I've done it a dozen times now in a half dozen different ways, and I'm relaxed enough I can sleep while I wait."

The voice continued, "But I remember the first time. Every twig snapping, every cold breeze rushing through empty branches was someone after me. But you needn't worry. Who wants to catch us? North, South, they need this exchange of letters, information. Nobody wants to catch us."

The first quiet voice responded, "I've heard of people being caught."

"Rumors, I assure you," the second voice proclaimed, confidently. "Don't worry so. Relax. Rest. You'll be safely wherever you're going soon." The voice paused briefly. "Where are you going?"

Don't answer him, thought Dante, listening intently.

"Delivering a package to my uncle."

"Well, you'll be fine," said the second voice.

The conversation died. Dante had been gathered during the afternoon with his two fellow travelers at a farm a few miles back. The family seemed to be Southern loyalists, and the travelers seemed to share the allegiance. At dusk, they had been brought through the woods toward the Rappahannock River that divided the two armies, abandoned in this small clearing and told to wait. Someone would come to ferry them across. They were assured it wouldn't be long, but they were left to define "not long" for themselves. In the minds of all three men, their wait had extended beyond any conceivable definition of the phrase.

Dante had said little to the two men who accompanied him, and he didn't want to. He was wary of everyone. He was acting as a courier for Matthew, carrying letters to Matthew's partners in Washington City. It wasn't the grand scheme Dante had planned, but it would get him north, and that was crucial.

He didn't know the content of the letters he carried, and because of his hesitation to trust anyone, he'd left their seals intact. If Matthew mistrusted him, whoever was to receive the letters might look for evidence of tampering.

The traveler who had broken the silence talked often and anxiously from the time they met, and the second traveler had spoken to calm him.

"What's in your package?" the second man asked the first in a conversational tone after a brief silence.

"Don't know I should say."

"Wise. Few you can trust these days, but we're in the same boat . . . or at least will be in a few minutes. Letter?"

"Why do you ask?"

"You've been so concerned about getting caught. Thought there might be something you don't want to lose. If there was anything like that, you take special care . . . and we need to know because we might be charged with you for carrying something . . . well, subversive. I don't carry subversive correspondence, but if you are, I want to know."

"Don't worry. Nothing I have is valuable or subversive. I just don't want to go to prison. I've heard horrible things of the prisons."

"Why would you be frightened of prison . . . if you weren't carrying something . . . Are you carrying something that would put you in prison?"

"I was thinking about going to prison because we sneaked through the lines."

"I already told you no one wants to catch us."

There was a rustle in the bushes. Someone approached. The men quieted, waiting.

"Is anyone there . . . in the bushes?" asked an unfamiliar voice in a hesitant tone.

"I'm Mr. Smith, and the water seems high tonight," the second man responded cautiously.

"What is that to me. I have no interest in going on the river," the voice responded, now confident.

Dante stepped from the bushes, followed by the other two men. The night was cloudy and moonless, but having long waited in the dark, their eyes could distinguish shapes, especially peripherally. A hand grabbed Dante's arm and pulled him toward the riverbank as a voice commanded, "Quick, now. Be quiet. The rest of you, stay put till I come back! Don't even breathe." The voice drew out the last word.

Dante walked by the man as he guided Dante down the riverbank's slope. At one point, Dante stumbled and was surprised at the strength of the hand on his arm that nearly lifted him off the ground to stop a noisy fall.

They made their way to a boat where a man waited at the oars. No one spoke as the hand guided him to a seat. Only when he was in place did the man speak again, this time in a quiet whisper, "The money!"

"Right here," Dante responded.

"Quiet. I just want the money, not conversation. If I wanted conversation, I'd live in Richmond."

Dante pulled ready money from his overcoat pocket and shoved it toward the man. The man effortlessly found Dante's hand and the money. After feeling the required coin, he pocketed it and returned for the others.

Barely had the currency been passed for the third passenger when the boat pulled from shore. Dante looked into the darkness of the river. It was not broad, and he thought voices drifted across from the far shore. He held his breath, trying to listen. But with the soft sound of the boat cutting the water, the oars gently, methodically breaking the surface, and the quiet, controlled breathing of the oarsman, he couldn't tell if he'd imagined them.

When they reached the middle of the river, his inexperienced travel mate cried out, "My hat! It fell in."

"Shut up, man!" came a deep, firm and quiet whisper from the oarsman. "You've lost it, and if you even breathe, I'll throw you in the murky Rappahannock. Once you're in, there's nothing you can do. You're trapped, the prisoner of river flow. She'll carry you in darkness where she will. She won't care who you are or your business . . . or whether you're alive or dead. She does the same to all she captures in her dark breath."

There followed an uncomfortable, tense silence. Dante was ready to throw his fellow traveler into the river if he made more noise, but again the only sound was the water parting and the oarsman again rowing, breathing rhythmically.

In spite of the river's narrow width, time—compounded by the stress of the lost-hat commotion—seemed interminable before they reached the north shore. Once there, the three men were told in that deep, firm voice to climb the sharp embankment. Someone would be at the top to meet them.

As they struggled up the bank, no one spoke but the men still made considerable noise as they pulled on barely visible exposed roots and straggly bushes to aid their ascent. At every sound and grunt, Dante remembered the voices he thought he'd heard. Did they wait at the top for three grunting Southerners?

After climbing the bank, the trio met what in the dark looked like an old man, beckoning them with a skeletal hand. Without a word, he led them quickly on foot for nearly half an hour before Dante saw light. It glowed from inside a small cottage, and with the soft light, he could finally confirm they were led by a human, male, old, slim, with emaciated face, worn clothes and a crippled hand.

The old man led them to the cottage door, knocked five times with his good hand, then opened the door. Inside was an old woman who took a pipe out of her mouth to extend a disgusting, unnerving wanton smile, as she patted a shotgun resting at her side. If it hadn't been for the warmth of the room and the hope of rest, her gappy smile and scant remaining, deeply discolored teeth would have compelled Dante to run. But the warmth intoxicated him, and once he overcame his revulsion, he luxuriated in the roaring fire's heat, moving quickly to it.

"Ya'll from Richmond?" the woman asked as soon as the door closed. She replaced the pipe in her mouth.

"I am," spoke the nervous man immediately. The other man indicated he'd come from Danville.

Everyone's eyes turned to Dante. He had to speak, and he did it curtly, "Yes."

"Got me folks there," the woman said.

"You'll want the news then," offered the first man.

"Don't need none," the woman said, the gaping hole smiling again, eyes staring at the first man. "We see bodies . . . and they're all atellin' us what's going on. Bodies want to pass from both sides. We like them from the South, so them from the North, we make 'em pay more. When they're here, we're atellin' 'em how we love Uncle Abe . . . that Baboon." She cackled, and Dante shivered in disgust.

"We don't call 'im that, not whiles they're here," the man quickly added, cracking a wide smile on his cadaverous face, revealing he too had no front teeth.

"Got supper for y'all . . . on the stove," the woman said cordially. "Get what ya want. Don't go scrimpin'. Take all ya want—then git out to the barn for the night. In the mornin', go on north. It's easy from here."

Dante looked lovingly, remorsefully at the fire, realizing it was only for the cabin's monstrous occupants. He moved to the stove, lifting the pot's lid to peer at a thin stew which he ladled into a nearby bowl, all the while wondering what was in it. The nervous traveler moved immediately to the door. The host, seeing only two men approach the soup, offered again. "There's plenty!"

"No . . . I'm fine. Had supper earlier."

"Suit yourself."

The man led them to a shed, leaving them to make their own beds in the dark on the straw-strewn, cold ground. Dante ached, anticipating a frightfully cold night, the thin straw, sleeplessness and the stew.

He sat in a corner and ate. The stew was greasy and hot, but he couldn't identify its contents and tried to distract himself from bits of what floated in it.

Seeking comfort, his mind wandered back to Staunton, the comforting blaze of Betsy's drawing-room fire, their conversations. They'd mostly talked about the business he feigned to manage for her. But the topic didn't matter, he just enjoyed being with her.

One of his traveling companions found a moldy blanket in the straw and shared it with his traveling fellows. The three men huddled tightly together through the cold night.

When Dante awoke the next morning, sunlight already filtered into the shed. One companion was gone, and Dante stretched, yawned and stood up. His movement aroused the third sleeper, the nervous man from the night before who had lain next to Dante. He woke fitfully, then jumped up, demanding, "Where's our friend?"

Dante responded, "Up and gone. Sun's up, and he probably didn't sleep any better than me."

"Ah," the man said, "the comfort of sleeping in the middle. I slept better . . . a lot warmer."

Dante picked up his satchel without responding, slung it over his shoulder and stepped out of the shed. He yawned again in the cold sunlight that greeted him, then heard, "Where's my package? It's gone!"

The door had already closed, and Dante didn't return to the shed. He knew the answer. A sharp blow landed on his back, and he stumbled to the ground.

"Give it to me!" the fellow screamed.

Dante rose to his feet as his assailant was picking up a large tree branch for a second assault. Dante's back ached where the man had punched and pushed him, and he craved breaking the man's thin neck.

They faced each other defiantly, and the nervous man demanded, "Open the bag! I knew there was something about you. Never talking. Secretive. Thief. Open it!" As he spoke, he waved the branch menacingly.

Dante struggled to repress his anger as Matthew's warning echoed in his mind. He had to control himself to get what he wanted. Hurting this man would jeopardize what Dante really needed. But if the man hit him again . . . .

"Open it!"

"I'll not open it for you or any man."

Out of the corner of his eye, Dante caught the glimpse of the old man approaching slowly, casually.

"You'll open it, or I'll open it for you. I'll call the other fellow. We'll take it from you."

Dante felt no threat from his overnight host who, now close enough for comfortable conversation, commented, "Don't think that'll help ya none."

"Sir?" the nervous traveler said. "This man stole my package. It's in his bag!"

"Doubt it," the man said, calmly. "If he was athievin', he'd be gone . . . like the other fella. Gone 'fore sunrise."

The nervous man's expression crumbled to despair as he moaned aloud, "What am I to do? I'm done for."

Dante sullenly observed the exchange, then turned toward the road. The old man called, "Don't want no stew?"

Dante stopped, "Breakfast would be nice, but I'm not eating near him." He glowered at the nervous traveler. "He can wait outside till I'm done."

"I do apologize, but I was sure it was you. The way you were . . . silent . . . suspicious. But the other fellow, he asked all the questions, didn't he? I regret accusing you."

Dante smiled. "I'm not harmed. Come, I'll eat with you."

"I'll not eat this morning. I may still catch the thief." He repeated forlornly, "The thief."

"Good fortune then," Dante said, nodding his head, as he moved toward the house for another portion of stew. He downed it rapidly thinking of Betsy, her smile, her touch. But a question kept intruding. What was in the packet so carefully stowed and hidden in his satchel?

Chapter 9

March 1864, Staunton, Virginia

Emily hadn't slept blissfully through the night in more than a week. But she was entitled to bliss. She was a lady of means—even though only one house slave remained, the rest having escaped her care. And she had her family's premier social standing. Certainly, she should have possessed sleep. But it too had stolen away.

The weather was ideal for slumber, with cold breezes from the northwest and a warm fire. Each night she would try to relax before retiring. She would read a favorite novel, drink warm tea, sit carefully on the edge of her bed. She would raise her legs and scoot into the bed's center. She would lie on her back, smile, breathe deeply, close her eyes. Then fear would grip her.

It had been there all day and made time a garden slug, moving slowly in the shadows, leaving behind a sticky, sickening goo. At night, excruciating memories and visions of horrid futures surfaced and lingered, trapped in time's stickiness.

The progression was similar each night. Fear would layer slowly until her whole soul was filled with it, smothering her frantic efforts to block horrific thoughts and stealing her breath. She would gasp for what air she could in small short pants, but fear had turned ferocious, debilitating, exhausting.

Soon she couldn't bear lying in bed. She would rise and pace the floor. Why couldn't she stop thinking? She shouldn't have to worry. It wasn't right. She deserved quietude. She would scream, but only in her head. Why couldn't this stop? Her thoughts? Her nightmarish life? She abhorred herself. She abhorred her thoughts. She abhorred her husband. She abhorred the sheriff, but most of all, she abhorred Betsy and her dear cousin Thaddeus for ever marrying Betsy. She detested Hank. All had conspired to make her suffer . . . and she suffered innocently. She hated Lincoln, Davis, Lee. She loathed Stonewall's memory. She should have been happy, but they had made it impossible. Trapped, unable to escape, she was carried wherever her fears flowed.

She recalled her faithfulness to Betsy. She'd told the sheriff only about Hank after the sheriff had made it clear Betsy had deceived her, used her, betrayed her, betrayed her own husband. Emily was beginning to understand how profoundly Betsy had harmed the nation. If the Confederacy fell, it was Betsy who had given her wretched Union lover—a traitor to the Old Dominion—the South's greatest secrets. The sheriff had been right in coming to her. Perhaps what she'd revealed would save the country. But new doubts arose. How could it be true? It was wrong! Betsy a traitress? No! It couldn't be.

The thoughts rotated faster and faster, with increasing energy and vividness, leading nowhere. She'd already done what she could . . . what she did. It no longer mattered. Right or wrong, it was over. She would breathe a sigh of relief, and her shoulders would slump in momentary comfort. It was settled.

Then the thoughts, string like, would wrap and spin her mind like a child's top. She would remember her faithfulness to Betsy. She only told the sheriff about Hank when she knew Betsy had deceived her, betrayed her, betrayed her cousin, her nation. If the Confederacy fell, it was because Betsy had given secrets to her grimy Union lover—a traitor, slave lover—he'd betrayed his soul for cursed pottage of Northern abolitionism!

The sheriff had been right to come to her. What she'd told him would save the country. But it couldn't be true . . . not about Betsy. No! But no matter. It was done. She could relax. She would close her eyes briefly, breathe deeply and smile. Rest was coming. She would climb back onto her bed, pull up the covers to her neck, sigh audibly and close her eyes. But she would see Betsy's face, smiling gently, and it would begin anew. Soon she would be pacing the floor, re-thinking the same smothering thoughts, suffering the same fears.

The first few nights, she was lucid enough to know she couldn't long stand the strain, but lucidity and awareness faded. Her mind and body deteriorated rapidly till decay was visible. But her husband, as was his recent habit, had gone to Richmond for an extended time. There was no one to no-tice her decline except her remaining house slave, Ruth. The slave, herself of a nervous nature, marveled at her mistress's complete focus on something . . . something inexplicable, unexpressed. Something was horribly wrong.

Her mistress would sit for meals, but never eat. She'd rise from the table to again walk the floor, and her lips would move as if she were talking, but she made no sound. It had been a week since Mrs. Graham had spoken to her, which meant she'd not been cursed for a blessed, precious seven days.

Ruth cleaned the house, ran the usual errands, prepared her mistress's meals and helped her dress and with her morning and evening rituals. But she spent every free moment fretting and watching her mistress walk the house.

She initially cherished the silence, intrigued by Mrs. Graham's unnatural behavior. But something was not right, and she soon worried for her own safety. She saw her mistress's drooping eyes, pale complexion, rapidly thinning body, her constantly fidgeting hands that mercilessly picked at her now scratched and scabbed face. How would it end? She imagined being whipped a whole week's worth in one day. She envisioned her mistress, in a fit of madness, choking her to death. Oh, that her master would come home soon. What was she to do?

Ruth despised her mistress. Mrs. Graham had mocked her, yelled at her, belittled her. Ruth couldn't remember a kind gesture from her. Years earlier she'd wanted to read and had found a woman willing to teach her, but the mistress got wind of it and whipped her savagely, leaving her unable to rise from her thin mattress for a week. Faint scars from the beating were still visible. Why should she care what happened to her heinous owner?

The new incarnation of Mrs. Graham was easy to serve, never yelled, never beat her. For all these things, Ruth was beginning to feel gratitude. Her mother had always told her, no matter how difficult her life, she should remember the blessings the Lord had given her. But she had been unable to feel gratitude for anything in her suffering and took no solace in religion like her mother and others, which made her feel guilty.

But everything was changing, and late in the week she began to relax and enjoy herself. She ate more and would sneak into her mistress's closet and try on different dresses. She slept in late, went to bed early. These good things might end anytime, and she determined she would savor them. If she were beaten in the end, she would have at least experienced something like happiness for these few days. She was grateful for the first time in her life, grateful something terrible was happening to her enemy, and she liked the feeling of gratitude and the pleasant days.

On the morning of the ninth day the crisis came. Ruth woke at her new after-sunup time. She raised her knees from the straw-filled mattress on the floor, breathed the cold morning air and smiled. Then she heard a rustle of activity below. An intruder? Should she scream? Should she flee the house?

She rose quickly, crept to the door, raised the latch and carefully peered down the stairs. She could see nothing. She walked carefully across the small landing, descended the stairs, one at a time, pausing to listen and peek from each step. She could still hear commotion below, and it ended with a sudden bang of the front door.

Ruth dashed to a window in the hall overlooking the street and, at first, glanced furtively out the window, hiding from any person who might spy her. Then she saw her. Ruth stood to her full height, staring at her mistress walking in the street. Mrs. Graham was barely dressed, hair dirty and unbrushed. No hat. She wore mismatched shoes, no coat. She walked in the middle of the street. Her mismatched shoes were already covered with mud and more from the road. Periodically, Mrs. Graham would stop as if to converse with someone beside her, but no one was there. Ruth was ashamed. She ran down the stairs, barefoot, dressed in a loose, shabby nightshirt, threw open the door and ran into the street.

"Ma'am, what brung yuh out here? Come, Ma'am. Come wid me. Come to de house. Somet'in' bad happenin'. Yuh can't walk . . . not in de road like yuh is."

She caught up with Mrs. Graham, grabbed her hand and pulled her homeward, but Mrs. Graham merely reached out and slapped Ruth's hand as if it had been a bothersome mosquito. Startled, Ruth let go. But moments later she was tugging again, pleading with her mistress to come home. People watched from the sidewalk.

Mrs. Graham slapped Ruth's face. She showed no anger, no condescension, seemed to be just trying to free herself from the thing holding her. They both pulled harder, and Mrs. Graham jerked free. Both fell into the street's mud and muck. The slave was instantly horrified, not at being in the wet filth herself, but at her mistress sitting, mud covered in the middle of the street.

She reflexively closed her eyes for the coming blow. She deserved it. Oddly Mrs. Graham still seemed unable to see her or the muck on her own clothes. She rose as if nothing had happened and walked on.

Ruth opened her eyes and stared in horror. What was she to do? Her mistress was walking down a prominent Staunton street covered in mud and literal muck.

Emily had crossed an unseen threshold. She was unaware of her state of dress and her wrestling match. She knew only that she must get to the provost marshal. It was her purpose in being born—to save the Confederacy.

It had to be her, because it was the wife of her beloved cousin who had betrayed the nation. She alone was worthy to atone for such a great sin. Who else could muster the courage to fight against such power? She would strike the fatal blow against the sinful Union. When their most cunning spy was unmasked and the source of the stolen secrets stopped, the North would retreat and sue for peace.

She had despaired when Stonewall had died—a terrible tragedy. There had been no hope left once the Almighty had taken him. But now God had heard their prayers and raised another savior, a new immovable Stonewall. God had given Virginia another chance. She, with heroine's mantel, was the new General Jackson, Lee's greatest arm. She was God's tool. No matter the outcome or cost, she would trudge forward. She was invigorated by his strength pulsing through her, and she marched now a Christian soldier, doing God's work, saving the mighty nation of the Christian God, the new Israelites.

With her help, God would crush the invading hordes, the nation of hypocrites, the idolatrous Canaanites. She remembered Joan of Arc. Joan's spirit filled her. But hadn't Joan been betrayed, captured, put to death? Thus be it. She would join Joan, the Baptist, Stephen, Peter, Paul as a martyr for Jesus.

She didn't notice the looks, laughs, murmured comments and street-urchin catcalls that accompanied her. She had to reach the provost marshal. She had to tell him that Betsy was a spy. Then it would be over—her turmoil, the invasion, her sleepless nights. The South would be a great nation, built on principles fellow Virginians had crafted a century before for an ungrateful race of debauched Yankees.

She marched on, feeling as if she carried a rifle on her shoulder . . . no, it was the flag of the South, the stainless banner with its cross of St. Andrew and a great pure and white field. She was the great general, the perfect private, the color-bearer . . . and she was running out of energy. She could feel it and fought it. It was the Devil, holding her back from destiny . . . from God's will.

But if it was the Devil, he worked to her purpose for she was within sight of the marshal's office when she felt the first wave of confusion and dizziness. She tried to ignore it. A few more steps and it hit again, this time stopping her in the street amid the mocking crowd. She'd eaten virtually nothing for more than a week. She hadn't slept. Her body was shutting down. But food, sleep, even her body no longer mattered. She took another two steps before the confusion overwhelmed her.

Her last memory was of the paunchy sheriff running anxiously to her. Ah, she thought, he knows I'm the savior. She fell face first into one of the road's muddy ruts.

Only when she was unconscious on the ground did the sheriff reach her and pull her face from the diabolical mud drowning the heroine. The sheriff and a provost guard lifted her filthy, dripping body and carried her by happenstance into the very office she'd sought.

Chapter 10

March 1864, Just Outside Staunton, Virginia

Ruth, still barefoot, mud covered, cold and dripping wet in her nightshirt, arrived at Betsy's plantation well after Emily collapsed in the street. She, likewise fell nearly senseless on the front porch, and the clatter of her fall brought John to the door.

He knew Ruth but didn't recognize her at first. When he did, he knelt, wiping the mud from her face before he lifted her. He struggled to carry the slim, limp, cold body into the house, where he immediately lowered—nearly dropped—her to the floor.

"Mrs. Henderson," he cried, again bending over the girl. He took her frozen, wet hands in his as he examined her body, trying to assess what she needed and what had happened. She stared at him silently, wearily.

Mrs. Henderson, not used to slaves addressing her unless it was in low, reverent tones, was shaken by the cry and came quickly. She saw John kneeling over a girl's body. Had a servant collapsed? The creature was filthy, barefoot and barely dressed. She wasn't a house servant.

John nodded at her and answered her unasked question. "Mrs. Graham's girl, Ma'am."

The news startled her. Why would Emily's servant come to her house, especially in this condition?

Other slaves had gathered, and John looked at Betsy, expectantly. She looked back, blankly. Only after John cleared his throat did she realize he was waiting for instructions. She bent beside him and touched the girl's forehead. She expected a fever, but it was cold and wet. "She's frozen."

"Yes, Ma'am."

"We've got to get her into warm water. Not too hot, not too hot."

"No, Ma'am, not too hot," he responded. He ordered a tub brought to the kitchen and water warmed on the stove. He directed one slave to find clothes for her, another to bring blankets. He scooped his arms under her body again, ready to lift her. He stumbled as he tried to rise, and Betsy stepped forward to help him, reaching her arms under the girl. The cold and wet instantly permeated the layers of Betsy's clothes. Together, mistress and slave shuttled awkwardly carrying the frightened, spent slave into the kitchen.

By the time they got her to the edge of the kitchen fire, the slave sent earlier for blankets had returned with several. They laid one on the floor, lowered Ruth toward the blanket, as one woman said directly, "Get her clothes off. She can't get warm if she's not dry."

They worked to hold the girl up, while Betsy and others undressed her. John, discreetly, left the room.

Wrapped in warm blankets, the girl's awareness increased. Ruth moved, shivered, moaned. John reentered the room, having changed into clean clothes, and studied her. Betsy, still in her wet and soiled bolero jacket and skirt, watched compassionately. She turned to John. "What's the girl doing here?"

"Don't know. And why was she dressed like that and covered in mud?"

Betsy's mother, Rebeka Richman, entered the room. She'd been in her bedroom when the commotion began and ignored it for a long while. But when an unending stream of slaves noisily ran up and down the stairs without correction, her irritation brought her to the kitchen. "And who is this," she asked condescendingly.

"Cousin Emily's girl," Betsy responded.

"Why is she wrapped in blankets in your kitchen?"

Betsy looked at her impatiently. "I don't know."

The tub was being filled with pot after pot of hot water.

Betsy inquired, "Why are you here?" She expected to hear Emily had beaten her again, locked her out of the house or thrown cold water on her. A part of her wanted to hear it. Speaking for the first time, Ruth recounted Emily's lunacy. In Ruth's panic, she could think of only one person who'd ever shown her kindness and had come hoping Mrs. Henderson would know what to do.

Betsy assured Ruth she could stay with them until things were sorted out, then rose from the slave's side and directed John to have her carriage made ready. She would look for Mrs. Graham. Betsy left the kitchen, climbed the stairs and disappeared into her bedroom suite. She emerged quickly, clothed for a winter drive, gloves already on, and directed John to fetch her winter cloak.

Her groom met her with the carriage. It was odd, but the sight of groom, carriage and horse brought back memories of her father's slave, William. Hank had been fond of William and treated him with a respect Betsy found, at the time, peculiar. When she was a girl, William would have met her with horse and buggy, and because of his connection to Hank, nostalgia overwhelmed her briefly.

The slave assisted her into the carriage, and she directed it to the road.

Shortly after entering the road, soldiers on horseback and with a wagon blocked her way. One horse-mounted soldier approached. "Mrs. Henderson?"

"Yes."

"You are under arrest."

"Me?" she asked incredulously.

"Yes, Ma'am. Will you please step from the carriage? We will take you to . . ."

"I'll not step down. What's going on?"

"I'm to arrest you for passing secrets to the Yankees."

She looked at him sternly. What was happening? Why would anyone think she would help the enemy? Then she saw him, leering at her from his horse. His balding head covered by his soiled hat—the sheriff. So he knew about Hank. Why wasn't he arresting her? Who were these soldiers? "I've given no information to the enemy."

"Step from the carriage, Mrs. Henderson."

"Who are you?"

"The provost guard."

"Why doesn't the sheriff arrest me?"

"It's a military matter, Ma'am. You're charged with disloyalty, and we deal with traitors."

"May I return the carriage and horse to my house . . . tell them what you're doing?"

"No, Ma'am. You're not to speak to anyone."

"I'll want to send a note to my lawyer."

"You'll need no lawyer."

"I insist."

"I, also, Mrs. Henderson, insist. Step from the carriage. You'll ride in the wagon. If you don't do so immediately, we'll carry you to the wagon."

She was humiliated, but not overly concerned. The sheriff had made a vague charge that would be easily refuted. They had no proof, because there was no guilt. She pressed her lips together, tied the reins to the carriage and stepped to the ground. As she did, she was surrounded by members of the guard who escorted her to the wagon. The sheriff approached on horseback.

"I'm sorry about this," he said with a serious look on his face. "But, under the circumstances, I don't suppose there was an alternative."

"Sir, it will be sorted out quickly. But the circumstances don't require this, nor should you have done it. This is most offensive," she responded harshly.

He removed his hat, tilted his head respectfully and pulled his horse back from the wagon.

Chapter 11

March 1864, Eastern Kentucky

"M . . . M . . .Ma, he's a . . . aww . . . wake," Adam cried out as he ran from shed to house.

"Quiet, boy!" His mother said severely as he entered the kitchen. "Do you want everyone in Kentucky to know he's hiding in our shed? What should I do with you?"

Adam looked at the ground and offered, "You could . . . could tie my mouth shut."

She laughed softly. "How would I do that?"

"If you wrap a rope around my head, from the top to the bottom . . . if you tttie it tttight, I couldn't open my mouth. Then III wouldn't get that man caught."

"I appreciate the suggestion. I do, but do you think it would work?" She paused, then added playfully, "I'll think about it." She loved the boy. He wasn't old enough to require complete segregation from the white community and his enthusiasm endeared him to many. Perhaps their hearts were softened by his stuttering speech.

"You could ask the jjjudge." His head rocked forward, his mouth opened widely, rigidly, to get the last word out. "He could tell you if it would work."

"Yes . . . I suppose I could. Perhaps next time I see him."

"BBBut Ma, that may be too late. I might yell out again before that."

"It can wait." Her eyes sparkled as she gazed dotingly on him. "But," she said softly, "if you yell again, I'll drop this very pan on your head."

He looked thoughtfully at his mother and at the cast-iron frying pan she held in her hand, and offered somberly, "I think it bbbetter to ask the judge."

"Come, child," she said putting down the pan and pulling him close. "Is he really awake this time?"

"He is. III saw his head move and came fast as I could . . . ttto tell you. Come, MMMama. YYYou'll see." His head again jerked. He took his mother's hand and pulled her out of their small kitchen, down the worn wooden step leading from the neatly painted blue house. He stopped abruptly, and his mother bumped into him. "Shhh," he whispered with a serious expression before he, more slowly, led his mother to a small outbuilding 30 paces from the house, hidden in trees and shrubs.

As they approached the shed, his mother looked cautiously around. Her joviality was gone, and she stopped the boy. When she was convinced no one watched, she stepped to the shed, lifted the latch and pushed the door. She pulled her son in quickly, then closed the door. The shed was filled with barrels of grain and dried legumes, and a few tools hung neatly ordered along the back wall.

Even with the door closed, enough light filtered into the shed that her eyes quickly adjusted, and she could easily see the trapdoor that covered a cellar where she kept root vegetables and more grains. She bent down agilely to open it. It had no hinge, but rested on the surrounding framing. She raised the door with both arms and leaned it against two adjacent barrels. A rough, short ladder, anchored on the trapdoor-nesting frame, descended to a dirt floor below.

She crouched carefully, slowly, looking keenly into the chamber. She moved quietly and was irritated when her wide skirt caught the edge of the framing. Adam stood motionless and silent as he watched her. She unhooked her skirt from the snag, moved her hands to grasp the parallel sides of the frame, and her chest heaved a last sigh of resolve as she lowered her feet, dangling them until she located a ladder rung. She shifted her weight to the ladder, grabbed the top rung and descended. Barrels lined one wall, and a slight light shifted faintly near the floor between them. She smelled melting wax. She looked up and smiled when she saw Adam silhouetted above her. She listened. Had she heard something? There it was again. She didn't move. Moans, shuffling—exactly the sounds she imagined a haunting spirit would make.

Suddenly a raspy voice said, "I done killed him."

Her eyes widened. She took another deep but silent breath and listened for more. Silence followed. Adam had only left a few minutes earlier. Had someone come down that quickly and killed the man? Was she too late? Was all this in vain? Was her freedom forfeit? To whom was the person talking, and why had they killed him? Her fear threatened to propel her up the ladder. She'd throw the heaviest barrels on the door and run. She fought the fear. Something didn't make sense. Two people wouldn't be able to sneak into the hidden room so quickly. But still she wanted to run—the voice, the words.

She heard movement again, a deep scream, the gravelly voice. "He's dead! I done killed him!"

Was it the Devil, come to slay the man? "Absurd!" she thought. "The Devil would use better grammar," she whispered.

Another scream. "Oh, my Heavenly Father, I'm dead! Oh, dear Lord," the raw voice prayed in thick misery. "And for . . . for my sin, I'm done been sent to hell. Oh, sweet Jesus, deliver me from hell. Deliver me like yuh delivered yor great King David. Oh, God, deliver me! I knowed yuh freed David, pulled Jonah from the whale. Save poor William, who ain't done nothin' but kill that sinful man." She could hear someone flopping around, flinging himself from one side of the tiny vestibule to the other, and his voice rose almost to a scream. "I know what I done. Hell! Oh, I'm in hell. Oh, Jesus, forgive yor servant. I know he was white, but he was bad."

She heard something fall, and the light was gone.

She smiled and glanced at Adam who was still standing silently in the shed above. She couldn't see his expression, but imagined him petrified, unable to move. She breathed audibly, calmly, and called out clearly, "Sir, you are not dead . . . and not in hell. Now that you've knocked over the candle, you are in the dark. But it's not hell, and from the ruckus, I'd say you're still quite alive."

The commotion on the other side of the wall stopped. "Who's there?"

"Are you feeling well?" she asked, ignoring the query.

"Are you a debil, hopin' . . . If it ain't hell, it's like hell!"

"I'm sorry for that. I was hoping to be here when . . . as you awoke, so you wouldn't be frightened. But," she almost giggled, "I'm too late for that."

He spoke in despair, "I see light . . . comin' from below. It's hell! I'm sinkin' to hell." He loosed a deep, woeful moan. "I'm sinkin' . . . right through the floor. I can't move my legs!"

"You're not sinking to hell. You've nothing to fear. You're among friends. I'm sorry you're frightened." She chuckled softly. "You are safe. And I can help you get out . . . if you calm yourself. But you must be calm."

There was a period of silence before a softened voice asked, "Then where am I?"

"Before I tell you, I heard you say you killed someone. Who did you kill?"

"Knew it." the voice rose in agony. "Yuh're a golden-throat angel sent by the Debil for me to 'fess, so he can have me. Oh, the light . . . it's agettin' brighter! Oh, pitiful man. It's hell fire. I can feel it. My feet, they're aburnin'."

"Stop this at once! I like to think of myself as an angel, and that's kind of you to suggest. But I'm not here to force you to do anything. Nor are you being lowered anywhere. . . and it's not getting hotter." She waited, but lost patience. "And if it is getting hotter, it's not the fires of hell. It's my temper, which is much worse! I can get you out. But first tell me who you killed!"

"Can't I come out 'fore I 'fess. Just want one last look . . . at the sun 'fore yuh deliver me to yor marster." Panic rose again in the voice. "Ohhhh, the light's gettin' stronger. He's gettin' closer. That Debil. I can feel him tuggin' at me . . . at my leg. Oh, dear Savior, won't yuh please help a poor man. Deliver me! Yuh know I killed him just to save young Hank. The boy would'a died. Would'a died. I killed the man . . . but he was a demon. He shot that white woman. I knew they'd hunt me for killin' him, but, Jesus, don't send me to hell . . . not for that. He was white, but I had to do it. He would'a killed Hank like he killed the woman." He groaned deeply.

"Man, you're not in hell!" She spoke tersely. "Calm down. You're as safe as you would be in your mother's arms. We hid you in case someone came looking for you. You're safe. It's just a hidden room in a cellar." Her anger was abating as she considered what the man must have been feeling. She imagined how terrible it would have been to awaken unaccompanied. She, Adam and slaves from the judge's farm had taken turns being with him in the tight alcove to comfort him should he awaken.

"MMMama, should I get the judge?" Adam asked softly.

She looked at Adam, but the man spoke again. "Oh, oh." She heard him fall again onto the tiny room's narrow cot.

"Are you all right?"

"I don't know," he responded quietly, drowsily.

"Lie there, rest a while. You've been sleeping a long time. You must be weak," then she added softly to herself, "from your frenzy." She raised her voice again, "You haven't eaten for a long time."

"Asleep?"

"Yes, we found you . . . or rather my son found you. You've been unconscious for days. What's your name?"

"William . . . William," he said weakly. The energy he'd expended in his mania had drained him.

"William, it will be much easier for you to get yourself out, than it will be for us to get you. There's not much space, and it was hard to get you in." She awaited a response, but he said nothing, and she began to fear he'd again lapsed into unconsciousness. "Can you hear me?"

"I can hear yuh, but I am tired."

"William, we dug that room to hide people. We made it . . . for someone like you. Let me tell you how to get out."

"Repent," he said weakly. "Oh, Lord, I know! Torment me no more. Save me, a wretched soul."

She smiled. "Don't waste your strength talking. Listen!" He didn't respond. "The room you're in is tall enough for a man to stand, long enough to lie down and wide enough for a cot and a person to sit by the cot. We left little ledges at both ends to hold the litter. Someone's been sitting with you since you arrived. That's why a candle burned.

"Where's the door? There ain't no door! Just one to hell . . . beckonin'. Oh, I'm gettin' so hot! Fallin'. I'm fallin'."

"No, William! Hush! Listen. There is no door . . ."

"Knew it," he responded in barely audible tones. "There ain't no door out a' hell." He moaned again. "It's so hot. It's burnin' my skin. I'm sweatin'. The Debil's lowerin' me right through the earth. I'm fallin'. He's pullin' me down. The light's bright now! I can hear the Debil singin'. I'm his, all because . . ."

She crouched. Then remembering her skirt and petticoats, she stood, unhooked the braces that held the skirt up and carefully let it down. She removed two petticoats and lay all three neatly on a nearby barrel head. She pulled several barrels from the wall, squatted, squeezed in between wall and barrels, nimbly lowered and stretched her body flat on the ground, parallel to a long, narrow opening under the wall. She rolled through it until she was trapped tight under the stretcher with the man sagging on her.

She hated this—being in this tiny room. She'd hoped, at hearing his voice, she'd never have to reenter. She'd already decided to fill it up. Everything about it made her uneasy, and now, squeezed under the man, her heart raced. She sidled beyond him by pushing up on his passive body and wiggling under. After squeezing into the small space on the other side of the cot, she labored awkwardly to stand.

"Sorry," she warned in the dark as she pulled the near side of the stretcher upward.

Rising as she tugged, it trapped the man between the wall and litter, and he meekly said, "What're yuh doin'?"

"Getting you out." She leaned over and, with a hefty pull, yanked the other side of stretcher from its place against the wall, releasing the man's body. He fell hard to the floor and moaned. She winced, put her hands on the side of the man's body and pushed. He didn't move.

"Are yuh tryin' to move me?" his whispered weakly. "What if I try? Be easier . . . than killing me like this."

"I'd like to kill you, but I can't. You're in my way. Just slide out."

"Yuh ain't takin' me no place worse, are yuh?"

"I'm going to let the Devil take you if you don't slide under that wall now."

William slowly scooted under the wall, then struggled to stand. The woman was close behind and soon they were face to face in light filtering from above. William, seeing her for the first time, smiled. She was heavenly, no diabolical angel. The Lord had saved him, but the room was moving, spinning. He was wobbling. Strong arms wrapped tightly around him, steadied him. The Savior had heard him. He'd forgiven the murder, and she—his angel—had been sent to fly him through the clouds to Heaven. Joy in death. He was happy as he slipped blissfully again into unconsciousness.

She called to Adam, but he was gone. She vaguely remembered him asking if he should go for the judge and imagined he had when she didn't answer. She hoped he had because she alone could not lift or pull this man—William— up the ladder. She looked at him, slumped, heavy in her arms, and chuckled thinking of the comic scene they'd just survived.

She couldn't hold him longer. She was uncomfortable with her tight embrace and his weight. She slowly lowered him to one of the barrels and twisted him around to rest over its head. When she was sure he wouldn't slide off, she let go, breathing a rapid sigh of relief. Her arms and shoulders ached, and she felt a slight pain in her back.

She again squeezed between the barrels and wall and rolled into the hidden room. In darkness, she felt for the candle broken in William's panic and her beloved push-up brass candle holder. She collected candle bits, then raised the cot to rest against the back wall of the tiny room. She tightly grasped the candle bits and holder and slid clumsily back under the wall.

She placed the candle holder and remaining wax on one of the barrels, grabbed her petticoats and soiled skirt from the floor where they'd fallen. They'd been rolled and walked on, and the dress was surely stained, dirty and ruined. She was just as filthy, as she always was after sliding into the hidden room. She tried to ignore the smell she'd picked up from William. When she finished dressing, she bent down to push the barrels back against the secret opening.

She considered the unconscious man, then climbed a few steps to peer out of the cellar to ensure Adam had closed the shed door. When she saw he had, she reached for the trapdoor and struggled to place it on the opening. As it settled, complete darkness enveloped them.

She felt her way to William. With careful hands, she pulled him gently, attempting to lower him to the ground, but his weight was too much for her, and he fell the last few inches, thudding on the clay floor. She grimaced, imagining the bruises he'd wake to. She reached down, adjusted his body into what she imagined would be a more comfortable position, then felt her way to the ladder. She sat on a middle rung to wait for Adam and help.

She smiled, amused by her situation and her incongruous feelings. She was in a dark cellar with a man she didn't know, probably a killer, a runaway slave, and she was enjoying everything about it.

Chapter 12

March 1864, Eastern Kentucky

William woke to a dark, moist physical world. He was hungry and vaguely remembered being saved from hell by an angel wrapping her strong arms tenderly, lovingly around him and flying him upward. But where had she left him? This seemed no better than where he'd been. He moved, and it hurt. He'd been beaten.

The Devil tore William's shirt from his back and lowered a wooden paddle with dangling leather straps into a water pail that sizzled and glowed red as it wet the straps. Noise was everywhere—clanging, shouting, crying, screaming, wailing, disorder. William was still, watching the water glow. The demon pulled the leather from the water with a nefarious laugh and whipped down hard, mercilessly on William, and William heard himself scream as fire scorched his back, driving salt deep into his pores. William—suddenly deaf—watched as Lucifer picked up a whip and cracked it again across his now-blistered back, tearing the blisters. Unendurable agony. Over and over, the Prince of Darkness brought the whip down, till with one last howl of delight, he picked up the pail of sizzling, glowing water and sloshed it over William. Fire again as water, salt and pepper found every open wound.

William, unbound, urged himself to run or fight back, but he couldn't move. Paralyzed by hellish power, he bellowed in frustration.

Once again he rested in the cool darkness, the Devil was gone. The scorching pain miraculously healed. The clatter and cries of hell had merged and dwindled into his own breathing—raspy, shallow, exhausted. He tried to move. More pain, but not the agony of a diabolical beating. Soreness. Wherever he was—he smiled to himself—he was not in Hades. He stretched out on the cold ground and sighed.

"Awake?" A voice. He remembered it from somewhere . . . the angel's voice. She was still with him.

Breathlessly, he responded, "Yes, 'am."

"You were screaming."

"Debil was beatin' me."

"Ah . . . a dream."

" Where am I . . . we?"

She could tell where he was going and didn't want more talk of hell. She replied quickly, "A root cellar."

"Who are yuh, and what are we doin' in a root cella'?"

"It's my cellar."

William lay thinking a long time before he asked, "What am I doin' in yor root cella'?"

"Quiet. Just lay there . . . rest till help comes."

"What's the smell? Horrible!"

"You."

He tried to remember what had happened. "What help we waitin' for?"

"Friends."

"Yors or mine?"

"Mine. Judging from your condition, I'm not sure you have friends."

William moaned slightly. "Must have a few." Momentary silence. "Where . . . don't know."

"Do you want to talk about it now or later?"

"'Bout what?"

"Who you killed?"

William lay silent, reliving the moment at the old woman's house. He flinched remembering the woman blowing backward, crumpling to the ground as the man shot her. He remembered wrenching the white man's neck as he choked Hank. They hadn't buried the man. He and Hank had fled quickly—Hank to Staunton, William to . . . . His memories became wispy. Vague images, odd emotions passed—hiding in the woods, digging roots to eat, fear, the white man collapsing limp on the ground. They'd hunt him down, hang him for killing that worthless white man. The dread of hanging lingered in the cool cellar.

She waited quietly. Weakened as he was—he was no threat. She could fight him off, escape up the ladder if he attacked. But she was curious. Nothing about this man spoke violence.

He finally spoke, "Killed a man . . . a white one."

"Your master? Did he beat you like the Devil?"

"No!" he was disgusted at the suggestion. "What do yuh think I am? Didn't kill Marster Richman."

"Then . . . tell me again who you did kill."

"Again?"

"You already confessed, but you were in a fever."

"Killed him for a friend."

"Glad to hear you have one." She smiled. She liked this man, who went mad because he saved a friend.

"'Fore the war, lived in Winchester. Mars Richman bought me when I was 'bout twenty. If you have to have a mars, he was good. Good wife. Good daughter—just a little thing when I come. Cared for the horses. I was an ostler, that means stable boy."

"I know what it means," she said, as if offended.

Feeling rebuked, he quickly added, "Ain't sayin' yuh didn't. Just sayin'."

Embarrassed by her unkind remark, she didn't answer.

He continued, not able to see her but still imagining her the dream-like angel who had flown him from hell. "Was there a long time, years . . . with the Richmans. Liked 'em, especially Mars. But he done died, the war come 'long, and everything gone crazy. Mistress . . . she gone mad. Miss Richman got married . . . not to Hank, to some other fella. All wrong. She become Mrs. Henderson. Moved up to Staunton. Hank . . . he disappeared—everyone thought him dead. I thought he was dead, right after the row."

"Wait . . . wait. You're going too fast. Where did this Hank come from? How did he get in the story?"

"Saved Mars' life once. All of us loved him. Servants, Mars, Mistress, especially Miss Richman . . . loved him most."

"What's your name?"

William was surprised with the abruptness of the question. "Name?"

"Yes, what's your name?"

"William, Ma'am."

"Yes, I know that. Your surname?"

"Ain't no sir, Ma'am."

"No, surname . . . your last name?"

"Surname," he said slowly, trying to memorize it.

"Yes, what's your last name?"

"Don't worry 'bout that much."

"Why not?"

"Don't seem important."

"Oh, William, it is important. Everyone needs a last name . . . to know where you fit. They took your family—mama and papa. You need a name."

"Still don't see no good in it, but if yuh gotta know, it's Richman."

"Does that bother you, me asking?"

"No, don't s'pose it does."

"Good. I wouldn't want to hurt you with questions."

"Like yuh askin'. Not many ask me questions."

It was odd, she thought, that they sat here in the dark chatting now as if they were in her sitting room and intimate friends. "You got your name from your master?"

"My best marster."

"Now, I'll be able to introduce you to my friends . . . if they come."

"If?"

"They'll come. I'm just tired of waiting, but I'll introduce you as Mr. Richman. More dignified than just William."

"Ma'am? What's yor name?"

"Victoria Parrot," she said proudly.

"Victoria." He pictured the angel in his dream. It was an angelic name and face. "That's beautiful."

"Thank you." She paused briefly. "Named for a queen. Now, William Richman, tell me the rest of your story."

"Story?"

"You were telling me about murdering . . . murdering a white man," she said mischievously.

"No . . . no. Never said 'murdered.' Said 'killed.'"

"Tell me the rest . . . so I don't call the sheriff."

"Oh . . . I do smell bad."

"Of course you do, but don't think . . . don't talk about it. I'm smelling it, too, and I don't want to think about it. The story."

"What was I sayin'?"

"You were talking . . . about Hank—the one everybody loved so much."

"Hank used to visit the Richmans, 'cause he loved 'em . . . specially their daughter. Spent time with me . . . teachin' me . . . sharin' things. Knew my wife . . . my children."

"You have a wife?" Victoria said, surprised.

"She died. Don't know what happened to the children. She wasn't my first."

"I understand."

William paused, remembering his last wife, Molly. Being with her made his life joyous, even living apart as they had. "Should I say more?"

"If you're willing."

"I've been talkin' a long time," he said, suddenly aware of a consuming thirst and hunger. Where were her friends?

"Finish later. Just rest now."

"I'd be happy to get out o' here."

"Well . . . I'm sitting on stairs that lead to a shed, but I'm not strong enough to push or pull you up the ladder. So we're stuck . . . till help comes."

"I can get up any ladder," he said.

"Are you sure? You're tired . . . just talking."

"Talking takes thinkin'. Thinkin' takes strength. Climbin' a ladder . . . that ain't nothin'."

She heard him rise slowly from the ground.

"I'm standin'."

"It's so dark, I can't even tell if you're still in this cellar."

"Where's the ladder?"

She moved from the ladder, seeking tentatively his hand. She bumped into him.

"Yuh're real." he said.

"Give me your hand." They both reached out, eventually finding and grasping hands. She pulled him gently to the ladder. "Oh, I've got to open the hatch first."

"I'll do it."

"I don't think you could. I'll open it. Then . . . then we can get you up."

He stood motionless, feeling exhausted, while she climbed. She pushed on the door and it rose, flooding the cellar with what William was sure was the brightest light he'd ever seen and a bit of fresh, cold air. His eyes burned, and there, in the middle, surrounded by unendurable light was the angel. He was dizzy and grabbed the ladder.

Victoria climbed farther to lean the door against a barrel above. He could still see her form and watched it with admiration and gratitude. Strange that an angel would dress so human.

She was quickly back down, standing beside him again, and asked, "Can you do it?"

Without answering, he reached for the ladder, raised his foot to the lowest rung and pushed up, raising his body. He was sweating. "Let me rest. Old . . . I'm feeling old. A ladder, and I can't hardly climb one step."

"Be quiet and rest. For three days, all we get are moans and groans. Now I can't keep you from talking."

He laughed. "Gunna try the next one."

"You're strong enough," she encouraged.

He pushed his right leg up again, this time to the second rung, and pulled his body up, but she could see him collapsing. Without thinking, she climbed to the lowest rung, wrapped her arms around his body and under his arms and grabbed the ladder. She held him tight against it so he couldn't fall. "Are you all right?"

"No more steps . . . not yet."

She laughed, "What are we going to do then?"

He didn't answer, but she heard noise outside the shed. The door opened and in walked Isaiah, a lean, dark-skinned slave. Cold air poured into the shed, wafting into the cellar.

Isaiah looked at the pair, with William held tight between Victoria and the ladder. Isaiah, bundled in a bulky overcoat, scowled, and Victoria—for whom he felt a new strong attachment—could tell he was irritated and wanted to say something.

"Thank you for coming," she said.

"What y'all tryin' to do, here?" he asked hostilely.

"Climb the ladder, but he's exhausted. Pull him up."

"That'll be easy . . . skinny ole man. Give me both yar hands!" He said harshly.

William, held tight against the ladder by Victoria, was free to raise his arms and quickly extended both upward. Isaiah pulled, backing toward the door of the shed. Victoria eased the pressure against his body as Isaiah pulled, and she began pushing from below till William was lying with his upper body on the floor of the shed, his legs still leaning against the ladder below.

"Man . . . you smells," Isaiah said, raising his own hands to his face to see if his hands had picked up the odor. "And now it's on me."

"Sorry," William said humbly.

Victoria—still trapped in the cellar—encouraged both to move. Isaiah grunted, reached under William's arm pits and pulled him onto the cold, winter-hibernating undergrowth outside the shed. He again smelled his hands and looked at William with disgust.

Victoria climbed the ladder quickly, replaced the trapdoor and moved opposite Isaiah, looking at William.

Isaiah didn't take his eyes off Victoria. "Ya smells as good as yar friend."

"Isaiah, you must have studied the art of compliments." She looked for Adam, who was standing behind her. "Adam, where are you?"

"He . . . he . . . here, Mama."

"Oh, good." She reached toward him, pulling him along-side her. "Adam, this is William Richman, just over from Winchester—the man you saved."

William nodded his head at Adam, and Adam smiled broadly at the exhausted man as he lay on the ground. "Hel . . . Hello," Adam forced the words out with an extraordinary effort. "I tttold you Mama, he was a nnnice man." He screwed up his face to force out the last words.

William, who was now freezing on the hard ground, said only, "Thank yuh, boy."

Her introductions continued, "William Richman, this is Isaiah, the man who braved pattyroller insults and violence for you."

Isaiah, suspiciously watching William and Victoria for signs of affection, said, "How come ya come from Winchester? Didn't do no work? Marster threw ya out? Get all starved over there? 'Cause ya don't look like ya' been fed . . . ever. Ole, ugly . . . skinny."

William tried to rise, and Adam knelt to help him up. "Thank yuh," he said again.

Adam looked at his mother, "Is that all he kno . . . kno . . . knows how to say?"

Victoria laughed, feeling the stress of the last hours lifting. "I think he knows a few more words." She looked at Adam seriously. "I've been down there a long time. I've been able to teach him quite a few words."

Isaiah interrogated William further. "Why come over here?"

William answered guilelessly, "Tryin' to get to Maryland . . . or Washington City . . . to enlist in the army."

Isaiah snickered, "Well, ya come the wrong way."

William looked at him questioningly. "Wrong way?"

Isaiah sneered, "You came southwest. You gotta go northeast."

"Just a day's walk, just 'cross the Potomac at Barry."

"Don't know what he be talkin' 'bout, Victoria," Isaiah responded, appraising the woman in her soiled clothing. "It ain't no quick trip to Maryland . . . and what's Potomac?"

Victoria, a puzzled look on her face, answered absentmindedly, "A river near Washington."

William looked confused. "How far is Winchester from here?" Then with eyes scrunched in disbelief, he said, "Never heard of the Potomac?"

"Why should I? Ain't 'round here," Isaiah said.

Victoria said quietly, "It's probably 500 miles from here." She bent over the emaciated man and asked hesitantly, "Where do you think you are, William Richman? You are from Winchester like you said, aren't you?"

William shook his head, "Don't know. S'pose I'm . . . confused . . . or maybe . . . oh, it's all like a dream. But Winchester ain't more than 50 miles from Maryland."

"Ya're a lunatic!" Isaiah declared a little too loudly, then added, "or maybe just ole . . . too ole . . . and ugly."

Victoria ignored Isaiah. She knew what was driving his animosity, and she wouldn't acknowledge it. She spoke patiently, "William, what state are we in?"

William looked at her, distrust in his eyes. "Virginia."

Isaiah guffawed, "Ya're in Kentuck." He whistled. "And ya're in trouble if ya ain't from 'round here. They'll sell ya a slave 'fore ya can breathe . . . and they'll beat ya, just for bein' here . . . if ya ain't from here . . . if ya ain't lyin'. And if ya's alyin', I'll beat ya." Isaiah was more animated with each word and his grin widened with pleasure. "If ya're free in Giny, they'll sell ya a slave in Kentuck."

Victoria was disgusted by Isaiah's rejoicing, and she tried to soften the atmosphere by compassionately adding, "William, you've wandered hundreds of miles out of your way. We're near Winchester . . . Kentucky."

Chapter 13

March 1864, Eastern Kentucky

Isaiah sat at the small table in Victoria's tiny kitchen watching her. "What we gunna do wid de ole man?"

"Old man?" Victoria responded coldly.

"De ole man upstairs."

"Isaiah, he's just tired." Victoria responded wearily.

"Long as ya had 'im in de cellar, nobody could 'a found 'im. But now . . . he be dangerous. Put 'im back. Give him a little food, water till he be strong." He stopped to think, adding, "Don't think de man was ever strong—looks scrawny, weak . . . ugly, too."

She dismissed his irritating belittlement of William and spoke reflectively. "He can't go back down." She paused remembering the tight space, the close air, the horrible smell. "I'll never go back down. It was torture. I'm not sending anyone down there again. I'm going to fill up that hole and try to forget it."

"Somebody's gunna see 'im. Den we'll be . . . all o' us . . . put in some jail what's worse than that hole."

"Isaiah, don't you ever say good things?" She looked at him sternly. "We'll keep him hidden."

"What 'bout de man bein' here . . . wid ya and Adam? Ain't right. Not Christian."

"Just be quiet. Let me think. Besides, if we hide him well, no one will ever know."

"De man shouldn't stay here."

Victoria, bored with his jealousy, didn't respond as she verbally considered their predicament. "It will be hard to separate Adam from him. The boy thinks he's found an injured squirrel . . . wants to nurse it to health." She smiled at the image.

"Gotta 'gree wid Adam. De man be a squirrel . . . a wounded squirrel. Let's shoot 'im . . . but we ain't gunna get no meal out o' 'im. Got no meat on dem bones."

"Isaiah, why I allow you at my table . . . ."

Isaiah raised his hands to a defensive posture, "Just thinkin' o' ya and yar boy. It ain't right, 'im stayin' here."

"If you've got a plan, tell me."

"Let de judge decide."

"Oh." She was angry. "The judge? That's no plan. Think for yourself! You're human, aren't you?" She paused and added, "I'm sorry. I should be more patient . . . but don't depend so much on the judge. What's he going to do? Secretly add a hidden room on my house? Tell people to stay away because we're hiding a fugitive?" Her expression softened. "Strange, Isaiah, I think you're right. Actually, Isaiah, you're wrong on everything but one point. William Richman can't stay here."

Isaiah's eyes glowed with victory, but shifted to suspicion. "Ya think I be right?"

Victoria was still thinking aloud. "He can't stay here. He'd be seen. He's out of place. We were fortunate no one saw us bring him so carelessly in from the shed."

"What'll we do?" Isaiah asked.

She looked at him harshly. "You're the one convinced he's smarter than every white man. You should have ideas by the baker's dozen."

"Baker's what?"

"Dozen—at least 13. But don't worry about it. I shouldn't have said it. It was unkind."

He shifted nervously, embarrassed by her apology. "Ya're not no slave, Victoria. Ya don't know what it be like."

Her eyes blazed. "I was a slave. I know its inhumanity." Her voice warmed slightly. "I hope you'll be free soon. You're not far from it now."

He looked at her, returning her now-gentle gaze.

She smiled at him out of guilt and a desire to be kind. "Well, Mr. future freedman. What will we do? He's not a slave, not legally, I suspect. He was in Virginia. So, according to President Lincoln's proclamation, I think he's free . . . a free man. Alas, in Kentucky that's all the worse for him."

"Can't they make 'im a slave . . . just bein' here, a free man from another state."

"They can put him in jail. They're scared of us, of freed blacks. If a master takes his Kentucky slave to visit a free state, the slave can't even come back. It's tough to be slave or free . . . in Kentucky. Don't suppose it's easy to be white right now either. I know it's not for the judge. Surrounded by enemies no matter what he decides . . . or says or does. But what to do with Mr. Richman?"

"Get 'im out o' Kentuck . . . soon."

"Oh, Isaiah," Victoria said exasperated. "You're in a great hurry to get rid of him. But he's in no shape to travel . . . by foot or any other way."

"Hide 'im at de judge's farm . . . least den, he'll be 'way from yar boy."

She was talking to herself again. "I don't think they're looking for him, at least not near here. He'd have to be crazy . . . he was crazy to come to Kentucky when he could have just gone north to freedom. Hiding him can mean two things. Physically, so no one sees him—that's hard. Or hide him in plain sight and hide his freedom—a tree in the forest. Hiding him at the judge's is a good idea, Isaiah."

"Ya don't want 'im near ya, then?"

"Oh, I wouldn't say that," Victoria said merrily, and quickly continued, "That's what we ask the judge."

"If ya want de ole man near ya?"

"Course not," she responded impatiently. "We ask him to accept William as his slave."

"'Cept 'im . . . a slave?"

"You can enslave yourself in Kentucky . . . anytime."

"Don't make no sense. Why be a slave to de judge? If I be free, ain't never gunna be no slave no more."

"Isaiah, you're a slave in name only. The judge pays you wages, doesn't he? Only reason you don't leave is you know you might end up in the army. Then the judge wouldn't be able to help you."

Isaiah looked at her defiantly, "I wanna be free."

"Course you do." She saw she'd offended him. "But you're biding your time. It won't be long before you sneak off to join the army." Under her breath, low enough that Isaiah couldn't hear her, she added, "I hope." She raised her voice, "Then you'll be free. Yes, I can see you a soldier."

"S'pose." His tone brightened. "Ya want me to do that?"

She looked vacuously at Isaiah and said, "Isaiah, I've enough problems looking after Adam . . . thinking for us. I'm not about to think for you. If you want to join the army, do it. If you want to stay at the judge's, stay." She stopped, stared at the wall behind Isaiah as she reverted to thinking of William. She smiled. This plan was revenge on the slavers. "We'll hide our escaped slave in plain sight at the judge's . . .

right under their noses . . . and they won't suspect a thing. The judge can draw up papers showing he's a free man who asked to be the judge's slave." She smirked.

"Just get 'im 'way soon. Better for 'im if he be gone."

Isaiah was always tedious. Again she spoke sternly, as if to a naughty child, "Why? He's not dangerous to us."

"Well . . . I don't think de same. 'Trollers might . . ."

"It won't matter. He'll be a slave of the judge."

"Maybe he says somethin' 'bout de judge . . . and yuh . . . and how de judge feels 'bout slaves."

"He doesn't know anything to say about the judge." She laughed. "Besides no one in the county doesn't already suspect the judge's feelings."

"Adam."

"Adam?"

"S'pose he be caught up in it."

"In what?"

"S'pose, they come after de judge 'cause he's helping dis freedman from Giny and Adam's wid 'im."

"Why would they come after him if they think he's the judge's slave? Enough! If you say another word . . . I think you're just jealous of William." She gazed upward with a feigned, distant, dream-like expression, adding, "He's a strong, fine looking man . . . the kind a woman likes."

"That's . . . ." He turned to look nervously out the window. "He be too ole for ya."

"We must be thinking of different men. William Richman is a loving . . . handsome . . . young . . . man."

Isaiah squirmed, but they were distracted by noise outside the cottage and moved quickly, nervously toward the front door. They hoped it was the judge, but wanted to meet whoever it was before he got to the house.

They crossed the threshold as Adam and the judge descended from a carriage. The judge smiled at Victoria, stepped onto the porch, put his arms affectionately around her and held her tightly. She returned the embrace. When they released arms, he said, "I understand our guest's been saved from hell."

Victoria glanced at Adam, smiled and said, "I'm glad he's told you everything."

"I understand he stunk before his bath. Isaiah was disgusted by his smell. He's weak and apparently naked as Adam insisted we bring Isaiah's best clothes for him."

Isaiah looked put off. "Not my clothes!"

"That's what Adam said we should do. Was he wrong?"

Victoria laughed delightedly, "Adam, you're wonderful. You told him all the important things."

Adam smiled shyly, stepping to his mother's side, and she pulled him tight.

Victoria directed the party into the sitting room and asked the judge if he wanted anything to drink or eat.

"No, I'm fine. A little cold. Can we go in the kitchen?"

"Of course," she responded, leading them and arranging three chairs at the table. Isaiah remained standing nearby.

"He's weak, then?"

"Very," Victoria responded.

"To be expected."

Isaiah spoke boldly, "We want 'im to be ya slave."

"My slave?" the judge looked confused.

"That be what Victoria thinks," he said, nodding approvingly, knowingly, at Victoria.

"Isaiah, I don't want another slave. Besides, he's already got a master, hasn't he?"

Victoria responded, "He's from Virginia, Judge. He won't really be your slave. Remember the Kentucky law?" The judge looked at her blankly, and she added, "The one where a freedman can choose to be a slave for anyone . . . for life."

"The 1860 Act Concerning Free Negroes, Mulattoes, and Emancipation. Yes. He's a freedman, then?"

"I think he is."

"Think?"

Isaiah chimed in, "He's crazy . . . thinks he be in Giny."

"Virginia? Why?"

Victoria responded, "He was trying to enlist."

"In the army? I don't understand."

Victoria said, "Let me tell you his story, then guide us."

"Guide you? That'll be the day." The judge chuckled.

"Here's his story . . . at least all I got between dreams and hallucinations."

"Hallucinations?"

"He was definitely lost somewhere in his mind. He's an escaped slave from Virginia. He escaped a while ago and wanted to get to Washington . . . or Maryland to enlist."

"Why not enlist in Virginia? Why come to Kentucky?"

"I don't know why he didn't enlist in Virginia, but I do know he thought he was in Virginia . . . here in Kentucky."

"So, to him, Kentucky is a hallucination," the judge said, laughing. "Right now, I think it's more a nightmare."

"It be that for me too, Massa," Isaiah added.

The judge frowned.

Victoria continued, "I thought since the Emancipation Proclamation applies in Virginia, that he's free."

"Some parts of Virginia. Applies to parts not under Union control, but since it's nearly impossible that his owner will pop up like a devil in a box, I think we can treat him as a freedman. If he wants to attach himself to me, he'd be legal here, and it'd be easier to get him out of Kentucky."

Isaiah followed quickly. "Just what I be telling Victoria. Gotta get 'im out o' here."

"I'll prepare a document. If he'll sign, I'll have another slave, but only long enough for him to recuperate. I'll bring papers tomorrow. Keep him hidden. Don't let anyone in the house. Just you and Adam. Oh, I'll need his name."

"William Richman," Victoria responded.

"No middle name?" asked the judge absent-mindedly as he took out a pencil and a small notebook.

"I was lucky just to get a first and last name."

"CCCan't his middle name be Adam?" Adam contributed. "Then I'd bbbe named after him."

Victoria looked sadly at her son. "Yes," she said, not taking her eyes off Adam. "His middle name is Adam."

The judge smiled affectionately at Victoria. "I'm going home." He replaced the pencil and book in his jacket, rose, pulled his overcoat tighter around him as he moved toward the front door and away from the warmth of the kitchen stove. "Come, Isaiah. Victoria, take care of our new friend."

Isaiah mumbled, "Ole man."

Isaiah and the judge climbed into the carriage and rode from the cottage.

When he could no longer see the carriage, Adam climbed the narrow stairs to the small bedroom—usually his own—where William slept soundly. It was evening, and the boy sat in the dark doorway, listening to his namesake breathe deeply, slowly.

Chapter 14

April 1864, Eastern Kentucky

The two black men walked in the easy gait they would have used to meander on a slow Sunday to hear the slave minister in the woods. But it wasn't the Sabbath, and they feared being questioned. They wanted any who passed to see them as reluctant slaves sent to work at a neighboring farm, slaves with no desire to get anywhere quickly, as arrival would only mean hard work benefiting someone else. But contrary to their charade, they were on an urgent errand. The decision had been made the previous night, and William already regretted it.

For weeks, Isaiah had berated William for agreeing to be enslaved to the judge, declaring at every turn that he must escape immediately. Did William have no self-respect? He had been free and yet knelt—willingly—to be chained again as white-man chattel. Isaiah, his face distorted with disgust, would rhetorically question how William could do it. He would emphasize that no woman, especially Victoria, could respect such a man.

Well after dark the day before, a slave whispered that Union recruiters from Camp Nelson would be at a nearby town the next morning, and Isaiah immediately began badgering William. This was the chance to escape all Kentucky masters, to claim freedom in the army.

"Ain't it what ya wanted?" he'd asked William enthusiastically when he saw William's hesitation. Isaiah assured him they'd be safe, he knew the roads. They'd leave early, before they were found out.

William wanted to enlist but still suffered spells of exhaustion and fear. Isaiah dismissed William's resistance and spoke exuberant words. This was the chance! Escape slavery! Join the cause! It was an answer to prayer. William had been too tired to resist and conceded approval.

Well before dawn and without awakening the other men in their small cabin, the pair set out in a cold fog to join the voracious, engorging Northern military behemoth. William tired early in their journey but convinced himself he couldn't stop or go back. He pushed on, struggling to keep up with the younger man, even at their leisurely pace. Each step depleted William's energy, and he grumpily resented Isaiah's persistence.

Further consternation followed when William realized Isaiah's tone had changed. Isaiah had started talking about how much William was going to like the army, the experiences he'd have, the glory he'd gain. This new emphasis birthed the impression that Isaiah wasn't enlisting. Could it be he never intended to join? This preacher of slave liberation planned to return to the horrors he railed against! He led William on this exercise merely to get him out of the way. William remembered something Victoria had read to him as he lay exhausted in Adam's bed. "O, that's a brave man! He writes brave verses, speaks brave words, swears brave oaths and breaks them freely."

William's frustration was compounded by mental exhaustion. He was recovering from his bow to lunacy, but he could still see in his mind the white man's head jerk fatally sideways. He'd overcome the guilt of killing, but there were times when he succumbed to intense fear—manifested as mental images of his own body hanging from the limb of a big, picturesque white oak tree.

In the early days in Victoria's home, she'd often laughed him from his gloom, ribbing him, encouraging him, beckoning him back from the precipice of fear. Her spiritual nursing was a candle, illuminating even the deepest crevices of his mind, exposing and destroying almost every filament of his madness. The light, at first weak and wavering, now shone stronger, brighter; and even in his dispirited morning march, he could feel her guiding him toward sanity.

Unknown to William, his convalescing weeks had tried those around him. Isaiah continually lobbied the judge to get William away from Victoria, telling him William was trying to steal her heart from its rightful place. He was sure the suggestion would infuriate the judge and prompt him to turn William over to the county. And, if that wasn't enough, Isaiah reminded him that William—an escaped slave—might destroy the judge's standing in the county. What if William's owner were to descend in a fury?

When Isaiah found an excuse to be alone with Victoria, he assured her William was a menace. He'd murdered someone, hadn't he? He might strike Adam. Certainly the old man would mean no harm. Or would he? What did Victoria really know about him? Maybe he'd killed many men and women . . . and children. Maybe that's why he had been running . . . if you could call his labored efforts running. What mother would let such a madman near a child?

Both the judge and Victoria had shown no interest in Isaiah's fantasies. They knew jealousy drove everything he was doing and independently refused to feed it. But their ignoring him only increased his hatred of William.

As William's health and mind improved, he moved to the judge's farm and began working periodically in the stable. The judge had quickly taken him aside, encouraging him to rest more. William was embarrassed that this gentle man would worry about him.

William finished the memory, then noticed how tired he was. He hoped this walk wouldn't put him back in bed.

Thoughts of bed brought images of young Adam sitting at his side the two weeks he lay prostrate at Victoria's. William would doze, then wake to the boy staring at him, waiting to hear stories of what it was like in Virginia. William had told Adam of his childhood. They began as mostly happy memories of pleasant times with few worries, abundant free time, play and wandering with other young boys, white—the master's sons—and black.

But as time passed, the stories turned darker. William told Adam how his life had changed in one day. He didn't remember how old he was, and no one had warned him. They knew—his mother, his numerous unrelated aunts and uncles—but no one prepared him, and the sudden change left William feeling betrayed.

One day William had been unexpectedly sent to the master's stables to learn to care for horses, wagons and coaches. At that unforeseen moment, his freedom of movement and friendship with the master's sons ended. Only later did he realize the hasty change trained him for docility and compliancy like the horses he would learn to break.

It also groomed the master's sons. Quickly, his separation from them was so complete they gladly beat him for slight mistakes, hesitation or subtle belligerence.

William recalled his own mother being forced to watch as the master's youngest son whipped him. She wept and shrieked as she tried to get to her son. But her struggles were met with menacing warnings from the white boy to get back or he'd beat her, too. Slave men had to hold her to keep her from intervening. William's eyes watered as he told the story. "The marster . . . he was teachin' my mama that I—her flesh and blood—wasn't none of hers at all," William had told Adam.

Later, as his mind cleared, William was ashamed he'd introduced such horrors to a child. As he walked with Isaiah, he cringed and grimaced recalling stories he'd told. He chastised himself for a loose tongue and craved Victoria's forgiveness for the terrors he'd embedded in the young mind. Suddenly he stopped walking. A thought came, and he smiled. In spite of the awful memories he recounted, Adam had never shown any fear. Quite the opposite, the more he told the boy, the closer he'd hovered, awaiting the next semi-lucid moment and story.

As he dragged himself toward the army, William relived pleasurable evenings with Victoria at his bedside. Sometimes he was unaware she'd entered his room—she was just there with her hand resting warm on his shoulder. He was strengthened by the touch, enlivened by the smile. Nothing but excitement and encouragement streamed from her. On his best days, he understood he had put her in great peril, but he never saw anxiety in her eyes.

She would read to him, pausing periodically to look into his face. He remembered her reading stories from the Bible and from a man with the odd name of Shakespeare. She'd stop once in a while to make sure William followed what she was reading. Sometimes he didn't, but he didn't care because he loved the sound of the words delivered in a voice that reminded him of the young Richman girl, Betsy.

Later during their time together, she read from the Psalms. She loved the songs of King David. She told him they gave her strength when she was tired and weak, that they were a healing balm to her soul, and quickly described balm when she saw his confused expression. He still remembered one song. "For thou wilt not leave my soul in hell; neither wilt thou suffer thine Holy One to see corruption." "Ah," he said when she read it, "it was God then that saved me from hell, and you his . . . my angel of light." She had smiled shyly without comment.

Night after night, she happily read words that left him lighter, almost spiraling upward. He'd heard of Jesus often in his life, but he'd felt nothing for him, not till he lay motionless in the boy-sized bed. He felt a love emanating from Victoria and from within himself that warmed him. The Holy One of God, Jesus, was filling him with it. In those weeks, he enjoyed a peace he'd never felt before. Jesus had delivered him from hell and healed him with a loving balm.

William was reveling in his memory of the feeling, and remembering it, the warmth came again. "Ah," William inadvertently said audibly. He was in the hands of his Savior, even on what had become a heavy-legged, slow-witted trudge to the Union Army.

William's chest was heavy, arms leaden. His legs rose with less bounce virtually in each step. His breathing was loud, labored. He couldn't keep up anymore and began to lag, walking slower and slower. He was not well, not nearly well enough for this. But still he surrendered his will to Isaiah. He had to go on. He tried to suck in air slowly, but it escaped in gasps. He was dizzy.

"Dere's de town, William," Isaiah shouted as William was ready to collapse. "De town." William was almost invigorated by Isaiah's enthusiasm. "I see de recruiters."

"Recruiters." William repeated. He looked at the town's rough buildings, but saw only the long 150 yards he still had to walk. He moaned.

William glanced sadly at Isaiah, who smiled at him and said, continuing his excited tone, "Brudder, this is where ya join de army . . . like ya wanted. A soldier!"

William was sure of Isaiah's plot. It should have been obvious earlier, but to a man saved from death by kindness and an angel of light, one who'd been born of Jesus, he hadn't expected betrayal from a brother. He was hurt, angry, tired, but showed none of it. He lowered his eyes and walked slowly toward the town. He had to get away from Isaiah.

"Goodbye, ole man," Isaiah shouted cheerfully, offended by William's lack of response. He was beginning to feel slight guilt, but ebullient thoughts of Victoria without William flushed regret from him. Now only the judge kept him from Victoria, and he would find a way around him. He smiled to himself as he watched William move slowly toward the recruiters. "Huzzah, huzzah, huzzah!" he called, hoping William would acknowledge it with a shout of his own. But his vanquished foe didn't respond, and Isaiah had a notion to grab and lead him back to the judge's.

The humane impulse passed quickly, however. Isaiah stifled it with an image of both men returning, and Victoria running to William, embracing him, crying at his suffering. Isaiah angered. Why hadn't the brat left him to die?

Fortified by jealousy, he watched William until he'd made it. He began to feel a giddiness, a lightness. Thoughts of Victoria enveloped him. The day was suddenly brisk and clear, the ground firm beneath his determined steps, and his pace energetic. With William gone, he could envision Victoria grateful he'd helped the pathetic old man get to the army.

Unfortunately for Isaiah, the recruiters had attracted patrollers and general miscreants to the daylight, and the normally nocturnal predators had already beaten a dozen escaping slaves. They came on Isaiah swiftly.

At the sound of galloping horses, Isaiah scurried toward underbrush at the road's edge. But they were on him before he could hide and acted quickly without accusation or questions. There were four of them, and they quickly surrounded him and dismounted. He tried to dart behind a tree to elude one, but the others hemmed him in.

He felt a whip lash from behind and turned to face his attacker as another lashed at his side, then another stroke fell. He turned toward one, but a whip stung his back. He spun again, but that cracker had withdrawn. Then the whips began to fall in earnest, coming down systematically, further tearing clothes and skin. Whips snapped on his back, hands, head and his bleeding face where one eye was already swollen closed. Desperately he plowed with full energy into the man in his front, only to realize his strength was matched.

The whipping stopped, but the punches began. He cowered and was knocked to the ground, and the blows and kicks continued, harder, faster. He curled into a fetal position. The blows were unrelenting. His head. His back. His belly. His legs. He was dazed, and his mind was slowing down.

Chapter 15

March 1864,
Washington City, District of Columbia

Hank Gragg was a son of Virginia's Shenandoah Valley and an immigrant to Indiana. He mustered in the latter state's 19th Infantry Regiment, an original part of the only Union brigade composed of western men fighting exclusively in the Eastern Theater. It fought stoically at Second Bull Run, Antietam, Gettysburg and more. Now monikered the Iron Brigade, it had been forged under murderous fire into a legend symbolized by their unusual-for-the-infantry tall Hardee hats.

But the legend was now bigger than the remains, for the Iron Brigade and the 19th had diminished with each battle until Gettysburg, where it had been decimated. The brigade waned still further as many veterans chose home-fire comfort when their three-year enlistment ended. And in a perceived insult to the fabled brigade, the army mixed the residue with regiments of eastern soldiers.

When regiment veterans had passed through Washington City for a quick excursion at the end of an official furlough, a well-dressed man at the Capitol had asked Hank how his regiment fared. He'd responded—hesitating, somber, nearly tearful—that he thought a quarter of the men dead, another half gone home disabled.

For Hank, the experience was worse than the statistics. He'd lost his messmates, those closest to him with whom he lived and ate—two in battle, one of disease, one had gone missing early, probably deserted. Hank alone survived, feeling isolated.

However, a furtive solo trip into enemy territory had buttressed him against such sorrow. He had miraculously seen Betsy Henderson, the woman he'd loved years earlier. And in her presence, he recaptured distant, forsaken feelings and found he still adored her.

Their reunion, nonetheless, was complicated by her dedication to the Confederacy in the heart of a rebellious state. Their only quarrels during his brief clandestine stay at her home in Staunton, Virginia, were about Southern secession. Did the South have the right to secede? Did the North have the right to invade a sovereign republic? The couple's arguments were tinged with desperation, driven more by abhorrence of coming separation than by ideological passion.

During the regiment's several-day stay in Washington, the men explored the town—the city both sides had wanted for their capital to buttress their claims to a direct link to the first American Revolution. Hank and his brothers-in-arms walked the grounds of the President's Residence and pushed through the field of cattle to explore the partially completed monument to George Washington.

Hank smiled as he reached the monument's abridged walls, remembering a ribbing from Betsy:

"Yes," she had said in one conversation about the war. "I know all about the Union's great love for the general. The Yankee nation built that great monument to General Washington . . . the one near the President's Residence. No, that's wrong. They could only muster half a monument because,"

she paused meaningfully, "they weren't faithful to his vision . . . the liberty he'd won them."

Hank quipped, "They have a completed monument to Washington in the city."

"Do they?" She looked suddenly bored. "Glad to hear it."

"Yes, he's on horseback."

"Oh, I've heard of it." She still looked bored. "The one that was unveiled only after our wonderful equestrian statue adorning our Capitol."

"Not my Capitol," Hank responded, yawning. "But I have heard of it. It's not quite finished, is it?"

"His statue's complete . . . along with those of Patrick Henry and Jefferson. I think that's quite enough to count. You've forgotten, perhaps, who those pure Virginians were . . . what they did."

"I'd like to forget what their children have done."

"All of them?"

He smiled, "Not all. I'm fond of a few." He looked softly at Betsy, who refused to acknowledge the familiarity. When he saw she was not giving in, he added, "But you're diverting the conversation. I've heard that New York has a statue . . . an equestrian statue of Washington, and it's completed. No extraneous statues of those who . . ." Hank stopped, worrying he pushed too far.

When he stopped mid-sentence, she prodded him, "Finish, sir. I want to hear what you have to say." She looked gruffly at him, then softened. "But before you do, remember where you are, how quickly I could call a company of Confederate patriots. They'd know how to handle such invading hordes."

"Hordes?"

"Yes, but please continue. I do want to hear what you'll say to offend your kind, patient hostess."

He grinned, "I think it unwise for me to continue for I've nothing to add. Do I need to swear it? I just wanted you to know about that first completed monument to General George Washington . . . the one in New York. That's all. I said it awkwardly. Sometimes I speak clumsily. Would a generous Confederate lady forgive me that?"

"Sir, you do speak awkwardly when you twist mind and mouth to defend indefensible coercion. And, Sirrah, I do pity you when all you can find to support your cause is some silly statue in New York." She stopped abruptly, leaning her head sidewise, smiling at him gently, "That is New York, isn't it? What have you or I to do with New York?"

In small groups, the regiment also enjoyed tables filled with memorabilia and marvels and period rooms at Washington's Sanitation Fair in the Patent Office, before moving across the Potomac to Alexandria. Soon they reunited near Culpeper with their Iron Brigade brothers from Wisconsin and Michigan.

There Hank wrote to a woman with whom he'd often communicated in the past. Always before, however, he'd corresponded with her as Betsy Henderson, wife of dead Confederate officer Thaddeus Henderson. Only during his furlough did he learn she was also Betsy Richman, formerly of Winchester, who had always held Hank's deepest affection. He wrote carefully to her, coding thoughts and feelings. He would worry about how to get it across the lines later.

Tenth of March of 1864
Dear Mrs. Henderson,

You are continually in my mind and heart. As poets must have scribbled, you are, if I may be bolder than I ought, the very air I breathe, the grass that softens each footfall and the breeze that brushes my cheek and reminds me that I am alive and that somewhere the world is beauty and peace and love and you. I am your humble servant and pray God will not keep us apart forever. That friends can be reunited and glow in the warmth of affection does honor to all who love God.

I have little to write, for we idle away in Virginia awaiting resumption of action that will surely come with spring and summer. In the meantime, we huddle in our winter hovels, trying to keep warm, with nothing to do. I do not complain. It is getting warmer by the day and will soon be hot enough in temperature and action. We have plenty of food. My only misery is that with little to do, I have scarcely anything to occupy my mind but memories of dear friends and moments shared in happier times not far distant. As they say, the Devil finds work for idle hands, so I have begun learning about base ball. It's a rather gentlemanly game, and quite enjoyable. But it is still often too cold to play, and then my idle thoughts return to friends. My only consolation at such times is knowing friends are safe in home's comfort.

On our way down here, we had a few days to visit the cities of Washington and Georgetown. They are busy places, especially Washington City. They warned us to stay away from some areas and activities. Soldiers passing through the capital cause a fair number of problems.

So many bodies have come to the city that it is bursting with excitement, activity and trouble. We went to see the Capitol and actually saw a few senators and congressmen. They looked rather normal and seemed decent fellows.

I would have been happier had close friends been with me. There are many wonderful places to walk and picnic in the hills around the city. There is yet much open space in Washington and nature seems to thrive there, even this year.

I want to tell you about the fascinating Patent Office. It is a wonder with its high vaulted ceilings and glass cabinets full of all kinds of contraptions and inventions. One of the ladies' groups is holding a Sanitation Fair in the building, so it is a hive of activity. We spent a pleasant afternoon at the fair. They organize them to raise money for the army. They charged twenty-five cents to enter. There were all kinds of displays. There was a massive bazaar room where you could buy different things, from clothes to candles. There were rooms decorated as they would have been in George Washington's day, before there were statues of him in North or South, with furniture and paintings, old fashioned kitchens, ladies dressed in the clothes of the day, but I was not interested. I was fascinated by a machine they had that washed clothes for you.

They had dancing, quilting bees, and you could even vote for your favorite general. I voted for General Thomas from Virginia. Many soldiers attended the fair. Some were ill, some with grievous wounds. I believe they were invited to help them keep up morale. There was quite a bit of singing. We joined in singing all the best patriotic songs, although I did not dance. There were rooms displaying weapons and trophies and selling autographs from famous people and blood-stained flags from various battles and wars. It was good to see that the nation is still fully behind us, especially before we returned to dreary winter camp in Virginia.

That is about all that I have to write. No, there is one more thing. It raised my ire, but I most likely just imagined it. On our way to winter camp, I saw someone who looked like that fellow Walthrope, without a beard. At the time, I was sure it was him, but I could not see him clearly, and that is probably just as well as I would have probably attacked him and gotten in trouble. I am convinced now that it wasn't him. It was just a man who looked like him. He was moving north on horseback, hardly the direction he would go. I should not have mentioned it. Please forgive me if it upset you.

I have not confided details of our friendship to anyone. Always know that I cherish you and look forward to our reunion. I am most grateful to our Heavenly Father that you are safe by your hearth and fire.

Your Faithful Servant,
Hank Gragg

Assumptions in Hank's letter were inaccurate in two ways. The man he'd seen on horseback was Lucius Walthrope, now Dante, and he was mistaken imagining Betsy safe in her home. For at the very moment he penned the letter, a field slave spied Betsy's abandoned carriage in the road and set off a frantic search for the mistress.

Chapter 16

March 1864,
Washington City, District of Columbia

Dante eventually made his way to Washington where his first days' efforts succeeded beyond anticipation. He delivered letters to Matthew's partners, received documents for return delivery—payment to come from Matthew. He spent a day scouring shops and markets for items scarce in Richmond and salivated anticipating the prices he could charge in the Southern capital.

His fortunes had turned, and he with pleasure fantasized Betsy hearing of his success, his influence. Closing his eyes, he imagined her smiling at him and tried to picture her scar, his brand. She was his to do with as he liked.

He'd taken special care of the package lifted from the traveler, leaving it unopened till he was alone in the city. He was at first disappointed to find no money in it. Instead he found seven letters written by Richmond residents to Washington City occupants. The letters were subversive, identifying letter recipients and other active capital-resident conspirators. The letters were better than money. It was a perfect theft.

He was tempted to blackmail each addressee, but concluded it would be foolish in this mixed-allegiance and violent town. He imagined a core of Confederate-loyal citizens organizing quickly to kill a lone blackmailer. No, he'd give this cache to the Union. It wouldn't raise the money possible from blackmail, but it might open influential doors and would be safer than extortion.

After brief inquiries, it became clear to Dante that he should present the letters to Colonel Lafayette Baker, a powerful man in the city and operator of his own secret police force under the supervision of Secretary of War Edwin Stanton. Reportedly, Baker at times even met with the president—the original baboon, Dante remembered with a smile.

Baker was infamous, hated and feared by the capital's citizenry, both for his legal efforts and rumored less-than-savory coercion. Dante suspected, however, the city really appreciated Baker's work. People liked order. Oskar Dante had seen that. They wanted to go about their daily lives—eat, sleep, enjoy themselves. If someone protected that, people were happy. As long as interrogations and torture didn't get close, they needn't acknowledge them. Surely reports of torture were just Confederate lies anyway.

He spent several days investigating Baker. During his probe, he felt queasy several times for, as he asked questions about this most chief of detectives, he felt eyes watching him and suspected quiet conversations asking who he was and what he was about.

After his research, he let it be known he had information useful to Baker. Well before dawn the next morning, two soldiers arrived at his lodgings uninvited. Ignoring the other boarders, they roused and escorted him without comment to a two-story building labeled merely 217 Pennsylvania Avenue, where he was left waiting in an empty room without explanation. He waited patiently, having expected mistreatment to test his mettle.

With nothing to occupy his mind, it wandered to his last memory of his father. The troubling image often lured him, but he usually quickly banished it with a drink, conversation or plotting some scheme. But as he waited for Baker, he was filled with an inner emptiness and uncertainty, and the recollection refused to leave.

He stood outside his family's cabin. His father, drunk again, greeted Dante with vile curses and despicable names as the boy arrived from working a neighbor's field.

Dante ignored him—he'd heard it before—until the man blocked the entrance to their hovel. Dante was tired and hungry. With little effort and no thought, he shoved his father aside and opened the door. Angered, the man grabbed a shovel left against the outside wall and swung it with his dissipated strength against Dante's back. The unexpected blow knocked Dante into the cabin.

Unable to think of anything but the pain in his back and his father's continuing laughter, Dante raged, lunging at his attacker and knocking him to the ground. He jumped on him and pummeled his face with his fists, crying audibly as tears dropped onto the inebriated, struggling man. The drunk was no match for his maturing son, and when he no longer resisted the blows and Dante had vented his wrath, the young man rose, tears still dripping from his eyes and spat on his father. Seeing the shovel on the ground, he picked it up and with one hand brought it down hard on his father's head.

Only then did he see his mother at the door watching, fear and tears in her eyes. She said nothing and made no move to aid him or her helpless husband who was sucking in short, raspy breaths. Dante detested her. He wanted to strike her, too. How often had she stood by as Dante's father had mercilessly beaten him? How often had she hit him for some small mistake. He shook his head, tossed the shovel onto his father's midsection, where it bounced and settled, balanced between beaten man and the ground, and walked away.

Still well before dawn, a man with sandy hair and red beard strutted into the office, jerking Dante from morbid shadows and the tears welling in his eyes. Dante did not rise to greet him, but nonchalantly rubbed his eyes to inconspicuously clear his tears. The man moved quickly till he loomed over him.

Forcefully Colonel Baker said, "Mr. Dante, you've been asking about me . . . everywhere citizens of this great national city gather. I assume you wanted to meet me. So . . . here you are." Baker proceeded to outline what Dante had eaten for breakfast the day before, who he'd met since arriving in town and where he stayed. "Mr. Dante, what are you doing here?"

Baker was trying to intimidate him, humble him, control him, but he was not going to arrest him. Baker wanted to know what Dante had for him.

"Colonel," Dante began softly, "I'm here for one reason only, and that's to meet you . . . to help you."

"That's two reasons."

"Everything I've done here was for this introduction."

"Should I be honored? I'm a busy man. I don't have time for social calls. We're at war. Why did you want to meet me?"

"Colonel, you live up to your reputation."

"Your point?" Baker still towered above Dante, staring down on him, forcing Dante to raise his head uncomfortably to look the agent in the eye.

"I have letters warning of Southern sedition," he said as he pulled the stolen letters from his overcoat.

Baker jerked the letters from Dante's hand as he replied, "We already have Southern sedition." Without moving, he pulled the first letter from its open envelope. He read it carefully without comment. He then opened a second and gave it the same careful review. "They all like these?" he asked in a more cordial tone.

"Yes."

"Mr. Dante," he said looking at him for the first time since grabbing the letters, "These are useful . . . valuable." He stepped away from Dante, walked behind a desk in the office and sat. "How did you come to possess these . . . letters? Were you the courier? Do you betray someone?"

"No. I had nothing to do with them. I took them from a Southern agent on his way to Washington."

"Did you know what they contained?"

"The letters? No. But the courier was so nervous, I knew he was up to something . . . some harm to the Union."

"You stole the letters, sneaked through the lines and brought them to me because of your love for the Union?"

"Nearly."

"Nearly?"

"I'd heard of you. You're well known . . . feared in Richmond. But I wasn't sure you were . . . the right person."

"So you asked questions . . . lots of questions."

"Yes."

"Cautious."

"Yes."

"Not so cautious I wouldn't hear, though."

"No."

"Virginian?"

"No, from Tennessee, but I have no Southern loyalties."

"Why?"

"I'm angry . . . at the Confederates."

"Offend your honor, did they?" the colonel mocked.

"Yes," Dante responded, in an uncharacteristically revealing comment. He had to be as honest as possible. Baker was likely getting information about goings on in Washington and Richmond. He might check out Dante's story. "I offered to spy." He paused. "They refused my offer."

"For rejection, you change allegiance . . . without hesitation . . . so quickly."

"I'm a proud man."

"Proud, eh? Why not just challenge him . . . or gouge his eyes?" Baker said smiling.

"The South is folding. Spend a few days in the capital. You come away knowing . . . just a matter of time."

"Be on the winning side, then? Sit quietly while I finish these letters and figure out what to do with you."

"That's clear."

"Not to me. I have many options, Mr. Dante. I could put you in the Old Capitol Prison. As an inmate there, you'd have enemies everywhere from Secretary Stanton . . . the provost marshal, even Wood—Wood runs the prison. Without agreement from all of them, you'd never get out."

He paused, scrutinizing Dante slowly before continuing. "Secretary Stanton would want to interview you. I tremble to think what he might find out about you. The others would interview you, too. I would want my turn. How long would you keep your secrets? You have them, I'm sure. Let me read the rest."

When he'd finished perusing the letters, Baker walked to the door, closed it, returned to his seat and visited far more cordially with Dante. He asked no more questions, but assured his guest he knew how to deal with Southern traitors and was delighted to get the letters.

It was clear to Dante that Baker was also delighted by the clean-shaven man who proffered the cache. Baker pulled money from his desk drawer and paid him handsomely in praise and greenbacks. More would be available, Baker told him, if such material surfaced again . . . or better yet, information on the enemy's army. Stanton would like that kind of information especially.

He quickly excused Dante, explaining he was fully occupied at the time with final details of an investigation into theft and incompetence at the Treasury Department and, most delightfully, into proven prostitution among Treasury Department girls. Secretary Chase had asked him to investigate the goings on in the department. Baker's eyes twinkled as he told Dante his investigation had uncovered much more than the graft the secretary had expected.

How to spend the coming evening after such a glorious start to his morning and Northern alliance? He'd spent several days asking questions about the man most responsible for dampening vice in Washington. The side benefit was Dante knew exactly where Baker had succeeded and—more importantly on such a night—where he had not.

He'd fight the tiger at one of the better gambling establishments, and then, perhaps, should he augment his earnings, he'd visit Mary Hall and spend the winnings on her attractive family in the woman's famous three-story residence, just south of the Avenue. Maybe he'd visit Mary Hall's brothel even if he lost at the gaming table. This is what he should have enjoyed in Richmond, if only they'd accepted his offer. But tonight he would not quarrel with the Confederacy. There was too much to celebrate.

Chapter 17

March 1864, Staunton, Virginia

Betsy cried, but they weren't there to see it. They'd questioned her for hours, then left.

Who did you pass military secrets to? Never mind. We know. Why did you entertain a spy? Why didn't you alert the military when a Union soldier visited you? Was he a deserter? What was his name? You don't need to answer. We already know. What did you tell him? Surely you were duped by the Northern scoundrel.

They kept her in a tight room, with two chairs, a small table, the provost marshal and two provost guards. The marshal questioned her rudely, but it seemed whenever Betsy was near collapse, her upper body ready to fall forward into a wet, panting heap on the table, he would step from the room, leaving her alone with the silent guards.

She would hear him, just outside the office, talking with someone in soft but disagreeable terms. Only once did she glimpse the other man—the peevish sheriff. She involuntarily shivered as she realized the seeming simpleton had been her undoing. She'd misjudged him. Now he coerced the marshal into forcing her to confess fabricated deeds. Why did the sheriff persecute her?

She told the broad-shouldered, side-burned marshal repeatedly of her innocence and demanded . . . then begged him to let her go. She would bring witnesses to support her claims. But he refused, saying in clear frustration, "What good would that do for anyone . . . but you?"

She looked at him incredulously. "Isn't that what this is about? Finding the truth . . . about me?"

He looked at her disgustedly. "That's what y'all do. Spy on neighbors . . . on the army, then claim the right to protection. Wealth doesn't protect the wicked. We have proof of disloyalty. We could execute you for it."

"I've worked for years to support the army . . . the government. Now you take the word of some vile creature . . . that all I've done only hides what I really am."

"I don't think you hid it that well." He smiled smugly. "There were always the rumors . . . stories about town. I heard them. You and your accomplice speculating while soldiers suffered. You held back vital food stuffs, wool, cotton, armaments till you could get your price. I have a dozen witnesses I could call, and each will suggest you used your noble position—desecrating the honor of your dead husband—to enrich yourself and your paramour. Just rumors . . . till a witness revealed it."

"Paramour?"

"Do you claim innocence?" He yelled at her for the first time, and she understood he was treating her as a strumpet. "Yes, claim innocence, but my witness has vouched for everything . . . given us every detail."

"You're loathsome!" Her eyes were afire.

"Me? No, Mrs. Henderson, we loathe you. You claim to be better than us. Yet . . . you betrayed us. How many men died because you wouldn't give them the materiel they needed to defend us? You claim some man . . . suddenly disappeared . . . defrauded you . . . that you knew nothing of his exploits"—his voice softened—"yet, it went on . . . and on.

And when you tired of him—your paramour—you didn't call the sheriff. Why not?"

"I was wrong," she said meekly.

"Yes, you were, but you were deep in deceit. You couldn't call on him because your partner knew too much, that you stole from the government. Instead, you did something more subtle . . . evil. Why call the sheriff when you had someone who would help you quietly . . . a Yankee. Why would he help you? I wondered that. Then I realized it was because you'd been a toady for the North all along, sneaking secrets to the enemy. You called in Mr. Gragg to kill Mr. Walthrope."

"Walthrope? Paramour? Killed? Most imaginative."

"Don't mock me! We're not talking about buffoonery played for entertainment. It's theft . . . sedition . . . murder!" His ire was up, and she perceived she shouldn't push him further. She shook. She couldn't imagine anyone treating her this way. He was still speaking, "But the confrontation didn't go as planned. Mr. Walthrope was smarter than you thought and had the wits to attack you before Mr. Gragg killed him. With one murder to your credit—the factory foreman, Mr. Stokes—what would a second matter? No one has seen Mr. Walthrope since he arrived at your house. One of your deceived admirers tells me he's been seen. But no eye witness has come forward." He paused, and spoke softer as if to himself. "If only we could find his body."

She was stunned. Unimaginable. Who could have created such a story? Eyewitnesses would have told it as she had. The sheriff had misconstrued everything, then convinced the marshal that everything that was, wasn't, and everything that wasn't, was.

He continued, "You entertained Mr. Gragg. Was he another paramour? I see you now for what you are—a common fancy woman desecrating a great family's house. You entertained Gragg a few days . . . enough time for him to look around, to spy on the valley. Then you sent him away, safe with his secrets . . . those he'd seen and those you revealed. But you had a problem. The mills . . . and especially the factory. How can you claim innocence? And this, Mrs. Henderson, is where I begin to see your devilish nature."

He stopped briefly before continuing. "It's not enough that you prey upon the good name of your husband—a dear friend of mine, but you call in a man who's sacrificed a leg for the Confederacy to cover your foul deeds. You're kind to him . . . a broken soul. You win him over with attention . . . maybe more . . . till he'll do anything for you. You clean up the factory, put him in charge . . . and suspicions of you and your work are covered by his cloak of honor. 'What we've heard can't be true,' everyone says. 'He wouldn't be involved in anything untoward . . . not a man who made such a sacrifice!' And the truth is, if asked, he'll say whatever you want him to say . . . because he's faithful. Something you know nothing of!" He sighed and looked at the small table that separated them. When he spoke again, it was in a reflective voice, "It's so evil."

He reached into his jacket and pulled out a tin cigar case. He opened it, pulled out a cigar, put it in his mouth, closed the case and put it back in his jacket. With his teeth clenching the unlit cigar, he mumbled, "If you were an active party to all of this—and to that, I have no doubt—you were surely in on the deaths of Mr. Stokes and Mr. Walthrope." He grinned at her with the cigar still in his teeth. "If spying isn't enough of a capital offense, your murders will hang you." The marshal leaned against the back of his chair, ignoring Betsy as he pulled a packet of lucifer matches from his jacket and went through his ritual of lighting the cigar.

She was desperate. If they believed all he'd said, she was undone. Traitress. Murderess. She was surrounded by hungry, growling wolves nipping at her, waiting for her to weaken and tire. If they even hinted of their suspicions in Staunton—true or fabulous—her neighbors would burn her house and lynch her in spite of her sex.

She took advantage of the man's preoccupation with his cigar, answering forcefully, "Sir, I am aware of my rights. I'm entitled to a lawyer. These are false charges and innuendos. I admit I love a Union soldier known to me before the war. I've not spied with nor for him. I've not conspired with him in anything but in things of the heart. I'm as loyal to the Confederacy . . . as you are. I don't know why the sheriff would tell these lies, but that's what they are. I thought him honest, but I'm cleared of any misapprehension. You may put me on trial for loving a Yankee—I know of no law against that. Everything else . . . everything the sheriff has claimed is mere fabrication."

The marshal puffed on his lit cigar, then exhaled leisurely. "The sheriff will be sad to hear your low opinion of him." He paused, smiling again. "I fear for you, Madam . . . knowing what awaits you. But you want a lawyer, the protection of the legal system . . . a trial."

"I insist on it."

"Yes, I would if I were in your shoes, but . . ."

She interrupted. She could tell where he was going and wanted to stake claim to patriotism before he cited it. "I know we're at war with an invading country, a country that daily violates the rights of its citizens. But that's not who we are . . . what we fight for. President Davis has not stooped to the level of the Yankee president. We still have prote . . ."

He interrupted her, pulling the cigar savagely from his mouth. In fevered pitch, he said, "Don't lecture me about the Confederacy . . . when you betrayed it!" He rose, signaling with his head for the two guards to leave. He followed them without acknowledging Betsy again.

Only then did she allow the tears. Everything had converged into a picture of guilt, and she was devastated by the marshal's treatment. Gentility, kindness were no longer offered because she had fallen from good society.

But crushing her spirits most was the horrible realization that someone had betrayed her, telling the sheriff of Hank's visit. It hadn't been Caleb, that was clear from the provost marshal's comments. It must have been a close family member or someone from her household. A slave? She thought of Ruth in her mud covered panic. Was it Emily? It had to be Emily, turned lunatic. In some frenzied nightmare, Emily was dragging Betsy down with her . . . not into madness, but into suspicion . . . and death. Betsy shuddered at the image of hanging. No, Emily couldn't have done this. They would have seen her madness, dismissed everything she said.

It was the sheriff! He'd done all this! He'd learned just enough to create this damnable heresy. Her mind focused on the interrogation. Early on, she'd told them about Hank, from the beginning of their relationship to his arrival at her house and his confrontation with Walthrope. She thought the story so innocent it would win them, but their minds shaded it differently.

She understood their misunderstanding. If she saw only what they could see, she could have easily believed in her own guilt. Her version would seem naive, outlandish. It would appear as cover to blind them. Instead of seeing love disrupted by war, they wrested the facts just slightly, but it left her a Northern spy, profiteer, saboteur, traitress, murderess, safe harbor for a Union-sent spy.

Worst of all, she saw how they could conclude that she had used her feminine advantages to snag and control the men around her . . . and lure them to their deaths. This would come out—not her version, not the truth, but their reformulation. And once it came out, she would have no friends or business in Staunton or in the South. Beset by enemies, she would have to leave Staunton immediately . . . as soon as they released her.

Chapter 18

April 1864, Washington City, District of Columbia

Washington bustled as never before.

Visitors prior to the war found the capital reminiscent of a small country village with great stretches of forest enveloping sparsely populated, muddy streets, home to meandering animals. Only its outsized Federal buildings and the area on the north side of Pennsylvania Avenue—the Avenue—with its hotels, houses, churches, the city building and Patent Office, had suggested a city.

The unfinished stub of the Washington Monument lay on a triangular plot of land bordered to the south by the Potomac River and to the north by the Tiber Creek. The castle-like Smithsonian Institution sat farther east and south of the Washington Canal—the city's open sewer, carrying filth and overpowering stench from the Tiber Creek eastward directly toward the Capitol, which still awaited a new dome—then southeast and eventually south to the Potomac's Eastern Branch. The President's Residence and surrounding Federal offices were north of the creek and canal. All these grand buildings and partially finished projects in a small, mean town suggested the beginnings of something great.

With war now washing over the town, it had exploded into activity. Droves of underpaid government clerks crowded boarding houses, temporary shelters and tent cities. Job aspirants overflowed the President's Residence and other Federal fortresses like swarming fire ants.

Building in the capital was constant, filling empty sites that otherwise would have remained undisturbed for decades. Gangs of roughs had roamed the city before the war, and they were now joined by new rowdies and thieves who saw the crowd-besieged capital as a town of promise. Southern sympathizers, omnipresent and often silent in Washington, came out in jubilation at any hint of good news for the South or "their" armies. Prostitutes, nurses, soldiers—healthy and invalid—and families searching for invalids added to the capital's cacophony.

Washington was perfect for Oskar Dante because hiding would be easy in the turbulent town. He spent days finding a dozen places into which he could disappear, from down on the Island below the canal and Swampoodle north of the Capitol, to the prosperous Northern Liberties and English Hill neighborhoods. No one was looking for him, but he'd be ready when they did.

Early on, he visited the Executive Mansion to see its odd occupant and discovered the president fully met his expectations and security at the mansion did not. Dante laughed at how easy it would be to kidnap the president . . . or worse, and his laughter became guffaws when he remembered being introduced to the chief executive. The new arrival thought the president not stupid, just out of place. As Dante overheard the president rattle off an insipid story about a parrot, he realized but for the greater wealth of the Union in men, industry and money, the South would already be free.

He'd long suspected there was no leadership north of the Potomac. He knew Northern generals were vain, ineffective, political, judgment-lacking, cowardly. Now he met an ignorant peasant dressed as president. He was no better than his generals. Yet Dante remembered his own disgrace in Richmond and refused affection for the Confederacy. He would do nothing to harm the Union . . . nothing beyond mocking the executive buffoon. He had and would continue to use the South, but the Union was the future. He reminded himself that he was a man of the future. But, at the oddest times, he'd be pulled to the past, remember Betsy and regret losing her—which made him angry. But ire would pass as he recalled that she would remember him with every glance in a mirror, and that he still had plans for her.

Dante had not changed Washington City, but it seemingly had changed him. It began the night after his fateful morning meeting with Baker. He'd celebrated his new connection with a few hours in a house with closed curtains, just south of the Avenue where bankers dealt winning and losing cards in faro, then wandered off for other amusements.

The next day, he'd awakened lonely, thinking of the previous night and Betsy. He buttressed himself against her memory by focusing on the faro—the hand of the banker grabbing the card as the box released it, the excitement, the creeping warmth, the rapid, shallow breathing stopped just briefly . . . as he waited for the player's card.

He'd bet the winning card as often as he'd bet a loser, and he'd lost just a little more than he'd won. But as he remembered the evening, the money didn't matter. It was the feeling . . . the anticipation . . . the question: Had he played the winning card? The card would fly from the box with the answer. Winning elated him, losing briefly angered him, both left him craving the next deal.

To celebrate the joy, to dampen the anger, to push away memories of Betsy, he would try again, again, again. He'd leave his bets, move them or place another, all to feel it again. In the beginning, the banker was a woman. He hadn't minded losing to a woman, but soon forgot the banker's sex, craving only the thrill. Win or lose, it came.

He was sure he could learn to win all the time if he stuck with it long enough and, in a moment of desperate inspiration, he understood that an obsession with the game might be useful to him. Thus, on the second night, he stayed a bit longer, the third night till two o'clock, and each succeeding night till early morning.

Two weeks passed and faro seemed to consume progressively more of Dante till he appeared to have no interest in taking messages to Richmond, in unmasking new traitors for Baker, or in selling the hard-to-come-by trinkets he'd accumulated in Washington.

His new interest didn't go unnoticed, and one very late morning he was awakened by a brusque shaking. "Get up!"

His room was empty but for two men. Fellow boarders had long since left to spend their day clerking in various government departments. The men, dressed in dark suits, bowlers still on their heads and muddied boots, looked sternly down at him. They weren't rowdies, but seemed as tough.

"We want to talk to you!"

He wanted to remind them they were in his room, that they should leave and return at a more convenient hour, but he held his tongue. He roused himself, swinging his legs over the edge of the bed, refusing to look at either man. The room was cold, and he imagined the floor even colder, immediately envying the men their coats and muddy boots. He rubbed his eyes, but they didn't focus fully. "What do you want?" he demanded, not looking up.

"We've come to talk to you."

"Then talk," he said gruffly.

The men almost looked like twins. Tall, stocky, broad black sideburns, large noses, dark eyes. Dante had never seen them before. One of the men looked passively at Dante and spoke, "Time to leave."

"Leave? Don't tell me Mrs. Ferguson sent you. I've paid for my room to last week. I'll pay her the rest tomorrow. She needn't worry."

The man spoke again, "We're not interested in Mrs. Ferguson, but it's time for you to go back to Virginia . . . Richmond."

"Who are you to make demands?" Dante queried defiantly. I'm not sure I want to leave . . . not yet." He excitedly thought of his favorite gambling establishment.

"No demands. We're here to give you a choice, but if it's not . . ."

"Not what?"

"Get dressed, eat something, get on your way. We'll give you safe passage across the lines . . . then you're on your own again."

"Ah."

"We don't want you here."

"Because I . . ."

"Because you can never tell when a gambling hell will be raided, and it would be better if you were . . . gone."

Dante smiled. "Come now, you haven't closed down any hells lately."

"The past, Mr. Dante. The past is not the future."

"Ah, a philosopher. Thank you for letting me know. Thank Colonel Baker."

"The colonel doesn't know. If he knew you'd spent every night in . . . you'd already be in Old Capitol."

"Why the warning?"

"You gave documents to the colonel revealing Confederate loyalists, but we think you're actually sympathetic to the South."

"Not in the least."

"Perhaps we think you should . . . and will be sympathetic to our cause."

"Your cause? I hadn't expected that. What do you want?"

"We've watched you, know what you're doing. Gambling's still illegal in Washington. What happens if Baker learns his new friend gambles nightly?"

"If you should suggest such a thing to him, I'll identify you as traitors." He leered at the man who had spoken, then sighed and chuckled. "Stalemate! Do me the courtesy of leaving, and I won't mention it to the colonel."

"You're right, Mr. Dante . . . or whatever your name is, and we're checking that out in Richmond. Neither of us can afford to be revealed. I . . . we . . . and I emphasize the 'we,'" nodding to his companion, "can never hope to checkmate you, and you . . . right now, can't even put us in check. Remember there are three witnesses to this conversation. Two will tell the same story . . . smuggling, gambling . . . prostitution. We have evidence—witnesses who . . . for a little leniency might . . . You know how hard it is to clean up these vices. While the colonel is busy on bigger matters these days, he'd be delighted to punish someone as an example of the evils in this city . . . and who better than a spy."

"Spy? Ha."

"Let's not quibble with words. We'd weather a few accusing lines from a desperate criminal . . . traitor or spy . . . a shiftless gambler. But you can't afford to offend us. Don't think you can betray us. Washington's dangerous in the dark.

For you, it would be your death . . . should you do anything inappropriate."

"The task?" Dante was beginning to shiver, thinking he should just stay in Richmond.

"Take this note," the man pulled out a sealed envelope from his overcoat, "to a friend in Richmond."

"Deliver the letter? Easily done. I already have one I'm late in taking there. Will I get paid now or in Richmond?"

"Money? Of course not. We won't insult your dignity with such an offer . . . but we could keep you from dying accidentally . . . in Richmond or Washington."

Dante looked at the floor with a resigned smile and a quiet "humph."

"Shall we arrest you now or. . . ."

"I'd be pleased to carry your note to Richmond." He smiled at the detectives. "It will work out well. I'll have clear passage through the lines . . . and once beyond, I'll have a crucial letter for the Confederacy. How better to assure I get safely to Richmond to sell my knickknacks?"

"Leave tonight."

"Tonight I'll go . . . down to old Dixie." He looked pleasantly at his two guests. "And may I ask your names?"

"We'll give them if . . . we ever come to arrest you or . . . ."

Chapter 19

April 1864, Richmond, Virginia

The enormous black dog in the corner frightened her. She'd heard much about the beast in the last few days. Nero, she had been told, was trained to attack anything dressed in blue, that the warden let him attack prisoners to intimidate them, that the giant had killed prisoners, that even the commandant had to whip him to protect himself. As she sat in the office alone with the monster, she was grateful she rarely wore blue. Determined to sit perfectly still, she tried to control her breathing, keeping it calm, quiet, predictably regular. She would give the dog no reason to pounce.

She sensed he was looking at her and her hands trembled. Were earlier prisoners killed by the canine guard likewise left alone with it? Was this how they justified the deaths? Did they plan that for her?

Her hands trembled more. She shut her eyes to block traumatizing thoughts of being bitten, but closing her eyes only focused her mind firmly on such an attack. She imagined the explanation. "Our backs were turned . . . just for a moment. He's uncontrollable." She shivered and felt sick, but she'd been sick daily since her arrest.

She waited, hoping someone would come, but the wait wore on. She tried to divert her fear by humorously imaging the large-jawed omnivore a direct descendant of the insane, like-named Roman emperor and wondered which paws he'd use to fiddle if Richmond ever burned. Richmond was the new Rome, built on her seven hills, the Capital of the greatest republic man had ever organized, direct heir of Greece and Rome. Richmond was the only legitimate claimant to the birthright of the American Revolution, for it had never descended to tyranny as had the North. Fiddling dog? Nonsense, merely a momentary distraction.

But Betsy couldn't distract herself longer from the terror of the dark dog staring at her . . . or at least she thought she could feel his stare. She opened her eyes and carefully pivoted her gaze just enough to see him. Suddenly there . . . it was! Enormous. She turned to look directly at him—perhaps too firmly—into threatening, cold eyes. This was how they did it then. No trial, no lynching, just a dog challenged by an inevitable stare.

She stiffened her body and felt an urge to bolt toward the closed door. But she knew he'd have her from behind. Instinctively her hands rose to protect her already-scarred face, but he just stared at her. She smiled. His expression wasn't ferociousness. Dark eyes gazed at her, but there was no brutality there, just gentleness and something resembling curiosity or anticipation. He seemed to want her to call him.

A sigh and her smile only made him more animated, giving her complete, welcome relief. She slowly lifted and turned her chair around so she could see him more easily, and he responded, rising on all four long legs, greater excitement yet in his gentle eyes.

An involuntary gasp escaped as she realized he was the largest dog she'd ever seen. She'd heard he was a Bavarian Boar Hound and easily pictured him hunting boar.

In spite of his gentle expression, his massive size—height, length, mammoth square head—and black coat made him formidable and frightening. They looked at each other.

Without realizing what she was doing, she extended her right hand. With no hesitation, Nero bounded to her. He sniffed her hand, then moved closer, shoving his majestic head into her lap. She laughed and called out, "Wait, wait."

But Nero would have none of it and pushed tight against the chair and any part of her body he could reach. At one point, he tried to sit on her lap, and Betsy only escaped by shoving him away, standing and stepping backward. As she did the dog followed, and she laughed again, petting and talking gently to him. He twisted around and leaned heavily against her. His head rested in her hands which were extended upward.

She spoke again, "So this is how you killed them . . . knocking them down, crushing them . . . licking them."

The dog whined for more strokes.

"OK . . . OK." She giggled. "Sit . . . sit."

The dog ignored her, still pressing hard against her side. She braced herself, with her legs extending at an angle toward the floor.

"Sit," she commanded more forcefully, and the dog obeyed, looking up at her with unabashed affection. "Killer! Hardly!" She smiled, then grimaced at the slobber covering her hand. She wiped her wet hand on the dog. "It's yours anyway. What are you doing stuck in here? You ought to be outside doing something useful."

She hadn't noticed the office door open and Captain Lucien W. Richardson, commandant of Castle Thunder—Richmond's prison for deserters, escaped slaves and traitors—slip into the office. He left the door open and watched as she petted the long, tall hound. He was silent until she wiped the drool on the dog. "Who's going to give him a bath . . . now you've slobbered on him?"

Enjoying the physical contact with the dog so much, she wasn't startled or offended by his comment. "I'm sure a nearby horse stable could give him a good scrubbing," she said jovially, still looking at the canine guard.

Captain Richardson addressed her by name, "Mrs. Thaddeus Henderson?"

She looked up, still slightly nauseated, and said, "Please call me Betsy. Betsy Henderson."

Captain Richardson wondered at the answer. "But you're widow of Thaddeus Henderson."

"I am. And he's dead for the cause of the Confederacy. I, on the other hand and for the time being, am alive. Although perhaps the government—which is set on persecuting me in my innocence—wishes I weren't."

"Please sit down, Mrs. Henderson," the captain said sternly. "Nero! Corner!" The dog looked at the captain, regretfully at Betsy, and moved slowly, settling in the corner.

"Thank you, Captain, for such a sweet guard."

"Most of them aren't."

"I dreaded this introduction, but he's charming . . . although slightly smelly."

"He's not always like that . . . not with everyone. Consider it a compliment."

"It's nice to have one friend . . . one compliment."

"Mrs. Henderson, if you hadn't betrayed the Confederacy . . . spied for the Yankees, we would all have been your friends. We were your friends . . . which I suppose makes it all the more difficult for us to understand."

Betsy responded sternly, "I've betrayed no one, spied for no one. I've told everyone that for weeks."

"Your protestations may make you feel better, but I've heard everything and don't see that you can be innocent."

"Then . . . Captain, bring me to trial, give me a lawyer, show me the evidence . . . the charges . . . the accusers . . . "

He interrupted. "Mrs. Henderson, I'm not arresting nor accusing you. I don't bring anyone to trial. I don't know . . . not really . . . that you're guilty. I don't think you're guilty of murder. If it helps you feel better, I don't think anyone does. But I'm responsible to keep you in Castle Thunder . . . keep you safe while you're here. Let's not cavil about guilt or innocence. Let's cooperate. You'll be much more comfortable. Maybe you won't have as many enemies among the guards and detectives."

"You propose a truce?"

"I suppose you could look at it that way."

"You won't ask me to declare my guilt . . ."

"You won't weary me with endless declarations of innocence. It's tiring to hear so many profess innocence."

Betsy looked at the captain. He seemed reasonable. "I accept your terms."

"Of course . . . there is an alternative."

"To the truce?"

"To being here at all."

"That is the most appealing thing I've heard since being torn from my home."

"You can take the oath of allegiance . . . to the Confederate Government. I could get you released almost immediately. Especially . . . considering your statement that you've done nothing wrong."

"But Captain, that's the whole point, isn't it? I'm here. I haven't done anything wrong. I am a loyal citizen. I've long supported the Confederacy. Why must I swear an oath?"

"But perhaps I could release you."

"Perhaps? You already seem less sure."

"The issue of the murder . . . I'd forgotten that."

"Murder? But you just said . . ."

"The suspicion of murder—even if no one believes it—it makes it much harder. I forgot about the murder."

"How could anyone imagine it true?"

"We all see things now—too many things—unthinkable not long ago. I'm sure it will come to nothing. Perhaps a willingness to take the oath would help."

Betsy stared at the urbane commandant blankly, thinking about what was left for her in Staunton. Neighbors would never trust her again. They would suspect her every action. She was trapped. She couldn't go back. She was caged in an old tobacco factory with a seemingly fair commandant; a huge, smelly dog; a clear conscience; and her only care was an enemy soldier. She was faithful to the Confederacy. To take the oath would suggest she needed to prove her innocence. No loyal citizen should be subjected to such indignity. "I won't take an oath, Captain, regardless of the torture."

He chuckled. "Torture!"

"Captain, for weeks, my ears have been filled with tales of Castle Thunder torture—bucking prisoners, whipping them, hanging them by their thumbs. They promised I'd be secured with a 30-pound ball and chain in a cell full of women of disrepute. I've been threatened with a barrel shirt. So don't act surprised. I fear torture."

He smiled kindly. "Mrs. Henderson, they have tried to frighten you."

"And have succeeded. But . . . Captain, do you pretend no one's tortured here?"

"Gentle lady, there were rumors of such treatment . . . in the past. Former commandant Captain Alexander, he did some of those things . . . but there was an investigation . . . congressional hearing. Remember many of the people jailed here were cutthroats and thieves. They didn't just incarcerate traitors and deserters in the early days. The prisoners were dangerous—dangerous to the guards, the city, the country, to each other. Surely Captain Alexander did what he thought best . . . and was fully exonerated."

"Then I won't be forced to wear a barrel shirt?"

"No, no barrel shirt," he said, then added mischievously, "Not till it becomes the style in Richmond."

"I fear it will come to that. Horrendous stories just to coerce me to lie?"

"Or . . . admit the truth."

"But . . ."

"All of this takes us back to my . . . our truce. Let us talk no more of innocence or guilt. No threats of torture. I won't even send Nero after you." He smiled warmly at her. "A mutual understanding . . . between you and me."

"That, I can do."

"Good, then we can be friends."

"May I ask a question?"

"I suppose . . . if it doesn't break our truce."

"Captain, I can remember its terms for at least a day."

"The first day should go well, then. Your question?"

"There's a sheriff in Staunton."

"Uh huh."

"Do you know him?"

"I met him . . . yes."

"I thought I saw him outside when I was brought into the prison. Was that him . . . or am I losing my mind?"

"It may have been him."

"Let me ask, then: Why is he so persistent in following me . . . in fashioning false accusations?"

"Is he?"

"Yes. He's followed me here, hasn't he?"

"I don't know that he followed you."

"He came to my house and started this. He was there when I was arrested. I heard him arguing with the provost marshal. I'm sure he was forcing the marshal to arrest me. And he witnesses my imprisonment here."

He smiled wryly. "Doesn't look coincidental."

"No. Why is he set on proving me guilty?"

"Uh."

"I'm sorry."

"I would try to answer your question if . . . if . . . What I can tell you is he's sheriff in Staunton . . . with no official standing in Richmond. He did mention you, but gave me no direct information about your arrest. The provost's office gave me information . . . about your case."

She sensed he hadn't told her everything, but said, "Thank you for being honest with me."

"My pleasure. Now, let me tell you about our prison."

"Tell me only the good things. I've heard the terrible."

"Just fear-mongering. It's not bad at all . . . other than the food's not good and the straw mattresses aren't comfortable. Personal needs are more difficult to deal with, especially for our female inmates. We are at times overcrowded, we have an ongoing war with vermin, both human and otherwise. There's been violence and viciousness toward the prisoners, as I said, but that was before my time . . . and I'm not interested in that . . . other than using Nero to intimidate prisoners."

Betsy smiled and looked over at the dog.

He continued, "It's really three prisons—all were tobacco factories."

"I remember. I visited Richmond when I was a child. My father brought me down by the canal and showed me Tobacco Row, the factories, Tredegar's."

"I remember my daddy bringing me to Richmond . . . showing me the same. It's changed a lot . . . mostly lately."

"As they marched me over here, it didn't feel the same as it was—many more people, all of them rushing about . . . or stopping to gawk at me."

"The buildings are different. But let me finish telling you about Castle Thunder, then I'll send you to your lodgings."

"Lodgings."

"Nice word, don't you agree?"

"Maybe if I weren't to be lodged."

"Yes, but please let me continue. Do you remember Whitlock's? That's where you'll stay. It's for our women prisoners and arrested slaves. Palmer's factory . . . that's for deserters . . . or at least Yankee deserters. Finally, this . . . the main building here on Cary Street, it was Greanor's Tobacco Factory. We've got the assistant provost marshal's office, all the police, clerks . . ."

"And the room where I lost my meager possessions."

"Good to hear you're not bitter, Mrs. Henderson." He grinned good naturedly and kept speaking. "We have storerooms, armory and, yes, the room you've already seen—one of the halls for confiscation. Prison's above us . . . mostly Confederate soldiers or others gone astray."

"Where do you eat . . . and what if someone's ill?"

Captain Richardson looked concerned, "Are you ill, Mrs. Henderson?"

"I'm fine, Captain. Just curious."

"The hospital's nearby . . . food made by slaves. Some prisoners mess together. I think you might like to mess with other female prisoners."

"Can I walk outside?"

"If you mean outside . . . on the balcony, I'm sure we can arrange that. I doubt, however, you'll walk the streets of Richmond anytime soon."

A bell rang in the office, and the captain looked up at it. "Part of Captain Alexander's plan for Castle Thunder—a whole system of bells," he explained. "But honestly, Mrs. Henderson . . . and please, this is a confidential confession, I don't know what they're saying. I just wait till someone tells me I'm needed someplace or something important is going on. Other than that, I ignore all the tintinnabulating." He smiled, paused and looked with resignation at her. "Please consider me a friend. Let me know should you need anything. Are you sure you're well?"

"I'm fine," she said, lying.

"Then the detectives will take you to your lodgings."

"That word again."

"Yes, that word. It's been a pleasure, Mrs. Henderson. I'm sorry you're here, especially after our visit. But now I know where I can go if I need someone to control Nero."

"I'd almost like to have him stay with me . . . but for the slobbering . . . and smell." Her eyes brightened. "Could he?"

"Unfortunately, Nero likes full run of the place. He loves the kitchen, changing of the guard. He loves the inspections. I don't think Nero would like the cells, Mrs. Henderson. Why don't you wait here with your friend while I get the detectives?"

Richardson stood quickly and left before Betsy could respond. Left alone, she turned to Nero and held out her hand. The monster leaped to his feet and ambled to her. She enjoyed the contact, forgetting briefly her sickness.

Chapter 20

April 1864, Richmond, Virginia

"Who are you?" the woman asked curtly as Betsy passed the transom.

The door grated closed behind Betsy and the sound ignited a flash of loneliness. She looked at the woman with a slight squint and tried to imagine why this woman was in the cell. After an uncomfortable silence, she responded dismissively, "A prisoner . . . like you."

"I guessed that," the woman snapped, irritated at Betsy's attitude. "What are you here for?"

"Can't you guess that, too?" Betsy answered sharply.

"Spying then," the woman said, more softly.

Betsy considered not answering, but replied also in a softened tone, "For a trumped up charge of disloyalty."

"Guilty?"

"I said it was trumped up."

The woman's voice turned accusatory, "They don't put innocent people in here. You're a spy . . . traitress—like me."

"If you're a spy, I'm nothing like you. I've nothing to admit . . . but perhaps a sudden dislike for current company." Betsy turned to the woman and squared her shoulders.

The woman stared toward the ground, saying with resignation, "All right. I understand." Her own shoulders slumped forward. "I've been rash. Forgive me. Here, let me help you." Moving forward, she extended her hand for Betsy's bag which held items not confiscated for safe keeping by the guards.

Betsy ignored the offer, glancing around the cell, then at its occupant. She was a bit older and much larger in height and breadth than Betsy, with dark hair pulled back in a bun. Her dress was blue, soiled and shabby. There was something genteel in her manner, but her gentility seemed faded and worn like the dress. Desperation seemed to lace her questions and push her beyond well-bred manners.

The room was small for two people, yet Betsy was surprised to see it crammed with old, grime-covered furniture—a wooden table with two chairs; two small beds covered with several thin mattresses and still thinner blankets; a threadbare, ornate Victorian Rococo chair. An empty bucket sat in the corner, and Betsy tried not to imagine its use. On the table was a second pail half-full of water, and several clean but dented plates, metal bowls, cups and utensils were neatly stacked nearby. A small, unlit stove stood at the end of the room.

The space was stuffy, pungent with the smell of human sweat and filth. A gas lamp hanging from the wall was extinguished so the only light in the cell filtered through horizontal slats of wood and vertical bars just outside the room's only window. Betsy moved quickly to it, lifting the lower sash and pushing her face to the bars, breathing in the cool spring, seeking escape from the stench of captivity.

The woman behind Betsy commented despondently, "After a while, you forget the smells."

"The smells in here . . . or outside?" Betsy responded sarcastically, continuing to inhale the fresh air. But even as she greedily sucked the air into her lungs, nausea overwhelmed her. The cell's odors were too much. She wanted to die. Her heart was racing. Oh, to be outside. She breathed deeply but couldn't get rid of the fetor. It was all around her, beginning to smother her, her pores soaking in the stink until she was sure the stench was her. How would she survive? How could she endure?

She remembered the captain's offer to set her free . . . maybe . . . if she'd just take the oath. At that moment, she ached to take the oath. There was nothing in it that would soil her conscience. She wanted her own bed, her own drawing room, her kitchen, her fresh-scented water closet, cleanliness, and frantically breathed the outside air. But still her stomach rebelled, and she remembered the bucket and ran to it.

Her fellow inmate watched wordlessly. Betsy didn't see it, but guilt and sympathy shown from her eyes, and she walked silently to Betsy, put her arm around her, raised her from her squat position in front of the bucket. Betsy responded instinctively to the embrace and rose. Her companion walked her toward one of the beds. They stopped at the bedside and Betsy watched, emotion and energy expended, as the woman straightened the blankets. The woman helped Betsy sit, then crouched down, lifting Betsy's feet to the bed. Leaving her fully dressed, she tenderly covered Betsy with a soiled blanket and stepped back to look. Betsy was already asleep.

The woman called softly for a guard, and after a few minutes, the door to the cell opened cautiously.

"Asleep," the woman said softly.

"You best come with me," the guard responded.

"I don't know anything . . . not yet."

The guard sniffed the air and motioned toward the bucket. "Bring that."

She crossed to the bucket and lifted it by its handle.

"She sick?" the guard asked.

"Just . . ."

Betsy shifted in her shallow sleep, and both the guard and prisoner froze. Betsy shifted again, opening her eyes. She took in the guard and woman in one alert glance across the room, pulled the covers back and rose to her feet. She reached out for the bucket. "That's mine. I'll do that."

"No, it's all right," the woman said softly. "It's a shock . . . that door closing for the first time. I understand. I'll do this. You can do me a favor some day."

"Hurry. I've got things to do," the guard interjected impatiently.

The woman hastened into the hall.

The guard pulled the door noisily into place. Betsy was alone, locked in the cell. This was her present and, she feared, her future. Loneliness overwhelmed her, but she refused the emotion and forced herself to think of Hank. But the captain's offer distracted her: Sign the oath . . . and maybe they'd free her.

What was war that it should hinder happiness? She was trapped in the war as she was in Castle Thunder. Her will belonged now to someone else, and they had already abused it. There was no hope for freedom, not as long as—at the slightest whim—a woman or man could be arrested and pulled from home to answer charges imagined by some angry, miserable, spiteful sheriff. Was it her wealth? Had she treated him badly? Was he so petty as to seek revenge because he didn't like the teacakes . . . or weren't there enough? Or the coffee, was it too bitter?

Panic seized her, and she stood quickly and walked back toward the window. She bent low, shoving her face into the space between the bars as far out the window as she could and breathed.

"Get your head in that window before I shoot it off," yelled a boy below.

She was startled by the cry, but instead of obeying it, she peered at the young soldier. He glared at her, raising his rifle and taking aim.

"Isn't it enough you've locked me up," she called. "Now, I'm threatened for breathing."

"Breathe in your cell. You gave up your right to fresh air when you entered the Castle. I won't give another warning. If you were a man, you'd already be dead."

"Would that be so bad?"

"To be a man?" the boy asked curiously.

"To be dead."

He lowered his gun slightly and looked at her inquisitively. "You'd rather be dead than in there?"

"At least I'd be free . . . if I were dead."

"But dead? There's no coming back." He further lowered his gun. "Men have been shot for sticking their heads out the window. Please, Ma'am, I'll get in trouble for talking to you . . . for letting you stick your head out."

She nodded at him, appreciative of an honest conversation, took one last breath of rich, sweet air and pulled her head in. With fresh eyes, she examined her befouled surroundings. She could conquer this.

Chapter 21

April 1864, Eastern Kentucky

Victoria heard a horse approaching and quickly left her kitchen, passing through the parlor to the front door. She opened it, crossed the small covered porch, descended the stair and waited. She smiled at the judge as he approached, but noticed the smile was not returned. Without a word of greeting, he dismounted, tied the reins to a porch post, removed his hat and smacked it against his thigh and brushed off his pants and coat, all the time avoiding her gaze.

"No good tidings?" she offered.

He looked at her, tightened his lips, took a long breath, and said, "I'm sorry."

She grunted an acknowledgment.

"I don't know how to tell you this." He was more nervous than she'd seen him in years. "Of all the stupid things I've ever had to report . . . I hope you won't worry."

"About what? If you'd just tell me what I shouldn't worry about."

"Well," he said, watching how she would react, "Isaiah and William have gone missing."

"Missing?"

He saw no emotion. "They left early this morning."

"Do you mean missing . . . or did they leave?"

"They," he waited for a long time before finishing, "left."

With the hint of a sad smile, she responded, "They can do that."

The judge looked at her sternly. "They were my slaves."

"You can say that about Isaiah . . . perhaps, but you can't . . . not honestly, claim William. And even Isaiah . . ."

"Why do I let you talk so much?"

"I don't know why William would go . . . not yet. I thought he could barely stand for an hour at a time."

"Isaiah pushed him to it, you can be sure."

"Do you know what happened?"

"I've pieced some together. Not all. Union recruiters have set up shop in the area . . . created quite a stir." He paused. "Did you know?"

"No, nothing."

"I'm surprised. At any rate, word spread to our house. Isaiah and William . . . mostly Isaiah . . . must have heard about it and figured it was their chance."

"Their chance? Ludicrous! Grown men!" She was disheartened to hear they were gone, but she hid the emotion. "When will we know they've enlisted?"

"Never, probably." He softened his answer, "I suppose when they write wanting something . . . or when they write to you. I could approach the government and demand compensation. Maybe I'd learn something that way, but probably not. The army won't let me see them, I'm sure. The army doesn't care if they have my permission or not . . . not anymore. They just want conscripts."

"We don't know they made it," Victoria offered reflectively, a trace of hope in her voice.

"We don't know they went to enlist."

She felt anxious. "I didn't think William would leave . . . at least not without saying goodbye. Doesn't seem something he'd do. I'm disappointed . . . sad we didn't hear from him . . . with Adam . . . ."

"I thought that would bother you." He glanced away from her. "Will you tell him?"

"I'll wait a few days . . . see if we hear something. I'll tell him then. He'll be hurt. He'd begun to think of William as a father. Disappointed again." Her eyes watered. "I thought the attachment was mutual." She looked out on the road, wondering where William was. "Maybe we'll hear news soon. Then I'll know what to tell him. It'd be better to have something specific to say. I hope William's fine." She wasn't just hurting for Adam, and she remembered the surprising melancholy she'd felt as she had watched William being taken to the judge's house. During his weeks with her, he had filled something in her life, something she didn't know was empty.

"Adam may hear."

"Maybe. But I'll wait anyway. If he does hear, I'll tell him what I know."

"I'll tell everyone at the house to keep quiet till then, so he doesn't find out anything . . . at least from us."

She sighed, "Thank you for that."

"For you, almost anything." He smiled sadly.

"Almost?" she responded, grinning playfully.

"We'll leave it at that, my dear. Where is the boy?"

"Off exploring something, somewhere."

Adam was playing nearby, close enough to hear the horse arrive, and he crept to the corner of the house to overhear the conversation. He wasn't sad. He was proud William would be a soldier and wondered if he was old enough to join . . . to be a drummer boy.

When Isaiah awoke, it was getting dark. He couldn't move. His body didn't feel like his own. It was not a body at all, just pain. Only one eye would open and his vision in that eye was blurry, especially at dusk. He tried to get up, pushing downward with his arm, but instead of raising his body, it collapsed and he fell, moaning as he hit the ground. He pulled himself up with the other arm. It too ached, but it raised him briefly before it also collapsed.

He was frightened. He wouldn't make it back to the judge's by sunset. Patrollers might set on him. He couldn't fight them in this condition. What had happened to him? His head hurt. The judge would be angry. Had he fallen from a horse? Who would let him ride a horse? Where was he? How had he gotten here? He'd get behind on his work. He was supposed to help with the fence in the large pasture. He'd have to work doubly hard tomorrow, and he suspected the judge would withhold his pay.

He remembered something hazily, something about William. Had William done this? William had been trying to steal Victoria from him ever since he'd arrived, and Victoria had seemed to confuse William's weakness with a desirable trait. She took such good care of the old man. And he was so old.

An impression crossed Isaiah's consciousness, something about the army and William. Hadn't he planned to get William out of the way . . . in the army? William must have found out and beaten him. Where did he get that strength? Now that he'd beaten Isaiah nearly to death, he would get Victoria. Conniving old man! William must have beaten him while he was sleeping and then dumped him in the road.

Isaiah had planned to court Victoria once he was freed. Then the judge couldn't stop him, and Isaiah knew he could win her from the judge . . . if he were free.

Isaiah drifted in and out of consciousness. He lay prostrate, unable to move, at the mercy of anyone. He hoped again the pattyrollers wouldn't find him. At least it was nearly dark. They wouldn't see him so easily, and maybe he could make his way to the roadside. In the dark, they'd never see him, unless they got the dogs out. The dogs! Odd—it didn't seem to be getting darker. In excruciating pain, he finally pulled himself to the side of the road. He cried. Fear mingled with the pain to overwhelm him. He whimpered. Maybe William would come back . . . have a change of heart and come back.

It seemed as if hours passed, lingering longer than Isaiah could stand, yet it was still dusk. Why didn't the sun just set and be done with it. Did pain stop time?—he wondered in his confusion. If the sun didn't set, he'd shortly and surely be a patroller' feast. A feeding frenzy. And he wouldn't be paid for the day.

He vaguely recalled a whip and fists and kicks. How could William do that? The blows, he now remembered, seemed to come from every direction. William was strong and fast. Where did he get the whip? He felt a slight tremble beneath him and heard voices. The tremble grew—it was a horse and more patrollers. This was the end.

"What'll we do with him?" a uniformed man asked as he climbed from a buckboard.

A second soldier, still in the wide seat of the wagon, responded, "Alive?"

"Think so."

"Put him in the back. We'll take him to Camp Nelson. He was probably on his way to us anyway. They got him . . . before we could." The man tied off the horse's lead and climbed from the wagon.

Isaiah saw movement, black boots and blue pants. Soldiers.

Had he been a soldier? Was he wounded in battle? No. He was the judge's slave. William—that woman thief—had beaten him. Or was he a soldier? Had he fought at Port Hudson, Milliken's Bend, Honey Springs, Fort Wagner? Had he proven that a black could and would fight? A fight. A dim vision passed of William beating him.

"Look at that face," one soldier commented.

"I bet his mama wouldn't recognize him. Almost doesn't have eyes.

Chapter 22

April 1864, Eastern Kentucky

William did make it to the enlisting exercise, and there he met a Captain Bensen.

He had dragged himself to the gathering crowd of black men. He looked for recruiters, arriving just as Bensen stepped to a wooden box and began a discourse. Excitement surged within William. He could enlist in the army. He wouldn't have to be servant to the cocky Union officer in Virginia who'd once employed, but never paid, him. He'd be a soldier, a man—free, toting a gun. But he was tired and sat down at the back of the crowd.

Bensen, a heavy-set, black-haired man of average height and pocked face, spoke in a deep, bellowing voice that reached to the soldiers who encircled the gathering.

He spoke in a casual, happy manner, but there was no question of his authority. "Men! I'm pleased to call you that. There's a great war upon us, and it's best to stand now and fight. You can stay here in the comforts of slavery and your crowded little cabin and be told what to do—when to eat . . . when to sleep . . . who to marry . . . when to work. You can stay for your next beating . . . or you can become free men . . . making your own decisions. You can . . . today . . . not tomorrow . . . not next week . . . not next year . . . today . . . yes, today, you can be free! This great nation has work for you. If you do it, you'll be men. I'm not from Kentucky. I'm not. I'm from that great state of New York, and in New York, men just like you are free. No masters beat them. They are their own masters. But your masters don't want you free. Why someone this very morning tried to shoot me . . . to stop me from meeting with you. They don't want you free.

"Some say you won't fight, that you're timid . . . weak . . . chickenhearted." The captain pulled his forearms up, his elbows to his body and began to flap his arms up and down. He raised the tenor of his voice. "Cluck . . . cluck . . . cluck." His voice lowered again and he stopped flapping his arms. "Yes, that's what they say. You won't fight . . . you'll run." The captain had mesmerized his audience. "Like chickens?" He looked over the crowd. "Chickenhearted?"

He scanned the audience one person at a time. "No . . . no. I don't see the chickenhearted. I see men, men like their brothers who have already fought. They found freedom with us . . . in the army. Join us. Can you feel the shackles falling from your legs?" No one answered, and he continued without waiting. "We'll give you a uniform, if you'll join us in this great war to save the Union . . . to free the slave. Is there a man among you who isn't brave enough to join the cause? Perhaps you prefer the lash. It's up to you, but I see no cowards . . . only men whose blood pulses wildly to hear the word liberty.

"The army will work you hard. It will do that, but you'll be free. You'll earn your own money. Do you want your own greenbacks? Will you be the army's sable arm? Don't ask your masters what to do! They want you in chains. They want you in shackles. They want your wife, yes . . . your wife. They want your children. Remember these?" Bensen held up a rusty neck iron.

Some remembered them, anchored on long lines of trudging slaves, stepping together, stopping together, tethered together.

"Don't look to your wife for the answer . . . because she's already been sold. Don't look to your children. They've been sold down the river. Look to yourself. Deep inside. Do you want to go on doing another man's bidding . . . another man's work? Do you want to labor day after day, knowing your work is his wealth? Can you look yourself in the eye . . . if you don't act like men today?"

He smiled, "Those of you . . . men . . . who want to enlist, move inside to Sergeant Cook. He's right there inside. He'll tell you what you need to do. You'll make fine soldiers . . . and free men. You may not have another chance. Your masters may hear you want to enlist, put you in chains . . . send you to Mississippi. Move in there to the sergeant. All of you. That's right. Keep going."

His gaze rested firmly on a few men who hadn't moved. "It appears we do have lambs among the lions. Look at them. I see weakness in their eyes. They're slaves . . . and will always be slaves."

His encouragement and prodding bayonets locked on rifle barrels moved everyone but one man toward the awaiting sergeant. William still sat in the dust of the street, exhausted. The captain looked bemusedly at him. He stepped down from the box and approached him. "You don't want to be a soldier, then? You'd rather sit on the ground, a slave? Did your master tell you to sit there? You're the only one. I know there are some with slavery in their souls, but I hadn't taken you for one."

Angered by the words and names the captain mixed into his conversation with him, William nonetheless looked up and responded respectfully. "Been waitin' for this day . . . this very day . . . all my life. Done walked hundreds of miles . . . from Virginia . . . just for this. I'll join yuh."

"Then get in that line to see Sergeant Cook."

"I will . . . but I need a rest . . . just a rest," William said, still out of breath.

The captain examined him carefully for the first time. "From Virginia just to enlist? You're a runaway, then? Contraband?"

"A slave from Winchester . . . in Virginia, but now a slave in Kentucky."

The captain's pitch turned conversational. "You didn't come from Virginia today?"

"A few weeks ago."

"You're ill?"

"Just tired."

"Come by yourself?"

"No . . . with another slave."

"Which is he?"

"Ain't here. Left me."

"Ah, I see. And where is this man now?"

"Goin' home."

"Where's home?"

"Why are yuh askin' these questions? I'm sorry, but I'm tired o' talkin'."

"I see that." The captain watched William carefully trying to determine the slave's intent. Was he lying? Was he as weak as he appeared? He had plenty of recruits for the day without this emaciated man. He would be more bother than he was worth. "I ask because we can go find that man . . .

help him enlist. Are there a lot of slaves where you live? Is the fellow that brought you strong . . . healthy?"

"The strongest . . . but it's a long way."

"And you're tired from coming?"

"I am. Let me rest . . . just a bit. I'll join up."

"We want to get as many of you enlisted as we can, but . . . You're ill. Go home, get your strength. You're a good . . . brave fellow. We won't stop recruiting for a long while." With no further word, the captain left William on the ground and walked toward the recruiting activities.

William was dazed. He hadn't anticipated this outcome. All he could do was turn his head toward the road. He imagined the walk home. How would he get there? He raised his tired body and slumped homeward as a buckboard wagon carrying two soldiers passed him slowly on the road.

Victoria stood on the porch, looking north along the road that passed her cabin. It was growing dark. Her emotions included a touch of anger and a heavy portion of fear. He wasn't home, yet. Where was he? What was he doing, that son of hers? She never could control him, but the strict rule was to be home by sunset. Looking up the road, she worried. She was comfortable with him roaming the town and nearby woods, but not up the road. There were many men about who would do harm to a slightly dark-complexioned boy.

Kentucky seemed more difficult now than ever. Slavery was legal, although she'd heard the value of slaves was falling sharply. Union alliance, Confederate allegiance, they mingled among the good citizens, but those loyalties also were held by citizens less good. The Confederate aligned sabotaged Union troops and Union supporters, and the

Union sympathizers shared in the horrors, destroying their neighbors and former friends. And now, her son, the only publicly recognized relationship she had ever had as an adult, was wandering in the dangerous dark. Her beloved son. She was emotionally frozen, unable to do anything. If she went to look for him, who would be here if he arrived home? No one, and he'd go off looking for her. If she didn't look for him, he might be left in some stranger's mischievous hands. But where would she look? Why couldn't she control him? Why was she such a terrible mother? He was just a child.

She wanted to control the sun, will it to stay above the horizon. She remembered the words of Isaiah the prophet when King Hezekiah was dying and quoted them aloud. "Behold, I will bring again the shadow of the degrees, which is gone down in the sun dial of Ahaz, ten degrees backward." If only she could move the sun backward 10 degrees, 20 degrees, enough that he could be home before it bowed below the horizon. She felt foolish. Bits of words came effortlessly again to her mind, "I have all faith, so that I could remove mountains." Ridiculous, she thought. Perhaps she did have great faith, certainly she had known the mercy of the Lord, but she was no Isaiah, no Paul, no prophetess. But she couldn't stand helpless and watch the sun lower her hopes.

Raising both her hands toward heaven, she shouted, "Lord, I cannot stop the sun, but thou with thine mighty hand canst save my boy. Save him, Lord. Save him!" Her upper body rocked as she prayed.

Suddenly self-conscious, she looked around to make sure no one had witnessed her plea, but her embarrassment annoyed her. Why fret who saw her?

It was almost dark, and she again began wishing the Lord would hold back the sun. She couldn't do it, but he could. Just for an hour . . . or two. She prayed aloud, no longer caring if anyone saw her. "It's not for me, Lord, to decide how thou dost save my son, only for me to ask that thou wilt. How can the creature command the creator? You're a foolish woman, Victoria. A foolish woman." The sun set, and the boy hadn't come.

Hours passed. Victoria didn't try to sleep. She moved into the house as the evening cooled and sat in darkness at the window, face close to its panes, looking into the dark for signs of something moving, something that might be Adam. Her anxiety didn't make her restless because paralyzing fear overwhelmed her.

She couldn't fathom where he had gone, if not after the men. Perhaps he caught up to them, and they were bringing him home.

If he'd followed them, it was to enlist. Normally she would have chuckled at the thought, imagining him trying to muster in, but not tonight. She couldn't be sure he'd made it safely or even that he'd gone after them. Perhaps he'd been injured playing in the woods and lay dying somewhere nearby. Perhaps her empty threats had come true, and he was shackled with slaves, marching toward Alabama. Nonsense, she thought.

Periodically, tears flowed unwiped down her cheeks, clinging to her neck till they were absorbed in her tight collar. She kept up her conversation with God. She reminded him of Jacob, how he'd wrestled with an angel all night and prevailed. She warned him she was going to stay right there and wrestle if need be with the Almighty—not just one of his angels—just to convince him to save her child. She reminded him about Moses and how he'd parted the sea so the children of Israel could escape Pharaoh. Couldn't he divide the darkness and let her boy come home. She recounted to the Deity a story of Moses holding up his hands so Israel could subdue their enemies, and she raised her hands and shouted praise in hopes her son might prevail over the enemy of darkness and slave traders and patrollers and thieves and murderers.

She saw something in the dark. Movement. Was it him? "Praise God!" she exclaimed audibly, unable to suppress her excitement, thinking it had to be him. But it wasn't, and her praise faded as four horses approached, each carrying a white man.

Chapter 23

April 1864, Eastern Kentucky

William was spent, but not dead. He was coherent, grateful he hadn't lapsed into an other-world insanity loitering nearby. He'd trudged the road from army recruitment, leaving behind again his long-held but now diminishing dream of soldiering.

Each step from the recruiters required conscious effort. He thought about raising his foot. He willed it. It rose, but not as high as he'd commanded. He was relieved it rose at all and that it fell, pulling his body forward. Then it was time to think of the next step. He imagined his opposite leg moving upward and forward. He willed it, and it rose hesitatingly and fell. He suffered, step by step. So slow. Tired. Sweating profusely.

His disappointment at army rejection evaporated completely and quickly. He wanted only bed, sleep and the enveloping happiness of his budding life in Kentucky. He craved a woman he now dreamed of when he was awake and asleep. The dreams were all the more adored because they replaced nightmares of lynchings, murder and starvation that had so long accompanied him. William was beginning to feel hope. Perhaps all was not lost.

At some point, it came to him that his exhaustion at the recruitment meeting came as much from internal emotional resistance as from physical fatigue. In spite of following Isaiah to the recruiting excitement, his heart no longer countenanced being a soldier. He realized his greatest fear had been that the army would take him, separating him forever from Victoria and Adam. He needed Victoria. Yet he knew her love was impossible because of his oldness so often pronounced by Isaiah.

He continued slowly and methodically to think through each step till his body was ready to break. At that point, he stumbled into the obscurity of the woods that paralleled the hard-surfaced dirt path. How odd, he thought, that it should be so difficult to make a leg move. He looked for the softest natural bed—wet decaying leaves piled up—and fell on them, lapsing instantly into sleep.

Roused naturally at dusk, he was surprisingly rested and refreshed. He was not a soldier—hallelujah—and perhaps something happy awaited ahead. His damp clothes clung uncomfortably cold to him, but he was returning to the judge's farm, dry clothes, a bed . . . and Victoria. He was giddy with hope, but subdued it, reminding himself that night brought new perils. He'd have to stay off the road, but near enough for it to guide him in the dark.

In the back of his mind, he worried that he couldn't find his way home. Isaiah had brought him on several roads and through several crossroads that morning, and William hadn't tried to memorize them because he never expected to return. To suppress his anxiety, he visualized Victoria in morning light.

A random thought passed in his mind—the judge would beat him for leaving. He imagined Isaiah fabricating a story of William running off and trying to convince him to follow. He'd probably say he had followed, but only to bring William back, leaving Isaiah framed for the judge as hero and William as scoundrel. The weak fraternity he'd felt with Isaiah yesterday had been replaced by repulsion and anger. His only hope was that, even if the judge did believe the Judas, he would not beat William. His thoughts returned pleasantly to Victoria, and he admired his memory of her profile.

William was ready at the slightest sound or movement to slip deeper into the woods or the yet-to-be-cultivated fields that at times abutted the road. Periodically, he'd trip, stumbling over some unseen obstacle in his path, but he never fell and kept going.

Men's voices ahead broke the silence. Warily William slowed his steps and strained to hear a conversation that was jovial, yet harsh and mocking. He moved away from the road to await their passing, but they weren't moving. Anxious to get home, William began to creep quietly through the trees to quickly skirt by the men. He was uncomfortably close, but still couldn't see them. He could hear them clearly, which meant they'd hear him if he tripped or sneezed or coughed. He suspected from their tone they were patrollers pounced on a hapless victim.

"You stupid . . . ."

William didn't hear the rest of the curse as he was concentrating on his own careful movement to avoid discovery. The voices were dangerously near. Visions of Victoria, his rescuing angel, at his bedside burst upon him and physically turned him toward the road. How could he abandon the unfortunate quarry when she had never forsaken him?

"Don't . . . don't . . . don't call mmme . . . don't call me that!" exclaimed a child's voice.

Lightning jolted William's body in a shock of fright. He instinctively wanted to run to the boy, but reason led him to a less reckless approach. He listened for clues and details. How many men? Where was Adam? Were there dogs?

A gruff voice responded to Adam's demand. "Well, we got ourselves a bold little . . ."

The man's words broke abruptly as William heard what sounded to him like Adam striking the man. Was this the crisis? He held his breath, ready to charge. Perhaps he could give the boy time . . . a chance to run.

Adam yelled in pain, and William moved cautiously closer. He could faintly see a man grab Adam by the hair and lower his own head to peer eye-to-eye at Adam. He cursed him, "I'll call you whatever I please, you . . ."

William crouched, searching the ground. He needed to save the boy now, or they might beat or . . . . He wasn't yet ready, but time was running out. He dragged his hands quietly along the ground looking for something, anything. A second screech of pain terminated William's search. It was time, the crisis was upon them. He strategically took aim and tossed across the road one of the oblong, potato-sized rocks he'd gathered. It struck what sounded to William like a larger stone.

All conversation stopped.

"What was that?" one of the patrollers asked, immediately, pin-pricked alert.

No one answered. They knew someone was nearby. Rock hitting rock was not the sound made by a nocturnal animal. At that instant, William wished he were a skunk, able to scatter the men without a face-to-face encounter.

Letting go of the wish, William pulled his arm back, aiming once more at the other side of the road, but to the opposite flank of the group. He heaved another potato-sized rock, this time high into the air over the men, and it came down through the sparse early spring leaves, rattling them as it descended to hit the ground in a loud thump.

No one moved.

William lofted a larger stone into the air across the road. It descended, tearing through young leaves, bouncing against branches and thudding as it landed.

Adam, who listened with everyone else, felt the man's hand loosen from his head, and he lit off, running homeward. As he ran, he bumped into one of the horses which, without a rider to steady him, bolted. The man let Adam run, still trying to determine what evil was in the woods. William watched briefly, then let go of a large pebble. It struck a second unmanned, already-nervous horse, and it also broke in terror. William smiled. He always had loved throwing stones.

"The horses! Get the horses!" someone yelled.

The patrollers were off on foot and horseback in pursuit of the panicked steeds, which fortunately traveled in the opposite direction from Adam's flight. William moved from the woods onto the road and walked quickly after Adam, using energy he didn't know remained. He breathed heavily but tried to control the noise, struggling to hear any clue of where Adam had gone. He had to get to him before they returned. The patrollers wouldn't let Adam's escape go unpunished.

As he moved along the road, and in spite of the torrential use of his remaining energy, William wondered, then worried, that the boy might not know his way home. Then he remembered he had no idea where he was going. His anxiety crescendoed as he came to a crossroad. He stopped. Which way had they come? Which way had Adam gone? In the daytime, he might have ventured a guess, but in the dark nothing was recognizable. The crossroad appeared to be every wilderness crossroad he'd ever come to—two roads converging, tall stands of wood on each corner, extending in slight, suggestive nighttime shadows as far as the eye could see. He felt claustrophobic, with trees towering threateningly above him.

"Stop this," he demanded out loud. He strained to recall anything from his and Isaiah's hustled morning march. Nothing came. He turned around, facing the direction he'd just come from, and tried to imagine it as if he were coming. Which way had he turned? Had he turned at all? He did remember turning left at some point in the day. Was it here? He turned.

As he moved through the crossroad, his thoughts shifted to finding Adam. Even if they never got home, at least they'd be together. Adam wouldn't be lost and alone. A guilty thought had come to him earlier—the boy had come looking for him. William's remorse deepened into an ache as he half walked, half ran down the new road.

He hadn't gone far when he heard soft, pathetic crying. William slowed and called out softly, "Adam." The crying stopped immediately, although William heard a sniffle. "Adam," he called again.

"William?" came a whisper.

"Where are yuh?"

"RRRight he . . . he . . . here," the now excited, stuttering voice responded so close to William that it startled him, and he involuntarily jumped.

"Boy, yuh done scared me." Adam could see better in the dark than William, and before William could find him, the boy had wrapped his arms around his waist. William reached down and returned the hug, again feeling very tired, "Yuh all right?"

"I . . . I'm fine. I wa . . . wa . . . was scared." He paused, thinking. "HHHow did you know where I was?"

"The Lord, he was lookin' out for yuh. He done led me right to yuh. Better get goin'. They'll be lookin' for yuh 'gain 'fore we know it." With that, William took Adam's hand and the two began walking quickly down the road.

The boy didn't respond for several minutes, finally asking, "What dddoes he look like?"

"Who?"

"The Lord."

William's confusion continued. "Don't know. Got a beard. Why yuh ask?"

"You said that he shhh . . ."—William could feel the boy struggle as he tried to force the word out—"showed you where I was."

William smiled, "That ain't what I meant. No, not at all. The Lord, he don't show yuh like that. He just sort o' leads yuh in yor mind . . . yor heart. Yuh just know where to go."

"Oh."

"Understand?"

"No." He was silent briefly. "WWWilliam?"

"Yes."

"Why dddo they call me that?"

William looked toward the small figure. "Call all of us that. Just a way they want to talk, I s'pose. Makes 'em feel better. If they don't never call us that, then they'd be more scared o' us, thinkin' we was as good as . . . no, better than they was."

"NNNot that. They always call me stupid. I knnnow I can't talk, but I'm not ssstupid. Mama tells me I'm . . . I'm . . . I'm not stupid. Why do they do it?"

William squeezed Adam's hand affectionately, "Cause yor too smart for 'em, and they know it. They don't want yuh to know it, so they call yuh that. Maybe they're tellin' themselves talkin' is the way to see someone's smart. But they done forgot the papa o' John the Baptist . . . the Baptist himself. Couldn't talk, not at all."

"Not at . . . aaall?"

"Nary a word. Not till the Baptist was born. So maybe yuh're like that. Yuh can already talk better than the Baptist's papa. Maybe something special gunna happen to yuh . . . something special like happened to John's papa."

"DDDid they call his father ssstupid?"

"Don't know . . . maybe just thought it. Couldn't talk at all. Why yuh can talk all yuh want. Just takes a while . . . 'cause yuh have somethin' important to say. But him, couldn't talk . . . nary a word."

He whispered, "You think there's something good's going to happen to me?"

"Think it will. I done known yuh was special the first time I seen yuh. Yuh saved my life. That makes yuh special. Ain't many 'round that done saved a man's life. No doubt 'bout it. Yor special . . . like the Baptist and his daddy. Why . . . almost forgot."

"Wh . . . Wh . . . What?"

"Moses. He was slow o' speech, just like yuh. Yor mama read it to me."

"William, you're sp . . . sp . . . special, too! You just saved me."

William laughed, "Oh, Don't know nothin' 'bout that. Yuh were doin' good when I come."

"William?" the boy whispered.

"Yes."

"Why are we walking this way?"

"Goin' home. I'm mighty tired. Just want to sleep a bit."

"But ttthis isn't the way home."

"What?" William said sharply. "Yuh was goin' this way."

The boy whispered, "I was just hiding from those men."

"Why the wrong way?"

"III think they know where I live."

"What do yuh mean?"

"There aren't any other bbboys that ssstutter like me."

William could feel his body tense as he pictured Victoria confronting the men in the middle of the night. He groaned inadvertently and said, "We best get home. Quick! Which way?"

"The wwway we came. HHHere I'll show you."

Adam pulled William's hand. A passing wave of exhaustion swept through William, but was quickly replaced by a surge of adrenaline as he again imagined the men . . . and Victoria. Their pace increased, and they walked openly without attention to danger along the way.

They rapidly returned to the crossroad where William had earlier turned, and Adam pulled him directly through the intersection. William picked up his pace, and Adam matched it till they were nearly running.

Adam was quiet for a long time, and William was concerned. "Yuh all right?"

He could feel through Adam's hand the young boy turn his neck upward and to the side to get his best look at

William. Adam was trying to force words out, his arm jerked, "YYYeah . . . bbbut sad."

"Sad?"

"I wanted to jjjoin the army with you . . . and IIIsaiah."

"That's what yuh was doin'?"

"Yeah."

William smiled, but said nothing.

"Where is Isaiah?" the boy whispered.

"Reckon home . . . sleepin' in bed."

"But . . . but . . . but they sssaid you both ran off."

"He went to help me 'long." He answered charitably, but added with increasing bitterness, "Make sure I joined up . . . to get me out o' the way."

"BBBut you didn't . . . jjjoin?"

"Didn't get no chance. They thought I was . . . ill."

Adam whispered, "That's what mama said."

"What else yor mama say 'bout me?"

Still whispering, he responded, "She was sad you went without saying goodbye. Think she was a little mad."

"She should a' been. Yuh thought yuh'd join with me?"

"YYYeah. It would have been just you and me, since I . . . I . . . Isaiah didn't."

William grinned. "Let's us get home tonight. I can get stronger, and yuh older—then maybe we'll try 'gain."

"I'm old . . . eeenough now, but we'll get you better."

They hurried on in silence, both breathing heavily, refusing to slow their pace.

William heard something. "What's that?"

They both stopped walking, straining to hear the sound.

Chapter 24

April 1864, Richmond, Virginia

Betsy felt physically better than she had in several weeks. She hadn't been nauseated all day, and for that she was grateful. Checkerboard-patterned sunlight made its way stubbornly through the cell's window, and in the light, she reread an English translation of the popular French novel "Les Miserables." In her innocence, she felt a new kinship to Valjean, and she hadn't even stolen bread.

She'd overcome her revulsion at the filth that covered her bed, the cell's furniture, the floor and walls. But she was convinced she would never get used to the bothersome bites suffered each night and the rats that sometimes scurried across the floor in the dark.

Caleb and Marie Ann had visited her, bringing her items she once took for granted: books, newspapers, a letter and edible food. Betsy was losing weight on prison fare because she couldn't bring herself to eat much of it, and even if she had, there weren't enough calories in the meals to sustain her.

Marie Ann had smuggled in a letter from Hank and the 13 dollars Hank had originally sent to Betsy, secreting both in a pocket she'd sewn into her petticoat. Betsy had already read the letter so many times she had memorized large chunks of it, and she savored every hidden message and emotion the letter conveyed.

Betsy's mother, Rebeka, hadn't come with Caleb and Marie Ann, and Betsy instinctively worried at her absence.

Caleb explained that Rebeka hadn't taken news of Betsy's arrest well and had retreated into emotional confusion. He assured Betsy she was recovering, but what he didn't divulge was that what she was recovering was her past delusion that her now-years-dead husband was alive and expecting her to be at their home in war-ravaged Winchester. Rebeka had already insisted on returning to Winchester, and Caleb sent John, Betsy's most trusted slave, to protect her in the troubled town. But even John, Caleb knew, would be tempted by freedom of the nearby North.

Caleb dissembled to buoy Betsy up, to reassure her that her mother hadn't abandoned her. Betsy, under usual circumstances, would have probed for details of her mother's condition, but she asked no questions. Caleb took her passive acceptance of the news as proof sorrow was defeating Betsy. She was now an emotional beggar, desperate for help, no longer able to give it. He was grateful they could visit her, but it wasn't enough, and he fretted that Betsy was already following her mother into fatal fantasy.

Their conversation had turned to Hank and his letter. Hank didn't know—and Betsy demanded that Caleb and Marie Ann never tell him—she was imprisoned. Why tell him? What could he do? It would only worry him or worse— he might undertake some hopeless attempt to rescue her, one that would end in Shakespearean tragedy. Betsy knew she couldn't send him letters, not to a man in the North, not when she was under suspicion of treason, not from a prison for traitors, not even if she wanted to tell him that she was in a family way.

Shocked, Caleb had asked pointedly, "Is it true?"

"No."

Caleb ignored her denial. "Do they know?"

Betsy looked at him. How could she respond? Her face was pale, emotionally cold. "Probably . . . maybe. I feel odd. Things aren't normal." She breathed. "I suppose if I am, it will be clear to everyone in the end . . . from jailer to jailed— my whole world." A sad smile crept across her face as she unconsciously patted her still-slender waist. Tears beaded in Marie Ann's eyes. Betsy looked at Caleb. "I'm sorry to speak of such a delicate topic, but I can't share my thoughts . . . my feelings . . . my suspicions with Hank. I have to share them with someone."

Caleb gathered his wits in a deep breath and diverted the conversation from the uncomfortable topic by saying he'd write to Betsy with Staunton news and reported—with eyes downward—that everyone in the town was concerned for her. "No one believes the rumors. You can see that in their kind treatment of Marie Ann and me."

The couple did continue to be included among the town's social cream, but only because of Caleb's sacrifice for the South. Staunton had totally abandoned Betsy, judging her guilty, and Caleb's obvious lie inadvertently but clearly communicated the truth to the prisoner.

Betsy asked about her estranged cousin Emily, and Caleb responded, "She's mad. You need to know that. She caused your arrest, but I don't think she knew what she was doing. She is rabidly insane. Her husband put her in Dr. Stribling's care at the Western State Lunatic Asylum. He diagnosed it as dementia."

"I've met Dr. Stribling," Betsy commented. "He seems kind. He told me he believes the most important thing he can do for patients is encourage them to worthwhile activities. Maybe he can help cousin Emily to garden."

"That's one reason no one believes these vile rumors . . . because Emily is so obviously crazy," Caleb mumbled.

"Regardless of Emily's lost sense," Betsy replied, "some will suspect me . . . and more will hope I'm guilty."

Neither visitor responded, knowing townspeople believed Emily had broken down specifically because of the emotional trauma of exposing Betsy as a traitress.

The couple spent an hour with Betsy, promising to return before taking the train to Staunton the next day.

Memories of their meeting distracted Betsy from reading, but she enjoyed thoughts of her friends and the words in Hank's letter, even if both left her depressed in the end. She could still see Caleb and Marie Ann's faces when she had revealed her family suspicions. She understood their revulsion, but she was grateful for the child. She would have someone she loved close, someone to care for and be with as others abandoned her.

The cell door opening with its usual grinding caught her attention. She grimaced at the sound, put down the book and looked toward the entry. A guard entered and said kindly, "You've a visitor."

She looked at the guard, returning his kind tone in her expression. "A visitor. Extraordinary, don't you think? Two visits in one day, when I've had none before."

Before he could respond, a thin woman pushed past him. She was meticulously dressed in a dark jacket and skirt. Her blouse was trimmed at her neck with a collar of white lace partially covered with a large brooch. Her dark hair, under a small hat, was pulled back. Everything about her was refined, and Betsy looked at her inquisitively. When the woman said nothing, Betsy asked, "Have we met?"

"We haven't." She turned to the guard. "Thank you. We'll be fine if you could leave us." The guard nodded and disappeared behind the door. The woman turned and with a shifting, systematic stare examined Betsy.

After an uncomfortable wait, Betsy again questioned her guest. "May I ask who you are?"

"Yes, of course. Excuse me for this intrusion. I imagine you hoped for family or friend."

"I certainly hope you're friend."

The woman smiled briefly, perfunctorily.

"And you are?" Betsy added, persisting.

"Florence Morrow."

"It's a pleasure to meet you. I'm Elizabeth Henderson."

"Mrs. Henderson, a pleasure. Of course, I know who you are." She looked again at Betsy for an unusually long time before adding, "You're not as I expected."

"What did you expect? And why would you expect anything?" Betsy was irritated. "Do you perceive me a traitress and imagine I, like Richard III, must have some defect in my soul reflected in malformed body parts?" In spite of her irritation at the woman's terse conversation and visual inspection, Betsy was curious. She imagined this visitor sent like the pathetic woman who at first had shared Betsy's cell. Feigning to be a prisoner, the woman tried for days to coax a confession from Betsy only to disappear when Betsy would admit nothing. Betsy wondered what role this woman was playing and stared coldly at her.

The woman looked back, still seeming to analyze Betsy, but her countenance softened. "Please excuse me," she said formally. "I've never been in a prison before, and it's different than I'd imagined."

"Are you here to hear confession?"

Miss Morrow looked slightly amused. "I don't think so. I'm surely no priest . . . as you can see. I've come on my own . . . to help . . . support."

"Your first visit to prison? Why visit me?"

"To be forthright, I'd heard the widow of Thaddeus Henderson . . . was in a woman's way."

Betsy's head tilted back in surprise at the news and at this stranger mentioning it.

Miss Morrow continued, "I've come . . . as I said, to give support."

"Where did you hear that?"

"I'm not here to be coy. It's broadly reported."

"Broadly?"

"Yes, I assumed you knew and that your plethoric state was obvious. I'm sorry to be the one to tell you. I find little trace . . . not enough for the public to know. Are you suffering the sorrow of our sex, Mrs. Henderson?"

Betsy flustered. "What has it to do with you?"

"Nothing . . . but if you had been in such a state, I would have offered assistance."

"Assistance?"

"Yes. I'd help you escape."

"Why?"

"Because I don't believe this prison . . . or any other, is an appropriate place for a lady . . . a lady like you . . . to be as you approach your time of trial. Under the circumstances, I think it will be particularly unpleasant."

"If I were going to have a child."

"Let me be direct. Richmond believes you carry the child of a Yankee spy . . . and murderer. That's the proof, they say, that you're guilty . . . that you spied for the North . . . that you are a murderess."

"No one's mentioned it to me . . . here. I just had friends visit, and they said nothing."

"Remarkable."

"Remarkable?"

"Remarkable that no one mocks you for it. I can't fathom it. A woman charged as a spy. I came believing that what I'd heard was unimpeachable truth and that it would be obvious. Now I find you not in a family way. All untrue. Forgive me. I've come errantly and offended you on such a personal topic. I regret it and will leave immediately."

Betsy was shocked by the rumor but wanted to know more and longed for company. "Don't leave . . . not yet. I have so little news of what goes on outside these walls. I've had only two visits—both this very day. My only pleasure is my daily walk in the courtyard with Nero . . . or Hero as I like to call him. Even if you've come under misapprehension . . . or even to spy on me, please stay . . . stay and visit a while. Tell me news of something. Anything. They keep me so isolated now."

Betsy could see the efficiency melt in her visitor's visage. "May I sit down?"

"Please . . . yes, of course." Betsy glimpsed the woman's hesitation to sit as Miss Morrow noticed for the first time the grime that covered every surface in the cell.

After quickly considering her seating options, Miss Morrow, who wore black gloves, pulled a chair from the table and sat down, facing Betsy who still sat on the edge of the bed. "Why not more visitors?"

"I suppose no one wants to associate with a woman held for treason. But never charged!"

"Ah, well perhaps others would come, but they can't. Perhaps they won't let them see you. I had to bribe the guard to see you."

Betsy looked surprised. "You bribed him?"

"Yes."

"Why?"

"I told you. If you'd been in an expectant state, I would have done much to get you out of here . . . get you to the North."

"The North?"

"Of course. With the stories I've heard, I can't imagine you'd want to stay in Richmond, even if you were released. The story is you killed—I don't believe it for a minute mind you—a man . . . or was it two . . . in Staunton. The stories vary on the number."

"People believe that?"

"Mrs. Henderson," she smiled at Betsy, "I don't know if anyone believes it or not, but they like to think it's true because . . . because people like to think the worst of everyone else, especially if they believe you're the enemy. Isn't that one of our worst traits? Hope the worst for others, the best for ourselves."

"What else do they say?"

She smiled, reached out to take Betsy's right hand in one of her gloved hands as she stroked it with the other. She spoke looking off into the room's corner as if to avoid Betsy's eyes. "That you killed the man because he was going to reveal your ill-got wealth—something about hoarding and something else. What's it called?"

"Speculating?"

"No, not speculating. Smuggling. That's it."

Betsy leaned backed and pulled her hand gently from her visitor's grasp. "If they believe I've murdered a man and betrayed my country, they'll hang me."

"I'm not sure of that. They haven't hung any women, yet. They still need evidence of guilt. I had hoped you were in that special way, for they surely wouldn't hang a woman in such a state."

Betsy looked sharply at the woman, "Have you been sent—like that other woman—to get me to confess?"

Miss Morrow looked at her compassionately. "Mrs. Henderson, have I asked about guilt?" She waited. "I'm not interested in it. I haven't been sent. Remember, it cost me money to get in here, my own money. I came because I can't imagine being in here . . . not if I were . . . I came out of pity . . . no, out of sympathy . . . in hope of helping."

Betsy looked at her thoughtfully, analyzing the situation, "You were ready to leave, but I kept you."

"I was leaving." She paused. "Even though you're not in that way, I can help."

"How?"

"How do you want me to?"

"I'd like to go back in time before it all happened, and do it again . . . better. If what you say is true, I know there are here—and in Staunton—those who will always see me now as the woman who spied . . . who killed a man."

"You're right. Then go to the Union."

"Do I have a choice?"

"Not really."

"But I've done none of it—the spying, the smuggling."

"It doesn't matter."

"It matters to me, and no, I don't want to leave the country. This is my home. I don't want to be driven out by a mad woman and a mean-hearted sheriff."

"I have an idea. May I visit again?"

"Of course," Betsy said, almost desperately. "Anytime."

"You're not in a family way?"

Betsy pursed her lips and her eyes shrank.

"I would not condemn you. If you are, it might help getting you to the North . . . if that's what you want."

Betsy's eyes blazed. "Is that what they want to know?"

"Who?"

"The commandant! He's sent you to detect if I'm . . ."

"I believe he already thinks he knows. Even the guard told me you are in that way . . . but he was more crude. He also said you were always sick."

Betsy's expression relaxed. "But I'm feeling better today . . . for the first time."

The woman looked at Betsy with her efficient expression. "Then you are. Good! It will be helpful."

"How? One young girl already brought forth favorable issue in Castle Thunder. They won't care if I do."

The woman smiled, "But I don't think they'll be so quick to hang you." She waited, watching Betsy who looked serious. "That was meant as humor."

Betsy laughed awkwardly. "Yes, forgive me. I was thinking you're probably right."

"A child is the best news we could hope for, but I've got work to do. You must tell no one of our conversation."

"What do I say . . . if they hear of it . . . ask about it?"

"Say I came to comfort . . . to encourage you to seek the Lord . . . to seek forgiveness."

"Seems blasphemous."

"It isn't because I do sincerely encourage you to seek the Lord, his blessing . . . and forgiveness of your sins."

"I'll say it, then."

"Good." She rose from her chair and walked to the door and called, "Guard. I'm ready." Then speaking more softly to Betsy said, "This is a bit exciting . . . being in a prison. Thank you for this adventure. It's so unlike the rest of my dull life." Again in a louder voice she called, "Guard!"

They heard the footsteps, the keys, the grating door. The guard stepped into the cell.

She turned once more to Mrs. Henderson. "Thank you for letting me see you."

Betsy bowed her head slightly in response, and both the guard and Miss Morrow disappeared into the hallway.

As Miss Morrow and the guard reached the ground floor, she said, "I'd like to see the commandant, now."

"Will he want to see you?"

"I think he'll see me."

"You won't mention the . . ."

"No, of course not."

"How will you explain our letting you see . . ."

"I won't tell him I've seen her. He won't know. You'll have no problem with the commandant. Escort me to him, if you'd be so kind."

Chapter 25

April 1864, Richmond, Virginia

A few streets to the north, Dante was ushered into the same room where he'd earlier been mocked and rejected. The same captain, clearly irritated to see Dante again, said coldly, "I thought you weren't to come again."

"I've brought you something . . . from Washington."

"Something useful? More useful than Miss Van Lew?" He smiled disdainfully.

"This is for you," Dante said hesitantly as he pulled the letter from the Southern-aligned Northern detectives.

Dante offered it standing at the officer's desk, and the man took it without rising. "Let's see what you bring." He reached into the center drawer of the desk and pulled out a letter opener. He slid it carefully under the seal and pulled out the multiple-page letter. He smiled, put it face down on the desk, leaned back and waved his hand toward a chair. "Sit down."

Dante sat.

"Mr. Dante, do you know what the letter's about?"

"No."

"Do you know who gave it to you?"

"By sight."

"Good. This is most helpful, worth my time to see you. To be honest, I expected you. If you hadn't come, we would have looked for you. I know you betrayed our friends in Washington." Dante shifted nervously in his chair, and the officer saw him. "Don't worry, I hear you're now willing . . . to help us."

"I offered earlier."

"Yes, but that was different. I'll send you to Washington in a few days. So quickly do whatever you need to do while you're here."

"I'll take letters to Washington, then?"

"I'll have several things for you, but it will be a few days."

"I'm staying at the Ballard House."

"I thought you'd stay in a gambling hell . . . from what I've been told. Ballard House will be better, and don't go near any gambling. Police are trying to clean up the city, and they don't need immoral citizenry . . . like you . . . making their work harder." The captain smiled sarcastically.

"I understand," Dante responded grudgingly. "But I do ache to sit again at the faro tables. They are wonderful. Have you tried it?"

The Confederate looked blankly at Dante.

"No, I don't suppose you have. Is that all? May I go?"

"Leave? Are you hurried? Urgent appointment? Somewhere you need to go? Oh, I did want to mention I'm glad you've recovered use of your arm . . . so permanently useless the last time we met. A modern Christian miracle."

Dante hated this man. He was angry and tired of being humiliated. He felt the familiar urge to reach across the desk, grab and strangle him. Instead he lowered his eyes and remembered Matthew's caution. Dante had to keep control, or it would be his undoing. He slowly raised his eyes and offered meekly, "I've nowhere I need to go, but I don't want to encumber your day further."

"A thoughtful fellow," the captain said smiling brightly. "With that attitude, I won't need to remind you we have a prison for those who betray us . . . if they live, a prison right here in town where we keep traitors. And no one is above the law. Right now, they even hold for treason the widow of a fallen soldier. Although her case is interesting and unusual, involving two paramours—a Mr. Stokes and a Mr. Walthrope. Evil is everywhere, Mr. Dante. But be it as it may, my point is they show no special courtesy to Mrs. Henderson. They'll surely show none to a villain like you."

The names tickled Dante as the captain mentioned them. "Yes, I've heard of those ghastly murders. I knew Mr. Walthrope. A fine gentleman. This flagitious Mrs. Henderson you mention . . . she deserves harsh punishment . . . for such heinous crimes. Will she hang?"

"For treason and murder? She gave information to a Yankee spy and killed two men. They say she's with child by the Yankee. An exceptional scandal, Mr. Dante, even amidst all the horrors of war. She won't get away with it. They'll make sure she pays. There's a rumor she'll hang, baby and all. She'll be the first. A strong warning shot, Mr. Dante, to anyone who considers crossing us."

"I'm under your control, sir. But Mrs. Henderson surely should hang for doing what she did to honorable Mr. Walthrope. Is there more, sir?" Dante said respectfully.

"No. I'll send for you in a day or two." Dante rose, and the captain looked at him, smiling widely again and said, "Good day, then."

Chapter 26

April 1864, Richmond, Virginia

The day was warm and sunny, and she was savoring her short time in the prison yard. She was in a pleasant mood. She had plenty to worry about, including her mother's emotional decay. Betsy had realized during Caleb and Marie Ann's second visit that they deceived her about her mother, just as she hid her circumstances from Hank. She could do nothing for her mother or Hank but petition God for their safety. On this glorious day, she would let no worry dissuade her from this happy escape from her cell.

She was not allowed in the yard for daily exercise—so important in her state—when the men were there, nor was she allowed to associate with other women inmates. So her brief, solo daily constitution in the yard or on the prison's balcony was her only diversion, and regardless of her mood or physical discomfort, she never missed it and the accompanying freshest air she could enjoy in the Castle. Even when disgusting kitchen smells wafted in the yard, it was better than her fetid cell.

Each day a guard—a young boy or old man—would lead her to the yard, and her walking companion, Nero, would bolt from the prison entrance to join her. He'd nuzzle her hand as they proceeded, and she would talk to him—her only confidant—constantly.

Today she told him about the wheat and corn grown on her farm, friends, and in a thrilled whisper, of her coming escape from the Castle. Miss Morrow's interest had resonated through her soul. Yesterday's prim visitor had gifted her hope, and she was reveling in it as she chatted with her slobbering giant.

"So . . . here's where I find Saint Betsy."

The familiar voice shocked and repulsed her. She wheeled toward the man, hatred inflaming her complexion. He was in the entrance, twenty feet from her.

He smiled when she turned. "Yes, I see it's true. You're scarred. I was so afraid Staunton would turn out badly, and now I find it is just as it should be . . . you are branded mine."

She glared. "I'm glad they finally caught you. Shouldn't you be in your cell?" Noticing for the first time there was no one in the yard and no sentinels on the walls, she called out, "Guard."

He laughed, "Cell? No, Mrs. Henderson, if that's your real name. Prison has been hard. You're confused. I'm no inmate. I'm not charged with smuggling, spying . . . murder. I'm free . . . at liberty to do as I please."

"Guard!" Where was the guard?

"We're alone. Haven't you dreamed of this moment? I have good money—your money—to keep guards away . . . so we can be together again . . . alone."

"What do you want?"

"For now, to gloat . . . mostly. You gave up my love and freedom for this, a Yankee lover, treason . . . murder, prison. You even murdered me. How wicked!" He laughed.

She didn't dare turn her back on him, but said nothing.

"I hear you're in a family way. Oh, the shame of it. Is it mine?" He laughed again.

"Guard!"

"I don't know what to do with you."

"Guard!" At her side, Nero pushed against her wanting to continue their walk. No guard appeared.

"You see the freedom I enjoy." He spread his arms in a smooth, wide expansive motion. "Marvelous, isn't it? Here you're penned up . . . like a cow . . . branded like a cow, and I'm free to travel from capital to capital. I should give evidence in your case. It might be enough . . . to hang you."

"You're a fool, Walthrope."

"A fool? Who, my dear, is free? Who the fool? The traitress, I'd think. But who am I to answer such a question? Merely a free man . . . rejected by a wanton woman who dared suggest I was unworthy of her. Oh, Betsy, my love, you are the fool. But I'm willing to forgive you . . . to help you escape the rope . . . if . . . you'll come back to me."

"Guard!" she yelled in intense fear. "Guard!"

"My dear Betsy. I'll not leave yet," he said in his suavest voice, strolling closer to her.

Her body went rigid, and she didn't move. "Get away!" she yelled. In response, Nero turned away from her and leered at Walthrope. She yelled again, "Not another step!"

"What are you afraid of . . . dear, dear Betsy?" He put out his hand as if to cradle her cheek.

"Not you," she sneered.

The sneer angered him, and he slapped her. But as he did, he heard a snarl and felt himself being pulled by a sharp pain and tug at his arm. A horrendous clamor erupted—it seemed to him—from everywhere all at once. What was happening? He was lost, confused. The tug on his arm had stopped, but there was pain in his leg, and he still was being dragged backward, then downward to the ground where he screamed as the dog grabbed his face and neck with his powerful jaws. Walthrope looked up, his pleading eyes rising to meet Betsy's, who watched in horror as her gentle friend bit and pulled at her menace so rapidly she could do nothing.

She covered her eyes and yelled, "No, Nero. No!" Instantly, even in the direful cacophony surrounding them, the dog stopped his attack and returned to her side, still glaring at the foe. But the deafening, maddening noise continued. Betsy, also confused by the racket, looked around her. It was as if the whole world was ending with one last shriek of death before all creation collapsed into nothingness.

Walthrope's clothes were torn, his arm, face, neck and leg bleeding profusely, as he shuttled backward, struggling to his feet. Betsy held the dog's head as she rapidly, firmly stroked its top. Neither she nor Walthrope said anything as he ran unevenly, with darting glances backward, from the enclosure.

The noise around her was organizing, becoming murmurs from all the windows, gradually waning till one single voice shouted, "Three huzzah's for Nero!"

Responding from windows that looked out on the yard, which was now filling with guards and cooks, "Huzzah! Huzzah! Huzzah!"

The voice again, "And three for our widow!"

"Huzzah! Huzzah! Huzzah!"

Betsy smiled sheepishly. They'd watched. They knew who she was. How odd.

Her escort guard reappeared and hurried her. "Time to return to your cell, Ma'am."

She looked at him, angrily. "Where were you?"

"Ma'am, don't know what you're talkin' about."

"I'll see the commandant!"

"Back to your cell!" insisted the aged guard.

"I'll see the commandant!" She was yelling now.

"Ma'am, back to . . ."

A voice shouted, "Commandant! Commandant! Commandant!" It again was joined by dozens of other voices."

With a frightened look, the guard hesitated, not knowing how to handle the ruckus and uneasy with the money still stashed in his pocket. Other guards who had filled the yard looked confused, scanning the barred windows of the three prison buildings. The cooks, all of African descent, had left the kitchen and were in the yard, pointing to the windows, laughing. One boy guard, frightened and flustered by the commotion, swung the butt of his rifle into the midsection of one of the cooks and all chanting and laughing stopped. Anger and fear mingled in the crowd. The prisoners above watched as best they could from their windows. No one dared move, no one spoke. Betsy with Nero at her side stood helpless.

Captain Richardson appeared in the doorway. There was silence. He calmly took in the scene: Betsy sided by a dog with blood dripping from its jowls, the guards gawking at the prisoners and cooks, and the cooks standing humbly, spread unevenly across the courtyard.

"It's nearly time to eat. You must have much to do. Be off and do it," he said to the cooks, who moved back warily, toward the kitchen, watching the guards. Richardson commented, "With so many guards in one place, there must be posts unattended."

The guards, except for the one with Betsy, moved away. The captain breathed deeply, and said to no one in particular, "Much better." He looked at Betsy. "Mrs. Henderson, a word, if you please. Bring Nero, if you would be so kind."

Cheers erupted from the prisoners, and the captain glanced upward with a face betraying no emotion.

Betsy, with Nero close, followed the commandant. The guard trailed. No one spoke till they reached the office, where the commandant invited Betsy to sit, ordered Nero to his corner and directed the guard to close the door. Betsy was surprised the guard remained.

"Now, everything is quiet and back in its place, except for you, Mrs. Henderson. I hope whatever happened is important . . . that you didn't create this commotion just to get an audience with me," he said sternly.

His tone angered Betsy. "The man who committed the murder I'm accused of attacked me in your prison!"

He smiled. "Mrs. Henderson, we do everything we can to assure your safety here. I'm sure only you . . . and the cooks had access to the courtyard. Isn't that so, guard?"

"Yes, sir."

"Captain, the man was in the yard. Only Nero saved me. Look at his face . . . covered in blood."

He watched disgustedly as the dog licked the fresh blood from his coat. "Have you been in the meat again?"

"Captain, am I to go crazy?" She was exasperated.

"Calm yourself, Mrs. Henderson. I do believe the prisoners yelling, the guards rushing the courtyard . . . I understand it made you hysterical. Surely you are prone to that. I don't fault you. It's a weakness of your sex. But do you expect me to believe the man who committed the murder you're held for is a prisoner here, too?"

"He's not a prisoner."

"Not a prisoner? Mrs. Henderson, please. It's not the time nor place to exhibit the sensitivities of your fair sex.

How would you know who's a prisoner and who's not, unless it was someone as famous as General Lee? You don't know all the prisoners . . . although apparently they know you."

"Captain, you're not listening!" Her anger exploded. "Check the guard for money . . the bribe."

"I will not," the captain responded firmly. "It's you, Mrs. Henderson, who's not listening. I don't know exactly what happened out there, but I do know no one from outside this prison was . . . or could have been in the yard with you. If there had been, this guard would have seen him as surely as I'm confident he would never take a bribe."

Betsy looked disgustedly at the guard and mumbled, "Check his pockets."

"That won't be necessary," the captain said sharply. He addressed the guard. "Did you see anyone out there?"

"No, Captain. I don't know what she's talking about. She's alone all the time. That can't be . . ."

"I didn't ask you that! Did you see anyone in the court-yard other than Mrs. Henderson?"

"Of course. There . . . in the end—you saw it, sir—the cooks . . . guards. Perhaps there might have been someone who sneaked in with the cooks. It would be impossible to say for sure. You heard the noise, sir."

The commandant looked blankly at the man, then turned to Betsy. "Again, I don't know exactly what happened, but I know you're imagining . . ." He broke off the thought and redirected his comments. "Maybe he's right. Maybe you've been on your own too much. I've met someone who would like to visit you regularly, just to relieve your loneliness. Would you accept a visitor?"

Betsy gave up. "Captain, I can do nothing but accept your will. And it seems that although I'm under your control

. . . I'm apparently no longer under your protection. The blood on the dog's mouth! It's not from meat, but from a man . . . a monstrous man. Ask this mendacious guard how the dog got blood on his mouth." She raised her hand and sleeve. "It's even on me. All of it witnesses the truth. Will you believe a man who has . . . Oh, what good is this? Send me your visitor."

"The woman was quite insistent that she wanted to visit with you . . . to ease your burdens. I will send her. Is there anything more?"

"My only consolation is Nero left him injured." She paused. "Yes, that's right. He must have left a trail of blood. Go, look for yourself. Follow it, you may find the man."

The captain was looking at the dog. "Mrs. Henderson, I imagine at this point you're frightened. Perhaps Nero could stay with you the rest of the day . . . overnight . . . if you can get him inside that cell." He didn't wait for a response. "I know you're frightened, even if you imagined the whole commotion, and I don't want you to be scared."

Chapter 27

April 1864, Eastern Kentucky

In the dark, unfamiliar with the roads and paths, William had no idea where they were, how far they'd walked or, desperately more important, how far they yet had to go. He would have asked Adam, but he didn't want to further frighten the child. At one point when he thought they must be getting close to Victoria, William stiffened when he heard something. It sounded again. Just an owl. But it aggravated his fear. He was increasingly terrorized by repulsive mental images of what the men would do to Victoria.

William's anxiety had fueled his flight toward her, but now, with hours passed, anxiety and even terror weren't enough to sustain his strength. He was wearing out. He wondered how far he could go before exhaustion or exhaustion-induced insanity retook him. Frequently he'd glance nervously back as if lunacy trailed them.

As they hurried along, their senses were fully alert. The boy heard and felt first the slight rumble of slowly approaching horses. William took the cue from Adam's straining and turned his torso to peer backward toward the deep vibration. Neither spoke. William guided Adam to the side of the road, stepping carefully in the grass and through bushes in a way that would not leave tell-tale signs. They both crouched low. They could barely see the road in the opaque night air, but could hear the horses and soon saw a dim light.

The horses walked briskly. William could hear talking, and one horseman held a torch illuminating the road. He moved it quickly side to side looking for disturbed grass. The torch gave off enough light that William could finally see the men who had tormented Adam. They passed, and even before their trailing noise faded, William pulled Adam to the road, and they carefully followed the horses.

They balanced their speed to not lose their pursuers or to overtake them. They had to stay close to arrive in time to aid an unsuspecting Victoria. How could they help her? William didn't know, but his mind continued creating horrible images of what awaited Victoria. He knew whatever happened would never find its way into a court for justice. Neither he nor Victoria could ever testify against a white man. Justice had to come in their own resourcefulness and finally at God's coming Jubilee. "Courage," he exhorted in a whisper and kept going.

Soon he knew his body was failing him. He couldn't go much farther, and if he did, what difference would it make? Arriving exhausted as he was would only ensure he would witness whatever the devils planned.

At each forced but blessed pause in their travel, when they'd get too close to the horsemen, William would let go of Adam's hand, lean forward, rest his hands on his thighs, lower his head and pant uncontrollably, sucking in air greedily to feed his fuel-depleted muscles. He hadn't eaten all day, and while he was hungry, hunger wasn't his only bother. His body had nothing left to give. No energy from food, dehydrated, adrenaline long ago spent. He was walking into death. His head was pounding. He could barely keep his eyes open because of the pain. He would be of no use. He had failed again.

He looked sadly at the boy. He was ashamed, and he stumbled and fell to the ground. He didn't try to rise. Adam stopped beside him. William looked at the scarcely visible form above him. "Can't go on, Adam."

The child didn't respond or move. William could see in Adam's silhouette that he was watching him.

"Yor mama needs yor help. I can't give it. Yuh can."

The boy bent over him, lifted his arm and held his hand. He whispered to William, "I can help her, but we have to get you out of the road . . . so those men don't find you." He tugged on William, and William responded, exerting his will and remaining strength to stand once more, letting the boy lead him carefully from the road.

Once in the trees, William sagged to the ground, fully spent. "Yuh go rescue yor mama."

"What should I do?" the boy whispered nervously.

William tried to picture what the men would do when they got to Victoria's. "Yuh ready to listen good?"

"YYYes." His head jerked forward as he raised his voice in rising confidence.

William gave the boy his last instructions and said, "Now hurry. Not much time. If it don't seem right . . . what I told yuh, don't yuh go and do it. Yuh gotta decide when yuh see what the men are doin'. Now, get goin', stay just behind 'em, like us . . . like we've been doin'."

The boy was back on the road, and William could hear him trotting. William wasn't sleepy. The sharp jabbing pain in his head was relentless, and he lay there imagining the worst for his new-found family.

Family? An odd thought. He had believed his fondness for them resulted from their kind nursing, but it came to him as he lay there that his love was not merely a response to charity or even the smoldering passion that drew him to

Victoria, but reached deeper and encompassed him. How could he love them? How could they be his family?

He loathed himself. He couldn't lie inert in the woods during their moment of crisis. He had to help, or his thoughts of love for Victoria and Adam were the idle meanderings of a weak mind, a spineless creature, an old man. He would be nothing more than white man's chattel defined by their fear of him, weakened by his willingness to do their bidding. As long as he did nothing to save his family, they had won. He felt anger surge, blocking much of the physical pain and exhaustion.

He struggled to his feet, his head still throbbing painfully. If the men caught him, at least they'd be diverted from his new beloved family. His legs barely held him up. He was sweating again in the cool, wet night air. The darkness enveloped him, blinding his eyes and seeping as despair into his inner parts. He couldn't think, he could barely breathe, barely walk. He wouldn't make it in time. The air was thickening, and he struggled to respire the coagulated atmosphere.

The four horsemen approached Victoria's cabin. One held a torch. She recognized him, and a visceral rage burned within her. What was he doing here? They approached the house, stopped their horses. One of them cried out, "Victoria!" She reined in her savage emotions. She was frightened and didn't answer.

"Wake up, fool woman! Get out here!"

She didn't shift a muscle, holding her breath.

The man called again, "Victoria! Wake up!"

She waited.

"If you don't come out, we'll burn you out."

She saw the man with the torch waving it menacingly, a maniacal grin on his face.

"Get down here, you . . ."

She had to confront them. If they were going to kill her, she would die with dignity, not hiding and crouching before them. She whispered as she reached the door. "Give me strength, Lord." She unlocked the front door, stepped out and demanded harshly, "What do you want?"

The horsemen were taken aback by Victoria's sudden, aggressive appearance. One was so startled he backed his horse from her. The patroller captain recaptured his composure and made demands of his own. "Don't talk to me like that, you . . ."

"That's the only way I'll talk to someone who awakens me in the middle of the night, with my boy asleep."

"I warn you, you . . ."

"You can warn all night. You can threaten till sunrise. It won't matter. You'll do what you'll do, whether I . . ."

The man's voice changed to a more conciliatory tone, "Victoria, we're not here to harm you."

The man with the torch spoke for the first time, "DDDon't . . . pppromise that! SSShe's tricky."

She looked at the torch holder, her eyes scrunched nearly into tight lines, "What are you doing here?" Her anger and hatred seethed. "I told you long ago to stay away. You'll be sorry you didn't."

The man stuttered a curse, adding, "NNNo one's here to pr . . . pr . . . protect you . . . nnnot nnnow."

Victoria stood statuesque, defiantly staring at the man. Inwardly she shook in terror, but she would have no patroller know she was scared.

"Victoria," the captain said, softening his voice. "You needn't worry. We have no quarrel with you. We'll leave as soon as you bring your boy out." His voice turned colder. "Bring out your boy, or we'll beat you till you do . . . then we'll beat him."

Victoria stopped listening. She cursed him in her mind for claiming any right to beat her son. Adam was hers, and no one else would touch him. She'd seen mothers forced to watch their sons and daughters stripped to their waists, beaten by masters, stark reminders there was no humanity in these creatures. They saw their slaves as things . . . to be used, beaten, raped, killed. They were chattel, like a horse's harness.

Suddenly her anger passed. She realized these men knew something of her son. "Why do you want him?"

"There, you're being more reasonable."

"Why," she repeated sternly, "do you want to see him?"

The man with the torch spoke, "DDDon't yo . . . yo . . . you worry about what wwwe'll do to that st . . . stu . . ."

Victoria shot back viciously, "Don't you ever speak of my son." She stepped toward the torch bearer.

The captain said quickly, "Victoria, we ain't here for a fuss. Bring the boy out. If he's here, all's well."

"He's asleep."

"Wake him, and everything will be fine."

"I won't bring him out . . . not in the middle of the night."

"BBB . . ." The torch tilted far forward and downward as its bearer strained to get the words out, and the odd angle of the light created a demon-like look on the man's screwed-up face. "BBBecause he's not hhhere."

The captain turned his head to the stuttering man, "What's the matter with you, Thornton?"

Victoria answered in disgust, "He's scared, and I don't blame him. If I ever get him . . . ." She thought better of finishing the thought and left her intent lingering malevolently in the air.

The captain laughed. "I do believe she's right. You're frightened of this . . ."

"III ain't scared of no . . . no . . . no . . ."

Victoria didn't listen to the vile words as she tried understanding why they sought Adam. Clearly, they'd seen a young stuttering boy earlier and assumed he was hers. He must have eluded them. The boy was resourceful, but was she? Could she keep them from searching her house? If they got past her and found his bed empty, they'd track him and beat him, and she'd suffer horrendous indignities. She had to stall them. But for how long? Impossible. What would interest them more than Adam? At that moment, she saw the eager lecherous expression of the stutterer.

The captain was climbing down from his saddle, ready to push past Victoria into the house. There would be nothing she could do, no way to hold him back. It would be mere minutes before they'd be at her, and when they finished with her, they'd set off to find Adam. It was William's fault. If that man hadn't run off with that imbecile Isaiah, her son would be home safe, and she'd be asleep. But there was no time for thought-clouding anger. She had to think of some clever diversion, but her quick mind failed her. Belligerently she blocked the door.

The man said nothing as he approached the porch. As pointless as it seemed, she stepped forward to confront him.

When he reached the step, he lifted his slouch hat, and ran his hand over his dark, long hair.

She couldn't see him clearly in the dark with the torch now behind him. This man had been surprisingly genteel considering he represented the dregs of white society. She was sure he and his fellows were compassionless. They were county-hired thugs, but she was amazed by his hesitation and curious what he would do. One of his companions offered a whip, but he ignored him, looking at Victoria. She wished she could see his expression.

He spoke civilly, but with conviction, "Now, Victoria, you get out of the way . . . you must fetch him for us . . . now. You're just putting it off . . . and that riles us."

"What do you want with my boy?"

Thornton, clearly the most nettled of the four, answered, yelling "Your . . ."

Victoria forgot the man before her and turned on the torch carrier, "Get out of here! I don't want to see you."

One of the other two men who remained on his horse chuckled. "Thornton, she don't like you much, and I'd say she's got the best of you." He chuckled again.

Thornton was getting down from his horse. "SSShut up," he yelled at the man mocking him. "I got . . . I'll get the bbbest of her!"

The captain had taken advantage of the confusion to come onto the porch, but Victoria saw him and slid back directly in front of the door. She set herself for the blow sure to follow.

The man again stopped. She could smell his breath and was grateful he'd not been drinking. He smiled at her. "I admire you, Victoria. Always have. You're different . . . than the rest, and I know you're important to the judge . . . but that doesn't change what I must do."

She hoped the respect he showed was genuine, and oddly it made her feel good, but she'd seen it used as a trick before and didn't slacken her concentration. She tightened her muscles in anticipation of a blow. With half closed eyes she said again, "What do you want with him?"

"I'll tell you, and then I'll pass. We caught him—we think it was him—without a pass . . . doing no good, but he got away. We didn't pass anyone, so he didn't come this way. If he's in bed, it must not have been him. It's time to let me in or bring him out. If he's here, we go away peacefully. If you don't call him down . . ."

"How do you even know my boy?"

"I've seen him before . . . with the judge. I've heard him. The boy tonight stuttered like your boy. Now let us in."

"The judge won't take kindly to this visit."

"I'll explain it. No one wants slaves wandering about."

"He's not a slave."

"None the less, we don't want freedmen gathering, wandering."

"He's in bed."

"Then everything's fine." He pushed into Victoria, and Thornton, still with torch in hand and in a frenzied rage, pushed the captain from behind. Victoria resisted, pushing her forearm into the man's neck and her force was doubled by Thornton pushing from behind. The man gagged. Suddenly, he pulled away from Victoria and shoved Thornton backward. The latter flew off the porch, and the torch fell into the nearby grass, spontaneously raising the smell of burning grass.

The captain moved to hover over Thornton who lay on his back, shocked by the unexpected blow.

Neither man said anything, but glowered at one another in the dark. One of the other two pattyrollers got off his horse and picked up the smoking torch and stamped in the smoldering grass as a second-story window opened and a sleepy boy's voice called down, "MMMama, I can't sssleep. There's too much nnnoise."

The men were silent, but Victoria didn't let the miracle pass. "There . . . you woke him! Now, I'll be up the rest of the night trying to get him back to sleep." Without turning her back to the patrollers and without their response, she lifted the door latch and sidled into the sitting room, slamming and bolting the door behind her.

Emotionally exhausted, she felt like collapsing but was driven by a consuming desire to hold her son. She rapidly ascended the small stairs and found Adam watching the men through the already-closed window. He heard her come in and whispered, "They're leaving, Mama."

"Praise the Lord," she responded in whispered passion. "He is our safety and our hope." She approached quickly, putting her arms around him as they watched the men ride away. When they were gone, Adam turned to his mother who wouldn't let go of him, and said, "We've got to rrrescue William."

"Where is he?"

"HHHiding in the woods. He's ill again. He helped me, but he's not well. He's nnnot far."

"We can't help him now. We'll have to wait till dawn before we venture out."

"We have to help him," he whispered angrily.

"We can't," she said firmly. "It wouldn't be safe for us . . . or him. We have to wait."

Adam squeezed his lips together in a pout.

After a long silence, Victoria whispered, "What happened? Where did you go?"

Adam recounted that he had followed Isaiah and William after he heard the judge tell her they left. He had planned to join as a drummer boy but didn't make it to the recruiters before dark. Patrollers caught him and were about to beat him when William surprised them. He whispered, "But I didn't know it was William till he caught up to me, because I ran to get away." He continued the story, telling her William got weak, "But he told me to sneak into the house, pretend I was sleeping. I'm so glad, Mama—how did you know?—that you left the back door open so I could get in quietly.

She listened without interrupting, somber, considering everything he said. When she heard his last comment, she asked, "The back door open? Did you shut, lock it?"

"No," he whispered. "William told me not to make noise."

She looked at him briefly, rose and looked out the window again. Something was there. Was it her imagination? Had she seen something move around the house. She listened carefully and said calmly, quietly to Adam. "Go to bed. You must be tired."

"BBBut William."

"Now!"

Chapter 28

April 1864, Eastern Kentucky

Victoria moved into the tiny hall, closing the door behind her. She quickly descended the stairs between sitting room and kitchen. Her worst fears were confirmed as she reached the bottom stair. Something moved in the kitchen.

"Who's there?" she called, regretting it the instant she'd revealed herself. In response, she heard a brief terrorizing and recognized laugh. She stepped into the kitchen, demanding, "What are you doing here?"

"Ssso . . . you dddo . . . remem . . . remem . . . remember me." Then he whispered loudly, with mocking pathos, "I thought you'd forgotten."

She came as close as she could to screaming at him in a whisper, "I remember exactly what you were, are and always will be. Now, get out before I . . ."

"Befffore? YYYou always tttalked big."

"Get out. Never show your face again," she whispered furiously.

"It's nnnot so easy."

"Get out!"

"Aren't you jjjust a little afraid? HHHave you forgotten?"

Savagely, she moved toward the man to attack him and only at the last second did she see something in his hand. She jumped back.

"Ah. III'm not alone. I've come with my old friend. Do yyyou remember hhhim? He . . . he . . . he remembers you."

He took one step towards her and whispered. "He still remembers you obeying him. Yes, he . . ."

A sharp twang cut his words short, and he crumpled backward striking his head against the door frame as he fell, his knife clattering to the kitchen floor.

Relieved, she closed her eyes. What had happened? She didn't care. She only cared that he'd stopped. She was sweating, sobbing. Her heart raced. But then he grabbed her waist. She screamed and lunged backward. But he followed, clinging to her. They bumped against furniture, and she pushed him away, following close as he tripped backward. She was crying, screaming—no longer in a whisper, fighting him, beating him, hitting him as hard as she could, over and over again. He said nothing, did nothing to fend off her blows, but slumped, hitting his head on a small table and groaned.

The groan. It wasn't his. She knew that groan, and she followed him again, crouching by him, hugging him, crying, "William, William, are you all right? I didn't . . ."

He laughed softly, hoarsely, groaning at the same time. "Yuh're crushin' me," he whispered, barely able to get the sounds out for the ferocity of her hug.

She half-laughed, stood quickly, smoothed her dress and waited for her pounding heart to slow, then said matter-of-factly, "I'm sorry."

He lay exhausted, beaten, without saying anything, but breathing loudly, raspingly, with a periodic chuckle.

Frightened by what he'd heard, Adam had come down the stairs. He said nothing, but found his way to the kitchen stove and opened it. Without looking around in the light glowing from the stove, he took a sliver of wood that rested nearby and poked its end into the embers, pulling it out when it flamed. He reached up to a nearby hook and pulled down the old Betty lamp, put the flaming wood stick to the twisted-cotton-cloth wick. The material slowly flamed and gave a white dim light that brightened as it took hold. He tossed the stick into the stove and closed it, never noticing the unconscious man on the floor. He walked gingerly into the sitting room, giving the lamp a chance to burn brighter. There he found his mother standing by William who was lying on the floor. Neither said anything, looking intently at each other in Adam's faint light.

"Am I to assume you weren't trying to hurt me?" Victoria said quietly.

William, whose face was puffy, swollen, scratched and red, responded, "Thought yuh was fallin'. Just catchin' yuh."

"Yes. Am I to assume you feel as bad as you look?"

"Worse."

"Not all my fault? I hope."

"No, just my face and added some to the headache."

Adam watched silently.

"I beat you pretty well," she said, bending down to put her hand gently on his cheek.

"Reckon so."

"What happened to that monster?"

"Hit him with a shovel. Found it out back."

"Is he dead?"

Adam interrupted, excitedly, "What mmmonster? A monster!"

His mother looked up, aware for the first time he had come down the stairs. "Adam, what are you doing here? I told you to go to bed."

"I couldn't, Mama. I cccouldn't."

"Since you're here, let's use that lamp to see what we've got to do." She stood up, glanced at William. She said quickly, "You know I'm sorry . . . and thank you."

William, still on his back, didn't answer, and the boy and his mother moved to the kitchen where the shifting lamp light faintly illuminated the body, inches from where Adam had grabbed and lit the lamp. Adam shuddered, thinking about stepping on it in the dark. "He's not a real mmmonster," he said disappointed.

"Oh, yes . . . he is."

"Is hhhe dead, MMMama?"

"Seems like you and I are always trying to see if bodies are dead." She bent over the man. She didn't want to touch him, but listened for breathing. She heard it. It wasn't loud, but it was rhythmic. "He's alive, and his head is going to hurt in the morning. Good!"

"Wh . . . Wh . . . Where are we going to put him, Mama? We dddon't have enough beds. CCCan we leave him here?"

"No," his mother responded sharply. "We will not leave him here, and we'll not put him in a soft bed. He had no business here! No business being anywhere near here. We'll drag him outside."

She was already at the back door, which still stood open. She stepped down onto the ground, turned, reached for the man's hands and tugged the unconscious body.

Adam called out, "I'll help."

She shrieked, "No! Stay where you are! Don't touch him! He's the Devil."

Adam stepped back, frightened. He'd never heard such an outburst from his mother.

She grunted and pulled harder. The man's body bumped out the door, his head, buttocks and feet thudding hard on the ground as each cleared the cabin. When he was completely outside, she dropped his arms and frantically wiped her hands on her skirt. She shook her head, twisting her facial features in horror, stepped to his side and kicked his midsection. She glared at him and kicked again.

Adam watched without a word. He'd never seen his mother mistreat anyone. He stood motionless, waiting for a signal from his mother that her mood had passed or that she needed him to do something. Behind him, William had arrived. He put his hands on Adam's shoulders, resting his weight heavily on the boy. The boy shifted to hold the pressure. Victoria looked at Adam, surprisingly unashamed of what he'd witnessed. She saw William and asked, "What can we do with him?"

William asked, "'Live . . . still?"

Victoria bent toward the body and heard breathing. "Revoltingly so."

William was silent. He had to make sure no one suspected this man had ever been here, or if he had, that he'd left and been injured elsewhere. William finally responded, "Needs to go home."

Victoria replied sarcastically, "Shouldn't have come."

William smiled. "Where's the horse?"

"How should I know? All I know is he wandered into my house in the middle of the night. Some lunatic hit him over the head with a shovel. And some old man attacked me." She was laughing. "Definitely an old man!"

Adam relaxed as he heard his mother laugh, and William asked, "Adam, think the man that hit him is old?"

"III think . . . Hey, ttthat was you! YYYou aren't old."

"Oh, yes he is," retorted Victoria. "If he weren't, he'd already have told me what do to with this fiend."

William felt a deep anger in Victoria even as she joshed him and hoped it wasn't directed at him. He'd felt closer to her than ever just minutes earlier. What had happened since? "Find the horse."

"Why?"

"Find the horse, woman! Quick, 'fore he wakes."

Victoria looked at William, hoping to see his expression. Was he angry? She wasn't sure. She'd better search for the horse.

William turned to Adam. "Listen careful . . . real careful, Adam. Go to the woods . . . near the road or clearings. Take that lamp. Find dried vines from last year . . . on the trees . . . the trunks—the ones hairy like. Don't touch 'em with yor hands. Don't let 'em touch skin. Do yuh have gloves? Use gloves and bring 'em in. Just the hairy ones."

Adam was out the door, leaping over the body, running quickly to the shed. He moved so rapidly the flame of the lamp waned, nearly extinguished, then blazed hot. He was out of the shed quickly, running without hesitation into the woods. By the time Adam disappeared into the dark, Victoria had returned, leading the man's horse.

William entered the kitchen, opened the stove door for light, stepped outside, carefully stepping over the man.

Victoria saw him. "On him! Step on him! Don't you treat him that way!"

When William saw Victoria, he smiled, ignored her demand, and thought how much fun he was having. He took the horse reins.

"Are you . . . can you do this?" she asked.

"I got a little strength left . . . with you here."

Shocked by his answer, she didn't reply, instead asking, "What are you doing?"

William smiled mischievously without answering.

"You test my patience."

"But I love yuh."

Victoria stepped away from him, her visage softened, her shoulders dropped imperceptibly. "What?"

"I love yuh."

She didn't respond, but he didn't expect her to.

Adam came back almost immediately, with long, thick ropes of vine. He dragged them carefully along the ground.

William looked at the vine and grinned.

Victoria looked at Adam. "What are you doing? That's poison ivy. Now you're going to get a rash. Did William tell you to do that?"

"YYYes, but he told me to wwwear gloves. I kn . . . kn . . . knew what he wanted." His head twitched as he spoke.

"That'll do fine," William added. "Never gotten no rash in my life. Have yuh?" He directed his question to Victoria.

"Yes, and so has Adam, but he doesn't get it bad. But I do, so keep it away from me."

"Yes, MMMama."

Adam laid the vine down and carefully removed the gloves, dropping them on the ground.

William directed, "Bring that lamp over here. We're gunna try and get him in the saddle."

"Won't it hurt the horse . . . poison ivy?" Victoria asked.

"Horses don't never get poison ivy. Don't know of no animal gets poison ivy . . . 'cept men."

"Just people," Victoria said reflectively. "Because we already have so much poison in us."

"Adam, hold the reins! Talk to him real, real nice," William directed.

Without instruction, Victoria stepped toward William and together they struggled to lift and push the man till he was positioned in the saddle. When the man would moan or shift, she would push harder and cry, "Oh, shut up!"

When they had him in the saddle, William turned to Adam. "Go get all washed up—yor hands, arms—and change yor clothes . . . in case yuh touched a vine. Important no one gets the rash."

"You're getting mighty bossy with my son."

"Only 'cause I love yuh."

Victoria didn't respond.

William carefully wrapped the reins multiple times around each of the man's hands. He then wrapped two lengths of the vine tight around the man's neck and laid him against the neck of the horse, crossing both ends of the vine on the man's lips and open mouth, then braiding the four ends together in front of the horse's neck, leaving the braid loosely tied at the vine ends. He did the same around the horse's barrel and the man's midsection, stuffing part of the vine under the man's shirt and into his trousers. He again left the braids tangled but unknotted at their ends. Lastly, he wrapped the remaining vine multiple times around the man's thighs and the saddle's fender. He left the ends loose, but tucked them well up the man's pant legs. Victoria watched him without comment.

When he finished, William looked towards her. "Care for a stroll?"

"Where to?" she asked casually.

"Just 'bout. Beautiful night for a walk . . . and I might need yor help comin' back."

"I'm not touching you," she said sharply. Realizing it had come out differently than intended, she added, "Not till you've washed off . . . your arms and hands."

He didn't respond, but took hold of the bridle's throat latch and led the horse around the house and toward town. He walked the horse till the cabin would have been out of sight on the clearest day, then let go of the bridle. He walked along the horse's side, smacked its hindquarter, and the horse broke into a brisk trot.

Victoria had walked by him the whole way. Watching the horse bolt, she asked, "How long will the vines keep that man up there?"

"Ain't the slightest notion. Hopin' they come off 'fore he gets wherever he's goin'." He looked at Victoria, then began laughing.

Victoria shook her head but couldn't help joining the laughter. "They may figure it all out."

"Maybe . . . probably."

"And if they do."

"I'm the one that done it."

"We have to say the same thing. Adam, too."

"I think they'll come," he concluded heavily. "Yes, they'll come. Was he one o' the patrollers what grabbed Adam?"

"They know he was here."

"Victoria, I'm tired. Just tell me what to say."

She looked at his shape in the darkness. "Just say you love me, again."

Chapter 29

April 1864, Eastern Kentucky

Dawn broke a few hours after Adam, William and Victoria went to bed, and the light awoke Victoria. Why get up so early? She dozed, but the merciless light brightened the room till she was fully awake and restless. She sat up and stared vacantly out the small bedroom window into the ragged patches of blue sky visible above the trees behind her house.

She was unsettled but never revisited what had happened during the night. She rose, descended the stairs to the sitting room and looked out onto the road. All was quiet. Her eyes landed on the grass burned by the torch. Instantly, it unleashed a torrent of overwhelming memories cascading simultaneously through her mind. She leaped up the stairs, needing a reassuring look at her son. She jerked open his thin door. He was asleep, peaceful. He was safe. She watched him briefly, then closed the door and walked quietly back down the stairs.

She stopped at the bottom, noting that everything was in disarray—the kitchen table askew, chairs out of place, the doused Betty lamp sitting on the table. Half expecting it to be covered in blood, she looked at the floor—but it wasn't. She was relieved, grateful William's desperate blow to the man had not cut the victim. Divine grace, she thought . . . divine judgment on the head of the monster.

Straightening the table and chairs and replacing the lamp on the wall hanger, she worked her way to the back door, unbolted it, raised the latch and slowly opened it, peering at the ground for tell-tale blood. She saw only small bits of hairy vine strewn across the lawn. She stepped down and walked toward the shed, pushing the door open and looking at the floor where William lay softly breathing on a thick pile of straw. He didn't stir.

An impulse to hug him moved her, but she restrained it, remembering he needed rest above all else. As she watched him sleep, irritation crept in, and she wondered what had driven him to enlist. It was his passion for the army that had created yesterday's disaster. She hadn't yet made sense of what had happened or what it meant, and she didn't even know why William had come back. But Adam was safe . . . for now. She felt anxiety for him, but she didn't focus on it. They had survived the night.

Her mind came back to William. Regardless of what he'd done, he'd risked everything to save Adam . . . and her. She waited, hoping her presence and streaming sunlight would disturb him. She wanted to talk to him, be with him, touch him, but he didn't move. For now, she was on her own.

She quietly closed the door and began her normal morning routine. She drew water from the well, washed her face, then went inside to stoke embers for breakfast.

"Victoria," she heard from outside the front of the house. She wiped her hands on her apron and calmly stepped through the sitting room. She knew the pleasant voice. When she reached the front door, she opened it, but he wasn't there. There was sharp knock on the back door, and she flinched at the noise and moved toward it. She cracked the kitchen door cautiously until she was sure it was the judge, then opened it quickly.

"Heard anything?" he asked.

"Everything's fine. Come in. I'm getting breakfast."

"What happened?"

She breathed deeply, "I found the boy . . . and William."

"William? Splendid. Not Isaiah?"

She grimaced, "Isaiah? I don't care . . . not at this point."

He raised his head, looking at her inquisitively.

She continued, "Have you heard anything in town?"

"Town? Why?"

"It was exciting here last night," she explained, telling him as much as she knew about what had happened.

He listened soberly without interrupting. His jaw was tight. When Victoria finished, he looked out the still-open door towards the shed. "Still out there? Hum." He looked at her. "This is difficult."

"Do you think so? Won't it just pass . . . like a storm?"

He looked at her without affection. "This will come back on our heads. He won't let go of what happened to him . . . not if he's alive. And if he's not alive, they'll know where to look. No, this will come back on our heads." He stood silently thinking. "We've got to get you . . . both of you away . . . out of Kentucky. I've needed to go to Washington City for a while. I have business with the government. Maybe now's a good time." He stopped, looked intensely at her. "You need to leave now. There's no time for breakfast. What were you thinking? The longer you stay here, the more chance trouble—real trouble—will catch you." He frowned.

She adopted his deeply troubled expression.

"William needs to get to the farm now!"

"What about Adam . . . and me?" she asked in an uncharacteristically anxious tone. Her mood had shifted. The judge had shattered the deception of normalcy and visions of hope and love. His fear infused her. "What happens when they come back?" she asked desperately.

"You can't be here!" he responded emphatically.

Close to panic, she bitterly castigated herself. "What have I been doing? I've been walking around the house like nothing's happened. We shouldn't be here. We should have left in the night."

"We'll hide you at the farm . . . keep it quiet till we steal you away. You know they'll come to me if you're missing."

She could see his anxiety increasing. He wanted to be gone, to be away from her. He'd never been like this before.

Sternly he said, "Come quickly. It's not going to be easy, if the man died. They'll be looking at what happened to him, scour the woods, try to figure out who killed him."

"If he's alive?"

"He'll bring the sheriff to your door."

"If we run, we'll look guilty."

"Are you new to Kentucky?" He said sarcastically, looking at her coldly. "Guilt . . . innocence, they won't matter. Pack clothes—clothes you'll need to get started elsewhere. Don't bring them with you. Stash them somewhere safe. I'll send someone for them later . . . when . . . if things quiet down. Right now, you need to get to the woods and quickly to the farm. I'm leaving! I can't be seen here. Don't tell anyone I was here. No one!"

She was stunned by his commanding tone.

The judge stepped from the kitchen to the ground, vaulted to his saddle and rode hard from the yard.

Victoria, responding to new-felt horror, ascended the stairs two steps at a time, yelling, "Adam, wake up!"

The boy leaped from bed, jolted by his mother's cry, and by the time she reached him, he was distraught and shaking.

"Adam, get dressed. Get a change of clothes! Put them in my bedroom . . . on the bed. Now!"

"WWWhat's the ma . . . ma . . . matter?"

"We'll talk later. Hurry. Now!"

She ran to the window, looked at the dirt road. Everything seemed oddly peaceful, but she ran by the boy and his bed, leaving the door open as she crossed into her own bedroom. Her door remained open as she gathered a change of clothes, stuffed them and those Adam collected into a case and began carrying it downstairs.

She stopped midway down the stairs. "We'll need blankets. Adam, grab the blankets from the beds. Bring them to the shed."

Victoria didn't wait. She wanted to get the case into the shed before anyone saw her. She wanted to be away. She ran across the yard. She was sweating. It was a cool but very moist morning, and the sweat already on her skin and clothes refused to dry. She reached the shed door, opened it, and there still in a deep sleep on fresh straw was William. She admired him. He seemed peaceful. She whispered loudly, "William . . . William, we've got to get away. Wake up."

He stirred, stretched, opening his eyes. It took him a moment to focus. One eye was swollen where Victoria had punched him the night before, and his face was crusted with dried blood where she'd scratched him.

Controlling her emotions, she repeated calmly, "William, we've got to get away."

He rose to his feet, still groggy. "What's in the bag?"

"Clothes. Can you put them below?"

William immediately scraped the straw away, lifted the door and grabbed the case from Victoria. "Where's Adam?"

"Here!" Adam whispered.

William looked at him without commenting on the blankets in his arms and climbed down into the cellar, carefully holding the bag as he backed down the ladder. He faintly remembered his time with Victoria in the dark. "Trapped with an angel," he whispered to himself.

"What should I do with these?" Adam whispered.

She responded quietly, "Hand them to William."

The boy approached the opening in the floor waiting for William to ask for them, but his mother heard something from the road. Horses? A wagon? She didn't know.

"Just throw them in and get down there," she whispered.

Adam threw the blankets down into the hole, and William caught them, carefully laying them on the case to keep them as clean as possible. He was surprised to see Adam descend and Victoria follow. She paused on the ladder to listen again. No one said anything.

William thought of the straw on the shed's floor. If someone came looking for them, it would be a finger pointing to where they hid. Their only hope then would be to hide in the hidden room, and William shrank at the thought.

Victoria was motionless, holding her breath. Adam approached William, and he pulled the boy close.

Victoria glanced at William. She smiled, but she was silhouetted so he couldn't see her face. "You two are getting to be like glue," she said softly, turning again to watch and listen for anything that wasn't squirrels, birds or deer.

Minutes passed in silence. Finally William suggested, "Maybe we should go. The longer we stay . . ."

"Yes," she said and carefully ascended the ladder. She reached for Adam's hand. "Adam, come up. We've got to get to the farm."

William followed, and she offered her hand, but he declined, saying gently, "I'm better today."

He rolled a barrel over the trapdoor, dragged straw with his foot to even it over the floor, and followed the others outside.

They ran into the woods and were quickly shielded from the road. The undergrowth was thick and hard to penetrate. The trees, not fully leafed out, didn't filter the sound of travelers who drifted by, so to avoid discovery, no one spoke. Adam, who had spoken more since William appeared, felt the tension and stayed mute.

Victoria was considering their immediate circumstances. She periodically peeped at William and her attempted analysis of the situation would be lost in emotion. He walked silently ahead, clearing their path of brambles, vines and branches, holding them back as they passed.

He was an enigma. Barely able one minute to raise an arm, the next he was crushing a man's skull with a shovel. Minutes earlier, he had been sound asleep, unconscious to the world, now energetically he trail-blazed for them. She wanted to love him, did love him, but he left without talking to Adam, without discussing it with her. Was he whom she thought or were her feelings just a mothering reflex to care for a man recovering from illness? She remembered his declaration of love and thrilled with excitement.

Then she recalled that he—his foolishness—had brought this crisis. She was briefly angry at herself for putting Adam in danger by bringing this stranger into their home as if he were some injured wild animal to save. She was just like Adam, she thought. But she loved being with William. Even now, escaping with him through the woods invigorated her . . . and she felt oddly safe.

She shook her head expelling thoughts of William so she could concentrate on their danger.

Even when they reached the farm, they couldn't assume safety. They'd have to watch the field hands, house slaves, visitors . . . even the judge. Any one might betray them, given the right incentive.

For the first time in her life, she doubted the judge's loyalty. He'd always been exceptionally kind, loving and respectful, and they'd enjoyed a fulfilling intimacy. He'd freed Adam and her, but this catastrophe tested his affection because it put him in peril. It also threatened his ability to protect his slaves. He'd made informal manumission agreements with many, and they continued willingly to feign slavery while taking his pay.

He would allow anyone to permanently leave the plantation anytime, but demanded he or she meet with him before going away. He had been annoyed when Isaiah and William had left without talking to him, and she would have been angered by his attitude, but she knew it was just who he was. Even in his relationship with her, there were subtle signs in unconscious gestures, expressions and words reminding her that they were not equals.

A new suspicion flashed as they walked. The judge, following careful deliberation, might give all of them up if his safety were threatened. His rapid, nervous departure upon hearing what had happened told her their circumstances were dire. But she knew the judge loved her. Surely, he wouldn't give Adam and her up, but he might offer William to save the rest.

She glanced nervously at William as he continued forging their way. He was looking at her and smiled, but she diverted her eyes in an attempt to conceal her thoughts. Yes, she could easily imagine the judge giving him up. If she were in the judge's situation, she might do it. Was she then leading William to a trap? Again she peeked in his direction, dropping her eyes when she saw him gaze questioningly at her.

Even if the judge refused to give anyone up, he'd be under suspicion. Their relationship was well known, understood as master and mistress . . . that Adam was his child. If she went missing and was suspected of assaulting the man, they'd watch the judge until he led them to her.

William was hurt that Victoria had diverted her eyes. He wondered why, then remembered they were running because he'd been so easily . . . so foolishly led into trouble by Isaiah. He looked at Adam, briefly entertained by thoughts of the boy trying to enlist, but his mind returned quickly to Victoria. What was he to do?

He'd never felt for anyone the love he felt for her. He'd loved before, been married, but it was always under the watchful, directing, commanding, controlling eye of a master. But this time, there was no one cajoling him to court Victoria or demanding quick offspring for the plantation. No one was evaluating whether the two of them would produce offspring big and strong . . . and docile. He'd fallen in love with Victoria with no limits. He was excited at the love and the freedom. He felt a comfort in her strength.

All his life, he'd been relegated to a poor patch of emotional land where self-confidence could never sprout, and even now he couldn't tell if the ground had grown simple, tenacious flowering weeds of survival or new fruitful instincts and blossoming judgment. He kept telling himself he was smart, capable, strong, but the conversation died the minute he was confronted by a white man or woman who wanted or expected little of him.

Even the benevolent Richmans had made it clear he was not like them. He was their possession, and they'd be kind as long as he responded to their every demand, wish and whim. The Richmans had been charitable because they were gracious to everyone and everything—their friends, dogs, horses and slaves.

Victoria, in her freedom, seemed to flaunt her ability to be who she wanted to be, and she was ennobled by her expectation of respect. He'd felt fondness in their exchanges, especially in the last hours, and his body trembled at the memory. But he was troubled by Victoria's relationship with the judge. Was she in love with him? Was she still his mistress? Adam was his son. The boy's light complexion and his judge-like profile left little doubt. Did the judge demand favors of her, and did she accept the arrangement so he'd free and protect her and her son? Was her freedom really just a different form of coercion . . . a different face of slavery—submitting body and soul for the facade of freedom? How could she subject herself to this most iniquitous form of slavery? Yet, how could she resist it?

He'd seen other slaves struggle under this weight. It humiliated him to think these women, even his own wives and daughters, had no choice but to submit to demands made. And the demands had been made. How could a man retain dignity, knowing wife and daughters could be snatched or borrowed . . . to satisfy a moment's lust? How could a woman survive the very ordeal, the humiliation?

Perhaps, he thought hopefully, the judge's and Victoria's relationship was better than that. Victoria was wonderful, after all. Perhaps the judge really did love her and would have married her but for law and society. She was beautiful, with her caramel complexion, strong body, clear face, dark eyes, regal nose and well-shaped lips. He understood why the judge would want her.

But Victoria showed affection to William. If she consented to the judge's relationship, how could she be interested in another man? Was this some agreed-to feigned affection camouflaging their sin? Or was she less than what William saw in her? Had the judge humbled her and made her common? That was not his concern, but it had seemed in the early morning hours as if she loved William.

He frowned and pulled a vine from the ground. Why would Victoria consider him? He was 10 or 15 years older than her. He had little hope, and other than the now seemingly elusive and suddenly uninteresting goal of enlisting in the army, he had no plan at all. The judge, William guessed, was just a few years older than Victoria. He was a man with a plantation and respect in the town. William could feel his mood shifting from one supporting active flight—strong and fast-thinking—to depression. Why should he hurry? The judge would turn him in for striking the white man. What would be his alternative? He would above all else protect his mistress and son.

William realized he could serve no purpose but to protect the others. His depression rose to resignation. William would hide Victoria and Adam at the farm. He'd make sure they got there safely, no matter what he had to do. He glanced briefly at Victoria's face, hoping not to catch her eye but to admire her anonymously, and she obliged, looking down at a Carolina rose that had caught Adam's trousers. He waited, watching her gently pull his pants from the thorns and then hurry the boy ahead.

Just as she raised her eyes in William's direction, he dropped his to affect looking at a wispy branch he was now holding back for them. She saw him drop his eyes and was sorry they hadn't made eye contact. This was a gentle, kind man. Adam had perceived him correctly when he'd seen his despair in the woods. In the days he'd spent at their home and in the brief minutes they'd spent together since he moved to the judge's house, she'd seen selflessness, humility and kindness toward all, including Isaiah who had continually baited and sought to annoy and embarrass him. He'd allowed Isaiah to call him "ole man," without resisting. She knew the appellation was now used by many slaves at the farm and suspected it hurt William deeply.

Perhaps he was too patient, perhaps weak. But then she remembered last night. She still didn't know exactly what had happened, but he'd come back to save them. He must have used every bit of courage and strength to save Adam. Then he saved her. This was no weak man. She remembered his feverish confession of killing a man to save a friend. She suddenly ached to hold William's hand, but he was too far ahead.

Then there was his loving treatment of Adam. She couldn't doubt his love for her son, or her son's love for him. Her maternal instinct and gratitude drew her emotionally to William, and she looked again in his direction, hoping for a smile, a confident nod, a playful wink. But he was busy holding another bush out of their way, and she dropped her head still thinking warmly about him.

William was thinking about his last wife. She'd been his favorite. He'd not been forced to marry her. He'd chosen her—with approval and supervision of her master and Master Richman. He'd loved her and their time together—the brief Saturday nights and Sundays brought periodic happiness in a life of desperate loneliness.

But thoughts of loving Victoria without approval from anyone exhilarated him. His energy level rose suddenly, he felt like yelling out, and he effortlessly pulled a sapling from the ground and flung it to the side.

Yesterday, he collapsed after his early morning hike with Isaiah, now he could have barred an army. He smiled, feeling the power of being close to Victoria. Yesterday, he'd weakened with every step he'd taken away from her. Today, in her proximity, he could have felled a tree with a shove from his broad shoulders. His eyes met hers and held her gaze. A deep, powerful laugh exploded from him. Embarrassed, he was about to whisper an apology, but glimpsed that she likewise had forgotten their danger and had fully inhaled his passion.

But what of her relationship with the judge?

Chapter 30

April 1864, Eastern Kentucky

When they reached the farm, William stopped at the edge of the woods, looking into the fields around the manor house. Close by they could see the handful of slave cabins along the tree line. William pointed toward the cabins, and Victoria nodded assent. The trio moved silently, within the visual protection of the trees, to the cabin where William lived. The brightness of day hid them in the contrast of the forest shade.

William signaled to Adam and Victoria to stay put and moved casually from the woods toward the small cabin he shared with Isaiah and four other men. He breathed deeply, trying to conquer the fear that had settled on him. He expected the judge to suddenly appear with the sheriff close behind. He kept walking steadily as he made for the cabin. If he were caught, he'd warn Victoria with a shout so she and the boy could flee. He reached the cabin door and pushed it inward with his foot. It scraped against the floor, and he stepped inside.

Victoria watched him, praying constantly in a whisper Adam couldn't understand. Minutes passed before they saw William re-emerge. He didn't acknowledge them but walked toward a large wood bowl. He lifted it and carried it to the well pump. He raised and lowered the pump handle till water gushed into the bowl and over its edges. Adam watched intently as William rested the bowl on the ground, removed his shirt and shoes.

"What's he doing, Mama?" whispered Adam.

"Adam, we're about to see a man take a bath," she said dismissively. "He's telling us everything looks normal."

They could see William washing his chest, back, face, arms, tightly cropped hair. When he was done, he poured the water carefully on the ground, took a rag and dried himself off, ending with his feet. He slipped his feet back into his shoes, carefully picked up his shirt and walked again into the cabin. Victoria was impatient. She wanted to know exactly what was going on.

Dried, dressed in clean clothes and smiling, William reappeared. He didn't look at the woods, but walked aimlessly toward the big house. Victoria commented to no one, "He's very good at this. I'd never suspect he's frightened . . . to death. He looks like he just came in from the fields for the day . . . and he looks so handsome."

Adam smiled.

Halfway to the house, William seemed to change his mind. Instead of going to the house, he turned to the stables. Had he seen something? Was he now in a panic, but unwilling to show it? Was he trying to escape?

Adam whispered, "He's going to see if the slaves there have heard anything."

"That's right," his mother agreed, relieved and impressed with Adam's quick mind.

William entered the stables, but came out within a few minutes. Again he happily ambled toward the big house. When he reached it, he discreetly looked toward Victoria and Adam, flashed a grin, then disappeared behind the structure.

Once he left their line of vision, they were again in disconcerting ignorance. Victoria didn't know if some trap inside would clamp closed upon her new love, and as they waited without word or indication, Victoria's imagination turned to the worst possibilities. Would they hold him inside until Victoria lost patience and came to the house and nab her, too? Were they readying William for a whipping in the shadow of the house, where Victoria couldn't see? Would he soon howl in torture's agony? Did they know she and Adam hid in the shadows? Minutes passed. Why didn't he come out, at least give her some signal he was fine, that everything was going to work out? Even the judge could come out and give some sign. Or had the judge given him up.

Five minutes, 10 minutes, 15 minutes passed. Trap or not, Victoria wouldn't wait longer, and she took a step toward the house. She turned to Adam, pointed her finger sternly in his direction and said in her firmest voice, "Wait there! Do not move! And do not follow me!"

Chapter 31

April 1864, Richmond, Virginia

"**C**aptain Richardson, we have an obligation," Miss Morrow said sternly. She again wore a dark skirt and jacket and white lace collar, a different brooch at her neck. She sat straight, looking severely at the commandant, gloved hands folded properly on her lap.

"Obligation? Don't be silly," the captain responded, leaning forward, pulling his chair closer to his desk. "What you demand is not possible and is treason." He lowered his voice. "My duty is to keep her safe and"—he emphasized the last words—"behind these walls."

"Sir, I am not silly." She had taken offense. "I've never been called—nor considered—silly. I ask you to remember that. But we do have an obligation that goes beyond keeping her jailed . . . something higher. Captain, let's not forget, it was under your protection that she was attacked. Your avaricious guard . . . for filthy lucre sold her to the first bidder."

"Yes." The captain was agitated and shifted nervously. "No need to bring that up. We searched him, found the money. I dealt with him. He's a prisoner now."

"Rightfully so."

"She's no longer in danger."

"No one knows where the man who attacked her is."

A pudgy man in the office who listened patiently with eyes half closed interceded, "Someone knows. Someone's hiding him."

The commandant looked surprised. "You think some-one's protecting him?"

"How can a man chewed on by that thing," he glanced at Nero asleep in the corner, "go unnoticed for days in town? I've contacted the hospitals, doctors . . . anyone who might have seen him. He's nowhere. He's hidden."

Captain Richardson was visibly concerned. "Surely he won't try again."

The second man, balding with long gray-streaked hair, smiled. "Attack Mrs. Henderson again? I'd have thought him unlikely to try the first time. We can't predict what he'll do, what he's capable of . . . what he's driven to do. I doubt he knows himself."

Miss Morrow was impatient with the side conversation and blurted out, "The lady is in a family way."

"Surely, Miss Morrow," the captain said sarcastically, "you won't blame me for that, too. If she is, she was in that way when she arrived. We've treated her well. No harm's come to her." He turned back to the second man. "Sheriff, what do you mean you don't think he knows what he'll do?"

"Just that. I don't think he had a well thought out plan to see her last time, didn't think about whether it was good or bad, dangerous or safe. He didn't think at all . . . or he's mad and driven by insanity. If I were a betting man, I would wager he's mad and capable of anything."

The woman was not interested in understanding the man who tried to assault Betsy, but she did add, "He'd have to be insane to come into a prison to attack someone."

The captain was not impressed with Miss Morrow's observation, ignored her and spoke directly to the sheriff, "Are you saying he was walking by the prison one day and just decided he'd go in and see the woman he tried to kill? That's absurd . . . unless he is mad."

The sheriff smiled, ran his hand along the side of his head through his long, flowing hair. "This man is a murderer . . . no question. He's a juggler . . . a confidence man. He's comfortable with disguises, bribery. He's arrogant. He believes he's entitled to anything and everything . . . and that he better take it before someone else does. He believes, I think, that he's entitled to . . . perhaps owns Mrs. Henderson in some perverse way. He's insane."

Miss Morrow, sensing her opportunity entered the conversation. "There, it's settled. If he's mad, we have an obligation to help her. But what you suggest is disgusting."

The commandant again ignored her, except for raising his hand to gesture her to stop talking.

But Miss Morrow wouldn't stop. "She hasn't been out into the prison yard since the attack. She won't venture onto the balcony. She's frightened. She knows this man—am I correct, Sheriff?—better than anyone else. She knows what he's capable of, and she's frightened."

"Miss Morrow's correct," the sheriff confirmed. "He tried to kill her. We have witnesses to that. All evidence says he killed the factory foreman, too . . . killed him in a rage . . . a mad rage. He's followed a pattern since the war began— even before the war—of finding women who need comfort, wealthy women. He cheats . . . or woos them out of money . . . then disappears . . . no trace. Mrs. Henderson's no murderess, certainly not a spy. She's just trapped."

"The nature of war, Sheriff. But how do you know all this?" the commandant pursued in a harsh tone.

The sheriff smiled sadly. Miss Morrow waited as anxiously for his answer as the commandant. "Mrs. Henderson is here for two reasons. She was unlucky enough to fall in love—long before the war—with a young man who disappeared and suddenly arose from the dead when Mrs. Henderson craved love and comfort . . . after she'd lost her husband. Unfortunately, her young Virginia love resurrected as a Yankee soldier . . . a persistent Yankee soldier set on seeing her, regardless of consequences. He could have been killed or arrested in his obsession to get to Mrs. Henderson, but he put her at risk, too. If he'd been caught, she would have ended up here."

"And she did anyway," Miss Morrow said flatly.

"That's right," the sheriff said. "She ended up here, but not because he was caught. She's here because she was kind to a woman—speaking of madness—with nascent lunacy who has now completed her metamorphosis."

"What does that mean?" Richardson said shortly.

"Mr. Henderson's cousin found out—I don't know how—about the Yankee long before their rendezvous. Then she heard about their actual meeting after the Yankee had gone north. The irony is I'm sure it was Walthrope who told her. And somewhere in the dim light of her unstable mind, she created a dark conspiracy."

"How do you know this?" the captain challenged again.

The sheriff looked patiently at the soldier. "I'm committed to finding Walthrope and bringing him to justice. I've interviewed everyone who might know something. I've traveled from here to Staunton . . . even to its lunatic home a half dozen times. A new sheriff will be elected shortly, so I've decided to leave my duties to others so I can stop this man, before he harms other innocents . . . innocent ladies. But someone's protecting him while he recovers. I don't even know what he looks like. I've got various descriptions, but a thousand men in Richmond could fit any one of them. Right now, if I could find him, he'd be easy to recognize . . . as you say he's been savagely bitten . . . in the face."

"That's what Mrs. Henderson claimed—bitten in the face, yes." Captain Richardson responded.

"Then if I can find him before he heals, it'll be easier. He's used different names—Walthrope in Staunton. I'm sure he's using another now. No picture exists of him . . . that I've seen. And the cousin . . . her husband put her in the lunatic asylum."

He paused, but neither of the others moved, so he continued, "The provost marshal in Staunton was keen on catching a spy . . . any spy, and he ignored the weakness of his only witness—a mad woman. She was a spectacle. She arrived at the provost marshal's office shoeless. They'd been left behind, stuck in street muck. She was barely clothed, completely covered in mud. I advised to immediately call for Dr. Stribling from the asylum. But when the provost marshal heard she had a story of treason, he interviewed her, took her word as gospel . . . when everyone else said the opposite.

"I argued long and hard against even arresting Mrs. Henderson. No one—but Mrs. Henderson's cousin—would even admit a Yankee visited. Everyone denied it. He still doesn't have evidence the Yankee exists. Of course, he does exist, but is as innocent . . . and apparently as naive as Mrs. Henderson. But the marshal couldn't be shaken loose from his grip of the batty woman's testimony. He took it as proof beyond doubt . . . from an unimpeachable witness. And Mrs. Henderson's here because of it . . . and the ill will of others. The lunatic cousin—fearing she'd be implicated in the foreman's murder—even refused to admit she'd seen Walthrope after the Yankee had visited Mrs. Henderson. So the provost believes that Mrs. Henderson killed the very man who attacked her here."

He stopped, exhaling a forced puff of air. "Thus, Mrs. Henderson sits in prison with no way to prove her innocence. She teeters on a precarious caged perch, a target for a man no one can identify, a man she supposedly killed."

"We have to help her, Captain," Miss Morrow said, turning her body from the sheriff to look passionately at the commandant.

The captain straightened in his chair. "The father of the child then is this Union soldier?"

The sheriff nodded, "If there's a baby, it's the Yankee's."

The commandant grimaced. "The very facts confirm the charges, though they misrepresent the truth."

"Just so," the sheriff confirmed.

Captain Richardson turned to face Miss Morrow. "I'm sorry, but she'll never get out of here, even if she's innocent. Most women aren't kept here long. They're sent to the North or take the oath. But with her, it's different. Too many people want her kept. For some reason, they're particularly keen on keeping her here."

"My point exactly, Captain. We must help her."

"What do you propose, Miss Morrow? Did you not hear what I just said? Do you not fear being jailed for treason yourself?" the commandant said, exasperated again.

"I don't know." she responded, disappointed she didn't have an answer. "Sheriff, do you have suggestions?"

"Ideas on how to get her out of Castle Thunder?"

"Precisely," she said hopefully.

"That's not my concern. You sought me out . . . asked me to tell what I know of Mrs. Henderson. I've done that. But getting her out of Castle Thunder isn't my business."

The captain smiled, "You're convinced she's innocent, yet do nothing for her? Mrs. Henderson thinks you're the person persecuting her . . . not the marshal. Are you just using her now to lure this Walthrope? Is that why she's here? Not war and treason, but just to catch your murderer?"

The sheriff smiled resignedly. "I thought she might think me her accuser from what she said to me when she was arrested. But she is wrong. At any rate, Captain, your suggestion of using her as bait is a good one."

Miss Morrow persisted, "You, yourself, admitted you're trying to stop Mr. Walthrope from harming anyone. Sheriff, your task is to protect the woman he's most likely to harm. You can't use her as a trap."

Captain Richardson chuckled. "If Walthrope is captured, it all comes to an end."

Miss Morrow barely let him finish. "Only in part. Remember, she's innocent. You can't just leave her in here. It does no good, and she just might hang."

The captain raised his voice. "Then go talk to the president, the provost marshal, a dozen people besides me." His expression softened quickly, embarrassed by his own attitude. "I'm sorry. I should never have said that to you. Take consolation that no woman has ever been executed here in the Castle." He paused briefly. "If you find I can speak on her behalf with someone . . . someone where it might make a difference, I'll do it. If nothing else, Miss Morrow, you've convinced me she doesn't belong here."

"Wonderful, Captain. How about you, Sheriff?"

"Miss Morrow, your efforts are praiseworthy, but look elsewhere. I'll not get involved in your work."

She looked at him coldly. "I'll arrange for her release on my own then. I don't know how, but I will!"

Chapter 32

April 1864, Richmond, Virginia

The slave woman unlocked the door, then slipped swiftly into the windowless closet where a man sat on a bed that filled half the room. A gas lamp sat on a small table by the bed holding a wash basin and pitcher. A soiled chamber pot lay on the floor. The slave quickly closed the door with her leg. She stepped to the table and put down a jug of water, commenting, "You're up."

"What time is it? It's hard to tell in here."

"Nearly noon."

"I've got to get out of here. I'm going quite mad, just sitting here. Waiting. It's enough to . . ."

"The bruises and bites are healing. But you'd still be conspicuous. You're welcome to go anytime, according to my mistress. She wishes you would. As hard as it is to say, I think you ought to stay longer. Another week or so . . . so you won't be noticed."

"I've got to get to Washington. I can't wait that long. I'm going crazy. Send your mistress to see me."

"She won't come. She doesn't like having you here and wants nothing to do with you."

"Ask her if there isn't someone who could take me north in the dark, when my face would be hidden."

"You have no other business in Richmond, then? You could go right away? She asked me to ask you that." Without hesitation, he responded angrily, "I have unfinished business, but I'll return for that. My other business . . . my urgent business is now in Washington. I'm ready to go anytime . . . tonight. I need to get there soon."

"I'll tell my mistress, then."

"Get me a military uniform! I could use that . . . go at night. No one would see my face till I was out of the city."

Without emotion the woman responded, "How far do you think you'd get in northern Virginia in a Confederate uniform?

"Imbecile! I'd change it once out of Richmond."

The slave was shocked by his tone and his words. She wanted to walk out of the room. She didn't like the man and was only doing this because her mistress demanded it . . . and because he secretly paid her handsomely. Someone else was paying her mistress to hide him.

"I just want to get out of here . . . to have these bites healed so . . . I'm going crazy, locked in like a prisoner, no sun, no moon, no clouds, no rain . . . no other living being."

"They want you to stay till it's safe to go about your work, whatever it is."

He was surprised at how little this woman knew of him. He assumed her ignorance reflected her mistress's lack of information. Convinced that everything he confided to the slave would make it back to the ear of the mistress, he said, "My work. It's important. I help the government."

"The government?"

"Yes, important. Look at how they protect me."

"Yes, you must be important to be locked in a closet day and night," the slave said, with downcast eyes.

"They're worried something will happen to me," he said, instantly regretting that he was explaining himself to a slave.

"I'm glad you have such important work." He didn't like her mocking tone, but said nothing, and she continued, "As far as my mistress is concerned—she says you're a bother. They brought more letters and a package for you . . . said you would know what to do with them. My mistress is keeping them for now. Do you?"

"Yes, I deliver them."

"Oh . . . speaking of letters, this one came for you. The usual way." She put the letter on the table.

"Did anyone see it delivered?"

"No, I'm sure my mistress didn't see her."

She didn't look at him, but bent to lift the chamber pot carefully and moved toward the door. She was tired of the stench of the room, of chamber pots. She wanted the man gone, but cherished the money more. She opened and closed the door quickly as she carefully entered the hall. He heard the key turn in the lock and cursed her quietly, but knew he had to be patient and that he could trust no one beyond the influence of his money.

He was again alone, left only with his own thoughts, imagination and memories. This couldn't continue. He had to leave soon. No one would catch him. He'd make sure she got him a uniform, a colonel's uniform. Then he'd be off.

His thoughts turned to Betsy, as they always did—and he wrested real memories for his pleasure and purpose. He imagined Betsy as the lady he loved and who loved him.

"Still hidden?" the captain asked, as he sat at the desk where he'd earlier confronted Dante.

"Yes, but I think we should just give him up . . . or have him shot trying to get away," Matthew, Dante's sometime-friend, responded in his deep, pious voice.

"You'd be delighted to be rid of him."

"He's a scoundrel, untrustworthy . . . obsessed with faro . . . crazy."

"But useful to us . . . for now."

"There are dozens of couriers in Richmond. Why care about this one . . . after all he's done?"

"I have reasons."

"They are?"

"I'm not obliged to reveal them."

"He's lodged at my expense. The people keeping him are tired and are sure he's suffering madness. Others are busy hunting him. I want him to disappear . . . and not just from Richmond."

"But he has one valuable attribute. He's trusted in Washington by a man from whom he might get important information. Until he loses that man's trust, we'll use him."

Matthew smiled and mumbled, "Will that man—whoever it is—will he trust him for long?"

"How much of a problem can he be where he is?" He leaned forward. "All right, what do you propose?"

"He wants to go at night . . . wants a uniform to get out of Richmond."

"A uniform? Easy enough to find a private's uniform. I'll see to it." The officer stopped, and looked silently, as he often did, at the ceiling for an extended period of time. "No, our fellow needs to know he does not dictate to us. He'll sit longer. Then he'll remember although he may play a spy for the North . . . he's ours. We need to make sure he understands this. He'll wait."

Matthew was visibly vexed, but the Confederate didn't acknowledge it.

"That will be hard," Matthew said after pausing to consider what he should say.

"You'll do it though."

"Yes . . . but I'd prefer he disappear."

"Everything in its time." He feigned a smile at Matthew. "I believe our business is concluded. I'll fetch you when I'm ready to have your friend return to Washington."

Matthew clenched his teeth briefly, then said simply, "Thank you." He got up, turned quickly and without looking back, walked out, leaving the office door open.

The officer smiled smugly, opened a drawer, pulled out papers and began reading them. Periodically he'd smile again and look toward the open door.

Chapter 33

April 1864, Richmond, Virginia

Betsy had an early morning dream of falling into a black abyss. She awoke melancholy, with the sensation that she was still falling, leaving her slightly nauseated. She sat up but stayed wrapped in a filthy thin blanket. The fleas, bed bugs and lice were getting worse, and she found and scratched several new bites.

She gazed blankly at the wall across her cell thinking of Hank. Her beloved's child would be born in a Confederate prison, flea bitten, lice infested. It would know rats before meeting its father, if they ever met at all. It would surely be weak, sickly, starved for good food, fresh air, and die an untallied casualty of war.

Betsy was morose—more than ever—and she wallowed in the sensation. She let tears drip and her mood fall unrestrained. Her nose ran onto her soiled nightshirt and blanket, and she did nothing to restrain it. She was tired, frightened, ready to give up. But what did giving up mean?

Would she swear allegiance to the country to which she already hung tenaciously? Easy. She'd never considered turning from her native state. But the commandant had proclaimed swearing allegiance not enough.

Could she just die? How could one just die? Would she take her own life? She looked at the rafters above. Too high to reach easily, she thought, and instantly recoiled that she would entertain such thoughts. In spite of the darkness of her mood and the bleakness of the future, in spite of the emotional and physical pain, in spite of the itching and her knotted stomach, in spite of all, she was repulsed by the thought and shivered. The revulsion grounded her again. No, she had to keep going, and she prayed a five-word, heart-felt plea, "My Heavenly Father, strengthen me!"

She clasped her hands tightly and sighed, trying to control her emotions. A memory surfaced of the two weeks Hank had stayed with her in Staunton. He, much as she was now, had been a prisoner. He couldn't leave her home for fear some passing neighbor might see him and ask questions, so they spent every day by the fire in the drawing room talking about the past and their blissful future.

He was a better man than he'd been before the war. Quieter, more solemn, thoughtful. She loved him more. Gone were her superficial cravings and pride of youth, replaced by something deeper—not yet a happiness—but a desire to make him happy. The time together wasn't all pleasant. Some had been sorely hard. At night, he would cry out brief unintelligible phrases or wake in a cold sweat, and she'd be there beside him. One night she'd rolled over toward him and found him sitting up.

"What's wrong," she'd asked, lazily stretching across the bed, as she tried to focus her bleary eyes.

He was breathing in short, violent gasps. "I wasn't here with you," he said, and she could tell by his broken words he was crying. She sat up and wrapped her left arm around his back and squeezed him gently.

"But you aren't gone."

He was silent for a while, "But I have to go."

"Not yet. Just enjoy being here now. It's what we dreamed—belonging to each other. There will be time later to grieve . . . not now. Don't worry away our time together."

"We have no future. You know that."

"I don't, and neither do you."

"Well, it's not hard to see we're trapped, like everyone else. They do with us as they please, and there's nothing we can do. We're just pulled along . . . pulled down."

"We aren't trapped. We can choose what we want."

He'd stopped crying, rolled over and wrapped his arm around her, pulled her towards him and kissed her gently on the lips. "No, Betsy, we can't do what we want. It is so much bigger than we two. We can make any decision, but in the end, the war controls us, smothers our decisions . . . our hopes."

"I prefer to believe it's God who holds us in his hand . . . and perhaps we may never have the leisure and freedom we crave, but I believe he'll protect us . . . bring us together again, the two of us—a family."

"A family. How odd, even now, to think it." He was quiet again. He broke the silence in a brighter tone, "And that will keep me going . . . it will keep me alive."

"God will keep us both alive."

"And while he does, I'll be thinking of you."

She could feel and joined in his relief, and love surged through her.

She wanted to be there again, with him, feeling something like joy. She tried to visualize the three of them as a family after the war, but it led to the ever-irksome question: Where would they live? She didn't want to move to the North, but knew they couldn't stay in Virginia.

She longed to talk about it with someone, but there was no one. Marie Ann and Caleb had visited again, but their visit had been short and guarded, full of merciful lies. She feared what everyone thought of her, and worried people would soon have their suspicions confirmed because even this early—as she lost weight for lack of good food—her belly was beginning to bulge. Her face was thinner, her belly fatter.

The coming baby was the only thing they couldn't take from her. She imagined they'd try to take it. Then worse, she imagined that she, the mother, would die, and the baby would survive. It would be left in the hands of those who imprisoned its mother, raised like Marie Antoinette's royal son—taught and forced to curse and repudiate his own dead mother.

Twisting in the bed, she lowered her feet to the cold floor. The tears had stopped, and she wiped at her nose with a dirty handkerchief. She crossed the room to the table and poured water from the pitcher into a bowl and washed her face. The cold water shocked her. With her face still dripping, she sat, resting her arms and hands on the table and stared at nothing. Eventually she rose, stretched, dressed and dreamed of a bath in a tub. When she'd adjusted her skirt, she straightened the soiled bed covers.

She scanned a short stack of books that lay in the corner—books Caleb had brought. None enticed her. It would be breakfast soon, and her stomach ached—as it always did now—with an insatiable hunger. She sat on the heavily soiled upholstered chair in the cell and looked at the door, waiting for some sign of breakfast. She was not included in the roll call with other prisoners. Guards would check on her at breakfast, and that would be her first and only break of the morning. She watched the door and thought of Hank.

Noise outside the room, the key scraping in the lock, interrupted her thoughts. The heavy door swung outward, and Miss Morrow was there with a young guard.

Miss Morrow immediately turned to the guard. "That will do very nicely, young man. Thank you."

Stepping into the cell, she turned to the guard, lowered her head slightly as if to scold. He was about to say something, but her look deterred him, and he slowly closed the door. The women watched the door as the key turned and listened as the guard receded.

Betsy watched the woman, fascinated by her guest's authoritative presence and aware suddenly of a loaf of bread in her visitor's arm. She smiled and waited patiently.

For a long time, Miss Morrow frowned at the door, reminding Betsy that this woman never seemed to act until sure of her surroundings. About the time Betsy considered standing to greet her guest, the woman turned abruptly without saying a word, walked to the table, placed the bread on a plate and sat on a chair opposite Betsy. She then looked at Betsy for the first time.

Momentarily unsure if she should begin the conversation, Betsy decided to wait because she couldn't bring herself to say anything that sounded of polite, shallow social conversation. She looked bemused at Miss Morrow, and Miss Morrow returned the look twisting her face into a businesslike smile. She finally bowed her head slightly as her only greeting. Betsy had the impression that while Miss Morrow maintained eye contact, her peripheral vision and mind scanned her, taking her measure, assessing her condition, probing her thoughts, her feelings.

"You look as if you've been cooped up here since our last conversation. I've brought this bread. You seem thinner . . . not fatter each time we meet."

Betsy had wondered how Miss Morrow would speak. The tone, she thought, would tell Miss Morrow's intent. The tone had been warm. "I never leave this room, and I'm so hungry. Thank you for the bread and excuse my rudeness." Betsy stood and tore a piece from the loaf and stuffed it in her mouth.

Miss Morrow ignored her actions and asked, "You've stayed in by your own choice?"

Betsy smiled as she chewed and said, "By my own fear."

"The commandant has promised it won't happen again."

"The commandant," Betsy said with a mocking laugh, having swallowed the bread. "He assured me he'd keep me safe. That man should never have gotten in here. The commandant won't even admit I was attacked." She pulled off another piece of the bread.

"Yes."

"Miss Morrow, is that all? Just yes?" Betsy bit into the second piece. It tasted heavenly, the best bread she could remember.

Miss Morrow smiled, "Call me Florence."

Betsy waited until she had swallowed a large mouthful of bread. "Miss Morrow, the last person demanding I call him by his first name was the fiend in the courtyard. Funny, isn't it?" Betsy's voice was tight.

Florence could feel her anger. "Do as you please, but I'd prefer Florence."

Betsy stared hard at her, biting into a piece of bread again, but her anger subsided. She smiled. "Then I'll call you Florence." Without waiting for a response, she continued, still chewing. "When I saw him, I thought . . . just briefly, that they'd caught him! What unlucky fortune has brought me to the same prison as this man."

She stopped and reached for another piece of bread. Florence watched her closely, but said nothing. With her mouth full, she spoke, "To imagine him free—of all people— free to walk into this prison . . . that he knew where I was . . . that he'd not run off to Europe to hide. It was unbearable." She took another bite. "A murderer free, and me . . . held for his murder. He came at me. Why didn't I tell the sheriff when that mysterious woman told me everything? If I'd just listened to everyone and done that . . . just that, it would have all been different." She swallowed.

"Do you believe that? Wouldn't he have raised the alarm, told the provost marshal about your lover?"

"Lover?" Betsy clamored sarcastically, but quickly softened her voice. "Husband."

Florence would have straightened her back in surprise if it had not already been perfectly aligned. "Your husband?"

Betsy was amazed her comment was unexpected. Surely, everyone had assumed they were married. If not . . . ? She couldn't fathom it. But what difference did it make what people thought? In their minds, they'd only add adulteress to murderess and traitress.

In confinement, her imagination was getting stronger each day, and she was vaguely aware it was somehow distorted. Surely this woman was a spy sent to ingratiate herself, gain Betsy's confidence, then betray her. Betsy didn't care, not anymore. She, at that moment, didn't care about Hank or her baby. She wanted this to end and another piece of the bread. Her life had become a long string of disasters: Hank disappearing; living with Thaddeus' cousin while he went to a "brief" war; Thaddeus' death; Hank's awkward reappearance; Walthrope's evil; her own clandestine marriage to Hank and his required departure; her arrest; her imprisonment; her father's death; her mother's lunacy.

Hank had been right. They would never be together. She wished she lived in England, Brazil or anywhere far from this war, and smiled at the thought in spite of herself. "Yes, my husband."

"You're married, then?"

"Of course I am," she affirmed as she pulled again at the rapidly diminishing loaf.

"But everyone thinks . . ."

"Yes . . . I see now what they must think, but what am I to do? I'm married to the man they've accused me of spying for . . . or with. It doesn't matter what I say . . . or do." She put the bread in her mouth.

Miss Morrow regained her composure. "I understand."

Betsy shook her head. "I didn't murder anyone."

"I know, and so do the authorities. His reappearance and attack on you had that one positive outcome."

"Then why am I still here?"

"I suppose you're here because it's hard to get out once you're in. The doors open only one way . . . and there's still the charge of treason."

"Am I to languish here?"

"I'm doing what I can."

"Why?" Betsy asked, not elated at the news, but disbelieving, suddenly distrusting.

"You shouldn't be here. You mustn't go through that difficult time here. I am relieved you're married."

"It doesn't change much, since no one knows."

"I'm glad to know. What's your last name, then?"

"Gragg."

"Elizabeth Gragg. How long have you known him—Mr. Gragg."

"Hank." It felt good to talk to someone about him. Would she hang for it? "Many years." Surely this new friend, Florence, was here to measure her for a noose.

"You've loved him all that time?"

Betsy was surprised to hear Miss Morrow of the straight back talk about love. "Yes. For a while I thought him dead . . . before the war. Still I loved his memory."

"When you met . . . married him, was he the same?"

Betsy's eyes drifted. "No, not the same. Stronger, not so arrogant . . . sadder. No longer a boy."

"But you still love him?"

"More so."

"Why didn't you go with him?"

"I wish I had. But even if I had, I'd never see him. He's in some regiment from Indiana. I'm not from Indiana and no longer a Unionist . . . not since Virginia seceded. I cast my lot with the South. Can't see myself following the Union camp, making a meager living doing laundry."

"When this is all over, where will you live?"

"Will the war end?"

Florence smiled, "Of course. Won't be long."

Betsy sighed loudly.

"Would you be willing to live in the North, now?"

Betsy, immediately suspicious, answered cautiously, "I'm a Southerner."

"I understand, but you're married to a Yankee. Where can you both live?"

Betsy cautioned herself. This woman was another trap. "I can't leave Virginia. I'll stay here. I'm a loyal Virginian."

Miss Morrow was exasperated. "Can your husband live in Virginia?"

"He was bred here. He still owes allegiance to Virginia, even though he's made a mistake."

"Do you really believe that?" Miss Morrow said, with sudden hostility.

Betsy looked at her directly, trying to guess what the woman was thinking. Why ask these questions? Was she hoping to uncover hidden loyalty to the North?

"I'm sorry," Miss Morrow said in a softer tone. "I'm frustrated by our conversation, so please allow me to be direct. I fear that you think I'm trying to catch you in some indiscretion of loyalty."

"Aren't you?"

"No, I want to help you escape! But once you're free, where will you go?" She looked at Betsy and could tell she wasn't going to answer. "You must think about it. When the time comes, you're going to have to know the answer . . . and it would help me to know before."

"Why?" Betsy asked defiantly.

"To make arrangements. Now I'm not telling you anything you don't know, but it would be impossible to stay in Richmond—everyone knows of your imprisonment here. They know why . . . or more accurately, believe you're in Castle Thunder justly. The recent attack's even known. In one version, your lover came to the prison for a rendezvous, and only alert guards and Nero stopped him. So even if they release you, the stain's there."

With a pained expression, she asked, "They really believe that?"

"Richmond society believes it."

"Then I can't stay in Richmond . . . and I can't return to Staunton—they probably believe worse things."

"May I ask again, where do you want to go?"

Betsy looked resigned to her fate. "If I get out . . ."

"When you escape."

"I have no idea, and my heart is broken because of it. I'm homeless. This war has destroyed my life." She began to cry. "And I've done nothing wrong, betrayed no one."

"Would you go to the North? Would you be willing to go to the Union? To Washington City?"

"Is there an alternative?"

"That's what I needed to know." Miss Morrow said, still sitting with what seemed to Betsy uncomfortably straight posture. "I know you fear everyone at this point, Mrs. Hender . . . I'm sorry I've forgotten."

"Mrs. Gragg."

"Mrs. Gragg, you needn't fear me. I'm not a spy for Captain Richardson. I've become the proverbial thorn to him. I'm here to help you. So don't be discouraged. No melancholy. Your disease will bear fruit beyond Castle Thunder, and you'll see your husband—your husband, what a lovely thought."

Betsy looked hopefully at the woman as a silent tear rolled down her own cheek.

"The best thing you can do," Florence continued, "is to not worry . . . to hope. I don't fall short when I've put my mind to a task. Is there anything more you would want . . . other than more bread?"

Betsy wiped at her face, sniffed, smiled and said, "Can I take Nero with me?"

Miss Morrow laughed, her visage softened briefly. "Honorable Mrs. Gragg, I'm committed to your freedom."

"Is it only because I'm in the way of women . . . and unfairly charged? Or is there something more?"

Miss Morrow, slightly surprised by Betsy pushing the issue, answered vaguely, "I'm going to help you. The specifics of why and how . . . they're not important."

Betsy wanted to believe the woman. She imagined Miss Morrow most dogged and took hope from that, but there was still something nagging her. Why would Florence want to do something for a woman she thought bore a child out of wedlock, a woman who everyone believed had betrayed the South?

Chapter 34

April 1864, Richmond, Virginia

Dante hadn't yet received a uniform. It had been promised, but something had changed, and he fretted at the change. He no longer dared gripe to his hostess's slave.

He'd not been allowed to see a mirror the entire time he'd been confined. Judging from the healing of his arms and legs and the length and thickness of his beard, he no longer needed the uniform to go north. He could feel the scars—still tender—with his fingers under his unkempt whiskers, but they were hidden. He no longer needed darkness as an ally. If he could get a clean set of clothes, he could safely walk at midday in the middle of the road.

The slave had taken his clothes—for cleaning, she'd said. But she never returned them, leaving him with only a night-shirt. She told him in conspiratorial tones that someone didn't want him to leave yet, but she didn't know who it was. Today, he'd outwit them. He'd tell her he needed a mirror to trim his beard, a bath and clean clothes so he could feel like himself again. Any set of clothes would get him out of Richmond now.

"Good," he said out loud to no one in particular. He'd begun to talk aloud often, even consciously encouraging himself to do it. But much of his time was spent thinking about the only thing that made him happy now—imagining Betsy, the woman who he now knew as his wife. He had thought carefully through their marriage ceremony and the honey in her voice when she said, "I do." What would she think when she saw his scarred face?

He repeated to himself till it became part of him that the Confederacy was keeping them apart, keeping her in that prison cell, while she carried his child. He could have taken her earlier, and they'd be safe in the North, but for that dog. He pictured exactly how it would have been, embracing her in the prison yard, then fleeing the country.

He envisioned in great detail their lives in Europe. First in England, then on to the Continent. He loved her passionately. He knew they'd told her they weren't legally married, that he had tried to harm her, but she'd see the truth.

He thought often of, even in his windowless prison, how powerful he was. He'd smile, knowing he would rescue his love from the shackles of Castle Thunder. He rehearsed scenes over and over again of their reunion. He would entertain himself with a mental game of thinking through what he could do in the future with her wealth. No, no, they had married, it was now his wealth. He'd revenge himself on the nasty Confederate captain who had rejected him, on the two detectives in Washington who had turned him, even on Matthew for abandoning him in this one-room prison. He'd destroy them all. And he'd kill the dog. With Betsy's—no his wealth—bulging from his pockets, he would do all of this.

Ah, and the baby. He rehearsed the night in Betsy's arms and imagined how it would be to have his own son.

Yes, he'd get clean clothes without the gaping tears left by that dog. There was no humiliation in being beaten by it. No mortal man could survive such an attack. He'd always suspected it, but it was now clear. He was extraordinary, and he happily remembered beating his common father. He was proud to be extraordinary.

Chapter 35

April 1864, Eastern Kentucky

William reached the back door where a house slave thrashed a carpet. She glanced at him without acknowledgment. When she had hit the carpet several more times, she asked gruffly, "What do you want, ole man?"

"Want to speak to the judge," William said meekly.

"Do you, now? Get back to the stalls, boy! Harness the wagon or something. Ain't that what you're good for? You're the new boy, ain't you. Let me tell you . . . and you remember this. We can't have all of you coming up to the house, all high and mighty, expecting to see the judge. Humph."

"Still," he said firmly, "Gotta speak to the judge."

"And I want to see Mr. Lincoln, but I ain't going to Washington. You're a . . . ." She finished her profanity and stared hard at him, waiting for him to back down or at least acknowledge her superiority. When he didn't, she doubted that superiority and softened her tone. "Well, you don't have to be so highfalutin about it . . . not with me. Come wait in the back. We'll see if the master wants to see you. What's your name, ole man?"

"William."

She started toward the door, then looked back, condescension in her expression and threatened, "William, you better hope he wants to see you. Do you like being beat?"

William didn't respond, but followed her into the house and waited nervously. He didn't think the judge beat anyone, but he easily conjured images of being whipped, dragged out of the house and hung for hitting the white man with the shovel.

Several minutes later, the judge came through a door that opened into the hall. "Ah, you've made your way home."

"Yes, sir."

"Come in."

William said nothing to the woman who had let him into the hall. As she passed him, she looked disdainfully, with squinted eyes, at him. He followed the judge into what William now saw was an office. The judge stood by the door as William passed and quickly shut it after William crossed the threshold. He said nothing, but glanced at William with almost the exact expression the slave-woman had just given him.

Concluding the judge was waiting for him to say something, William opened his mouth, not knowing what to say. The judged silenced him by raising his left index finger to his lips. William closed his mouth with a barely audible grunt. The judge was silent for more than a minute, confirming in William's mind that a conspiracy was at work that would make him the biblical scapegoat one of his many uncles had told him about.

After the extended silence, the judge jerked opened the office door, and the slave who had let William in was kneeling with her ear to the keyhole. The judge, expecting her curiosity, ignored her awkward position and said simply. "Ah, there you are. Tell Mary I'll eat early this evening."

"Yes, Master. I'll tell her."

"Good."

He waited until she had disappeared into the back of the house before he closed the door and motioned William toward the far end of the office, to a small chair at the side of a large desk overlooking the fields. "Sit down, William. We don't have much time, and we've got to be careful."

William, still silent, quickly walked to the small chair, but sat down hesitantly only after the judge lowered himself into the big chair behind the desk.

"Are Adam and Victoria with you?"

"Yes."

"Good. Where are they now?"

"Just in the woods . . . by the cabins. Waiting."

"They'll be safe there. I stopped in town this morning, after leaving Victoria's. Nothing unusual was going on."

"That's good."

The judge, who had been looking out the window, turned to William. "Yes, it is good, but I don't know how long it will last. Something will happen, and when it does, you, Adam, Victoria, my slaves, me . . . we'll all be in a tough strait, unless we do just the right thing. Hopefully, fortune will favor us. Do you understand what I'm saying?"

William nodded.

"The best we can do now is get Adam and Victoria into one of the slave quarters till we can get them away."

William felt and looked uncomfortable, and the judge noticed but ignored it.

"William, what do you want to do? Do you have a place to go? People to go to?"

"No."

"Then we need to think about you, too?"

"No," William looked at the floor. "Don't go worryin' 'bout me none, Marse."

The judge studied William closely.

William continued, "When somethin' happens, give me up. Don't hide me none. That ain't the way."

"What are you saying?"

"Yuh've gotta get 'em out o' here, like yuh said."

"Why not you, too?"

"It ain't gunna do no good."

The judge squinted.

"They gotta blame some body. If yuh take us all, ain't nobody gunna be here for 'em. If I stay, they won't go lookin' for nobody else. They'll forget 'bout the others."

"Do you know what they'd do . . . if you stay?"

"S'pose lynch me."

"They'll hang you that very day, and they'll beat you almost to death before they do it."

"Good. No fury left to hunt the others."

The judge had never taken time to figure William out and had never had a conversation with him. He assumed the man was worried only for himself, his own safety, his own freedom. But what William was suggesting was not in his own best interest. Appreciation for William germinated. He thought carefully before responding. "William, let's not rush decisions . . . especially this one. We'll not decide till we know what's going to happen. Remember, everything's quiet in town. I don't know why, but it is."

William stared sternly at the judge—discomforting the master—and said, "We wait till they're lookin' for us, it'll be too late."

The judge weighed William's words, and responded slowly. He drew out his first word, "Maybe . . . but I don't think so. We'll have time, especially if we were to accept your offer."

"Judge, ain't got no choice."

William addressing him so intimately and the strength of his tone vexed the judge, but he appreciated what William was offering, so he let the emotion pass. "What do you mean?"

"I ain't gunna let Victoria and Adam . . . Them men . . . they'll be mighty angry. Ain't right, and I won't let 'em get Victoria . . . Adam."

The judge looked at him, chaffed by William's moral strength, but said softly, "Neither will I."

"I'll give myself up . . . hang myself if I have to."

The judge didn't respond. He looked away from William and into the warming spring light out the window.

"Won't wait for yor permission. I won't. It's my life."

The judge heard him, but ignored his comment, trying to relax. He gazed out the window hoping something outside would sooth his rising ire. He silently cursed the man. He was his slave and acted as if he were free to make decisions. Worst of all, he was making a morally superior—even heroic—decision. He said nothing, knowing guilt would follow if he responded in rage.

What he saw out the window, however, didn't calm him. "Oh, no. I should have known!" He leaped from his chair, charged the door, opened it and stepped into the hall, running to the front door.

William didn't move. He was frightened, but resolved. Had the trap sprung? Was he to be hanged within the hour? He heard disputing whispers in the hall. Was he to be given over so soon? Perhaps this discussion had been a farce, a way to keep him here and quiet, until someone came to beat and hang him. His words about dinner to the eavesdropping slave must have been a code sending someone to town to retrieve the mob. The judge had already betrayed him.

The whispers were heated, growing louder and coming closer. Why did they argue? Had they come too soon? Was the judge planning to hide Victoria and Adam safely before giving him over? His mind whirled, but he worked to slow it, to prepare himself. He wouldn't fight. He'd confess to anything, go peaceably, but he couldn't stay seated. They'd at least find him erect, proud, a man.

He stood up as the angry whispers reached the door. The judge was the first through it, his face was red with anger. He drew his lips together and glared at William. William's body tightened till it shook and his bones ached, muscles seized and cramped. He could now see his enemy. A woman? He didn't understand. It was Victoria. His enemy? He laughed quietly to himself, and the laugh loosened his tightened muscles.

The judge saw him laugh, and William could tell he didn't take it well. Then she was in the room. Victoria, in her full splendor. She looked at him, and he could see her countenance and body posture soften. "There you are," she said kindly.

The judge closed the door. "I told you he was fine."

"And I'm glad," she said, still looking toward William.

The judge's face was no longer red, but bore an expression of resignation. He said, "Slavery ought to be abolished just so I can be rid of you . . . of you both. I'd pay to put you on a ship to Africa."

Victoria turned to him, "Don't think you'll be rid of me when slavery's gone."

The judge responded meekly, "It was a prayer."

William could feel that whatever was going on between them, he should keep quiet, and he found himself examining a carpet on the office floor.

With the discussion over, Victoria rushed to William's side, taking him by the arm and reaching her hand into his.

He was embarrassed by this open affection in front of the judge and barely responded to her warmth.

The judge watched, a faint smile on his lips. "Well, now that you've made a mess of it, what should we do?"

Victoria peeked at William and said without hesitation, "I don't know what you should do, but I think I should marry this man."

William was startled, and she felt him stiffen.

Victoria expected it, and immediately continued, "I'm sorry, but you could never ask me . . . not now, not till things settle. But we're going to travel together and it would be easier . . . more appropriate—don't you agree, Judge?—for us to travel as a family . . . a married couple and son. What do you think, dear William?" While the first part of the explanation was business-like, her last phrase melted smoothly on her tongue.

William was speechless, and the judge came to his aid, "I believe she's suggesting an arrangement for appearances. She's not saying that you'd actually marry."

William looked at the judge earnestly. "Can we marry? A real marriage?"

The judge, startled by the question, responded haltingly, "If you were free, you could now have a legal marriage. Just been authorized . . . a few weeks ago by General Lorenzo Thomas. That's what I've heard. I don't know how it works, but we could figure it out . . . if we have the time."

"Then you must give him his freedom," Victoria said.

"Why do I endure you?" the judge answered sharply.

"Because we're entwined forever, but don't think it's always a pleasure being a slaveholder's sister."

William's eyes widened.

"I should never have admitted it. Knowing you as I do now, I certainly wouldn't have said anything. I should have given you freedom only if you agreed to return to Africa . . . permanently. It was only guilt that made me do it, and living with you has surely repaid any debt owed you of my father."

"I'm not from Africa, and it's too late." Then harshly, she added, "And don't forget the debt owed my mother." Her own tone bothered her, and she warmed it to say, "You'll never be free of me. Can we marry?"

The judge looked at her, clearly thinking about the details entailed in her question. "What we can do is perform a slave wedding now, and at some later time, we'll get it registered . . . make it legal. Will that suffice?"

William, totally left out of the conversation, was busy trying to process Victoria's familial revelation, the possibility he could marry . . . really marry this wonderful woman—not his master's mistress, but his sister.

Victoria answered, "It will have to do, won't it?" She quickly turned to William and stepped away from him, keeping one hand on his arm. "William, do you want this? I've been a bit brash here."

"A bit?" her brother commented wryly.

She shot him an angry glance. "A bit." She looked at William, "Is this what you want?"

William was embarrassed. He would have preferred to ask her, but he never thought such a marriage possible. He hesitated, and the delay hurt Victoria's feelings.

The judge sensed her discomfort and tried to ease it. "Victoria, we've just overwhelmed William. I think he needs a day or two . . . if we have that much time . . . to let it soak in. Will that be acceptable, William?"

William could see disappointment in Victoria's eyes and responded to the judge. "I delay in answerin' only to say the right thing." He regarded Victoria and said slowly, "My beloved, Victoria." He dropped to his knees. "I agree if yuh promise to be my wife as long as we both live, and yuh do it with all yor heart . . . not just for travel."

Victoria smiled shyly. She began to say, "I do." But before she could finish she was crushed in a hug that thrilled her.

The judge, watching with amusement, smiled. "Shall I get the broom, then?" he asked mischievously.

William responded without a hint of restraint and without letting up on his embrace of Victoria, "No broom."

Victoria was shocked by the harshness of his reply, but understood it to be a wrenching break from slavery and all its traditions, pretenses and coercion. She said firmly, "I couldn't have said it better."

The judge commented, "I do believe you've met your match, Victoria."

There was a commotion at the back door, and the judge went to find out what it was.

There he met the slave he'd sent earlier to gather gossip in town.

"News?" the judge asked.

"He's alive. They have him in town . . . and he's conscious."

Chapter 36

April 1864, Eastern Kentucky

The atmosphere in the office was tense. The judge had posted one slave near the road to watch for anyone who appeared headed toward the plantation. A second was positioned on the front porch to await a warning signal if someone approached. A third slave had been sent to town on business and was told to do it slowly while listening for clues as to the man's condition and what he was saying. Only to these three slaves, the judge's most loyal, had he confided the true circumstances.

Adam, Victoria and William had been at the judge's twenty-four hours, but were already waiting in the office for the happy ceremony. News of the nuptials had quickly trickled through the slaves creating an excitement that worried the judge, lest news of Victoria's whereabouts leak beyond the farm. The slaves rejoiced for Victoria and to learn that the Union now recognized marriages for freed slaves. Even the house slave who a day earlier badgered William had wished him happiness in a soft, respectful voice.

The judge stood at the window looking toward the road, uneasy at offering his office for a slave wedding that might end with people from town coming to hang the groom. Victoria and William sat nearby, while Adam continually ran between the judge and couple. Stress, lack of sleep, and physical hardship had worn William out, and he sat staring vacantly across the room. Adam stopped briefly, lit beside him and rested his head on William's lap. Victoria nestled quietly with her arm tucked in William's. None of the joyful anticipation of pending marriage showed in any of them.

The judge's attention, diverted from the road, focused on a slave dressed in an old-fashioned suit approaching the house. "He's coming," he commented quietly. He looked at Victoria. "Are you sure you want to do this?"

William shifted his head and eyes lazily toward the judge. Victoria responded, "Do what?"

"Are you sure you want to get married . . . like this?"

"Is there another way?"

"No, I don't mean that. Are you sure you want to get married at all?"

Adam had raised his head long enough to look at the judge and say, "Of cccourse."

The judge smiled, "Yes, just so."

The slave preacher disappeared behind the house, but was soon escorted to the office. The judge opened the door to him and said passively, "Here's the couple," as he waved his hand dismissively toward Victoria and William.

The judge liked the preacher, Sam. He was strong, a good worker, never gave him trouble—the sort the judge wished they all were.

He looked at his sister. They'd been raised together on the farm, till she'd been separated for training as a house slave. She'd always amazed him. She grasped concepts and ideas faster and more thoroughly than anyone else he knew. He turned back to the window again, still thinking about her. When they were children, he'd made the mistake of teaching her to read. It was his biggest mistake. He remembered the humiliation—he would read to her, showing her the new words he'd learned, and instead of responding with appropriate gratitude, she would correct his pronunciation or read words before he told her what they were, or, worse yet, help him with words he'd forgotten.

At one point, she realized his—their—father's library was full of books, and he'd see her sneak away one book at a time. It was always back before a day had passed. He'd often find her hidden, reading one of the books. Their father never noticed what she was doing, or he certainly would have blinded her so she could never read again.

Those experiences were before the judge realized he and Victoria shared a father. His father never admitted to a relationship with Victoria other than master and slave until he was dying, when the judge had forced him to admit it. Once the judge knew for sure, he couldn't keep Victoria as a slave—his own sister. Many slave owners did keep their sisters or their aunts or their children in slavery, but he couldn't. He manumitted Victoria as soon as he inherited the farm and slaves. He was glad he'd done it, but it created problems. He smiled affectionately and shook his head.

What galled him most was she assumed she had personal value, imagined herself as important as him and her concerns as important as his. She expected him to go along with her opinions and decisions. "Ingrate!" he mumbled smiling.

Everyone in town thought he kept her as his mistress, and they thought it was understandable, although they couldn't comprehend why he'd manumitted her. Wouldn't it have been easier to keep ownership? He'd let the rumor that she was his mistress settle deep into the community. Some things just weren't worth correcting, and this was one.

Adam's birth had been noted in the community. Surely the judge was the father. This only reinforced community conviction that he should have kept Victoria in slavery. If he had, the judge could have hidden the boy among his other possessions. Instead, Adam wandered freely, reminding everyone of the unfortunate, but never-mentioned, paternity. Everyone sympathized with the judge, but ascribed this embarrassing public reminder to the foolishness of freeing his mistress. Surely he'd never recognize the boy, not socially, not legally—he couldn't do that. When Adam was born, the judge had considered correcting the scuttlebutt, but it was too late. Even if he denied it, no one would believe him. Best just let it go, let them say what they wanted.

The judge had for a while thought the best remedy was to marry, and he'd courted several women. But it was so hard, just not worth it, so he just let that pass as well.

He loved Victoria—they had grown up together, playmates, and now siblings. One couldn't help but be enlivened by being with her. He'd seen it happen to everyone who met her in any circumstance that allowed her to socially interact. He took energy from her. Without her, he would never have gone in the middle of the night to save a man who'd starved himself in the woods. She'd steeled him for the job, sent him, and he'd meekly gone, mustering his own courage and strength only for his brief encounter with the patrollers, in defense of shiftless Isaiah.

He was glad Isaiah was gone. He hated having him around. He'd seen Isaiah's interest in Victoria, and the thoughts of Isaiah as anything like a brother-in-law, even if Isaiah never knew, disgusted him. He was grateful to be rid of the slave, even if he never got compensation.

But now, out of a half-dead shell of a runaway slave, comes this unexpected man who had won his sister's affection. So many, white and black, had tried to win her—some for a lifetime, some for brief use, almost proud of their lack of good intentions. But it never mattered for she'd resisted them all, except for one still-unexplained relationship that had resulted in Adam.

Victoria had refused to tell him who the father was. He'd harangued her in this very office many times, but she wouldn't reveal it. She sulked and cried, or yelled at him for bringing it up at all. "Who is the boy's father?" he would demand. She'd say nothing. He knew she would never tell . . . at least not him, and he was angry she wouldn't. Why was she protecting whoever he was? But he knew it wouldn't matter even if she did tell him. He couldn't do anything. It wouldn't do any good. The guilty man would deny it, laugh at the allegation, laugh at her, laugh at the judge . . . if he were foolish enough to confront him. No, he wouldn't make accusations. The judge just wanted to know. It was his right.

As always, she had won their confrontation, and he remembered sadly that anger had led him to imagine tying her to a post and whipping her till her back dripped with blood. How dare she treat him as an equal, when she was lucky to be free and ought to be obedient to her master. Yes, he'd freed her, but he harbored a sense that she was still his. It was so confusing to him. Most times he was fond of her as if she'd been his full sister, but sometimes he hated her as if she were his slave.

No wonder he never married. With this woman continually at him, he couldn't bear the horror of someone standing on the other side, claiming her own right to browbeat him. He would have no peace in his life.

Still there was no movement on the road, and the judge decided he'd turn his attention to this unpromising union. At least William seemed a decent fellow. In the end, it wouldn't matter. William and Victoria would scurry off somewhere. Maybe they'd stick together, maybe not. His obligation was merely to get them away from Kentucky, then it would be in their hands. He'd probably never bother to get the marriage recorded legally.

He was surprised as he redirected his thoughts and head toward the room's interior and the wedding. All the parties were in position, waiting for him. Victoria wore the dress in which she'd fled her home. William, in clean workman clothes, stood to her right, and both of them faced Sam who waited in front of a wall of books and behind a small, cloth-covered table on which rested two lighted candles. An excited Adam, who for the first time in his life was on the verge of having a father, couldn't hold still, moving from Victoria to William. He repeated the cycle several times as the judge watched, amused and pleased in spite of his ill humor. He never admitted it to himself, but he loved this boy as if he'd been his own and would miss him deeply after they left.

"Are we ready, then?" the judge asked.

"Yes, Massa," Sam responded, lowering his head respectfully in the judge's direction.

"Go on, then. Begin," the judge said condescendingly.

The preacher looked at Victoria, whose eyes were afire, and then to William, whose eyes looked tired and unfocused. The preacher took a deep breath and began the ritual, reading the Episcopal wedding ceremony:

"Dearly beloved, we are gathered together here in the sight of God, and in the face of this company, to join together this man and this woman in holy matrimony; which is commended of Saint Paul to be honorable among all men; and therefore is not by any to be entered into unadvisedly or lightly; but reverently, discreetly, advisedly, soberly, and in the fear of God. Into this holy estate, these two persons present come now to be joined. If any man can show just cause, why they may not lawfully be joined together, let him now speak, or else hereafter forever hold his peace." Sam looked expectantly across the room at the judge.

The judge wanted to object but had no reason to do so. Was it because he knew the marriage a sham or feared it might be real? The impulse was strong and sudden. He cleared his throat to speak, but happened to glance at Adam. The boy's excitement shamed him into silence.

The preacher, who had hesitated again when he heard the judge clear his throat, turned to the couple, saying, "I require and charge you both—as ye will answer at the dreadful day of judgment, when the secrets of all hearts shall be disclosed—that if either of you know any impediment, why ye may not be lawfully joined together in matrimony, ye do now confess it. For be ye well assured, that if any persons are joined together otherwise than as God's word doth allow, their marriage is not lawful."

William looked pained. The minister saw it and said, "William?"

The judge smiled, Adam glanced questioningly at William, Victoria looked at Sam as if nothing had happened.

William shifted.

"William," the preacher said, "if you know of any impediments . . . you got to speak or at the day of judgment . . . it's going to be most dreadful for your soul. Speak, if you know something. It's your soul."

"I do."

"I haven't asked that yet," Sam said frustrated. "Before I ask you whether you take Victoria as a wife, you have to tell me if you know of something that keeps you from marrying her. That's what you answer now."

"Just did."

"Oh . . . I see."

Adam's eyes were terror-filled, the judge's mood turned, and he forgot about possible messages and problems from town. Victoria, unperturbed, ignored the discussion and looked at the minister as if no objection had been made, waiting for him to continue.

"William, what are you talking about?" The preacher asked, then increasingly irritated, added, "Do you know what you're doing?"

"I do."

"Then tell me why you can't marry Victoria."

"I've had other wives."

"Are they dead?"

Victoria sported a grimace and glared at the minister.

William said meekly, "That's the problem. Don't know. Know 'bout one. Died not long ago. The others, don't know."

Victoria, in a soft but firm voice said, still staring at the preacher, "William, there is no problem. You weren't married legally to any of them."

William rocked his head sideways and grunted, "Um."

Victoria continued, "You didn't break vows because your masters . . . or their masters separated you. You know you can't possibly find them now, nor are you under obligation to them. Your masters broke your vows. But the vows, if you took any, weren't ever really yours. Did you vow . . . or just jump a broom? No, there were no vows to break. Your masters lent to you what they thought was their property . . . lent them to you for their purposes and . . . when their evil purposes changed, they took them away. You weren't free to keep your vows. You weren't free to make any. You have, William Richman, never been married."

William looked at her with tears in his eyes.

"And William Richman, you're the only man I know who would bring this up. You're a good man, and I want to marry you by taking vows . . . me to you and you to me." She smiled at him, "Can Sam continue?"

William responded with a melancholy smile, his eyes still wet. He said determinedly, "Yes." He turned to face the preacher. "No reason to stop. Just somethin' I was worried 'bout."

"Good," Sam quickly responded.

The judge scowled, mourning the death of his last hope for derailing this unfortunate union. Suddenly his disparate thoughts came together. He didn't want to stop this marriage. He wanted to stop Victoria from ever marrying, from ever leaving him. She was all he had. Without her, he'd be alone. He shook his head as he felt his eyes grow moist. He couldn't stand the thought that Victoria wouldn't be in her cabin when he wanted to talk to her, get her advice, see Adam. He almost envied William. William would be with her, and he would be left behind, left out . . . alone.

"William, wilt thou have this woman to thy wedded wife, to live together after God's ordinance, in the holy estate of matrimony? Wilt thou love her, comfort her, honor, and keep her, in sickness and in health; and forsaking all others, keep thee only unto her, so long as ye both shall live?"

"I do."

The preacher whispered, "Say, 'I will.'"

"I will, then."

"Victoria, wilt thou have this man to thy wedded husband, to live together after God's ordinance, in the holy state of matrimony? Wilt thou obey him, and serve him, love, honor, and keep him, in sickness and in health; and forsaking all others keep thee only unto him, so long as ye both shall live?"

"I most certainly will . . . as long as I live."

Sam looked sternly at Victoria, and she smiled back at him. He continued, "Who giveth this woman to be married to this man?"

The judge, still stood by the window watching the ceremony from a distance, responded slightly embarrassed, realizing he should have been at Victoria's side, "I guess I do."

Victoria looked at him, amused. This was going to be a wedding to remember, for all the wrong reasons.

The preacher directed William to take Victoria's hand in his right hand and to repeat the words, "I William take Victoria to my wedded wife, to have and to hold, from this day forward, for better for worse, for richer for poorer, in sickness and in health, to love and to cherish, till death us do part, according to God's holy ordinance; and thereto I plight thee my troth."

He directed them to let go of their clasp, then asked Victoria to take William's right hand and repeat, "I Victoria take William Richman to my wedded husband, to have and to hold, from this day forward, for better for worse, for richer for poorer, in sickness and in health, to love, cherish, and to obey, till death us do part, according to God's holy ordinance; and thereto to give thee my troth."

Sam announced, "I understand there's no ring."

William responded, in a hopeful tone, "Don't have one. Can we do without?"

"No, no, no! Wait!" the judge interjected forcefully. "Just a moment." He walked briskly across the room, questioning why he was doing this. He opened the door, disappeared into the hall, closing the door softly.

William and Victoria looked at each other. Victoria had anticipated everything to that point in the ceremony, but she worried what the judge might do. She'd noted his mood and feared he was working hard to delay the ceremony till he could figure out a way to permanently stop it. No one said anything. Adam was thoroughly disappointed with every delay, and shuffled off to look out the window while they waited.

The judge returned quickly with an old ring box. He stepped to the preacher and handed it to Sam.

Seeing the box, Victoria assured him she could not accept it.

He shrugged off her resistance. "If you won't keep it, use it for the ceremony . . . so it's proper. This ring belonged to my father's mother. I want you to use it . . . to keep it. I'll never need it."

The wide-eyed minister took the box respectfully from his master. He put the paper from which he was reading the ceremony down on the table, opened the ring box and extended it to William. William took out a narrow wedding band. He held it up so Victoria could see it. The magnitude of what the judge had done overwhelmed her, and she broke into uncontrollable sobs. This was her grandmother's ring.

The preacher let her cry for a time, then said quietly to William as Victoria continued to sob, "Repeat after me: With this ring I thee wed, and with all my worldly goods, I thee endow; In the name of the Father, and of the Son, and of the Holy Ghost. Amen."

William repeated the words, then took Victoria's left hand and gently pushed the ring onto her finger.

Sam continued the ceremony, "Let us pray. Our Father, who art in heaven, hallowed be thy name; thy kingdom come;

thy will be done on earth, as it is in heaven; give us this day our daily bread; and forgive us our trespasses, as we forgive those who trespass against us; and lead us not into temptation; but deliver us from evil. Amen."

Victoria was unable to control her tears. The minister smiled at the couple.

"Is that it, then?" asked William. "Are we married?"

"No, no, no. Not yet," Sam said nervously. "I've still got to bless you." And without pausing, he continued, "O Eternal God. Creator, and Preserver of all mankind, giver of all spiritual grace, the author of everlasting life; send thy blessing upon these thy servants, this man and this woman, whom we bless in thy name; that as Isaac and Rebekah lived faithfully together, so these persons may surely perform and keep the vow and covenant betwixt them made—whereof this ring given and received is a token and pledge—and may ever remain in perfect love and peace together, and live according to thy laws, through Jesus Christ our Lord. Amen."

The preacher reached down and took both their hands, joining them together and said, "Those who God hath joined together, let no man put asunder."

Victoria, in control of her emotions, had become impatient. "Are we married now?"

"No, not yet. Be quiet," Sam said, clearly increasingly exasperated by the interruptions. He turned to the only witness, the judge, and said, "Forasmuch as William and Victoria have consented together in holy wedlock, and have witnessed the same before God and this company, and thereto have given and pledged their troth, each to the other, and have declared the same by giving and receiving a ring, and by joining hands; I pronounce, that they are man and wife; in the name of the Father, and of the Son, and of the Holy Ghost. Amen." Anticipating another interruption, he hurried on, "God the Father, God the Son, God the Holy Ghost, bless, preserve, and keep you: The Lord mercifully with his favor look upon you and fill you with all spiritual benediction and grace; that ye may so live together in this life, that in the world to come ye may have life everlasting. Amen."

William said quietly, "Hosanna!"

But Victoria, overpowered by what she was doing, shouted, "Praise God. For he hath redeemed me and given me a man . . . a good man. Praise God, all ye men and angels. For he is mighty to save. Hosanna to the Highest!"

William, invigorated by Victoria's outburst, grabbed her around the middle and pulled her tight and kissed her. Adam, wrapped his arms around the couple. The judge quietly watched, no emotion visible on his face, and the preacher looked on enviously.

Chapter 37

Late April 1864, Richmond, Virginia

Matthew waited in a Confederate War Department office. He was annoyed the captain hadn't permanently rid him of Walthrope. Perhaps this rapidly arranged, unexpected meeting was to announce that Walthrope had stepped out of line and would no longer be a problem for him, but he doubted it. Such an urgent call early in the morning didn't bode well. He was glad he at least no longer hid the pariah.

Walthrope's "hostess" had reported increasing lunacy. She'd heard screaming in his secured room, shouting about murder, his wife and child, and his fortune made at the faro tables. He'd demanded through the locked door to see President Davis and General Lee and struck a slave who had entered to remove his chamber pot. His keeper was frightened that, now crazy, he would burn down her house, kill a slave or come after her. But that had ended a few days earlier at the direction of the Confederate officer, when Matthew had personally delivered a private's uniform to Walthrope. He hadn't wanted to see Walthrope and left the uniform at the house with a message that a government agent would call for him that evening.

When Matthew left the house, he was elated. He was through with the hellish fellow. Walthrope was now a ward of the Confederacy, and Matthew was delighted with the new arrangement. For the first time in weeks, he was able to enjoy the fresh April morning and wondered when the dogwoods would begin to bloom.

As he waited now for the captain, he tried to assure himself that this morning beckoning was a quick meeting announcing Walthrope—or Dante or whoever he had been at the decisive moment—was gone . . . for good. If Matthew was wrong, if the meeting didn't boast the good news he dreamed of, he would use his best arguments to convince this officer—proud, insecure and stubborn—of the danger of the lunatic bon vivant wandering freely.

The command to come immediately, then being left to wait, didn't anger Matthew as it usually would have. Under normal circumstances, he'd have already departed, but on this occasion he wanted to hear the news from the soldier's own mouth, he wanted to see Walthrope's corpse, to confirm his demise.

Matthew also knew, but didn't dwell on it, that he was not really free to leave. His continued business under the government's vigilant neglect, and even his personal safety and freedom, could quickly disappear if the captain, or others, willed it. Whatever was required, Matthew was willing to pay.

The widow in Castle Thunder came to his mind. What a lovely woman she'd been when he'd seen her in Staunton. Matthew loved beautiful things, and she fit neatly the category. He felt no romantic desire, just an appreciation for the beauty of the thing. He remembered her elegance and refinement, her rapturous profile, almost a radiance. He had enjoyed just watching her—so full of life.

Walthrope had defaced her in his fury, and Matthew pitied the woman, regretted the lessened beauty in the world and wondered aloud, "Why did he have to do that?" Now, innocent, she was in the prison with little hope for the future. Matthew couldn't see how it would work out well for her. Her only possible escape would be the government tiring of her, exchanging her. Of course they would, but there was that murder matter. Surely they didn't believe it, but would they try her for murder and use that and treason as an excuse to hang a lady in her state, a fat woman? Tragic. A forlorn lover caught in a less than civil war. Beauty was in decay all around him, and it saddened him, but it had brought him money and power. Why couldn't he have them without the untidiness? He sighed in resignation.

His thoughts were interrupted by a soldier who abruptly announced he would be seen. The soldier led Matthew to the officer, who sat at his desk, looking out a window.

"I'm guessing I'm not here to celebrate war's end," Matthew said, breaking the silence.

The officer jerked his head and glared sternly. "No, your friend's gone."

Matthew's excitement surged.

"Dante's disappeared, and no one knows where he is."

His excitement abated. It was not the news he wanted.

The officer continued after a brief hesitation, "We were escorting him north, as planned, but he slipped his escort. Vanished! Gone!" He paused again before asking, "Where would he go?"

"Go?" Matthew said absent-mindedly, busy thinking of the ramifications of the news.

"Yes, where would he hide?"

Matthew thought carefully about the man he knew and responded, "He won't hide."

"Not hide?"

"Not in the sense you're thinking. He'll just take another identity and melt away."

"Melt?"

"Yes, like ice on a Richmond summer day."

"That's good." The officer's voice lightened. "Then . . . it's not as I feared."

"What did you fear?"

"Never mind. Thank you, and please close the door as you leave."

"No! You called me here urgently, had me wait interminably. And that's it? There's something more to this."

The captain smiled, "No, everything's fine . . . as long as he disappears into some other person, in some other town. I'm not concerned."

"You were scared he'd come after you."

"Nonsense. Maybe a little. But it's nothing . . . nothing. You wanted to be rid of him. Now you are."

"I didn't want him to disappear again . . . not like this." His voice rose in anger. "I wanted to never . . . never see him again. They are not the same thing. This does not do, sir."

"You said he would vanish."

"Yes, but remember, he disappeared after Staunton . . . then used his invisibility to go after the widow."

"What are you saying?"

"He left comfort and safety . . . his new life . . . for revenge. He used his new identity to settle an old score." Matthew was expressionless. "I'm afraid he'll look for a chance to . . . ."

The Confederate's eyes flickered fear.

Matthew continued passionately, "He might think we mistreated him, humiliated him, imprisoned him. I don't think he'll forget. You can't . . . for your own safety, let him fade away. And now he's crazy! He'll be more unpredictable. You have to find him."

"What do you propose?" the officer asked desperately.

Matthew laughed. "That's in your power . . . not mine."

"Yes, I know that." For the first time, the man humbled his tone. "But I need your help . . . anything you can suggest. You know how to do this."

"I think it best to have him dead, regardless of how."

"What should I do?" the officer said in complete panic.

Matthew almost laughed again. This mean, controlling man was more cowardly than he'd believed. He was not like the soldiers or even the generals on the front line. He took courage only behind a protective desk in Richmond. For the first time, Matthew felt a fondness for the man. He responded civilly, quietly, "I know of a man who's been searching for Walthrope. A sheriff from Staunton. He actually interviewed me. Ask his help. He surely would have found him had it not been for lack of our cooperation. Mr. Walthrope's arrest is his reason for breathing, I do believe, and if you offer the help of the government and give him information you have, I think he'll track him down or die trying."

"I'll search him out."

"I believe Captain Richardson at Castle Thunder might help you find the good sheriff."

"Why the commandant?"

"I have developed a friendship with Richardson . . . to keep my eye on the situation . . . the widow. I understand from him there was a meeting at the prison—the sheriff and commandant . . . about Walthrope . . . Dante."

"Do you think the widow at risk then . . . from Dante?"

"We are . . . I fear, all at risk. Even the dog."

"Yes, the dog." The officer gazed out the window again, eyes glazed over, and Matthew turned his back on the man, walked out of the room, leaving the door open.

Chapter 38

Late April 1864, Richmond, Virginia

Miss Morrow was with Betsy again, sitting stiffly in the same chair she'd occupied a week earlier. She had brought a still-warm loaf of bread and placed it on Betsy's table. Her expression was again efficient with no suggestion of compassion, and Betsy wondered about what was inside the woman. She'd listened without comment to the woman's information. Betsy was to be taken to a doctor after sundown because of her sickness.

Florence had arranged it with the commandant who was concerned about Betsy's condition and wanted a doctor to confirm the ailment. Florence explained a few of the tests doctors, with their interesting modern techniques, were using to confirm prospects of a growing family.

Betsy didn't want to hear about them and grimaced when Florence described an examination—called a ballottement—in which the doctor palpitated the womb, and she was only slightly less uncomfortable when Florence told her about doctors testing women's urine.

"I've never heard of these. They're disgusting. I don't want any of them."

"I do agree with you, and you won't have to have them. But they're just what doctors are doing now for women in your state."

"I don't want a doctor at all. If I have a choice, I'll stick with a midwife."

"Don't give up on doctors. There's another test that appeals to me."

"Will I want to hear about it? I don't like the sound of the others."

"This one is pleasant . . . exciting. Doctors use their stethoscopes now to hear a baby's heartbeat.

"I've seen a stethoscope. That wouldn't be nearly as bad."

"No, and I understand the stethoscope is the most reliable way to tell. But it doesn't matter, Mrs. Gragg. You're not going to get any of these tests. No doctor really expects you. It's just an excuse to get you outside the prison. Of course, the commandant knows nothing of that." In detail she then explained the plan.

Betsy couldn't believe what she was hearing, but ambivalence consumed her. Out of prison. Out of Richmond. Out of Virginia. Out of the Confederacy. Among Northerners. In the Union. Closer to Hank. So many good things were possible, but all beyond her beloved Shenandoah Valley, outsider her native state.

Florence expected her to say something, but when she'd finished recounting the details Betsy said nothing. "Is there anything more I can do?" Florence added, hoping for some response from Mrs. Gragg.

"For me?" Betsy said flatly.

"Mrs. Gragg, are you well today?"

"I was."

"You don't want to do this?"

"I have no choice. I can't stay here to be hung for murder. I'm tired of the rats and the bugs and the spiders." She shivered. "I can't stand guards and guns and commands and firing squads. I can't bear the thoughts of my baby born in this squalor. I can't eat the disgusting and tasteless meat anymore."

"But something . . . part of you doesn't want to do it?"

"Not part, all of me. I'm no murderess . . . or traitress."

"But you're at risk of being tried regardless."

"Miss . . . Florence, I'm already tried. Whether there's ever a formal charge or trial, I'm already branded with that "A" . . . and a "T" and an "M". It's a wonder they can fit so many brands on me. I can take no comfort . . . in Virginia, but I am innocent . . . and it's distasteful to leave under such circumstances."

"Yes."

"I suppose . . . if I weren't with child, I would stay and make them confront their dishonesty, day after day, even if this place drove me to madness . . . which it is. I would make such a ruckus, they'd have to try me . . . or set me free. And if they hung me for something I didn't do, they'd bear that eternal burden in hell. But I'm not alone in this tribulation, and I often think of that saying, 'Sweet are the uses of adversity.' Something good must come of this . . . this nightmare. Does it change me into something better? Does it change Virginia and somehow make her more beautiful? Does it change the world and make it more livable? Does it better the world my child will live in? Is this merely a mother's sacrifice for her child?"

"And her husband."

"Yes, I think of him. He's in all of this, above it, below it, through it. He has his own trials, and I can't . . . I don't want to imagine what it must be like for him. I've heard of coming battles in Virginia, but I don't know what to make of them. The guards tell me the North is ready to negotiate . . . we've won. But I don't believe them, and when it comes to my poor husband, winning or losing the war doesn't matter, because it doesn't save him . . . either way. He's trapped . . . like me . . . like all of us in some dark hole without dimension . . . or maybe we're just falling one by one into eternal oblivion." She laughed at her own melancholy.

Florence felt a touch of guilt, watching with admiration this fragile woman of steel.

Betsy continued, "I'm grateful he doesn't know I sit here. I fear what he'd do if he knew . . . that I'm here and already condemned."

"But the newspapers."

"Don't you think I haven't thought of that? I dread it. I imagine him opening a paper and finding an account of a widow . . . a Mrs. Henderson held for murder or spying or for whatever they write. I've had nightmares about that every night for the years—that's what these few months seems like—that I've been here. And what would he do, if he found out today? Come to rescue me tomorrow night . . . when I'm already rescued? But he'd be caught, and I'd be free—another Romeo and Juliet tragedy. No, I don't believe it will happen . . . it can't. God who has been so merciful to me as I've been beset with enemies . . . he would not do that, too. No, my Father in Heaven has kept him in ignorance of my travails, and he's kept me ignorant of his suffering."

Betsy kept speaking. "Ah, to not know any of this. To be a child again. To see only the yard, the house where I lived and played. To know that papa and mama would protect me from evil. But those days are gone, and I live in a world . . . well, you know the world, Florence, and I have meandered once more into darkness."

"You've not meandered, my dearest. But the children know . . . too. They know. They play with toy guns, soldiering in the streets. Their fathers and grandfathers leave . . . and never come home. Or they come home mangled. They lose their homes, everything around them shakes and falls. They know, and it's a sober time."

"I've become so consumed in my own affairs I haven't even asked . . . I know nothing of you, so self-centered am I now."

"Not at all. I fault you in nothing."

"Then what of you?"

Florence smiled. "Mrs. Gragg, we all have difficulties, hardships. Mine are no worse than some and better than others."

"Why can't that be my answer? Why can't I at least lift my head out of this mire, breathe intoxicating air again and think of others . . . anyone . . . and help someone. I'm failing at loving my fellow man."

"You judge yourself harshly."

"Who better to know what I really am?"

"You spoke of him just now."

"Hank?" She laughed. "He's . . . was caught up in the romance of it all. He can't judge me fairly . . . honestly."

"It wasn't him. Not him. God can judge you. Only he knows your heart . . . and mine. I hope he will have compassion on us both. He sees our . . . your burdens. Perhaps he's sent me . . . just to alleviate part of the weight you bear."

Betsy gently looked at Florence. "Perhaps. You've certainly lifted my spirits . . . given me hope in this hellhole . . . you and my kind hero, Nero."

Florence smiled. "And how is Nero?"

"Good. He comes to see me daily now, and the guards . . . they even let him in here . . . which explains the dog hair everywhere. You'll surely leave with a part of him."

Abruptly Florence announced, "I must leave. It's likely we won't see each other again . . . not in this life. Remember what I've told you. Freedom is hours from now, not days, months or years. Don't despair . . . but do not celebrate. Be somber, patient. Hide your excitement . . . and your fear. You'll weather this. Yes, I've seen your soul, and you'll weather it . . . no matter the trials yet to come. You're stronger than you know. You'll overcome what awaits you."

Betsy rose, "Thank you." She stepped toward her visitor who also had risen. Betsy initiated it, but both women hugged each other tightly. "Oh, thank you, thank you!"

Florence eventually pulled away from Betsy's hug and without another word, turned her head away, sniffed and made her way to the door. She didn't wipe away the tears dripping from her eyes until she was beyond Betsy's gaze.

The evening was warm and moist. There was a refreshing breeze and fragrant air. It had been a long time. She looked down at her soiled, ill-fitting and worn dress, her dirty hands, and she was ashamed. She was being led from Castle Thunder's entrance, and she stopped to look back at it, hoping it would be her last view of its barred windows and brick walls.

Everything was happening as Florence had outlined. At dusk an unfamiliar guard came to her cell, opened it without warning. He told her she was to see a doctor by command of Captain Richardson. She willingly, but nervously, followed him as they passed other guards and out the front of the prison. She didn't know what was next and what role she was to play, so she just kept walking. He didn't bind her and walked alongside her. Only as the Castle Thunder door closed did she see Nero resting in a corner, but he didn't see her and made no fuss. She longed to call him and steal him away.

The guard said nothing, but turned right. They were both silent as they moved along Cary Street. At 8th the guard motioned to the right. She paid no attention to anything going on around them, fearing that everyone was glaring at her—the traitress, the adulteress, the murderess. She kept her eyes down to avoid their judgments. They walked another block and a half before a woman across the road screamed, startling Betsy. The guard grabbed her arm gently, stopping her.

She peeked at the guard, who said softly, "We'll wait."

The woman shouted, "He took it. Thief! He's got my money! Thief!"

The guard without saying more took off after an indistinct shadow now running a half block away. The woman was crying hysterically. "Someone help me. He's stolen all my money." The woman too began running.

Betsy was left alone. She could sneak away, but where to? She stood where the guard had stopped her. She heard a soft voice from behind her. She didn't dare turn around because she recognized it.

"My dear, you shouldn't be out . . . not by yourself in the dark. There are thieves and scoundrels about. Richmond is no longer a safe and quiet town . . . and you are so lovely." Silence. Betsy froze. He spoke again, "I'm so glad to have found you. I hope you're in good health . . . with our child."

Fear overwhelmed her. She hadn't expected this deception. Florence had acted so convincingly, even the tears on her cheeks. She must have been a stooge, acting at the whim of this monster. Betsy felt all was lost. She'd been freed from the prison by Miss Morrow so depravity could cut her throat . . . away from guard and canine protector. It had been so well orchestrated. She shivered and stepped away from him into the street.

"Where are you going, my love? I'll always be with you . . . and you with me."

She didn't reply but walked briskly toward the other side of the street. She was nearly there when a strong hand grasped her left arm firmly. She turned, swinging her right hand savagely, perceiving only at the last second—but well after it was too late—that the man was not the right height or race. It was not Walthrope. The man stumbled back as he absorbed the blow.

He laughed and patted his nose with a handkerchief he'd pulled quickly from somewhere. He immediately and humbly said, "Forgive me for grabbing your arm, Ma'am. But I needed to stop you . . . get your attention. I didn't know where you were going. I was afraid of losing you in the dark. I've been sent to meet you."

Betsy considered his comments carefully and whispered, "I'm sorry. I thought you were someone else. Will you be all right?"

"Yes, in just a moment. I've been hit harder . . . just wasn't expecting it."

"I'm sincerely sorry," she said with contrition.

"We don't have time. Come with me."

"I thought you were . . ."

"The man hiding in the doorway? I heard him talking . . . not what he said. He's gone now. He ran when I came up the sidewalk. Mrs. Henderson, we need to be swift. Please follow me, motioning her back toward Cary Street.

"Where are we going?"

"You're not to ask questions. I'll answer none."

He quickened their pace until they reached Cary Street. Turning right, away from the prison, they walked for several minutes. Suddenly the man stopped, saying, "I leave you here. A farm wagon will pass shortly. Climb in the back, cover yourself with straw when no one watches. Don't say anything—just get in the wagon. It will take you out of Richmond. Goodbye." He stepped away.

"Must you leave?" she asked desperately, frightened to be alone again.

He turned and said simply, "Take courage."

She smiled sadly. She would have been content to be alone and free, but for her unnerving run-in with Walthrope. How had he known she was leaving tonight? Had he been waiting outside the prison? For how long? Days? Weeks? She shivered again. He was mad. Something had happened to him. It would have been better to think he'd arranged her escape than that he'd been waiting for her. A chill passed as she remembered his voice. But it wasn't her memory. She was hearing it again.

"You didn't stay with your friend long . . . not long at all. Did he touch you? I'll kill him for that!"

Betsy didn't know what to do. If she ran, the wagon would never find her, but if he kidnapped her what difference would it make? She turned toward the voice, but still couldn't see him. "What do you want?" she called out quietly, defiantly.

"Now, that's more like my Betsy, ever concerned about what I want. A thoughtful wife. I'm most fortunate."

He was crazy. "What do you want?" she asked louder.

"My legal wife . . . my coming child . . . happiness."

"I'm not your wife."

"What? Have you forgotten? What have they done to you. Betsy, you and I are joined in holy matrimony . . . we are one flesh. But we can't be seen together in Richmond . . . not now. You must make your way to Washington as best you can. I'll follow, so don't worry about me. In Washington, everything will be as it should be. We shall be together . . . with our son."

"I'll scream, and if I do, they'll find you."

"Yes, they might. But don't scream. You'd reveal your escape, and they'd take you back. I couldn't bear that."

"You're a lunatic."

"Have they taken your memory and destroyed your love? Have patience, my lovely, till we're together again. In Washington, we'll rekindle the love we shared. They've made you forget me in their terrible prison. I shall find you, you shall turn to me, and I will heal you."

"Shared love? I mock you, sir."

"Oh, Betsy, you are lovely when you play these games of the heart. Yes, even before that bungling Yankee spy tried to spoil you . . . you always loved me. Yes, you loved me, and you proved it when you said, 'I do.'"

"You're mad! We never married. I'd never . . ."

"Don't tease this way. I know your feelings. You don't deserve me, but we're bound in holy matrimony. Have you so quickly forgotten our vows . . . at that beautiful church in Staunton. No, you haven't. You know you belong with . . . to me. I've condescended to love you . . . to marry you. Perhaps I could do better . . . especially now you have no friends . . . no standing. But I'll be true to my troth and honor . . . and know you'll do the same."

She didn't respond.

"Betsy, my love, you cannot deny . . . to anyone that we are wed. Yes, my fair branded one, you're in a difficult path, but I will save you. They can do you no harm."

"What do you want?" she demanded loudly.

"Please keep your voice down. You don't want to attract attention. Remember, you're escaping from prison. You were meant to be in a mansion . . . and there they had you as if you were a . . . a . . . I can't say it."

She repeated her question softly, "What do you want?"

"I've told you—the two of us together. Do hurry to Washington. I must leave to prepare your welcome. I cannot be detained longer. I shouldn't have stayed so long, but I delayed to see you—to reassure you, to let you know that I watch over you. All is well. Even though people have kept us apart . . . to poison you . . . to defile you, they cannot separate us . . . in life or . . . in death. I am your destiny, and you are my love."

"I keep us apart."

He laughed softly, "No, of course not, dear Betsy. Oh, what flirtations, even with your husband. How merry you are, even amidst trials. I ache to hold you in my arms, to look into your dear green eyes. It's hard to wait, my beauty." His voice had drifted into a dream-like state, but it suddenly turned hard. "No, but your mother, the Yankee, they have kept us apart, and they must each . . ." His voice softened again, "Oh, never mind that now, not when we're together like this . . . with so much to look forward to. Goodbye, love. I'll see you in Washington. There it will be as it always should have been." Silence.

He was gone, and Betsy crumpled to the ground.

Chapter 39

Late April 1864, Richmond, Virginia

Captain Richardson was thinking about Mrs. Henderson when he opened a directive he received the afternoon before but hadn't had time to read. It instructed him to prepare her and several other prisoners for exchange and transportation to the North.

He read the order several times, chuckling to himself. "Where is she?" he wondered aloud. She'd been lost during the confusion of a random street robbery the night before. The culprit had escaped with his bounty, but the victim—the woman—was grateful to the guard for acting so gallantly. She came forward willingly, reporting what had happened and the courage of the guard who in vain scrambled after the ruffian. In the disorder, Mrs. Henderson had fled.

Something didn't feel right about the whole affair, but there was nothing to do, especially now he'd received the order. He thought about rigid Miss Morrow and her interest in Mrs. Henderson, but didn't linger on the thought. He had other things to consider. Mrs. Henderson was somewhere safe. He wouldn't report her escape—no woman had ever escaped from Castle Thunder. Why muddy the record? He'd report she was lost during the exchange.

Sheriff had been on his way out of Richmond, waiting to catch the train to Staunton. He was in the station when the messenger came summoning him to the War Department.

His last weeks had been futile, and he'd concluded someone, somewhere, didn't want Walthrope found. He'd disappeared without a trace. Perhaps he'd been killed by some double-crossed business partner. The sheriff had concluded—uncharacteristically more in wishful belief than in well-reasoned analysis—that Mrs. Henderson was no longer in danger.

He still hid his deepest motivation for hunting Walthrope from everyone. He'd told them, and they'd believed him, that he was only interested in stopping the miscreant before he harmed again. But that had never been his motive. He'd done it for her—Mrs. Henderson . . . Betsy—because she made him feel young again, and because he wanted to protect her as if she'd been his own . . . his daughter, surely.

The messenger led him to a small room in the War Department where a captain rose to greet him warmly. The sheriff, curious and suspicious, was put off by the welcome.

"Thank you for coming so quickly," offered the Confederate. "Would you like some coffee?"

"Coffee?"

"Well, chicory coffee. Would you like some?"

"No, but thank you," the sheriff responded crestfallen that he wouldn't at least get real coffee out of the interview.

"Please sit down. We have much to talk about."

"Much to talk about?" the sheriff said dully. "A surprise to me."

"You've got questions. If you didn't, you wouldn't be the man described to me . . . the distinguished detective."

"Distinguished detective? Simple sheriff."

"Nonsense. I've heard of the investigation you've undertaken and hope it progresses well."

"You've heard of my investigation?"

"Yes, good things."

"Well, sir, I wish you'd share them, because I've heard nothing promising . . . and make no progress. This very morning, your sergeant found me on my way home for lack of success. So your praise sounds odd . . . a bit out of tune . . . to my ears."

"You've given up?"

"I never give up, but I've abandoned this investigation. Nothing more I can do."

"Why would you think that?"

"I've searched for a man for weeks with nothing to show. I heard rumors . . . thought I saw shadows early on, but now . . . now I hear nothing and the shadows are faded. My quarry has disappeared . . . so I leave feeling . . ."

"You needn't feel that," the captain responded brightly.

The sheriff was irritated by the officer's enthusiasm. He asked slowly, "Because?"

"I can help you . . . give you some direction."

"Why . . . why now?"

"Someone's been hiding him . . . your quarry—I like that word. Those hiding him aren't interested in him anymore."

"No longer interested in him?"

"Precisely. I can't tell you who hid him . . . or their motives, but they've changed."

"Motives have changed?"

"They have changed, and they've shared with me certain information about him. I do hope you can use it."

The sheriff stood up suddenly, smiled, and said, "It's too late, sir. I've determined to give it up and return to my wife in Staunton." He noticed the officer's complexion pale.

"I am sorry. I'd hoped I could help in your business."

"My business?"

"Yes, catching this scoundrel. A murderer is he?"

"He's a murderer, but there are many around. War breeds them like Richmond rats, and not one of them is worth a call from the Confederate Government." There was an uncomfortable silence before he continued, "Seems out of scale. Too small for you, sir. No, a murder and murderer . . . they aren't worth the time of someone of your stature . . . not while the Union Army covets all land between here and Washington City. This search is no longer worth my time. I'm returning to Staunton. I should never have come. It was a mistake. My time as sheriff ends next month. I'll give it up to another man, but he won't have time or the interest to search for Walthrope."

The captain persisted, his face turning still whiter. Sheriff perceived a slight shaking in his voice. "Sheriff, you must . . . recognize even one murderer loose in Richmond is too many. Surely you would not have us ignore such a villain . . . because we're at war."

"One villain among thousands of villains on the streets of Richmond? It makes no sense. But your interest in a murder a hundred miles from the capital—that peeks my curiosity. It's a strange dance we do here today, you and me. I'm not interested in dancing. I was on my way home, and I should . . . I will go."

Resignation entered the officer's countenance. "Yes, Sheriff, I admit I've played a game, but we desperately need your help."

"We?"

"The government."

"Still the game, then."

"No, no. I need your help. I'll give you the details . . . all the information I have."

"Good. Tell me why you brought me here? What's your interest in Walthrope? Why you protected him? And why you're suddenly so frightened of him?"

The officer smiled, "Nothing gets by you."

"Whether it does or not, isn't the corn."

"It's right to business, is it? That's right. I'll be direct if I can count on your discretion . . . your honor."

"You can count only on my listening. My discretion and honor are not to be offered in ignorance and will always be left in my power to govern."

"Well said, sir." The captain cleared his throat. "This Walthrope fellow . . . we were using him as a courier and scout of sorts."

"Where?"

"Washington City." The sheriff didn't reply, but the officer waited to make sure he wouldn't, then continued. Sheriff didn't interrupt or show any signs of listening as the officer explained carefully selected and edited portions of his involvement with Walthrope. Instead he turned his head and looked at the scene outside the window and thought how hot it was for so early in the year. He did listen, nonetheless, and nothing he heard surprised him. Little was added to what he already knew but for the small daguerreotype the officer produced from a drawer in his desk. At last, he knew what his man looked like, and he looked familiar. In frustration he remembered chatting with the charming fellow in a Richmond hotel.

He was irritated at the officer. All of this could have been avoided, Walthrope apprehended, if this man hadn't thought to protect him. He was concerned for Betsy. Walthrope wanted revenge, and he was now free to try another assault. His mind was drifting, but he brought it back to the officer's windy explanation.

"If I can be honest with you, Sheriff," the officer droned on. "My fondest hope is that the woman went north and that he'll follow her there . . ."

"What woman?" interrupted the sheriff.

"The woman, Mrs. Henderson—the one they had in Castle Thunder, the one he attacked."

"They had?"

"Yes. She's gone, been exchanged."

"Exchanged?" he asked in surprise as coldness settled in his heart.

"Yes, of sorts, but it didn't go well. She disappeared at some point. No one knows when."

"During the exchange?"

"Apparently so."

Sheriff's mind spun. Had Walthrope kidnapped her? He recoiled. It might be too late. She might be dead, buried in the pocked landscape of the war.

But if she wasn't yet dead—Sheriff felt his resolve returning—she was out there, undefended. The sheriff allowed the officer to finish telling him everything he knew.

"I'm counting on your discretion," the officer said.

Sheriff was annoyed and sniffed. "Thank you, you've been helpful."

"You'll handle it for me?"

"No, I don't believe so."

"I thought . . . Why did I go through the whole . . ."

"I'll find Walthrope."

"I don't understand."

"I suspect not."

"We are in agreement though."

"I don't believe we are, and I won't be your agent."

"I still don't understand your . . ."

"You needn't. Good day, sir."

Quickly Sheriff rose, raising his hat to his head, and stepped into the hall. He'd already forgotten the man he'd just interviewed and was planning his travel to Washington. If yet alive, where else would she go? She couldn't stay in the South. Mrs. Henderson would go to Washington to be near her Union lover, and Walthrope, hatred ripened to obsession, would search for her unrelentingly.

Then to Washington. He should have asked for a pass to get through the lines, but he'd not go back to the soldiering bureaucrat. He'd send the captain a note and demand a pass. At least he'd taken the daguerreotype.

Sheriff left the captain mumbling nervously to himself, more agitated than he'd been when the sheriff had arrived. The man's hands trembled, his skin was clammy, his mind foggy. He didn't know if he should be insulted by or pleased with the sheriff and wasn't certain the sheriff would help him. The officer was left in horror, imaging Walthrope tracking him down in his own office after he'd dispensed with the reportedly lovely Mrs. Henderson.

Chapter 40

April 1864, Eastern Kentucky

The sky had turned dark during the ceremony and as the wedding ended, rain pelted the roof. A sharp rap on the door interrupted the festive joy, and when the judge opened it, the slave who had been sent to town stood there looking grim, his clothes dripping wet. He waited to be invited into the office.

The judge looked at him, trying to guess his report. Was he to lose his sister in marriage and by flight the same day? He motioned the man into the room and dismissed Sam. He began pacing back and forth along the windows, eventually stopping abruptly. He gazed into the afternoon darkness where the intense, spring green of grass and trees was turned a shadowless gray. Finally, he asked, "What did you hear?"

"The man, he's awake . . . but can't say nothing. He's red all over and has blisters. Joe, the Brown's boy, he said he heard his master say the rash done proved he was a no good drunk. He got loaded and rode in the woods with no sense till he fell. They found him flat on his back by the road. Back of his head was crushed in . . . by the fall. He was holding on poison ivy vines. Lot of men laughing about it in town. They were saying his eyes was so swollen he couldn't see, his nose so big he couldn't breathe, his mouth so stuffed with blisters he couldn't talk none."

"What else were they saying," the judge asked patiently.

"Some body said he heard the doc say he might cut the man's throat so he could breathe. But that don't seem right to me. Cutting a man's throat kills him, don't it?"

"I think they're talking about a little round hole in just the right place to help him breathe. It wouldn't kill him."

"Well, if you say so, but he can't talk . . . not now. Joe said he heard the doc thought he might die."

The judge smiled. "That's all good. Tell Robert he can come in from the road."

"Yes, sir."

The judge considered their plight. William and Victoria still had time to safely flee. Maybe they wouldn't have to go at all, he thought, momentarily hopeful. But he knew they couldn't take that chance. Suddenly he laughed and turned to William. "That was an exceptional trick you played on the man . . . on all of them."

Trying to hold back a proud smile, William said humbly, "It was Adam that pulled the vines."

"William . . . Adam, it was very smart, smart indeed. You made him look guilty."

"He was guilty," Victoria interjected angrily.

The judge, shocked by her hostility, continued unperturbed, "Yes, I know, and William's . . . and Adam's ingenious plan made sure he looked guilty without involving any of you . . . any of us."

"Until he can talk," she responded.

"Yes . . . if he ever can. I doubt he will. I'd like to think he won't. And if he does recover, he may never remember what happened to him. I'd like to say you can stay." He hesitated for a long time before pronouncing, "But I know you can't . . . shouldn't."

The next two days were tense. Victoria, William and Adam moved into a vacant slave cottage and spent their time visiting, joking, playing games among themselves in the afternoon. Slaves from the plantation would drop by in the evening to chat. Every night visitors asked to see the ring. "Why'd you get the ring?" they seemed to ask with their eyes. Their expressions led Victoria to sadly conclude they believed it was because she was his mistress.

The guests asked about the ceremony, reporting the preacher thought it the loveliest wedding he'd seen. Victoria smiled, remembering that there was nothing lovely about the ceremony or setting, except her new husband and the ring—an unexpected gesture of her brother's love. The women always asked if it was true that it was a legal wedding, and Victoria took special delight in announcing the judge was going to have it recorded as quickly as possible. "Yes, it'll be a legal marriage." She couldn't help but add with solemnity in her voice, "It's not like a slave wedding . . . not like that at all."

The judge came down both afternoons and visited for a few minutes, giving them the latest news. He was making arrangements for them to get away. He had purchased a barrel of whiskey in Lexington and was modifying two tobacco hogsheads. The large barrels would be used to hide family members and luggage.

William, uncomfortable thinking about being stuffed into a barrel, asked if such expense and trickery was needed if the man couldn't talk.

Even if Victoria's attacker didn't speak for weeks, the judge explained, he had to make sure no one knew he'd helped smuggle them out of the county or condemnation would fall on him. If there was any chance the man would speak again, they had to hide their escape.

The judge had decided to postpone his trip to Washington because it might look suspicious. They'd be on their own. He would send Robert to drive the wagon and get them onto the Central Kentucky train in Paris. He'd ride it to Covington, where he'd transfer the barrels to the ferry for crossing to Cincinnati. The judge was contacting a friend, hoping he would meet the barrels in Ohio and release the trio. At that point, they'd be safe and would ride the B&O to Baltimore. From Baltimore, they could take the spur to Washington, and in the capital start a new life.

"Why Paris?" they'd asked.

"Lexington's too close to the farm. It will be safer if we put you on at Paris." He added, in a tone of self-pity, "You'll soon be in the capital and forget friends left behind."

Never discussed was the misery they would suffer in transit. William imagined being roughly rolled onto the train, then onto the ferry. No food, no water, no break. He wondered how the judge was planning to make the weight of the barrel feel authentic and concluded it would mean being cramped inside the barrel with some type of filling. William hoped it wouldn't be tobacco. Thoughts of its smell in such tight quarters nauseated him. He even dreaded the relative comfort of the long train ride from Cincinnati.

The news continued to trickle in about Victoria's attacker, and it suggested he was tormented. The itching, the severe headache was more than the fellow could stand. The judge had learned the man had lived in the area a decade earlier, was a bad sort, and he'd just returned—deserted, the judge surmised—from fighting under General Forrest in Tennessee.

Victoria commented that she'd met the man before and wanted nothing to do with him. What she didn't say was she wasn't dealing well with the man's return. She raged internally. She knew why, but she'd never tell the judge and didn't want to tell William till they were out of Kentucky. Then she'd explain it to him . . . maybe. She hoped he'd understand, but till then she would hide her agitation.

At the end of his last visit, the judge said haltingly, "In a day or two . . . maybe tomorrow, we'll get you out of here." He spontaneously grabbed Adam, pulled him close and hugged him. The small boy responded passively, not understanding what was happening. Neither said anything.

Victoria could see the suggestion of tears in the judge's eyes, and feeling her own aching sorrow at losing him, she rose to hug him. He returned the gesture briefly, but quickly pulled away, running his hand over his eyes and face, and said sharply, "It will be hard to lose you. It will be hard to have you gone." He turned and stepped into bright sunlight.

The next day the barrels were filled in the barn with a combination of secured weights and enough tobacco against the outer walls to ensure a tobacco smell should anyone get close. Adam, who had been increasingly quiet and restless as the days had passed, was chatty, excited. He wanted to be the first stuffed into the four-foot-tall barrel and, when he was, he gleefully demonstrated that he could almost stand up when they tested the barrel head.

"It . . . It . . . It's dddark in here," was his only comment when the top had been secured.

William asked the judge, "They gotta do this?"

He looked kindly at William, "Adam and Victoria—more than you—must be hidden. The man knows them. I don't believe you were formally introduced . . . though you certainly left an impression on him." The judge smirked.

William looked worried, but Victoria smiled and pointed inside the hogshead. "I'll be all right. Look, they built a nice bench to sit on, so we don't have to crouch the whole way." She smiled mischievously. "We've got to keep this secret, or it will catch on with the rich white folk. Barrel travel! The way all the best ladies get around." She looked earnestly at William. "It won't be bad . . . and I may someday be able to stand up straight . . . again. But just in case, take a long look at me now, so you can remember when I could stand erect."

She turned serious. "Don't worry. We'll be fine. A little discomfort is worth getting away with my son." She instantly realized she'd left out William—not because she'd forgotten him, but because she wasn't yet used to worrying about him. She quickly added, "I'm grateful we'll be with my husband and Adam's father."

William didn't want to get into the other hogshead. When he looked into the barrel, he only saw images of his nightmares of hell. He couldn't bear thoughts of descending into restricted darkness. He looked at the judge and asked, "You don't think I need to ride in that barrel?"

"I didn't say that, but you're barely known here. No one knows you were with Victoria that night. No one knows you saved Adam. You could easily ride up front . . . if that's what you want."

Victoria, trying to gauge what William was feeling, commented, "It would be much better for me . . . I'd like it . . . I'd feel safer if William weren't in the barrel. If any problems come up, he . . . you could help, rather than being helpless in a barrel. I'd like William to ride up front. Just put the suitcases and bags in the second barrel." She peeked at William to see if she'd said the right thing and noted his body relax.

The judge said, "It's up to you, William."

"'Cause Victoria wants it, I'll ride up front."

"Fine," the judge said absent-mindedly as he turned to Victoria. "It's time to get in."

Adam, still standing in the reopened hogshead, said impatiently, "CCCan we go, yet?"

Victoria smiled, stretched by the barrel and took a deep breath as William, who had followed her, lifted her up. She raised her legs high to clear the barrel's side. As she gathered her skirt and squeezed it as tightly to her body as she could, William put her gently into the hogshead. They both struggled and shifted to get her dress through the barrel head, tight next to Adam. Once inside, she commented, "This is close."

"Yes," the judge said. "But look here, by the bench, there are ropes. Tie them around you so you won't fall when the barrels are rolled. Remember, as long as you're in the wagon, you'll be riding on your back, and when no one's around you can shift to be more comfortable, but when they're rolling the barrel, you need to be tied in . . . tight."

"III'll get them," Adam responded.

"Tie them tight. Look here. When they're rolling you onto the train or ferry, grab these handles on the lid and sides. Can you do that?"

"I cccan."

"Good for you. Now, take hold . . . and take care of your mama in Washington. Will you do that for me?"

"Yes, bu . . . bu . . . but can we go now?"

The judge smiled sadly, looked at Victoria. "You going to be all right?"

"This will give Adam and me time to be as close as any mother and child ought to be." She smiled. "Visit us . . . sometime." The judge stepped to the barrel and hugged his sister with one hand while patting Adam's head affectionately. Victoria tearfully repeated, "Visit us."

The judge stepped back, tears already on his cheeks. He nodded to the trusted cooper, who raised the top of the hogshead. Victoria's head was barely under where the lid would fasten. She ducked further as they secured the top. When the lid was wound into position, Victoria realized it wasn't entirely dark. The cooper had discreetly drilled small holes at various places. One hole was immediately covered by what she imaged was William's eye.

"Yuh all right?" William asked gently.

"We would be," she answered, laughing, "if the fool who's blocking our light would move."

William laughed.

"We're ready, then," the judge said. "We're going to push you up on the wagon, so grab those handles. Victoria, can you feel the handles?"

"Wait just a bit."

"Did you find the handles?"

"Got them, we're tied in. But it won't make a difference. We're squeezed too tight in here to bounce."

"Ready? Here we go." The judge nodded to the cooper and Robert. "Gently!"

The two men carefully turned the barrel on its side and rolled it.

William stepped forward, saying to the cooper, "I'll do it. Be doin' it at the train anyways."

"That's true," the judge said.

"Get ready. We're pushin' 'gain," William said. The two men pushed, quickly gaining momentum. Even with the momentum, they strained to get the barrel up a short ramp into the wagon. As they positioned and secured it, they heard a woman's sigh from the barrel.

William crouched, futilely trying to look down into one of the drilled holes, "Yuh all right?" She didn't answer, and he added, nearly panicked, "Victoria, Yuh all right?"

"Of course," she responded. "Just a little dizzy from spinning and not being able to sit up. We're trying to get comfortable now. We'll get used to it. Now, it'd be best if you stop talking to this barrel of tobacco!"

William laughed.

The four men worked quickly to get the cases into the second barrel, securing them and adding weights. They rolled it into the wagon behind Victoria's hogshead and secured it. The smaller whiskey barrel was lifted and fastened upright at the back of the wagon bed.

When the work was done, the judge looked sternly at William and said, "Take good care of them, my friend." Without awaiting a response, he turned and walked slowly toward the big house, his head bowed. William watched him go.

Chapter 41

April 1864, Eastern Kentucky

They had traveled for several hours and were well along the road leading from Lexington. Paris loomed ahead, and they hurried to catch the next train north. Trying to distract Victoria and Adam from their miserable circumstances, William kept up a constant conversation with them without making it obvious he was talking to people lying horizontally in a barrel. Robert periodically joined the conversation. All proceeded as the judge had planned, and while Victoria and Adam were uncomfortable, they endured it because the boy was enjoying the adventure and Victoria rejoiced at the growing distance between her and the poison-ivy-inflamed man.

The latest conversation was Victoria and the driver describing an earlier Confederate attack on Cynthiana, up the railroad line from Paris. The Union forces at Cynthiana had sent men south because of a rumor Confederate raider Morgan was going to strike at Paris. Instead, Morgan burned the railroad bridge between Paris and Cynthiana and struck the remaining soldiers in Cynthiana. The Union men didn't have a chance, but Morgan paroled most, gave them a speech and sent them home for exchange. Victoria, in her muffled voice, said it was a couple of years ago and there hadn't been much Confederate activity in the area since.

William turned to speak to the barrel that held Victoria, but Robert cautioned him, "Don't. That ain't the way to do it.

Just talk like you're talking to me. That ways if anybody sees, they won't suspect what's in the barrel.

"Who's in the barrel," Victoria corrected.

"You is."

"I know I am."

"Then why ask?"

In the dark barrel, Victoria rolled her eyes, "Just wanted to make sure you knew."

William ignored the exchange, wishing out loud that Victoria could ride next to him in the train to point out the bridge.

She responded, "Won't be hard to figure out."

The wagon rolled on.

William was getting restless. He knew his new family needed entertainment. "Need a song! Need a song!" he called out.

The driver responded, "What you want ta sing?"

"Know the one 'bout Jacob wrestlin'?"

"Oh, I know that one. I know that one, that's for sure."

"We'll sing it then. Victoria," he said, looking at his bench mate, "Why don't you and Adam sing, too? Softly!"

"Is my singing that bad?"

William chuckled deep in his throat, then sang out, "I hold my brudder wid a tremblin' han'. De Lord will bless my soul. Wrestl' on, Jacob, Jacob, day is abreakin'. Wrestl' on, Jacob, Oh, he would not let him go."

"I lllike that one," Adam called out a little too loud.

"Quiet," his mother whispered.

William stepped in, "I like it, too. Let's do more of it." Again he sang, "I will not let you go, my Lord."

"That's it," cried the driver.

William continued, "Fisherman Peter out at sea." Everyone sang along, although quietly from the barrels, "De Lord will bless my soul. Wrestl' on, Jacob, Jacob, day is abreakin'. Wrestl' on, Jacob, Oh, he would not let him go.

"He cast all night, and he cast all day. De Lord will bless my soul. Wrestl' on, Jacob, Jacob, day is abreakin'. Wrestl' on, Jacob, Oh, he would not let him go."

"We sing it a bit different round here," Robert offered.

But William was enjoying himself too much to answer and kept singing, "He catch no fish, but he catch some soul. De Lord will bless my soul. Wrestl' on, Jacob, Jacob, day is abreakin'. Wrestl' on, Jacob, Oh, he would not let him go.

"Jacob hang from a tremblin' limb. De Lord will bless my soul. Wrestl' on, Jacob, Jacob, day is abreakin'. Wrestl' on, Jacob, Oh, he would not let him go."

When they had finished singing, William shouted, "Oh, that felt good."

"Oh, yeah. Felt good," joined the driver.

"You boys can sing," a voice called, and out onto the road ahead stepped a man in his twenties. He wore a shabby blue uniform, slouch hat and had only one arm. "All you . . . ."

William didn't hear the man's profanity as his mind was in a frenzy. Why was the wagoner stopping the horses? He saw fear in Robert's face, and only by leaning forward could William see the man had a pistol aimed at the driver. It was too late. The wagon had stopped, and the man was coming towards them. Two horsemen appeared up the road, blocking the way.

"You boys, step down. We'll take your wagon."

Robert was already down, but William didn't move, determined to stay on the wagon.

"Perhaps the . . . " again the profanity and pejorative names, but William didn't care. He was planning. "I know what you ought'a do," William said brazenly.

"You do? The . . . ." William listened again to the language and names. "I don't need no . . . ."

William didn't hesitate. "Just thought yuh ought'a drink while yuh talk things over. Got me some whiskey . . . from Bourbon County. Massa's best."

"Whiskey?" asked the man, with sudden interest.

"Sure. Yuh look mighty dry. Tap the barrel. Raise yor spirits with massa's spirits." William flashed a wide grin.

The one-armed man laughed. "Where's this whiskey?"

"In the back."

"What do you want to give us your master's whiskey for?" the man asked.

"Hopin' for just a little taste myself . . . 'fore I skedaddle."

"What else you got?" he asked.

"Only good thing is whiskey. Rest is just 'bacca."

"I am thirsty," the one-armed bandit said, smiling broadly to his two partners who had reached the wagon. One man grasped the bridle of one of the wagon team. "Let's take the whiskey, leave the rest," he said.

The other man on horseback nodded toward the hogsheads, saying, "The tobacco, too."

William thought about Adam and Victoria. Robert was gone. It didn't matter. He was Victoria's husband. He had to get his family to safety. Then he spied Robert hiding in the woods, watching. The bandit, as he made his way to look more closely at the whiskey, had seen the slave run and let him go. He called to William as he inspected the barrel, "You should run. I ain't giving you any of this whiskey."

"Just a little drink, Massa!"

The bandit said, "Not for you, you . . . ." He turned to his friend, "Let's take the whiskey and the tobacco." He'd finished inspecting the whiskey barrel and glowered at William, growled and said angrily, "Run, boy, or I'll up and beat you!" He opened his eyes wide and yelled, "Boo!" He frowned when William didn't move. "Suit yourself, but I swear I'll beat you, yet. You're a dumb one, ain't you."

"Yes, Massa, yes. They always says that 'bout me." William showed no fear and didn't move.

One of the men on horseback jumped down, picked up a large rock and ran at William screaming, the rock held above his head with two hands. William, opened his eyes wide, yelled out in fear and jumped from the wagon and ran toward Robert's hiding place.

"Let's get out of here. Tie your horse on back," the one-armed man said.

Victoria was in agony. She could feel Adam shaking. Her son couldn't fall into the hands of these men. She felt the jerk of the wagon as the horses began pulling and sensed their hurry as they were whipped to a faster pace, quickly putting distance between her and William. She looked out the peep hole, but could see nothing. Panic overwhelmed her. Her heart raced, her thoughts were uncontrollable, and, in the confined space, she couldn't move enough to remove the barrel head and attempt an escape.

Where was William? Was he to abandon her at the first hint of danger? Was he not what she'd thought she'd seen? Had she deceived herself? Was there no escape? What would these men do to her? What would they do to Adam? So many frightening questions, and no space for thought. She wanted to scream, run. Maybe she should climb out and attack the man driving the team. Adam, oh Adam! William, are you no more than a broken man, counseled only by fear? How had she been so wrong about him?

She knew bushwhacking had recently been increasing in the area and struggled to control anxiety and to quietly comfort Adam who cuddled silently, but still trembled. She only mastered her fear by weighing escape options. How could they do it? Would it work? It became clear they could not succeed without outside aid.

The hogshead top was snugly fitted, but in such a way that if she could free her arms she could unscrew it. She thought about removing the top, crawling from the barrel, leaping to the ground and trying to outrun the horses. But they would easily catch them. She almost smiled as she pictured trying to scoot out of the barrel in her layers of petticoats and skirt. How uncivilized to make women wear such clothes when they were escaping, she thought.

Consciously fighting her panic, she forced herself to think of William with hope. What was he doing? Did he have a plan? Was he trailing the wagon, waiting to pounce unexpectedly on the men? But she couldn't hold positive thoughts and soon imagined him slinking to safety, abandoning his new wife and child. Legal marriages were no better than slave weddings, she thought bitterly. How would she tell Adam they'd been abandoned? But regardless of her difficulties, she was glad to be away from her attacker. She hated him for what he'd done. She hated him for what she would have to tell William when they were again together.

"There," she verbalized in her mind, "I never doubted him. He'll come after us." The positive thoughts about William calmed her.

It hadn't been long, perhaps a quarter hour since this rapid run had begun. She imagined William following under cover of the woods, trying to keep up.

She had no idea how many men were involved or where they were. She knew there were horses ahead and behind because she could hear them. The wagon seemed to be slowing, making a turn and shortly thereafter stopped.

"Shall we go back for more? Or do you think someone will come after us?"

The wagoner responded, "That's enough for today. Those slaves ain't going home to tell what happened. They're scared of being beat. They'll probably use this as a chance to run north. Come on, I'm thirsty."

"A drink?"

"Yeah, a drink. We've got this fine Bourbon whiskey here. We'll take a sip, then move on."

"Just one drink," someone said enthusiastically.

"Look at that."

"What?"

"There's a tap next to the barrel. I think they were planning on drinking the whiskey themselves, those . . . ."

"I'd like to have been their master and caught them drinking my whiskey."

Victoria strained, listening to understand what the men intended and, for the first time, understood why whiskey had been loaded on the wagon. Her body was cramped, her lower back ached. She longed to sit up.

The wagon shifted and rocked. There was a loud thud that jolted her, then a second. One man cursed and another complained about someone's inability to tap the barrel. She heard a scuffle.

"Here let me have that. I'll get it. You got to hit it straight on," one said.

"I'd like to see you try, one armed. Just don't break the barrel—we don't want to waste any. Hit it just right."

"Get out of my way. You just about broke the barrel. I can't do worse."

More movement.

"Here goes."

There was a softer thud, a second, then a jovial cheer.

"Remember, just one drink each."

"One long drink," someone said lovingly.

"What are we going to drink it out of?"

"Open it! I'll drink from the tap."

"You'll waste half of it. Empty your canteen."

Victoria heard shuffling, liquid pouring onto the ground, then silence. The wagon bed rocked, followed by another round of cheers.

"Oh, that's good."

"Fill up my canteen . . . to the top."

"Be patient. There's enough for us all."

"That is good! Best I've tasted. Give me some more."

"I'm for that."

"Quick though! We've got to get going."

"It won't slow us down much."

"Here. Fill this one. No, just get out of the way."

Victoria heard another shuffle and was frustrated she couldn't see anything. Long minutes passed in silence before one of the men spoke.

"Oh, that's good . . . oh, good whiskey."

"I'll take another sip."

"Hey, who are you?" asked a heavily slurred voice after another extended silence.

Victoria perked up.

"Don't remember me?" asked Robert. Victoria recognized his voice.

"No . . . and I don't like you, you . . . ."

Victoria heard a soft tap on the barrel head, shifted her body and arms struggling to quietly wind the top off. She pushed it outward slightly, carefully to peer out. But once it cleared the edge of the barrel, a hand grabbed it and pulled it from her. She almost screamed and wouldn't let go of the handles. There he was—William—sweat beading on his face, his chest heaving, finger to his lips. He laid the head on the wagon floor.

William said nothing, but reached for Adam. He grasped the child's hands and pulled. Victoria helped, grabbing the boy and shuffling him outward. William lifted him clear of the barrel and set him on the ground. Adam, swaying slightly from being again upright, was frightened and didn't move.

The men's discussion had become heated. The three thieves now demanded the slave drink with them, even as they cursed him for his race. He refused the drink loudly, saying he'd get a mighty beating if he ever drank master's whiskey. They were insistent, he resistant.

William turned his attention to Victoria, who was watching him. He reached into the barrel and took hold of her elbows and pulled. Grimacing, she pushed with her feet, first against the bottom of the barrel, then against the small seat as she moved outward. When she was completely out of the barrel, William lowered her to the ground by the wagon and nodded toward the forest. Her legs wobbled as he set her down. They were hidden by the wagon and barrels from the white men.

William replaced the hogshead top and was irritated to see Victoria and Adam still standing by the wagon, waiting for him. He shook his head no. She frowned. William frowned back and pointed toward the tree line. She shook her head no. He mouthed the word, "Yes." She mouthed, "No!" He glared, pointing to Adam. She glared back, but he'd won, and she quickly led Adam to the woods.

The inebriated white men were still drinking from their canteens and trying to get the judge's slave to take a sip. William carefully climbed onto the wagon and to the top of the first hogshead. From there, he balanced watching the four men. When Robert, who faced the wagon, saw William, William nodded to him. Robert smiled and verbally accepted the invitation to drink. He stepped forward.

One of the men grabbed him, pulled him close, spinning him as he pulled. A knife was at the slave's throat, and the slave's eyes were wide with fear, looking back toward William for help. The man snarled, "I don't drink with no . . . ."

Before William moved, Robert's throat was cut.

William was stunned. Adam and Victoria, visually shielded from the murder, saw the body fall to the ground.

Without thought, Victoria ran toward the wagon. The drunken men heard her and as they turned, they saw William hovering over them from the wagon. They were startled, confused and bumped into each other, one tripping over the corpse as they tried to get to their weapons or William.

Instantly frightened for Victoria, William roared gutturally, jumped onto the second barrel, then leaped on the nearest thief, bringing his full weight down on the man's head. The man collapsed under William's weight, his neck snapping as he hit the ground.

William bounced up, charging the one-armed man who was stumbling in retreat, his head swinging wildly side to side as he desperately searched for his dropped pistol. His shaking legs failed him, and he stumbled, falling to his back. He pushed on the ground with his feet, still trying to escape as William reached him. He begged William to let him go. "Don't kill me! Take your whiskey! Take your wagon! I won't stop you! Just don't kill me! Don't kill me!" He whined, "I have a wife . . . children."

William said nothing. Begging now, later when sober, the man would come after them or send someone else— perhaps the law. They couldn't live in peace as long as this man lived. William didn't review the possibilities, feeling them intuitively. He searched the ground for the man's pistol. He glimpsed it back by the wagon and turned to retrieve it, but then noticed the third man wrestling with Victoria, knife still in hand. Adam was running from the trees to protect his mother. William half groaned, half yelled, forgetting the pistol and the drunkard behind him, and ran toward the life-struggle ahead.

Victoria was screaming, struggling. The man gasping, flailed widely with the knife as he tried to control her. Adam reached the two and grabbed in vain at the man's hand as it stabbed the air between the boy and his mother. But the child distracted him long enough that, with a whole-body heave, Victoria pushed the drunken attacker from her. He stumbled backward, and Victoria jumped on him, grabbing his neck. He reached back to stop his fall, still holding the knife. As he hit the ground, he groaned and twisted his torso trying to rise, both hands now grasping at his lower back where the knife had been driven by Victoria's weight.

Silent and in shock, Victoria released his neck and pulled herself off him. She leaned back on her forearms and elbows, watching in horror as the man writhed uselessly. His groans grew to screams, and Adam raised his hands to cover his ears, but he couldn't turn away as blood flooded the dirt.

Victoria glimpsed William running to her, dread in his eyes. She was still on the ground, crying, her chest heaving as she fought frantically for breath. The front of her blouse was bloodied, and only when Adam saw William's panic did he look at his mother.

"Mama," the boy cried, lunging on top of her.

She shoved him away harshly, still struggling for breath. William kneeling beside her, took her hand, not wanting to hurt her further.

She looked at him sorrowfully.

William heard a horse gallop, but ignored it.

Her breathing was slowing, her expression of horror decreasing. She said softly between her pants, "Don't you think you should go after him?"

"Don't matter, now." Tears wetted his cheeks. Adam was sobbing and had turned away from her.

"If he gets away, he'll tell someone."

"Won't matter without yuh."

"Without me?" She sat up briskly. "Without me? What are you talking about? Go after the man! We can't let him get away!"

"You're hurt."

"I'm out of breath . . . frightened."

"But the blood . . ."

"What blood?"

"All over yuh."

"Not mine." She pointed to the man now dead, open eyes staring at them.

Adam grabbed his mother, who put her arm around him and pulled him close.

"I thought," William continued, "Yuh was dying."

"I'm not, but . . . ." She didn't finish, looking sadly toward Robert, dead by the wagon. Tears welled in her distantly focused eyes. Still holding her son, she shook her head, turned to William and said, with the hint of a smile, "William, I think death and mayhem follow you. You're a dangerous man . . . to be with."

In response, William cried, resting his head on her shoulder.

She put her other arm around him and squeezed, saying gently, "You better go after him. We'll change our clothes and be ready when you get back. I love you."

He stopped crying, stood, glanced at Victoria, ran to the horse still tied at the back of the wagon, mounted it smoothly, turned toward the road and galloped after the one-armed man.

William was back within 15 minutes, leading a second, empty horse. Victoria and Adam waited by the wagon. They had covered the dead slave with a blanket from the buckboard and left him where he'd fallen. Victoria didn't question William, and he didn't volunteer information. He was grim faced, and Victoria watched him trying to gauge what he was feeling.

He dismounted just as the horse halted. He smiled perfunctorily at the pair who stood close together. They had been praying for him.

"Ready?" he asked.

"Yes," she responded. "I secured the barrel heads, but I left the luggage out. We rolled the whiskey barrel off the wagon . . . off the back."

He looked down at the blanket which covered the bloody earth and slave, glanced at the man he had crushed and over the wagon at the man who had died attacking Victoria.

"Freedom costs a lot of blood," Victoria proffered.

William responded, "And I'm ashamed of it."

She asked bitterly, "How much of our blood have they spilt in slavery?"

"Too much, and now too much blood is shed again."

Pulling Adam with her, Victoria stepped close to William, extending her free arm around him. He was sweating. She felt one of his arms wrap around her and the other reach down to touch Adam. Both lowered their heads to rest on each other and cried. Thoughts of escape and Washington City slipped from their minds as the new family grieved what it had already lost.

Chapter 42

May 1864, Washington City, District of Columbia

He was outside yet another man's office with feelings of a different ilk. He was nervous. This interview could end in interrogation at Old Capitol Prison or with a quick, dangling death. His hands fidgeted. He sweated.

The sheriff reminded himself that anxiety was useless as he'd already committed to his course of protecting Mrs. Henderson wherever she was and as long as he was able to do it. This meeting was his best plan to that end. He'd see it through. A soldier appeared after a brief wait and led him to an office.

"Colonel Lafayette Baker?" queried the sheriff, his ill-ease exacerbated by Baker's grim face and penetrating gaze.

"Robert Sheriff," Baker pronounced without answering, shaking his guest's hand firmly across his desk. "Your business, sir?"

"You got the daguerreotype?"

Baker laid Walthrope's picture on his desk. "This one?"

"I'm looking for that man."

"Why?"

"In being here, sir, I risk all I have. I hope you'll see my intentions are pure, based on duty and our shared mission of building a law-abiding society."

"That's one mission, but speak frankly. I warn you, however, I'm skeptical of anyone who announces pure motives, especially when I've no reason to suspect them. My experience is the opposite is usually proved . . . they turn out most impure."

"Regardless of experience, and I share that experience, my motives are pure, and I've put—perhaps foolishly—myself in danger being here . . . by seeking an audience with you, putting myself in your hands . . . with no hope of reward."

"Foolishness is no good trait." He'd been standing formally, but relaxed suddenly and said hospitably, "We can judge your motives later. What do you want of me?"

"Here, Colonel, is my danger. I'm a sheriff from Staunton, Virginia."

"Yes, I caught that. Am I to be impressed by your family . . . because it's from Virginia? If I am, you'll be disappointed. I've never heard of your family, nor am I prone to be influenced by aristocratic families from states in rebellion."

Sheriff chuckled, "There's a little confusion here."

"Confusion?"

"While my name is Sheriff, I also happen—and this is what I was referring to and the danger I willingly accept—I also happen to be the sheriff in Staunton . . . about to retire, but still active."

The hint of a smile hovered at the corner of Baker's mouth, as he repeated aloud, "Sheriff Sheriff."

"Precisely."

"Sheriff, a poor choice of occupation."

"Or parentage."

"I'm assuming then . . . you're here to tell me some news useful to the Union. A Unionist who's crossed the lines, hoping reward for some war-ending news?"

"I'm not really interested in politics or the war, Colonel, and have no information for you."

"Then why are you here, why do you have a picture of Mr. Dante . . . and why shouldn't I throw you in Old Capitol for spying? You did sneak through the lines."

"I'm entirely in your power."

"Then Mr. Dante . . . must be important."

"I'm investigating a murder."

"A murder . . . that occurred in Rebel-held Virginia? Interesting. Sit down. Tell me why I should care."

Sheriff had involuntarily lowered his shoulders as tension eased. He pulled his hand out from his pant pocket, and used it to help describe the foreman's murder and the murderer's passion for stealing widows' affection and money. He explained a woman, a Mrs. Henderson, held a prisoner in Castle Thunder for treason, had been lost during a prisoner exchange and probably was on her way to Washington. Mr. Walthrope—or Dante—would most likely follow her.

The colonel listened with an amused expression, then said, "What do you want of me? I can't stand by as an official of Virginia wanders freely in the capital."

"As I said, I'm not interested in the war . . . at least not now. I'm here to find and bring Walthrope to justice."

"Even if that were true . . . and let's assume it is . . . what would you do if you happened on information or witnessed something so interesting . . . that might help support this untoward Rebellion? If it would help Virginia, you'd surely report it. In your shoes, I would."

"I am here with the full understanding of the Confederate Government. They didn't send me for information or to spy. They desperately want Walthrope."

"That makes me . . . or maybe it should make me more suspicious. If the Rebels want him out of Washington, arrested . . . perhaps dead . . . Do they want him dead? If the South wants that, shouldn't I protect him? He may have valuable information for us. That's why you're here . . . to stop him from getting to me. I suspect he'll come eventually."

"I think you'd find information he has concerns just a few men . . . men who might be embarrassed because of personal indiscretions. Nothing more." The sheriff paused. "You'd realize they're not interested in war information, but worry about his recklessness, his unpredictability . . . uncontrollable anger and passion for . . . no . . . dedication to revenge. They're afraid he'll seek revenge on them."

"Sheriff, are you one of those men? That would explain a lot. Then I could understand your motives."

"I'm not. I don't really know the man. Until I got that picture, I didn't know who I was looking for. I'm here only because I want to see justice brought to this bloodsucker."

"Bloodsucker? The purest of motives only, then?"

"Pure I'm not, but I have told you why I'm here . . . and there's no duplicity or dissembling."

"Wouldn't a spy offer an interesting story . . . provide the same solid assurances? Wouldn't they say and do exactly what you've said and done?"

The sheriff searched for the right answer to this challenge, finally responding, "Probably. But he'd only give it if he were caught." He paused to let Baker consider the implication. "I hope you see a . . . the difference and its significance. He wouldn't . . . I wouldn't come to your office without invitation and tell you the plan. I'd hide waiting patiently for Walthrope, ready to kidnap him and quietly send him to the South through some network. Or I'd kill him outright and make it look like a street robbery. You'd never know I'd been here."

"I can't have you moving around the city unescorted."

"Put someone with me day and night. I might be able to use the assistance. And they . . . and you will see I have one interest—Walthrope."

Baker scratched his cheek. His full red beard twitched. "Mr. Sheriff," Baker began, "you have no official position in Washington, so you'll never again refer to yourself as a sheriff from anywhere." He stopped and chuckled. "That will be difficult won't it? You'll be with two of my men. One during the day, one at night. You'll be here in Washington for no more than two weeks. Then, if you've not already departed, I'll give you safe passage across the lines . . . or I'll hold you in Old Capitol if you've done anything suspicious. You may apprehend Mr. Walthrope, of late Mr. Dante . . . or whatever his name may be. If you find him, you'll bring him to me . . . and I shall decide what shall become of him. I'll need to question him. You'll not smuggle him to the South. If you do attempt such foolery, you'll share Mr. Dante's fate."

"This is more than I'd hoped."

"Good." His gray-speckled eyes glowed beneath his eyebrows. "I'll tell you what I know. Mr. Walthrope came to me as Mr. Dante, offering documents which identified Confederate agents here in the capital. They were filled with valuable bits of information, and I was interested in using Mr. Dante to obtain more. But he proved unreliable . . . morally corrupt, unable to avoid the few gambling hells which we still have here—far fewer, by the way, than you have in Richmond. Mr. Dante has no value to us, so find him quickly. You may want to spend a few evenings in some of those gambling houses. You never know who you'll see." He stopped speaking. "Does he know you're looking for him? Will he recognize you?"

"He may recognize me. We met at a hotel in Richmond, but I didn't know then who he was. I don't believe he knows I am after him."

"Splendid." Baker's voice was exuberant. "Then if you happen upon him, he'll be none-the-wiser, giving you the advantage. Mr. Sheriff, here's the picture of our friend. Good day. It was a pleasure to meet you . . . and very funny about your name."

The sheriff immediately rose, taking the image. "Thank you. I hope to see you again in days, not weeks."

"I'll be so much the happier." He rose, nodded to the sheriff and watched as his guest left. When he saw a soldier had met the sheriff to escort him from the building, he sat down.

Betsy was confused by the city's commotion and tired from travel and pregnancy. After being smuggled from one farm to another, she'd been brought with early crops by wagon to the Washington City market. Someone, they told her, would meet her, but the person never appeared, and she was left alone.

She had no change of clothes, no luggage, just 13 dollars in gold coins Hank had sent her with his first letter years ago, the same money Marie Ann had smuggled to her in Castle Thunder. She'd bathed before the final leg of the journcy but still felt dirty, and her clothes were embarrassingly stained. Her final host on the trip north, a small, nervous farmer, had shown little interest in her and had left her at the market without concern. He told her he was only doing it for the money.

With nowhere to stay or food to eat, she felt helpless and ravenously hungry—surely because of the child. Betsy was certain anyone passing would have noted her confusion and despair and mistaken her for a mad woman living on the streets.

Most people hurried among the market's worn sheds buying food as the fetid odor of the city's canal sitting behind the market mixed with the smell of fresh vegetables and fish. Flies traveled between the canal and sheds, partaking pestiferously of both. Soldiers were everywhere, and injured and maimed men mingled in the crowds. Many had somewhere pressing to go and moved at what was to Betsy a sickening pace. Others loitered, watching; leaving her suspicious she was the object of their menacing scrutiny.

Her night-time interview with Walthrope and his promise to meet her in Washington came to mind, and she shuddered as she scanned the market to make sure he wasn't there. When she didn't see him, she reassured herself that he was too insane to successfully follow her, too irrational to ever make it to Washington.

Fear of Walthrope wasn't her only concern as she wandered the market. As she'd come north, she'd seen ample evidence the war was heating up again after the winter lull and had heard the Union was set on taking Richmond. She didn't worry about the capital as she still believed Lee was invincible, but she did fret about Hank's safety, especially now that he'd be a father.

She tried to ignore her growing anxiety so she could consider what she needed to do. Where to start? She knew no one in the capital and worried there could be no unoccupied bed in a city with such madding hordes. This had been a mistake—coming to Washington. Still there had been no alternative, and she had expected a welcome and early help. Why had Miss Morrow's exacting arrangements unraveled on this end? Perhaps her Union contacts weren't as strong as those in the South. Maybe Betsy should move on—but to where and how? In her anxiety and in spite of her hunger, she never thought to use the money she brought to buy food at the market and walked away from the peddlers.

She happened to glance toward the majestic Capitol and the statue that stood on its dome, and her feet followed in that direction. Betsy had never visited Washington, but something about the Capitol drew her. As she walked along the Avenue, she peeked back at the market. There he was. No, it couldn't be. Had he actually followed her? She shook, then scanned where she'd seen him. Nothing. Men and women were coming and going, mostly men, but he wasn't there. Just her imagination.

Turning again toward the Capitol, she walked swiftly to elude her dreadful vision. She walked a long time, and as she climbed toward the newly domed edifice, she became increasingly depressed. Her attraction to the building had not changed her circumstances. She was still in an unfamiliar, unfriendly town, among strange people, with no place to stay, no food to eat. She heard a carriage slow beside her.

Robert Sheriff, his appointed Federal partner alongside, walked the Avenue from the Capitol toward the market. He was listening with interest to the confessions of one of Baker's detectives who admitted to being one of the men who had compelled Dante to work for the Confederacy. Walthrope was trapped, thought Sheriff, nowhere to go. Both

South and North had believed foolishly they could use him, but he'd failed them both.

What made the man tick? Why target vulnerable women? Why kill the foreman? Clearly intelligent, why not use his intelligence for good? He'd worked so hard to gain and exploit Mrs. Henderson's trust. Why not be a simple highway robber? It would have been easier, quicker, maybe safer. Why spend so much time pursuing women . . . especially Mrs. Henderson? The sheriff couldn't quite understand the man, and decided to stop wondering about his motives. Facts were Walthrope was alive and a threat to everyone who'd ever known him.

The sheriff didn't ask his companion questions or encourage him to tell him more, but the man didn't seem able to stop talking, thinking he'd found in Sheriff a fellow Confederate willing to do anything to salvage the fading Southern Cause. Perhaps the sheriff would do anything for Virginia, but not now, not while hunting. He'd exert all his efforts, thoughts and devotion to finding and killing Walthrope.

Chapter 43

May 1864, Washington City, District of Columbia

"It's her," Betsy heard a woman say loudly in a familiar foreign accent. "Ask her! She needs help."

She could hear a man respond softly in the same English accent, "It's not proper for me to address her. You'll have to do it."

Betsy stopped and looked directly into the hack that slowed beside her. It carried a couple, slightly older than herself. The pretty woman gazed at Betsy with sympathetic, brown eyes. Her modest straw bonnet was tied under her chin, covering dark hair pulled back in a bun. The man, a military air about him, sat tall in the buggy. He had dark hair and a mustache reaching to a beard that ran along his jaw.

The man spoke. "My wife," indicating the woman beside him, "she wants me to ask if you're all right. I address you at her insistence."

Betsy stared without responding, and glanced nervously at the hackman.

When Betsy didn't answer, the woman spoke directly to her, more softly than she'd spoken to her husband. "I couldn't help but notice you at the market. You looked . . . confused." She waited for Betsy to acknowledge some terrible plight, but when waiting elicited no answer, she continued. "Can we help you?"

Betsy studied the woman, intensely wanting this conversation to be real, but concerned it was only some hopeful hallucination.

"Please let us help you," the woman said gently.

"Why would you do that?" Betsy responded in a distrust-ful tone bred in captivity. She was sorry she'd said it. The couple would surely direct the driver along, without his pas-sengers giving her the help she so urgently wanted and needed.

"I think you're lost," the woman continued gently. "I think you're new to the city. Is there not something we can do? I know it's difficult to be new here."

The male occupant, clearly straining to hear the conver-sation, added, "Mary's been watching you. She's convinced you're a gentlewoman, down on her luck."

"Enough of that, Thomas," the woman responded more loudly to her husband. "Do you need a place to stay for a day or two, till you can find your way?"

Betsy was curious, concerned, wary that they knew so much about her. Surely they were Walthrope's agents, en-trusted to take her directly to him. "I'm fine," she said with-out conviction. The conversation was strengthening her defenses, helping her surmount confusion.

Mary spoke with surprising authority, "You're not," but then softened her tone, "and I . . . we want to help. I saw the wagon with the produce drop you at the market. You caught my eye right away. I don't know why. I just kept looking for you to buy something . . . to find someone . . . to look for someone. But you didn't. You looked as if you'd awakened in a strange, unfamiliar place . . . from a dream . . . as you wandered aimlessly through the market. I think you haven't a friend in the city, and you're tired, cold—well, maybe not cold—but hungry, and I . . . we will not leave without offering . . . giving you assistance. You need it. Please don't deny it."

Betsy liked hearing the woman's accent. It put her oddly at ease. Tears welled in her eyes. She began to cry, then sobbed till she could no longer control her feelings. She slumped forward to let her shoulders bounce freely in rhythm to her weeping. Sorrow, relief and anger simultaneously overwhelmed her till she felt a warm arm reach gently around her. Mary raised her, turning Betsy to herself, guiding Betsy's head to her shoulder.

Mary let her weep, holding her tightly until she thought the emotions shed. She said quietly, "Come, love. Please . . . get right in there . . . by Thomas." She was helping Betsy into the buggy before Betsy was aware of it. Someone again—like Miss Morrow—had shown kindness, and it was so rare that she couldn't resist it. "Come, we'll take you home tonight. It will be noisy, but we can feed you, and you can get a good night's rest. You need food. Everyone needs food. It's all I can think of now. I'm getting fat, or so says Thomas, and I can eat twice as much as he can." She raised her voice, "Can't I Thomas? I can eat twice as much as you."

"Yes . . . yes, you can, Mary. No disagreement on that point. I'd say twice as much as me . . . with the children ready to get a new companion." He chuckled to himself.

The impatient Jehu was already moving. With Betsy squeezed between Thomas and Mary, the three fell silent as they moved further up the Avenue. Minutes passed, each person waiting for some clue as to what should be said next. Finally Thomas said, "We should introduce ourselves and banish this awkward silence."

Mary said loudly, "Thomas, there's nothing awkward about silence. We were just thinking, lost in our own thoughts. But yes, Thomas, please introduce us."

"My name is Thomas Rathbone, and she my beloved, Mary."

Betsy sniffed and dabbed at her eyes and nose with a well-wetted handkerchief. "I'm Mrs. Henry Gragg . . . Elizabeth."

"Mrs. Gragg, I hope we can ease your current circumstance, as it's clear you carry heavy burdens," Thomas offered.

Betsy turned in the seat to look at Mrs. Rathbone. "Your children will have a new companion? Are you . . . ?"

"I am."

Betsy felt a growing bond with the English woman. "I have almost no money—not here with me—and no family or friends in the city."

"Mrs. Gragg, stay with us . . . till you put your affairs in order. We're now your friends. Our house is small, and we have young children, so you'll get no quiet . . . little rest. But it will be safe and out of the weather." She raised her voice again, "Thomas, don't you think that would be fine?"

"Whatever you feel appropriate, my dear."

Kindness at just the right moment, thought Betsy. Heavenly Father always planted it around her—the Graggs in her hour of need in Woodstock; Caleb and Marie Ann and Miss Morrow in the prison; and now the Rathbones in the Northern capital. She sighed audibly as she finally mastered her tears. All was not lost. Even tonight there was hope. A warm feeling of gratitude gently passed.

"Now, Mrs. Gragg," Thomas began, "our home is humble for now, but we are going to move to a bigger place. I've seen a house in Maryland. I've got plans."

"Not that now, Mr. Rathbone," his wife complained.

"And why not? Surely, now is a good time, as we've nothing else to talk about."

"A good time to bore our new friend?" Mary responded still speaking loudly. She lowered her voice to speak to Betsy, "Please excuse him, Mrs. Gragg. He's always thinking, my Thomas. Always thinking. But sometimes his thinking is a little," her voice rose for emphasis and so her husband could hear her, "too detailed."

"Nonsense. There can never be too many details, and you'll find it interesting, Mrs. Gragg. You're a lady of refinement, thought, and the house will please you."

The Rathbone's banter entertained Betsy, enabling her to push her troubles briefly from her mind as the wagon passed the Capitol and turned onto Maryland Avenue. This couple cherished each other, and she felt doubly safe. These weren't agents of any demon. "Please tell me your plans. Even the details would be interesting to me."

"Oh, goodness!" Mary offered in exasperation. "You don't know what you've done."

"Well," said Thomas, "I've been thinking about it for a while. I got the idea shortly after I came to Washington City. I'm an immigrant, but I'm sure you knew that."

"I thought it possible," Betsy said, with a sly grin.

"I've applied to be a citizen, joined the army."

Mary spoke softly, "That's where he lost his hearing." She raised her voice and continued, "One too many cannon balls, Mrs. Gragg."

Thomas ignored his wife's explanation, "I'm in the Provost Marshal General's Office now, clerking. It's a good job. My heart broke when I came to America. I had to leave my Mary behind in England. But, thankfully, she and the children arrived—was it a year ago, Mary?"

"Has it been that long? Goodness. We arrived Good Friday last year. Already been more than a year. Mercy."

"Why come now . . . with the war?" Betsy asked.

"Just a good time to leave England," Mary answered vaguely.

"Let me tell you about the house I'll buy someday, Mrs. Gragg," Thomas said, trying to get to his topic.

"Tell her about the shape of the house, Thomas."

"Yes, well, that's the intriguing part, don't you see? It's an octagon. Built before the war."

"An octagon?" Betsy said.

"Yes, eight sides. Interesting, don't you think?"

"Very. Where did you say it is?"

"Not far. Just over in Maryland . . . Hyattsville. We can't buy it yet, but someday. When the time's right, and it's for sale. You'll have to visit us there, Mrs. Gragg."

"Betsy. Please call me Betsy."

Seeing Betsy had mastered her emotions, he spoke. "May I ask, Betsy, where your husband is?"

Betsy stiffened. A probing question. An agent? But she remembered she was in the North, and her husband's identity and whereabouts would be welcome information, not sinister or traitorous. She smiled at her new freedom. "I don't know exactly, somewhere with the army."

"So many are," Mary responded resignedly.

"He's with the 19th . . . 19th Indiana."

"Indiana? Is that nearby?" Mary asked.

"No, love. It's out west," Thomas interjected.

"But is the . . . what was the number?"

"The 19th."

Mary queried, "Is it nearby?"

"In Virginia."

"The Army of the Potomac?" Thomas asked.

"Yes, I believe it is."

Betsy stayed with the Rathbones two days, and they proved exceedingly honest for their house was small and their three children noisy, but Betsy enjoyed her time with them more than she could have imagined. Mary had kindly and patiently helped her delouse without concern for her family and quickly helped her find a place to live. Betsy joked with Mary that she thought the two matters were related.

Betsy wrote two letters at the Rathbones, one to Hank explaining she was well, healthily expecting their first child and in Washington—closer to him. She also wrote to Caleb asking him to find a way to send money—coins—to Mrs. Henry Gragg in Washington City. Without support from her farm and factory, she was a pauper.

During her time with the Rathbones, Betsy also explored the dirty, hustling city. It had none of the charm of Richmond before the war. To her eye, large buildings had been thrown up in the middle of forests and vast open space. They had no connection to the rest of the city. A real city, Betsy thought, would have buildings and homes compressed in one area. In some parts of Washington, construction was underway on every street corner, but it was the roads that displeased her most. Roads haphazardly crossed one another with a grid pattern and something overlaid, so when Betsy thought she understood it, the pattern was broken by a circle and a great park. Streets converged on each park from every direction.

Mary Rathbone had cautioned Betsy about wandering the city. She explained there were places where a lady wasn't safe and that the city was pocked with gangs of rowdies.

Great stretches of the city weren't city at all and horrible things could happen in them. But Betsy was enjoying freedom too much to be concerned with ruffians and her time with the Rathbones had eased her mind and lowered her distrustfulness.

Searching the city was an adventure in liberty, one she cherished and had sorely missed in prison. Early on the fourth day, before breakfast, having spent a comfortable night in a rented room, she wandered aimlessly to the Capitol, then toward the Avenue as she tried to get the exercise she needed in her special condition. She was not entirely at ease, for every time she'd gone out into public, she'd thought she'd seen him lurking . . . but she now knew it was only her imagination and fear.

She even wondered if her fear as she fled Castle Thunder had engendered delusions of Walthrope, his voice and conversation. Perhaps he'd never spoken to her in Richmond. She'd never seen him. Maybe it had been only a hallucination caused by fear . . . or her illness.

She'd heard everything was different with women at this stage in life. She was beginning to believe that fantasies filled the minds of similarly fat women with images, voices and feelings. She'd ask Mary, who was going through it for her fourth time, about it soon.

It would explain why everywhere she looked, he seemed to be there watching her. She was capable of creating his face almost anywhere and anytime, and it was now becoming interspersed and twisted tightly with daydreams and images of Thaddeus and Hank.

The afternoon before, it had been Thaddeus whom she approached on the Avenue. But when she neared the man, he wasn't anything like Thaddeus. Earlier in the day, a uniformed soldier ahead of her was Hank's height, build and coloring. His gait was Hank's, and he spoke with Hank's gestures. She tried to catch him, and when she called his name, he turned. But it wasn't Hank. Together Thaddeus, Hank and Walthrope controlled her thoughts and feelings, and she couldn't shake off the tangle of love and hate, hope, memory and dread she felt.

Wandering on, she made her way along the Avenue, reaching the market. It didn't look as foreboding as she remembered it, and she smiled, knowing there was nothing to fear. She was in the North, close to Hank, had dear new friends, food and a place to sleep. She made her way through the market sheds, listening to the men hawk their products. At some point, she noticed a bridge over the dirty canal and crossed it, curious about what Mary had called the Island.

She was sweating, but it was a pleasant sensation. She remembered Thaddeus. Grateful for his love and kindness, she was sad he was gone, that she couldn't lean on him and enjoy the luxurious life he'd provided. She thought about Hank and worried about his safety. Mr. Rathbone reported a rumor that the new general—a General Grant from the west—was readying the army for another push to Richmond. Then she remembered how grateful she was to no longer reside in Castle Thunder.

Chapter 44

May 1864, Washington City, District of Columbia

Late the afternoon before, after Betsy left the Rathbone home for more permanent lodgings, Mary Rathbone answered a knock at her door. She was cordially greeted by a tall civilian, well dressed, bearded. He smiled gently.

"Good day, madam," he said in a refined, southern accent, removing his hat, tilting his head forward.

Thomas wasn't yet home, so Mary was careful not to open the door completely. She placed her foot securely behind it. "Good afternoon," she said curtly. "State your business."

"Madam, I believe you have a guest whom I know well and would like to visit. Forgive me for calling unannounced, but my circumstances are most unusual. Here is my card."

"A guest?" Her tone softened, taking the card without notice, hoping he bore good news for Betsy.

"Yes . . . or does she board here?"

"Who do you look for, sir?" Again, she mustered a short tone and ignored the children playing behind her.

"My name is Thaddeus Henderson. I seek my wife."

"There is no Mrs. Henderson here. Good afternoon." She began to close the door, but a foot slipped between door and frame. "Please, sir," she said as a hint of fear entered her voice.

"Perhaps she is for some reason using another name . . . for she thinks me dead." He described Betsy. "She's just arrived in the city. I must find her. I've lived too long without her and only recently am able to return."

Mary lost her breath. This would be wonderful news for Betsy. Her husband not dead. Of course, Mary didn't know he was supposed to be dead, but Betsy did. She had developed a warm camaraderie with Betsy, but Betsy at times had seemed closed and talked little of her past. Mary knew Betsy hid something painful. Was this it? Surely this would raise her spirits. Mary stopped pushing the door.

"Sir . . . your wife was here as our guest, but she's taken lodgings just off the Avenue."

"Thank you for that courtesy. I know the area. You don't know how happy it will make us both . . . to be together again. I'm sure she'd given up hope . . . perhaps she no longer even speaks of me. Can you imagine her joy?"

"May I ask how you knew she was here?"

"Little in this city stays secret." He, stepping away, bowed at the waist, removing and waving his hat downward as an extension of his bow. "Thank you, my dear lady."

Mary closed the door, pushing it hard until it seated in the frame. She quickly locked it as she reflected on the conversation with the stranger. Immediate doubts taunted her and crushed the excitement she had felt momentarily for Betsy. Why would Betsy use a different name? Hadn't she said her husband was serving with the army? Hadn't Mary seen a letter addressed to a Private Henry Gragg, 19th Indiana? As discrepancies arose, terror followed. How did the man know Betsy had been here?

When Thomas arrived, he had barely entered the door when she pounced on him, recounting her discomforting visitor.

Thomas consoled her. "How do you know he lied? Remember, we don't know much about Mrs. Gragg. You said yourself she's been reticent about her past."

"But, Thomas, I—of all people—should have been careful. We fled to America . . . changed our name—became the Rathbones."

"Yes, we did, Mrs. John Carling." He smiled at her affectionately.

"And why?"

"To avoid debtors prison for something we'd not done. I see what you're suggesting. Let's keep our wits, though. We can't assume her story is like ours." He considered possible scenarios and laughed at the thought of one. "She may have married a second soldier when she got news her first husband was dead . . . and become a bigamist."

"Nothing to laugh at there, Mr. Rathbone."

"I suppose not, but it is funny."

"We must warn her."

"First thing tomorrow, on my way to the office, I'll stop by the boarding house, let her know."

"Yes, it probably is too late tonight."

Betsy had left her boarding house early, driven by her cravings for space and fresh air. She loved walking with no walls to hold her in, no pungent cell to smother her, no guards watching. She was grateful for the fresh air, the trees, the early dandelions that caught her eye with cheerful yellow heads and tenacity. She wished Nero was with her, that he was her dog. What a pleasure it would be to take him walking.

Thomas reached the rooming house minutes after Betsy's departure. He stared vacantly at Betsy's new landlady when she told him she'd already gone out.

"Did a man call for her last night . . . or even this morning?" he asked urgently.

Her hostess was visibly shocked by the question. "Sir, I do not believe that I can . . . or should report on my young ladies and their lives."

Undaunted, he persisted, shifting his weight nervously from one leg to the other. "I understand and applaud your reticence, but I must tell you she is perhaps in danger. I must find her."

She looked at Thomas carefully, scrutinizing him for a long time before answering, hesitantly, "She had no visitors, neither last night nor this morning . . . not until you, sir." She eyed him suspiciously, but the expression passed.

"Can you tell me which direction she went? Was she going to the market?"

"No," said the proprietress. "We do the shopping. I am sorry, I can't tell you where she went. If you'd like to wait, I'm sure she'll be back soon and that she'll be fine."

"May I intrude?" asked a boarder who had been standing in the background listening.

Thomas looked at a young woman expectantly.

"I overheard your conversation. Forgive me, but I saw her . . . Mrs. Gragg go out. I stepped out briefly to gauge the weather before I go over to work at the Treasury. There was a man across the street, just standing about. I'd seen him earlier and thought it odd he wasn't going somewhere . . . doing something. But he wasn't, not at least until she came out. I watched her. She went toward the Capitol, and with what you said about a man visitor and danger, this is what I hadn't considered before. I peeked out the window a few minutes later. The man—he was gone."

"Gone?" Thomas asked.

"Yes. Probably just coincidence, but I thought I should mention it."

Thomas' mind floundered. What did it all mean? A husband. A man loitering outside her boarding house without coming to the door. A changed name. Mrs. Gragg going out before breakfast . . . alone. They knew so little of her, but he and Mary both felt an almost familial connection with her. "Thank you, thank you ever so much for your help."

The landlady and her boarder looked at each other questioningly as Thomas ran from the house, down the stairs and toward the Capitol.

Betsy, ignorant of the Rathbone's curious afternoon visitor and the morning commotion at her boarding house, continued her walk onto the Island. She stopped, looked over the trees at the distant Smithsonian and wondered where the Patent Office was, of which Hank had written. She ambled on. It hadn't rained, so no mud or bogs distracted her mind from dreams of Hank and their child together. Maybe they'd settle in Washington.

She wondered about her mother, now in Winchester, awaiting again the return of her dead father. She wondered about Hank's family in Woodstock, Virginia, and about Caleb and Marie Ann. Had they ever married? She'd never even asked. She wondered when the war—the senseless war— would end. She no longer believed in it. Slavery? It should have died already. The South? The North? She didn't care. She just wanted to be with Hank and their child.

She had a slight jolt, imaging for an instant that she saw Hank charging a Southern soldier, but smiled at her now-boundless imagination.

She heard something behind her. Someone shuffling, almost running. Abandoning decorum, she turned slightly toward the sound. It was happening again. Walthrope was running at her, and she calmly watched him, waiting for the illusion to pass. He was within 10 paces. When would his face change to that of a stranger? Ah, there it was. The man—unfamiliar to her—ran past without glancing her way.

But he diverted her from her daydreams and from noticing another gentleman, overdressed for the weather, sporting a stove-top hat and a light scarf around his neck. He was at her side before she saw him.

"My love, you've come," said a quiet, raspy whisper.

She jumped in surprise and turned to examine him more closely. Her heart pounded. It had been him, then—always nearby, watching. It had been him in Richmond. Why had he waited till now to approach her? She said nothing. Her feet were frozen, her mind leaping from one possible disaster to another. Her consolation, she reminded herself, was that he was mad and not dangerous . . . at least not to her. He thought they were married, thought he loved her . . . and she him. He wanted to protect her. His lunacy had tamed him toward her. She would go along with his madness till she could safely slip away. She suppressed an urge to flee and mustered a kind expression.

"I've been waiting so patiently for you," he said.

"Mr. Walthrope, why do you follow me?"

He looked shocked. "Why would I not? I watch over you, my angel."

He was close enough to grab her, but he didn't. She was right. He was no danger to her.

"You don't need to watch over me. I'm fine."

"Yes, fine now . . . now I've liberated you."

Her stomach twisted, her fingers trembled, but she remained otherwise outwardly calm. Could it be? She had to know. "You? Did you free me from Castle Thunder?"

He laughed arrogantly. "Of course. Who else could have performed such magic? Your Yankee spy? Your steadfast tin soldier, with his one leg? Your sheriff?" His voice turned hard. "Captain Richardson? No, none of them could have done it. Only me, my love. I love you . . . have always loved you." He smiled wantonly at her. "I did it in spite of our spat. Remember our spat? How silly it was, when I branded you forever mine."

"I remember," she said trying to compose herself and control her suddenly shallow breath. Surely he was mistaken. It was Miss Morrow who freed her. In his lunacy, he—like tortured cousin Emily—created fantasies. She decided to challenge him. "And how did you do it . . . free me?"

"Such a question when we're rejoicing in our reunion. Why does it matter now . . . now we're together?"

He hadn't done it. He knew no specifics and didn't care to discuss it. It was only the grandiose dreams of his madness. She breathed deeply, relieved her darkest suspicion was wrong.

He smiled. "Here, take my arm. Let us walk as lovers do."

She stiffened slightly, momentarily resisted, but didn't want to frighten or anger him. She took his arm, concentrating on steadying her trembling hands. They walked farther onto the Island as if they had been a young couple on promenade.

People passed them, and to each, Walthrope would doff his hat and tilt his head. "Betsy I'm so happy you remember it all now. I knew you would when we were together again—the church, our marriage, our devoted love. I knew you would remember."

His tone was almost pleading, soothing her fears. Crazy. Harmless. Desperately in love with her. She would be fine.

They walked on, neither speaking. Minutes passed. Walthrope broke the silence. "Would you like to know how I freed you?"

"I would," she said softly, curious to hear his delusion before escaping his grasp.

His voice was dulcet. "Because you are my faithful wife, I will tell you." His arm tightened, locking hers against him. She didn't resist the added pressure but fought a sudden desire to cry out and run. No one was near them. His voice firmed. "My dear, I had to bribe many people. Guards. I paid a king's ransom to Miss Whitehead. She's an excellent actress. Don't you think?"

"I don't think I know . . . a Miss Whitehead."

"Why Betsy, how easily you forget. You were there for her greatest performance."

"Can you remind me, gentle love?"

"Must I do everything for you?" If he hadn't been holding her arm so tightly, she would have pulled it from him and run. "Must I think . . . must I remember for you? Why Miss Whitehead gave a rapturous performance . . . as Miss Morrow, the beyond suspicion Florence Morrow."

Betsy blenched, her eyes suddenly wild with fear, but she tried to gain control of her nerves. She remained silent.

Miss Morrow was not real! Nothing, then, was real. Walthrope had created her world and moved her and everyone she touched in it as if they were marionettes. This was no maternal fantasy. If he knew of Miss Morrow . . .

"Ah, Miss Whitehead. You touched her heart . . . as you do everyone. She made me swear I would do you no harm. Imagine that. Me hurting you. Ridiculous. But she loved you, Betsy." He sighed and looked out toward the Smithsonian. "And she was an excellent tutor as well. She taught me everything I needed to know to prepare my performance."

"And what role did you take, my dear?" She was repulsed at the words she was speaking, poised to break free at any loosening of his grip.

"Oh, Betsy, are you so simple that you still haven't figured it out," he said impatiently. "You seem much less, now that we're married . . . now I'm saddled with you . . . that your money is mine . . . you seem much less desirable . . . less intelligent. Must I explain all to you? I suppose I must out of simple kindness for the weaker vessel. Betsy, I appeared as a man driven crazy by the woman he loved. I feigned dissipation and madness for you . . . and others."

Betsy was horrified. She tried to yank her arm from him, but he held it firm. She jerked it again, but Walthrope smiled and patiently pulled his other hand from his pocket. He held a small pistol and pointed it at her side. He leaned his head toward her, smiling gently.

"Yes, my dear, it didn't work exactly as hoped, but well enough. I pretended to be a gambler . . . unable to resist temptation. No one worries about a gambler. No one wants to be around one, unless they can win money from them. They're no good. They began to avoid me . . . hoped I'd go away. They shunned . . . cut me. They wanted me gone, disappeared—like the magician's handkerchief, egg, lemon and orange. No one looks for me now or cares what I do."

He stopped speaking, halted and turned his gaze lovingly into Betsy's horrified eyes, his grasp still iron tight. "As for us," he said softly, "I spent hours rehearsing in my head over and over again, every detail of our wedding, so I could convince you either that we were married—lunatic you—or that I was crazy . . . that I truly believed we were married.

"Everyone else began to see me as crazy, too." Starting with a lilting pitch, he said, "'Don't worry about him, he's a lunatic.' And now, I'm invisible . . . free to haunt you, to destroy your life . . . your friends . . . because of what you did to me." His voice grew more enraged with each phrase.

He turned closer to her face. "I see the question in your eyes, 'Why act a madman . . . why feign such a role between us who love so well?' Simple my dear. I ask a straightforward question. Could I have gotten this close—held you fast—if you'd thought me sane . . . if you knew I never believed we were married? Would you have let me near if you knew I crave only revenge?" He laughed. "Of course not. You'd never have come out for a walk alone on this beautiful morning. But here I am," he dropped his voice to a whisper, smiling thinly, "so close to you, and yet you don't run. You saw me as harmless . . . someone not to fear. Yet, it all hid the horror of what I really am . . . a very sane . . . calculating . . . revengeful . . . jilted . . . innocent lover." With each word, he brought his face closer to hers and hardened his features and voice.

Eying the pistol discretely, she questioned him, "Why such elaborate lengths?" The calmness of her voice surprised her. She felt terror, near paralysis. She knew she would die shortly, with her hopes, her unborn child and memories of Hank. There was no way out. Poor Hank. They were never meant to be together. Yet her question sounded curious, intellectual. Had she crossed into madness?

"You affect calmness well, my dear. Did Miss Whitehead train you, too? A marvelous performance. Bravo!"

"Why such elaborate lengths?" she asked forcefully.

"As payment in kind for what you did to me. To repay your gentle love . . . generosity . . . your wicked betrayal, I became a harmless madman. It wasn't easy. Things didn't work in every case as I'd hoped, and I had to change my plan a thousand times. But it worked just well enough. I always knew what was important, and I got you here, didn't I?" His voice became angry. "It all worked well enough but that dog. I hate to tell you my dear, but your dear husband—that's me in case that's not clear! I'm still pretending madness. Your beloved husband is scarred . . . my face, neck, arms and legs. I hope it won't disgust you." He smiled.

She was gaining strength from his verbose drivel. She would resist this monster to the end. She had to pull away, run, but she didn't dare try, not yet. There were no people around. It was just her and this sane madman. She must wait for the right moment, but she had to escape. She was shaking—now in anger—and he could feel it, but mistook it as fear.

"Are you cold, my love? You shiver . . . and on such a warm day." He moved forward, forcing her along. His voice turned darker, "Betsy, do you know what makes me happiest? I did all this with your money. And I'm still spending it!"

She attempted to wrench away from his hold, but he was quicker and grabbed her wrist with one hand, pushing the pistol into her waist till it hurt her. "My actress coached me so well on pretending madness, that there were times that I began to think we had married. I envisioned the scene over and over again . . . our marriage. Oh, my dear Betsy, it was a lovely event, with the crème of the Confederacy there as we solemnized our vows. I only wish you could have been there. You see, I wanted to think it out just right, so that you'd know I was crazy . . . that I really did believe." He squeezed her wrist tighter. "Was I convincing? Did you wish we'd married?"

She didn't answer.

"I have talked so long. Have you nothing to say? No greeting for helpful Miss Morrow?" His eyes sparkled sarcastically.

She looked at him, hatred in her eyes, betraying no fear.

"Very well," he continued. "The only big problem was that stupid dog, which makes the coming revenge so much sweeter."

"And the Rathbones? Were they there just to capture me . . . so you'd know where to find me?"

"Rathbones?" He looked surprised. "No. I know no Rathbones. It's good to hear of them, though. It may be handy sometime. No, I've needed no help since you came to Washington. I just waited for you in the market. I am a patient man. And you came to me, as I knew you would. But Betsy, my love, we can't go on like this." He smiled.

She couldn't endure it longer and jerked her arm impulsively, freeing herself from his grasp and ran. He raised the pistol. He laughed deeply, then called out, "Bang."

She glanced back at him as she fled.

He was smiling widely. "Not yet, my love. I just want you to know I'm near, and I'll see you again. Revenge is best when drawn out and savored. Yes, savored."

She ran toward the market.

"Mrs. Gragg, are you all right?" an English-accented man's voice called from ahead.

It was Mr. Rathbone. She was crying, shaking uncontrollably, gasping for breath when he reached her. She didn't answer immediately, and Thomas didn't press her. She considered him suspiciously. How had he known where she was? Why did he come just at the very moment Walthrope released her? Was Walthrope again manipulating everything in her world? She was stuck in a nightmare. She was terrorized by the reality of her foe and his dominating power over everything about her.

Thomas waited before he spoke again. "You don't seem well. Has something happened?"

She examined him, as if she were searching for a marionette string tied to his back, a string controlled by Walthrope. Her head spun, and she looked at the filthy canal. Was that her answer? It would be quick. Something she could count on.

Chapter 45

May 1864, Culpeper, Virginia

The Union's Army of the Potomac had changed. It was still directed by Major General George Meade, but he had someone peering over his shoulder—a general Lincoln had appointed to head all Union land forces: Lieutenant General U.S. Grant.

The depleted Iron Brigade had been augmented with the addition of the Seventh Indiana Regiment, but even before that addition, things had begun to turn earnest, preparing for what appeared would be a summer of war. In the middle of April, camp followers were ordered away.

But Hank was still bored. Camp life was always monotonous, leaving him too much leisure to think, remember, brood and dream of Betsy. He imagined the two of them on her plantation in Staunton. He knew it ludicrous to even consider living there, but it formed a convenient backdrop for hoped-for happiness and bliss with his beautiful wife. He was at times sad, moody and afraid for Betsy and would let his fears dictate his thoughts, creating images of Betsy in bed, barely alive. Why else wouldn't she write and smuggle letters through the lines? He ached to hear from her. But he hid his sorrow.

While the boredom of life without battle and fear for Betsy gnawed at him, his excitement at having a family—joined as husband and wife—overcame all discouragement, and that happiness made him a new creature, one that craved friends and society.

He was now constantly with other soldiers. He was loquacious with his new mess mates and couldn't stop smiling. He let no soldier song pass without joining in with gusto. He told no one of his marriage, but those who knew him before the furlough marveled at the change. The melancholy he'd once radiated was gone. Men he'd barely known before were now embraced as brothers, pulled into his sphere of joy.

He further evaded his fear for Betsy through his new pastime, base ball. Only in that game, born a gentleman's sport, could he put completely aside his worries about his wife. Only during the physicality of a base ball match did he forget her, the war and lost friends. So when rumor spread that they'd march southward May 3, Hank and many others wanted a last match on open, peaceful fields. Monday, May 2, was their chance.

His club nine took on their top competitor and battled them to a bottom-of-the-ninth 39 to 39 tie. Both clubs were totally engrossed in the competition. And Hank, as a dirty and sweaty striker, came forward to straddle home base. He grinned at the equally dirty hurler standing at the hurler's point. The hurler didn't return the smile, glaring at Hank.

The hurler, like all hurlers, wasted no time, rotating his arm behind his shoulder, bringing it down underhand and around smoothly, heaving the ball slightly upwards toward the striker's point. Hank liked the toss and with a foot in front of home base and one behind it, felt his muscles begin to contract as he saw the ball leave the small hurler's hand. He was completely absorbed in the spinning of the ball and its stitches.

A quietness enveloped him. There was no crowd of cranks, no war, no wife. It was only him, his slab of wood and the ball spinning toward him. He saw it perfectly. Closer. Closer. It was all becoming one thing. He was alive.

His club had countered everything their adversaries had hurled, thrown or struck at them. Now it was his club nine's final chance to put away this formidable enemy. Hank's mental focus allowed no consideration of what was at stake. It was simply a game, and the way to win was before him. No conscious thought—only instinct and practice—drove his actions. His shoulders and back tightened, his right side twisting forward following the pull of his right shoulder as it moved frontward. His arms, the right one leading the way, swung, rotating the slab of wood outward, then forward. The bat was him, the ball was becoming him. All was combined in one. His eyes followed the ball, watching it meld around the bat before being compelled—in a great shock—forward.

The ball was off, something separate again, bouncing across the field, and Hank followed its momentum, as they both bounded toward first base. The cranks screamed for him to leg it . . . faster. It skirted past the first base tender before he could react, and Hank could see the right field scout scurry as it leaped past him into the scattering cranks.

Hank had proven a natural for this rising sport. His informal club beat all adversaries, and some credit always landed at his feet. When he took his position astride home base, hearts swelled into shouts of encouragement. The sound of ball and bat coming together, the running—all of it resonated for him. He adored legging it around the bases. He ran them with abandon, and the muffs of other clubs and his speed meant he often scored aces by refusing to stop.

His fellow club members loved his recklessness because it was exciting, more often than not adding to the score.

Hank approached first base watching the scout still chasing the ball. He turned quickly toward second and knew he wouldn't stop now . . . he couldn't, regardless of the cost. Club mates and cranks yelled instructions, encouragement, worries, but he ignored them all. He was running past second, then third base without concern for the ball.

As he turned toward home base, he finally saw that the scout in right field had run the ball part way in, then launched it. The ball flew past the behind who waited at home base. The defender gave chase, hoping to retrieve it before Hank could reach the base. It was a race, both men exerting all they had. The behind, now with the ball in hand, was quick in his short strides. Hank ran with long strides at top speed.

Hank could hear the cheers and indiscernible instructions of mates and cranks. Faster and faster he ran watching the behind who was so much closer to the base.

The behind threw the ball at Hank. He ducked the throw, but neither man could stop. A collision sent both players into the air. Hank landed on home base, hitting the dirt, face down, tearing his cheek till it bled, while the defending club's behind lay unconscious, sprawled just beyond Hank. A gentleman's game? No more.

The ball had sailed over Hank, never touching him. The cheers were deafening. Hank's knee quivered in shock, but he laughed in delight. An ace! The cranks and mates surrounded both injured players.

After the game, still bloody faced and with a throbbing knee, Hank received his first letter from Betsy.

With memories of his last base ball game and savoring the news from Betsy, Hank—with gouged face and slightly bruised knee—joined the 19th as it set out toward a not-too-specific destination in the early morning sun. Marching again was a jolt to his system after months of winter-camp leisure. His rifle lay uncomfortably on his shoulder, and six days' rations weighed down his haversack. The rations and heavy ammunition-filled cartridge and cap boxes worried Hank. They were heading to battle. There was no turning back, no time for consuming daydreams of Betsy, no thoughts of Virginia or family. He—with the army—was throwing himself to personal destruction or victory.

The air was heavy with water and dust, and Hank choked on the mixture. He was quiet. Her letter changed everything. A father! He couldn't fathom it, but thrilled at the unexpected news. And Betsy was in the North. They—Betsy and their future child—were on the same side of the Rapidan River for the first time since he'd left Staunton. It no longer divided what, by the laws of God and man, should have been united. To be so close to her again intoxicated him.

His excitement and her proximity constrained him nearly as powerfully as orders propelled him from her. Every step southward hurt, and he measured each in second by star-tlingly slow second. March away from her—not again! Stop this! The formation turned one way and then another, finally stopping at the edge of the river. He gazed across the pretty little Rapidan—such a small thing to divide a family, he thought.

By the law of gravity, her attraction should have de-creased with each mile, but it didn't. Some higher law had intervened, pulling him increasingly toward her till he could almost not move with the Union advance. How could he cross this river, now? How could it come between him and his love again? Was there no end to this? His happiness turned to despair, and the river—that river, so faithful in keeping them apart—was ordered crossed.

He trudged forward only by assuring himself that their coming battle would be the final one, that in days or weeks at most, they would conquer the waning Confederates, and he'd be free to find her.

With a welcome order to rest, Hank, exhausted from resisting Betsy's pull and the unaccustomed marching, slumped to the ground and greedily devoured his mid-day breakfast. Then the march renewed.

Hank had pitied the newer soldiers who abandoned overcoats and blankets in the smothering wet morning air of early May. His empathy grew as he saw it was no longer blankets and coats, but the men themselves falling by the wayside—dispirited, tired, exhausted. He knew intimately the feeling. Perhaps he could feign collapse until the army passed, then return to Betsy. But the army behind him was endless and such schemes simple foolishness.

When the regiment reached its bivouac, it was still afternoon. Another mess was welcome as it meant carrying less weight tomorrow. Surely, they were marching around the enemy to get to Richmond. That's why they carried so much food. They'd reach Richmond before the end of the week, without ever fighting the foe. There would be no battle. He would be kept safe for his family.

The 19th moved out early the next day. They had traveled through and fought in this dark place before—the Wilderness, an endless scrub forest of short, thin-trunked deciduous trees, vision-blocking pines and brush, thick with wild irregular branches fighting desperately to get sun. All of it entwined in an ugly, foreboding, nearly impregnable barrier to any army. They pushed forward on a thin trail, hoping to quickly escape this brooding wood.

It was early when skirmishers ahead slowed under enemy fire. The Iron Brigade immediately began digging in. They no longer hesitated—as they once had—at throwing up a barrier of protection. Some began cutting down trees, others digging a trench with any implement they had at hand. If the enemy charged, they'd be prepared. Hank dug feverishly, without thought or conversation, with a small spade he'd brought.

He was sweating, but didn't notice as he scooped, scraped, and flung the dirt in front of him. Men were adding the downed trees to the quickly deepening trench.

The effort was short lived. The order came—Advance! Hank stopped digging, breathed a long, slow sigh, stowed his scoop and retrieved his rifle. He sat down and quickly took out paper and scrawled a note to Betsy, just in case. Its message was simple, "I love you and always have. Your ever devoted husband, Hank." His mind flashed back to finding her first husband's letter on his body, and he shivered at the eerie similarity.

The movement began, perpendicular to the trail and into the unkind forest. While the 19th tried to form a fighting line, they quickly reverted to marching in columns, leaving dangerous gaps between regiments and brigades. Marching straight into nature's clutter, they struggled to move forward, at times bending and crawling to penetrate the unruly growth. They were held up briefly by a group of soldiers ordered to their support which had somehow gotten ahead of them.

Hank no longer thought about his injured knee or Betsy. He grew nervous, agitated, excited and welcomed the feelings. It had been so long. Now, as in the base ball match, his senses were enlivened. His eyes were wide, glistening, his muscles taut, his mind raced. There was no sorrow or joy, just intelligence, alertness, exhilaration. Forward. Distance no longer mattered. He noted every noise. The breaking of twigs. Men's curses. The cries for men to form a line. They kept moving, and Hank became one with the soldiers around him. They were a single body with one mind. Forwa . . . a blast from the adversary, rifle fire. Hank fell to the ground, but he was not hit. Rising quickly, he scrambled forward, running, pressing on. The adversary was just ahead. The screams of men from all directions, from Hank's own mouth. The musket fire. The smoke on the field. And Hank running onward, smashing the enemy line, pushing Sesesh backward into a confused, desperate retreat.

"Surrender!" Hank commanded a dawdling Confederate.

"Why not," was the skinny boy Rebel's response as he laid down his weapon. He was nearly skeletal, with long, ungroomed hair and random patches of beard.

Hank sent him to the rear and Union incarceration. Then the Union private from Woodstock rushed again to catch the surging 19th. He was out of breath, but he was fully alive.

This was his natural element. So many months without it. It was overpowering. Exhilarating. Exhausting. How had he gone so long without this elation. He'd forgotten what it felt like. This was life. This was the joy of playing base ball magnified a thousand times. His adrenaline pulsed and thrust him ahead. All his senses were alert. He passed Rebel colors being taken back, and he pushed forward, still trying to catch the charge. He rushed through underbrush and trees which responded by pulling, scratching, scraping, bloodying his face again. Finally, he reached the main body of soldiers, nearly overrunning the charge as the unit paused at an opening in the woods. He looked at the men, all now tense, breathing without rhythm, trying to get themselves under control. Clouds of Confederate Minié balls flew above them.

The Union colors—seemingly of themselves—bolted forward, beckoning the men onward, and they followed, lashing hard into the adversary. Forward. Forward. Forward. No!

Retreat! The order was desperate, and Hank, conditioned to respond, turned quickly. But the guns fired at them from behind, from both sides, from the front. What was happening? Hank strained to comprehend. Was this one of the many night dreams he'd had of impossibilities becoming real in unnatural tones of color and light? Which way was forward, which toward the rear, which to safety? The firing continued. Had he been turned around? Was he advancing or retreating? Where were the Union units on their right and left? Where were the men they had passed minutes earlier who waited in support? Hank pushed harder. How far must he run? How many Rebels and lines must he pass?

A man . . . Secesh . . . was coming at him, yelling, "Surrender! Surrender!"

The battlefield irony—victor one minute, vanquished the next. Captor, then captive.

"No!" he roared and charged the Sesesh through crush of men and trees. He felt so alive as memories of Betsy swirled anew amidst the lazily rising smoke of encircling muskets.

O you leaden messengers, that ride upon the violent speed of fire, fly with false aim; move the still-peering air, that sings with piercing; do not touch my lord!

All's Well that Ends Well, Act 3, Scene 2
William Shakespeare

About the Author

Michael J. Roueche grew up in Virginia and has an indelible affection for the Old Dominion. Always a romantic, only in recent years did he discover the Civil War that had always surrounded him, thanks to Bruce Catton books from his father's library and a good friend who gave him a copy of Michael Schaara's Killer Angels. He is ever inspired by the examples of those who maintain their integrity as they persevere and overcome obstacles.

With a deepening background in Civil War history and prompted by an "odd" experience at Manassas National Battlefield Park, Betsy's story was born.

He and his wife of 36 years now live in Colorado, where they enjoy hiking and exploring the High Plains and Rocky Mountains, with their alpine vistas, aspen groves and evergreen forests, and amazing wildlife. They have five children and several grandchildren.

He is currently working on the third book in the *Beyond the Wood* series and invites you to join him at www.michaeljroueche.com or follow him on *Facebook, Twitter* or *Google+*.

Beyond the Wood

Book One

Winner of the 2012 John Esten Cooke Award for Southern History

A rejected marriage proposal propels young Hank Gragg into a turbulent and uncertain future. He abandons family, security and the South to enlist as a Union soldier, and later refuses retreat from his first bloodied action without proof he has been there. He takes it from a dying enemy.

Fed by the compassion he finds in the Confederate's last letter and his own unsettled dreams and troubling memories, Hank imagines a romance that drives him relentlessly toward an impossible rendezvous.

All the while, Elizabeth, the widow, struggles with burdens left by her husband, even as neighbors conspire against her. And what is she to make of this Union soldier — this enemy — so set on coming to her? Is there hope? Or is it merely a young man's futile fantasy?